Ibrahim,

rited.

The Disinherited

ALSO BY IBRAHIM FAWAL

On the Hills of God

Youssef Chahine

The Disinherited

VOLUME 2 IN THE PALESTINE TRILOGY

~~~~~~

a novel by

IBRAHIM FAWAL

NewSouth Books

Montgomery

NewSouth Books
105 S. Court Street
Montgomery, AL 36104

Library of Congress Cataloging-in-Publication Data

Fawal, Ibrahim, 1933-
The disinherited : a novel / by Ibrahim Fawal.
p. cm. — (Palestine trilogy ; v 2)
ISBN-13: 978-1-58838-259-7
ISBN-10: 1-58838-259-1
1. Israel-Arab War, 1948-1949—Refugees—Fiction. 2. Refugees, Palestinian
Arab—Middle East—Fiction. 3. Married people—Palestine—Fiction.
4. Arab-Israeli conflict—Fiction. 5. Political fiction. I. Title.
PS3556.A988D58 2013
813'.54—dc23

2012032514

Design by Randall Williams

Printed in the United States of America by
Thomson-Shore, Inc.

TO MY GRANDCHILDREN,

GEORGE, MATTHEW, ELIZABETH, NICHOLAS,

LUKE, ROSE, PETER, ELIE, ELLA, RANIA, CHARLES.

Previously in Book One . . .

J UNE 1947 was the eve of the end of the world for eighteen-year-old Yousif Safi, for Yousif is a Palestinian. Book One of this trilogy, entitled *On the Hills of God*, described the year-long journey of a boy becoming a man, while all that he has known crumbles to ashes. When we first encountered Yousif, he was filled with hopes for his education abroad to study law and with daydreams of his first love, the beautiful Salwa. As the future of Palestine looked increasingly bleak due to the pressure on the United Nations from the international Zionist movement, Yousif was compelled to think like a man. He was frustrated by his fellow Arabs' inability to thwart the Zionist encroachment and by his own inability to prevent the impending marriage of Salwa to an older suitor chosen by her parents. As Palestinians faced the imminent establishment of Israel, on May 15, 1948, Yousif resolved to face his own responsibilities of manhood. Despite the monumental odds against him, Yousif won Salwa's hand and his own happiness. But then the war came and his world was upended. He and his neighbors, friends, and family were forced from the homeland they had occupied for generations. They lost their homes, their possessions, and in some cases their honor and their lives. They became refugees on a desperate flight to sanctuary in Jordan. In the chaos, Yousif and Salwa were separated. In his heart, he knew she was alive, but how would he find her? As he and his mother adjusted to refugee life in Amman, Yousif vowed to win back both his loves—Salwa and Palestine—and create his world anew.

1

S ALWA WAS ON YOUSIF's mind the moment he opened his eyes. As
if having haunted him in a dream were not painful enough. As if
having turned the dream into a recurring nightmare were an ordeal
he could tolerate. There she was again slipping in and out and reasserting
her presence in his life as if he needed a reminder of the agony of their
forced separation. Wasn't life in exile already hell?

Yousif and his mother left the three-bedroom apartment which they
shared with Abu Mamdouh and his family to do some shopping. The
bedlam in the narrow streets of Amman increased day after day. Masses
crammed into the bottle-necked heart of the city. Veiled women, western-
styled women, and Bedouin women with tattoos on their faces and rings
in their noses mingled in the shops. Buicks and camels and donkeys vied
for space. Trinket-selling pushcart peddlers jostled with pedestrians,
shoeshine boys, beggars, and the lost. The jangle of traffic and the dour
faces made an already coarse city more unsightly. Every shop, every cafe,
every sidewalk was so crowded that within an hour both Yousif and his
mother had lost interest in shopping. But pots and pans and mats and
provisions were necessities. Beds were impossible to find and they didn't
even bother to look for them. With fewer than eighty pounds to their
name—and shrinking rapidly—it was ludicrous for them even to think
about such luxuries.

After helping his mother carry back to their apartment a skillet, a pot
to boil eggs, a kilo of rice, a kilo of lentils, two packages of spaghetti, a
bottle of olive oil, and half a pound of zaatar (all of which cost less than
three pounds), Yousif returned to the business district, hoping to run into
anyone who could tell of Salwa's whereabouts. None could, nor could he
tell them where to find their own loved ones. The marketplace seemed
like a large football field full of searchers. People he had scarcely known
in Ardallah embraced him. One tall, gaunt woman in ankle-length dress
almost brought tears to his eyes. He remembered when he and his friends

Amin and Isaac had been returning from bird hunting back in Ardallah and had run into her coming out of the local bakery with a tray on her head. How sweet she had been, he recalled, to lower the tray laden with freshly baked loaves and offer each of them a piece. That seemed a century ago, when in truth it was less than a year earlier. What a historic day that was! The three teen-aged friends were a Christian, a Muslim, and a Jew who strolled down the road in hilly and peaceful Ardallah without a care in their heads. Yet that day had been the infamous November 29, 1947, when the United Nations passed a resolution to partition Palestine, thus torching the boys' destiny. Less than six months later, the Zionists had attacked, the Palestinians of Ardallah had been forced from their homes. And in the chaos, Yousif had been separated from his beloved Salwa, his wife.

THE NEXT DAY AFTER the shopping trip with his mother in the tangled center of Amman, Yousif ran into Uncle Boulus smoking nergileh at Al-Hussein coffee house. And he discovered cousin Salman walking alone on an alley, his elbow almost scraping the wall. Poor Salman! He was still reeling from shock. Salman looked shabbier than most. His eyes were vacant, his hair uncombed, his face unshaven, and he was probably wearing the same wrinkled shirt he had on the day they were expelled out from Ardallah.

A family "reunion" of sorts was within reach, if only Yousif could find Salwa. What had happened to her and her mother and her young brothers, Akram and Zuhair? He hoped they were together, but hastily built camps throughout the Middle East "housed" half a million families that had been torn asunder. Finding one's loved ones would be a miracle in a land that obviously had run out of miracles.

Meanwhile, crowded living conditions occupied their minds. Then one night Abu Mamdouh announced he had located some friends and was about to move closer to them. Did they want his room, or should he rent it to others? They had no choice but to agree promptly to take his room, even if they worried over how to afford the fifteen pounds rent. Next day,

Abu Mamdouh and his wife and three children packed their few possessions and were about to leave.

At the door, Abu Mamdouh paused and looked at Yousif. "Before long
I'll have a place of business," he said. "I don't know exactly what it will
be, but I'll do something. You can be sure of that. When I do, I'd like you
to come and see me. You are a bright young man, and I'll have a job for
you. At least for a couple of days a week. God knows we all need income."

Caught by surprise, Yousif could only thank him.

"Promise you'll come and see me."

"I promise," Yousif said, shaking his hand.

Yousif's mother was filled with gratitude and showered Abu Mamdouh
and his family with God's blessings.

Within a couple of days Salman and his family, Uncle Boulus and
Aunt Hilaneh, and Basim's wife Maha and their children all moved into
the cramped apartment; Basim himself rarely came home. The first
evening together reminded Yousif of life in Ardallah, except now they
were cheerless. Before long, they hoped, when their "residence" became
known to some of their friends and acquaintances, they would gather
on the patio and sit till past midnight, reminiscing and commiserating
with each other.

Salman was no longer the life of the party. He sat subdued in a mental
fog. The radio was turned on and they anxiously waited for the 9 o'clock
news. They were shocked to hear that unoccupied Ramallah was bombed
by an Israeli air raid, the announcer said. So was Jericho. Caught in the
line of fire was a group of Palestinians still staggering out of their occupied
villages.

"They have a new name for us," Uncle Boulus said, flicking his amber
worry beads. "We're now refugees."

"I've heard it on the radio," Yousif agreed, sitting on the floor.

"I've read it in the paper," said Wajeeh Abu Hadi, a neighbor from the
refugee camp up the street. He was an outsider from a nearby village who
had lived in Ardallah but with whom they had never socialized. Prior to
the expulsion, he always traveled the countryside to inspect water wells.

He used to wear a khaki uniform with a wide, shiny brown belt and parade through town riding a horse. His erect posture on that magnificent horse was always a figure to behold.

In most gatherings, the subject of the lack of participation in the fight to save their homeland was often discussed. Yousif was the first to broach the subject.

"It's amazing how little fighting we Palestinians did," he said. "Were you surprised?"

Wajeeh drew on his cigarette and looked at Uncle Boulus as if to elicit support. Resting on his left elbow, a cigarette dangling from the side of his mouth and constantly clicking his worry beads, Uncle shrugged his shoulder.

"No, I was not surprised," Wajeeh answered.

"I know we were no match for the invaders, but . . ."

Wajeeh tapped his cigarette in an ashtray, seemingly irked by the implied criticism.

"Let's hope your generation will do better," Wajeeh answered.

"I'm sorry, I didn't mean to blame anyone. I'm just curious."

"You recall, I'm sure, that we were under British mandate for thirty years."

"And before that four hundred years under Ottoman occupation," Uncle Boulus reminded his nephew.

Wajeeh nodded toward Uncle Boulus and then turned to address Yousif's impertinent question, rather condescendingly. "Do you recall how they hauled us all off to churches, mosques, and empty school buildings and locked us there for a whole day while their soldiers searched our homes for weaponry? And you ask why we didn't fight? Fight with what? Besides, we had no army, no resistance movement, not even a band of guerillas to join."

Yousif was in an argumentative mood. "What about the Revolt in the 1930s? Our guerilla fighters hunted the British and the Zionists all over the country."

"Yes, there was a revolt," Wajeeh agreed. "And it lasted for a few years.

The best and worst part of it was the general strike throughout Palestine in 1936, which lasted for six months."

Intrigued by the paradox, Yousif waited for an explanation.

"The fighting was the good part because it deepened our sense of honor and heightened our hope. That's when our people had few arms to fight with."

"It also showed the whole world the threat we were facing." Yousif added. "What's bad about that?"

"Ah, don't forget that it also galvanized the British authorities to ignore that honor and crush that hope. They lost no time to clamp down on us, disband our guerilla fighters, and send the organizers into exile. Mostly to Iraq."

Uncle Boulus chimed in. "And that's precisely when they began locking us up and searching any cave they could find, even our homes, for armaments."

"Exactly," Wajeeh added. "By 1947 or 1948 we were in worse shape than in the 1930s. On top of that, from the start you knew that if you fought and got killed there was no one to look after your widow or children. Even if you were wounded while performing your patriotic duty, there was no doctor to treat you. You couldn't afford medical attention because you were out of a job and had no money. No organization, no general command, no support, no financial or medical security. The Jewish underground had everything. We had nothing. So, my dear young man, it was a lose-lose proposition."

Yousif knew all this, but his hunger for background information egged him on. "In other words, we were had from the beginning."

"Long, long before the beginning."

Cousin Salman spoke up for the first time. "It's a done deal," he said morosely, with his hands clasped between his knees. "What's the use? As they say: big countries decide; small countries obey."

Wajeeh expelled a deep breath and lit another cigarette. "And some of us think we'll be back by Christmas!"

"What a joke," Yousif said.

Another round of coffee, some idle talk, frequent sighs, lots of cigarette smoke, more worry-bead clicking, and the visit came to an end.

But to Yousif it was the beginning of his nightly brooding. He viewed the grotesque situation in colloquial terms: the menu was planned, the meal cooked, the table set, and the feast made ready to be served to the aliens. The hands of the big powers were there to see. And yet the pangs of not knowing enough to understand all the political currents unsettled him. At such moments he wished his father were still alive to guide his probing. There was so much to study and learn he wished there were a huge library for him to devour. And how he wished Salwa were there to alleviate his mental anguish.

After the visitors left, Yousif and his uncle and Salman slept on the balcony overlooking the street. The nights were usually hot and humid, but they did not mind the outdoors. The three bedrooms were for the women and children and occasionally to accommodate friends who had no place to stay. Congestion was the least of their worries. Yousif and the other two men went inside only to use the bathroom, stepping around the mats and sprawling children. Many a night Yousif heard his mother praying before going to sleep. She prayed for the war to stop, for Basim's safety in his travels, and for all the refugees sleeping in flimsy tents. Above all, she prayed for an early return to their homes. Sometimes Yousif would hear Aunt Hilaneh praying too. But never did he hear Maha pray for her own husband. Nor would she sigh whenever Basim's name was mentioned. She was too reserved, too modest, to admit her longing for him.

EACH MORNING YOUSIF STRUCK out on foot to look for Salwa. One day, he came across a hotel, a substantial old building on the edge of town, built of stone grayed with age. It was situated opposite what must have been a spectacular flight of steps on the slope of a hill. He was told that those steps were a remnant of the great Roman theatre which had been built in the third century B.C. The city of Amman, he soon learned, had been called Philadelphia after a Roman general—a name which had been later adopted by the Palestinian founders and owners of the best hotel in the country.

Yousif walked between the broken columns and up the steps to view the amphitheatre from a high point. The relics were relatively well-preserved, except for the inevitable cracks through which weeds were growing. The seating capacity must have been hundreds, he thought. From where he was standing, he could see atop another hill the king's imposing white palaces. But immediately to his right were clusters of mud huts and little shacks for the Jordanian poor—and now for the "luckiest" Palestinian refugees. Anything was better than a pathetic tent, he thought. He also remembered from history books that until the 1920s, this capital was no more than a desert outpost.

The light traffic in the courtyard emboldened him to venture inside the hotel. Perhaps Salwa and her mother were among the privileged guests. With a sudden burst of energy he crossed the street and climbed the short flight of steps up to the large front veranda. The dozen or more men and women sitting or standing around shared the same anguished look. And none of them had heard of Salwa.

The same was true in the crowded lobby. And the busy clerks behind the front desk were equally of no help. As he started to walk out, he looked inside the spacious and heavily carpeted sitting room to his left. Against the back wall and right in the middle of a big sofa was none other than burly Adel Farhat, whose arranged wedding to Salwa had been recklessly and bravely stopped by Yousif in the name of love. Yousif froze in place. The two rivals locked eyes but neither moved. Not a nod. Not a word. Even a national catastrophe, Yousif realized, could not override personal grudges or heal open wounds. Yet Adel's piercing stare was full of curiosity but no apparent rancor.

Bewildered by his morning encounter, and with no leads to finding Salwa, Yousif walked listlessly back to the business district, bought a newspaper, and headed home. The congestion had not abated, for more tattered refugees were still arriving. Headlines spoke of a second truce to be policed by UN troops. He found Uncle Boulus sitting just inside a warehouse not too far from the apartment. Two of the men sitting with him were from Ardallah, but the others he did not know. Except for a few burlap sacks lying near the front, the cavernous store was empty and dark. And not a customer in sight.

He did not need an advanced degree in psychology to read the gloom on their faces.

"The way we Arabs do things," the apparent owner, with rolled-up sleeves, was explaining, "there's no way of knowing when we'll go back. I thought I'd better try and have some income before we run out of the little cash we have."

Those around him pondered his predicament and nodded.

Yousif could only admire the Palestinian men who had lost no time looking for something to do. The merchants among them, like the proprietor of this store, had rented warehouses in hopes of building up a trade.

"It's better than sitting at a coffeehouse," another stranger remarked, puffing on his rolled-up cigarette.

"I never sat at a coffeehouse more than once or twice in my entire life," the wiry, high-strung proprietor added. "I never had time. I've worked all my life, and I can't stop now."

Yousif was introduced to the strangers. He shook their hands and remained standing, for there was no extra chair. The August sun was hot, and he was uncomfortable, even in the shade. He noticed that except for himself and the Ramallah man, Abu Fahmy, all were wearing native, ankle-length robes. Abu Fahmy was wearing a tailored brown suit, dark sunglasses, and a short red fez. To many he was known for his modest wealth, but to those who knew him well he was better appreciated for his sharp wit and sense of humor.

"What I love most are the rumors," Abu Fahmy said, removing his fez and wiping his forehead which was half pale and half sun-tanned. "We Arabs love to spread rumors. We collect them, we embellish them, and then we believe them. We believe our own lies. First, Jewish cowardice. Then, Arab bravery."

"Then people would start demanding invasion," one of the men said.

"Imagine that!" Abu Fahmy added. "It's too damned presumptuous of us to even use the word. We're as capable of carrying on an invasion as a camel is of turning into a canary."

They all snickered. Other men, Yousif thought, could say these things and sound like traitors; Abu Fahmy could say them and sound funny. It was his smile and his tone. He looked at Yousif affectionately, took the newspaper from his hand, and began to read. An item caught his eyes and his smile widened. Glubb Pasha, the Englishman who headed the Arab Legion, was in London asking for a two million pound subsidy for Trans-Jordan.

Abu Fahmy chuckled. "We're not only weak—we are destitute. A nation of bare feet. *Hooffa*. And listen to this: 'Moshe Sharrett of so-called Israel—ha!—is saying that 'the phenomenal Arab exodus would change the course of history.'"

"To hell with that," one man said, pitching his cigarette in the middle of the street.

"Exodus? Forced exile is more like it," Uncle Boulus echoed.

Abu Fahmy was calm. "The whole world is full of lies and liars. You expect the Jews to admit they threw us out? Hell, no. The thing is: they lie and back their lies with action. We lie and think that's good enough."

Yousif watched the men purse their lips, click their worry beads, and nod their heads. Abu Fahmy, still reading the paper, stopped and handed it to Yousif.

"Here. Read us what the poet says. The Jews fought us with ten thousand guns and we fought them with ten thousand lines of poetry. Tell us who won. Read us the poet's verdict. Maybe he knows something we don't know. Maybe we won after all."

Yousif did not read the poem. Instead, he folded the paper and rolled it. His lips felt tight against his teeth.

"You disagree?" Abu Fahmy asked. "You think poetry is proper at a time of war?"

Yousif stood his ground. "There's always a need for good poetry."

Sensing a reservation on Yousif's part, the store proprietor pressed on. "But . . . ? Go on."

"Each of us has a role to play. And poets are fighting the best way they know how."

Abu Fahmy was quick to redress his earlier position. "You're right about that. I'm not ridiculing the poet. I'm ridiculing—even condemning—our Arab nation in general. We should be tired by now from allowing foreign powers to keep kicking our asses one century after another."

Yousif returned the smile. "Amen to that."

As he started to walk away, he heard Abu Fahmy tell his uncle, "Your nephew is a bright young man. I'm sure you're all proud of him."

"Yes we are," Uncle Boulus replied.

WALKING HOME, YOUSIF THOUGHT about Abu Fahmy's cynicism. At times, he admitted to himself, poetry (especially bad poetry) did sound pretentious, or superfluous. It even seemed indecent when front-page atrocities were staring one in the face. Yet he wanted to confront all those jokers who had done nothing to protect their homeland. How dare they sit now and criticize and blame and belittle! What the hell did they do themselves? He knew of one poet who was relevant, a Jordanian, living in Amman. Ah, he would love to meet him. Almost as much as seeing Salwa again, or finding out where Basim was. He knew of this particular poet from his own father, not from school. A rebel from birth, this impassioned and radical poet was a devout nationalist, and a pitiless critic of the king's and his government's policies. Above all, he was infuriated by the Allies' breach of faith. The Arabs had been promised independence after World War I, but after helping the Allies win the war, they had been pilloried. The poet rebelled, attacked the throne and its allegiance to Britain, and was harassed and imprisoned. During his stormy lifetime he was in and out of jail as often as he was exiled. What a man! A true Arab who had refused to be silenced. A free spirit who aroused people with his impassioned, iconoclastic poetry. His poetry was more than relevant, Yousif felt. It was necessary.

At the end of the town square, Yousif turned onto a less-crowded street. It was a long street, full of small shops with considerable merchandise displayed on the sidewalks. Sacks of wheat were next to rolls of colored cloth which in turn flanked big brass trays of pastries from adjacent stores. Porters were there too, with bent backs from the heavy loads they were loading, unloading, or carrying inside the stores.

Suddenly, several jeeps approached, each full of colorful Bedouin soldiers with their guns at the ready, looking in every direction. Pedestrians in the street hurried to the sidewalks for safety. There was a flurry and all eyes turned to the direction from which the jeeps had appeared. Applause broke out as a convoy of cars advanced.

"Sayyedna . . . Sayyedna," the onlookers chanted.

A man noticed the puzzle on Yousif's face and pulled at his sleeve to let him know that His Majesty himself was passing. Yousif caught a glimpse of his profile as the sleek black limousine slipped by them. His white turban, wound around his head with one end hanging rakishly loose, was a style unmistakably his. No one else in Jordan wore a turban that way.

Yousif wished he could have had a closer look at the face of the Jordanian monarch whose every whim had such an impact on the fate of his people.

2

MONEY, WHICH WAS SO precious, melted like a bar of soap in their hands. The smaller it got, the more time Yousif had to spend reassuring his mother. The optimism he had to pretend almost made him puke. Yet every day he had to paint a less bleak picture. The job with Abu Mamdouh had yet to materialize, not for lack of trying. While waiting for the former tycoon in the orange grove business to line up a small fleet of trucks to haul citrus fruit from Jericho to Syria and Lebanon, Yousif worked a couple of weeks as a brick layer and less than a month as a house painter. The few pounds he earned pleased his mother, yet she cried. Had their circumstances been so reduced that her only son had to become a common laborer? What would his proud father say had he been still alive? No matter what Yousif told her, she cried. She was getting more edgy, her prayers more fervent, her fanning more frantic. And the suffocating heat did not help her blood pressure. Her face, Yousif thought, was often as red as a pomegranate.

Seated on a small settee in her bedroom, she told her son that the two hundred and eighty pounds they had when they reached Amman had shrunk by more than twenty-five pounds a month—not to mention the seventy-five pounds they loaned Uncle Boulus and Salman to start a grocery store. Even if they were more frugal, in three months they would be destitute. He reminded her of the seven pounds he had earned as a laborer and she shrugged it off as inconsequential. He felt agitated, yet he told her not to worry. He would do whatever it took to provide for both of them. No matter, she insisted, shaking her head. She needed to get a job.

"I need to apply for a job with the Red Cross," she said, trying to summon her will. "That's exactly what I'll do. When I tell them who my husband was—they may even know about him—they'll give me a job. Yes, that's what I am going to do."

"At your age?" Yousif said, searching for a better argument. "Why, you never worked outside the house one day in your life."

"What of it? There's always a start. And I have made up my mind. We're in a dire need."

What would people say, he wanted to tell her, then thought better than to utter such banalities. Anyone with common sense would respect her for it. Survival was at stake, was it not?

"No question about it," she continued, almost to herself. "I'm no longer the wife of a prominent doctor living in the biggest villa in Ardallah. Now I'm a mere widow of a forgotten husband and a homeless refugee. Come winter we'd be as hungry as a fasting man in Ramadan."

Sniffling, she reached for the handkerchief in her purse but couldn't find it. Yousif opened a small drawer, pulled one out and handed it to her. Then he sat next to her, put his arm around her shoulder, and let her sob to her heart's content.

He went to the bathroom not to relieve himself but to satisfy an urge to pound the wall. He did so until his knuckles ached and turned red. If he and his mother felt that desperate, he thought, how was Salwa coping? Yes, he could look for menial jobs here and there, but he also needed time and money to travel and search for his wife. Feeling suffocated, he opened the window to breathe fresh air. The sight of the rows upon rows of tents on the field facing him and the beggars on the sordid street below failed to impress upon him his good fortune. In comparison, he and his immediate family were living far beyond the means of those unfortunate tent dwellers. A prison was a prison, he told himself, no matter how clean or large. He and his mother were prisoners—they who had had more than ten thousand pounds in the bank, an expanse of fertile land, a villa that was the envy of anyone who saw it, a car in the gated driveway, and jewels under the bedroom floor. Should they not be able to pay their share of the rent, or Uncle Boulus or Salman not come to their rescue, they would end up in a dismal tent in one of those miserable refugee camps.

Maybe he should not object to his mother's seeking a job with the Red Cross, he thought. Maybe that was one way to help him find Salwa. He himself should exert more effort to find whatever job he could be lucky to get—clerk, waiter, even errand boy. Whatever. Some of his classmates were shining shoes for a meager living. Some didn't even have shoes to wear. He looked at himself in the mirror and hated his image. He hated himself. He was getting thinner. His long bushy hair badly needed cutting; instead, he drenched it with water and smoothed it down to postpone a trip to the barbershop. The humiliation of knowing that he could ill afford a haircut swelled and remained immovable in his chest; again, his fist pounded the wall.

"What was that?" his mother asked from behind the closed door. When he opened it, he found her standing anxiously just outside.

"I hit the wall," he told her.

"Why . . .?"

"Because I'm sooo happy. Listen, Mother. Forget about the Red Cross. It's volunteer work."

"Oh, no!"

"Still, go and see them. They might have changed their policy. Besides I understand they're trying to help refugee families reunite. I meant to go and see them myself. Now, you can ask about Salwa."

Her face brightened. "And what are you going to do today?"

"Continue my search from town to town. Today it's Zarqa."

But before he boarded the bus, he stopped and had a haircut. He didn't think his haggard looks would appeal to Salwa.

Zarqa was as dreary as any town he had seen in Jordan. It was warm and dusty and full of refugees: either in rows upon rows of tents or sitting on the sidewalks swatting flies. He moved from street to street, from shop to shop, from coffeehouse to coffeehouse. Though he did not run into anybody he had known back in Ardallah, he questioned anyone who would talk to him: "Have you seen Salwa Safi? Or her mother, the widow of Anton Taweel?" He even described their looks and mentioned the names of her two brothers, Akram and Zuhair. It was all to no avail.

Despondent, he returned to Amman. Against his better judgment, he stopped to see his closest friend, Amin, at the ramshackle Basman coffeehouse which had been opened above two or three stores. Climbing the outside steps to the roof, he debated whether he could afford three piasters for a soft drink or a cup of coffee. He might even get stuck paying for someone else's drink. Amin looked very busy weaving between tables with a tray of coffee to serve customers. Yet he mouthed to Yousif that he had something urgent to tell him.

"Have you seen Ustaz Sa'adeh?" Amin asked on his way back to the kitchen. "He's looking for you . . ."

The noise was too loud and Amin was at a distance, Yousif had difficulty hearing him. When Amin reappeared, he pinned Yousif against a wall for moment to tell him what was on his mind.

"He came here yesterday and this morning," Amin explained, taking a deep breath. "He said he's opening a school . . ."

Yousif looked surprised. "And . . . ?"

"You'd have to ask him. He wanted to know where you live and I told him I didn't know."

Amin went to deliver the cups of coffee and then returned.

"Frankly I was a little hurt," Amin confessed.

"Why?"

"He's probably recruiting teachers but didn't bother to ask me. I must not be good enough, although you and I were neck and neck in class."

Yousif empathized with his friend, not only because of his amputated arm but also because he actually had been one of the poorest students in school.

"We don't know what's on his mind," Yousif said, smiling.

"It doesn't matter," Amin said, "I plan to go to Kuwait where so many refugees are going. I'll probably make more money than all the teachers in the school put together."

In September Yousif became a teacher. He was assigned to teach the sixth and seventh graders Arabic, history, and sports, although the school-yard was no more than a rocky, empty stretch of land between ramshackle two-story buildings that had been converted overnight into a new school. Wearing a recently purchased jacket but no necktie, he arrived half an hour early. The mustache he had grown since his appointment added a couple of years to his face. His was a headlong immersion in school life, a fact that made him less self-conscious. A mammoth job was awaiting him and the other teachers, strangers who seemed to share his awkwardness and un-certainty. Students still had to be registered, classes had to be shifted from room to room. They accepted students in the order they came, dropped the minimal tuition whenever questioned, and qualified students on word of mouth instead of school records. Confusion and chaos were rampant.

A week after the school opened, a demonstration broke out. Through the window Yousif could see a mob of men and women approaching. Fists were flailing and voices were rising, but he could not understand a word. As they got closer, he went downstairs to see what was happening.

Seething with anger, hundreds of men and women surrounded the faculty. "We want to go home," the mob shouted. "We want to go home."

Yousif failed to make the connection. Another teacher shrugged his shoulders, equally puzzled. Within minutes Ustaz Sa'adeh himself came down to face the outraged demonstrators. Women, both villagers and urbanites, were shouting louder than the men. Apprehensive, Yousif moved closer to his principal.

"We want to go home . . . we want to go home," the mob repeated.

"Who doesn't want to go home?" Ustaz Sa'adeh asked. "We all do. What does this have to do with opening a school?"

"It's collaboration with the enemy," shouted a tall, lanky man wearing a tarboush cocked to the back. He shoved his way closer to where Yousif was standing.

"If you don't know what kind of signal you're sending to the enemy," hissed a slender woman in a blue dress, "you're not fit to be a principal."

Most people in the rowdy crowd were incoherent. Ustaz Sa'adeh climbed back to the upper step so that they all could see and hear him. He gestured to them to be quiet and listen, but they shook their fists and one insolent creep dared to call him a traitor.

"You're legitimizing our forced exile," protested a short man wearing a soiled jacket two sizes too large. Many seemed to know him, Yousif noticed, for they allowed him time to speak and gesture wildly with rolled-up newspaper in his hand. "It gives comfort to the enemy. It tells them we're willing to start new roots away from home."

"Y-E-S," the mob roared.

"It's like asking us to settle down and forget about Palestine."

"HELL, NO. HELL, NO."

"It's like replacing the temporary tents with concrete houses. We want to go back to what's ours."

"I have a key to my own home. I want to go back."

"We all have keys to our homes."

"WE ALL HAVE KEYS TO OUR HOMES."

Though in total agreement with them, Yousif felt the need to address their concern.

"You're absolutely right, but . . ." Yousif started, before they cut him short.

"But what?" a lady wearing a blue dress snarled at him.

"Until we do go home, we need to get the boys off the streets. We shouldn't let them waste their time. They need . . ."

"What they need is a lot better teacher than you."

"I beg your pardon."

"Like the rest of you. All you care about is your salary."

The demonstrators were now shoving forward in earnest. With the principal and the rest of the teachers, Yousif retreated inside and shut the front door behind. The crowd grew more boisterous and unruly. Fists pounded the door, and a few window panes were broken. Someone alerted the police. In half an hour the crowd was dispersed.

No sooner had the first group of demonstrators vanished than a bigger group of protestors arrived. They came in trucks and buses, and on foot. They came down the barren mountain, and up from the valley. They came dressed in suits or dimayas, wearing tarabeesh or scarves or with bare heads. They came old and feeble, young and strong—until the schoolyard and the street beyond became impassable. They were high-strung and nervous, looking for a target to vent their anger on. It was as if the opening of the school doors had paradoxically shut out their last hope. Some had been in exile for five months; some were recent arrivals. Yousif could tell from their accents and motley attire that some were from Galilee up north or all the way down from Gaza. But that morning, with the bluest sky looking at them indiscriminately they spoke in one voice and their hearts seemed to beat in unison.

Now that the initial shock was over, Yousif stood by his principal, soaking up the people's torment and filtering it through his own sensibilities. Ironically he sensed hope and felt joy. If the harmless opening of a school could unleash such a torrent of emotion, then his people would never surrender, would never accept defeat. They were ready to resist, and he loved them for it. In truth, they were protesting the wrong issue. But the act of protest in itself convinced him that they were misguided but not unaware. What they needed was a leader who would transform their untapped power, their wasted individual sparks, into one gigantic blaze.

Yousif had Basim in mind, but to his surprise the genteel and mild-speaking Ustaz Sa'adeh reappeared and suddenly the crowd fell silent. Yousif held his breath and hoped for the best. To his utter and most pleasant surprise, Ustaz Sa'adeh's commanding presence proved that he was a man ready to lead.

"Let it be said," Ustaz Sa'adeh said, his voice loud, "that the Palestinian is a learner, not an idler. A builder, not a destroyer. To us Palestinians, longing to return to our homes is more than a hope, more than a dream. It is the essence of our life. Life is not worth living if foreign forces decree that we are to be uprooted and to remain uprooted from our sacred land. Who should decide our fate but us?"

Yousif applauded and the restless mob seemed willing to listen. He could read softness in their glare.

Ustaz Sa'adeh paused to gauge their reaction.

"But how can we escape the darkness without using our heads?" he asked, his face crimson with emotion. "Education should become our motto. Our battle cry. There is no liberty without education. No liberation without education. No resurrection, no redemption without education. Speak of it in your tents and huts. Instill it in your children's hearts and minds. Sing it to your babies as you suckle them or hold them in your arms. It would be the height of folly for our enemy to think that the opening of a modest school is a signal that we have resigned ourselves to living in exile."

"Y-E-S," someone shouted back.

"It would be a pipe dream for them to think that we Palestinians will languish in the sun and rest in refugee camps while they—the foreigners, the trespassers, the aggressors—plow our fields, pick our oranges and apples and figs off our trees, pluck the grapes off our vines, harvest our wheat, shepherd our flocks, and press our olives. Everything we left behind we either bought or inherited from our fathers or our ancestors. We are the owners of the land. And we have the titles and the deeds to prove it . . ."

"And the keys to our homes," many screamed in unison.

"How dare they come after two thousand years and claim it as their own? How dare they bask in our gardens and live in our homes as if we had never existed."

"How dare they," the crowd roared.

"HOW DARE THEY!"

The resounding applause was started by someone other than Yousif. It was started by the hateful, abrasive woman with the blue dress who had earlier belittled him. Yousif did not know whether to welcome her sudden conversion or to dismiss her as being gullible. He decided to give her the benefit of the doubt and to credit his principal with the power to persuade even the uncouth.

"Let it be said," Ustaz Sa'adeh continued, his voice pitched higher, "that we Palestinians do not feed on rhetoric, or cheap sentiment, or hot air. Our new generation will thrive on pragmatism, on practicality. And as a practical man I should tell you what needs our immediate attention."

"Tell us and we'll do it," someone shouted.

"Thank you," the principal told him. "And I will thank anyone else who's willing to volunteer. You see that piece of land between the two buildings? Soon we hope to have it as a soccer field. But right now, as you can tell, it is full of stones and rocks. If someone has access to a pickup truck and wants to do something good for the rest of the community, I urge him to come forward and give us a hand hauling them away. All kinds of craftsmen are needed to make this place habitable for our children. The stone walls need mending. The walls inside the building need painting. The plumbing needs repairing. You name it—we need it. We certainly could use a couple of carpenters. We can keep them busy for a week or two."

"I'm a carpenter," someone said. "When can I start?"

"I'm a plumber," another added. "And I am ready to work."

"I am an electrician. Can you use one?"

The response was most encouraging and the principal beamed.

"There's one more thing I'd like to ask of you," the principal continued, waving at a mob that was no longer hostile. "I'd like for you to form a committee of six or seven men and women, if you will, so that we may address our mutual interests and concerns. Those in favor of such an advisory committee let them please raise their hands."

The arms which had come to fight an hour earlier were now stretched high in total cooperation. The facial muscles which had tightened with suspicion and hatred were now relaxed. The eyes that had darted like daggers were now void of malice. Soon the throngs that had assembled to disrupt were now dispersing, with disruption the last thing on their minds.

The funny little man with the soiled and oversized jacket was now clapping his hands enthusiastically and encouraging others to do the same. Many responded to his call.

As the atmosphere turned friendly, and the crowd stirred to leave, Yousif had an idea.

"One more thing, if I may," Yousif shouted, taking Ustaz Sa'adeh by surprise.

"Does anyone know a beautiful nineteen-year-old girl named Salwa Safi? Does anyone know where she lives? She's my wife . . ."

"Oh . . . !" one girl swooned mockingly. "You're married?"

"Happily married. But we were separated in the exodus five months ago."

"And you miss her, of course," another girl teased him.

"I miss her very much. Please let us help each other find our loved ones. Thousands of us are in the same boat."

The crowd began to depart with a glee on their faces. Yousif's romantic appeal seemed to have drained the tension out of them. But the one thing Yousif did not anticipate was the unlikely sight of the lady in the blue dress approaching him.

"If I were younger I'd wish you and I were in the same boat," she whispered in his ear, smiling.

The glint in her eyes revealed a charm he would not have expected.

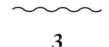

3

SEVERAL GOOD THINGS EMERGED out of the principal's meeting two days later with the advisory committee. Yousif was among the few faculty who had been asked to attend. Ustaz Sa'adeh not only convinced four men and three women that the opening of the school was in the best interest of their children, but that ultimately it was in the best national interest as well.

"The decision to return home belongs to none of us," he said. "It's in the hands of governments and we all know how slow that can be. While waiting for the ministry of education to triple or quadruple the number of schools needed to accommodate the influx of refugees and the country's natural growth, it would be a shame to let the children suffer more than they're suffering already."

From Yousif's point of view, common sense reigned and quiet filled the room.

"Right now," the principal added, "we should concentrate on what we can do and not on what we wish would happen. The minute we realize that returning home is imminent—or is an option—I'll be the first to strike the tent, so to speak, and head back to Ardallah. Until then we should do what we can to educate our children. Wasting a mind is a crime."

Yousif observed that the committee members were much nicer in private than they had been in public. Around the shoddy rectangular table in the faculty lounge, they listened and spoke as one family. Yes, they agreed, there was no need to let children miss school. The only thing that troubled them was giving the enemy the impression that they were willing "to settle" outside Palestine. As the principal spoke, the men nodded and the women tightened their lips or folded their arms.

"Personally, I'd like to apologize to you," a thin woman in her forties said, removing her glasses and dabbing her eyes with a lacy handkerchief. "Instead of trying to find out what was on your mind, we rushed here as if we were storming the Bastille."

"These are dark days," the principal answered. "I understand your anxiety."

Tariq Ayyash, the greasy little man with the oversized jacket, fidgeted in his seat. Everyone turned to look at him. Yousif was offended by the sight of black crud under Tariq's fingernails.

"With all due respect," Tariq said, "I still think opening the school at this time is unwise. It's bound to upset whatever secret negotiations that might be going on. If I were a Zionist in Tel Aviv I'd be dancing in the street. I'd be thinking the Palestinians are already making adjustments to live outside their homeland."

"They're not that naïve," a lady said, with a pale smile.

"It's possible," Tariq defended himself.

"That's a good point," Yousif argued. "But what if the hypothetical negotiations you speak of drag on for years? As I'm sure they would. What then?"

Tariq was not convinced. "Okay," he said, gesturing to quiet the rising chatter. "What if someone else starts a big farm to teach families how to cultivate the land and grow crops to make a living while waiting. And what if someone else starts a vocational school to train men in some kind of trade? How would the enemy read or misread our intentions?"

Ustaz Sa'adeh decided to close the discussion. "Tariq has raised legitimate questions. However, each of us must do what he or she is qualified to do. We do what we know best. If I were a prime minister of long standing and privy to the high drama being played behind the scenes, I might think otherwise. Right now I'm primarily an educator and you are proud and responsible parents. In these capacities I feel it's our collective duty to take our children off the streets to make sure that they continue learning. They need to know more than just how to read and write. Or to do math. Or to know basic history. Above all, they need to know how to think for themselves so that they can cope with the enormity of our catastrophe."

"Amen," Yousif said.

The rest solemnly nodded their heads or expelled a deep sigh. A robust man with a shock of white hair pulled out a pack of cigarettes but, seeing the disapproval in others' eyes, quickly put it back in his pocket.

Questions began to fly. "What about books? What about a budget to run the school? What about a school for girls, not just for boys? What about . . . ?"

"That's where you can be of great help," Ustaz Sa'adeh told them, flashing a forced smile. "We'll discuss that in our next meeting."

As a student, Yousif had often waited for the teachers to come to class and talk about politics. Now he was a teacher, meeting with the other teachers in the makeshift lounge and participating in their discussions. At the moment, however, his mind was on his first session with his seventh-grade students. There were twelve and he was ready to meet them. If only Salwa could see him now, he thought, as he opened the door to the classroom.

He started the session by introducing himself and giving them a brief summary of his background. Then he went around the room asking each one of them to do the same. One by one, they mentioned their place of birth and gave some information about themselves. All the while he was jotting down notes by which to remember them.

When they were through, he looked pleased and told them so.

"Now for our first assignment," he said. "When you go home, I'd like for you to write an essay about yourselves. Simply expand on what you have just told us."

One student in the back row raised his hand. "How long?"

Yousif told them to write as much as they could and to bring it in a week from that day. "As we go along," he added, "we'll take a good look at what you have written. Each paper will be considered a first draft. Then we'll start the rewriting process. Or what some refer to as revision. We will enlarge on some points, and delete others. By the end of the term each of you will have six or seven segments on the same theme: yourselves."

"Wow!!" many said.

"Is this a composition class?" one student wanted to know.

"Yes it is," Yousif told him. "As you can see we don't have textbooks yet. So reading will have to wait. For the time being, we're going to concentrate on writing. Actually we have no choice."

Most students seemed agreeable. Except one.

"We can read newspapers. They don't cost much."

"A good idea," Yousif agreed. "We'll try it. I might even bring some magazines and pass them around."

The students' approval was unanimous.

"As to the essay," Yousif said, "here's what I'd like for you to do. I'd like for you to tell me all about yourselves, your families, your towns, your friends. But avoid generalities. I prefer details. I insist on specifics."

A student with curly hair wanted him to explain what he meant.

"Draw me a word-picture and let me visualize what you're talking about," Yousif elaborated. "For me to get to know your father, I'd like to know his name, his age, and the kind of work he does. Or did. Tell me what town or village you come from. The number of brothers and sisters you have. Tell me what your parents are doing now. Name and describe your refugee camp. How congested is your tent at night? How many people sleep on the floor? Four? Six? Ten? Again, draw me a word-picture and let me visualize how you manage in that small crowded space."

At the end of the session, Yousif commended their cooperation and frankness.

"Obviously, what unites us is our love for our homeland and our shared dreadful experience. Record your vivid memories. Write down your feelings and the feelings of those close to you, who made an impression on you. This will not only teach the art and craft of writing, but will be useful to you in other ways. In the future you'll be able to share it with your children and grandchildren."

The students snickered and began to whisper among themselves.

"Who knows, some of you might become writers who one day will shatter the eardrums of those who pretend to be deaf to our misery. Or prick the conscience of those who claim to have any, for allowing this unprovoked injustice to happen."

He had them in the palm of his hand.

"One time I asked my father, what did we do to end up refugees?" said the boy from Ramleh.

"Excellent question," Yousif replied, truly impressed. "What did he say?"

"He said he wished he knew," the boy answered.

Yousif was delighted. "Your question and your father's answer are at the core of the problem. We will discuss them later at length. For now, I'm simply proud of your probing. Your wanting to know. Your curiosity. Your search for the truth."

At the sound of the school bell some students rose to leave, others raised their hands. There was no more time, and Yousif told them to ask them again next time.

But one question, shouted by the boy from Gaza, stopped him on his way out. "What's the title of our essay?" the chubby boy asked.

Once again Yousif was impressed. "Call it 'Lest We Forget.'"

"Lest we forget," the boy grumbled. "What does it mean?"

His hand on the doorknob, Yousif's smile widened. "It means so that we may never forget."

The students felt amused and left the classroom, murmuring: "Lest We Forget."

OCTOBER WAS WITNESSING A new assault by the enemy. Now they were directing their attention to Egypt and launching a full-scale offensive against her. They captured Beersheba and surrounded Faluja in the Negev Desert.

"You'd think Jordan would be helping the Egyptians now," teacher Hikmat Hawi said, turning the pages of the newspaper he was reading.

"Not a chance," Yousif replied, leafing through a book of essays, "even though the Jordanian forces are still intact and in a position to attack the left flank."

Teacher Hassan Mansour softly tapped the table with his pencil. "Jordan would not commit her forces in a serious battle."

"We knew this when they abandoned Lydda and Ramleh, and when they failed to capture Jerusalem," Hikmat added. "I know for a fact that when Lydda and Ramleh fell, a delegation from surrounding towns and villages came up to Amman to see the king. They were worried that he might withdraw his troops and leave them unprotected. His answer was shocking. And I heard this from someone who was in that room. The king told them he'd withdraw any time his army was endangered."

Everyone around the makeshift conference table stopped whatever he was doing and was now in rapt attention.

"He couldn't have been more honest," Yousif said.

"Or more blunt," Hassan corrected him. "That Englishman who heads his army, what's his name?"

"Glubb Pasha," Yousif told him.

"Yes, him," Hikmat continued. "Glubb, nicknamed Abu Hnaik, wouldn't stand up and fight to the last man. Never. He'd test the enemy, and at the first sign of danger he would order his soldiers to stop."

"And carry out England's wishes."

The teachers had heard stories like this before and seemed nonplussed. Most were Yousif's former teachers, except Hikmat Hawi and Murad Al-lam. Murad was an older man, dressed in crisp pants, with an air of dignity that bordered on fastidiousness. He was, Yousif had been told, a man with dashed hopes. After two years in England pursuing a medical education, he had been recalled by his family for lack of money. In the subsequent thirty years in the classroom, he never once was a real teacher. His bitterness over not having been able to become a doctor stood in the way.

Of all his colleagues, Yousif felt closest to Hikmat Hawi. Hikmat was in his early twenties, born and raised in Haifa, and educated at the American University of Beirut. He had studied mathematics but at the end of his third year he had to rush back home to be with his family as the troubles escalated throughout the country. His circumstances reminded Yousif of Izzat Hankash, who just before the forced exile had been a tenant in Yousif's home in Ardallah. Hikmat was of stronger build, and his nostrils were slightly more flaring. He and Yousif had taken an immediate liking to each other, and in less than a couple of weeks they had become fast friends. They visited each other's "homes" and were introduced to their families. Their dwellings were so inferior to what they had been accustomed, neither could tell who was less fortunate.

To Yousif, Hikmat's family had a diversity of looks. Hikmat was handsome but with a flaring nose. Fareed, the older brother, was fat and had a glass eye. Their mother was of medium height and must have eaten a lot of starch in her life. Their sister, Ghada, was flat-chested and homely. She looked older than her brother Hikmat, although she was three years younger. Fareed's wife, Leena, was more seductive than beautiful. Leena caught Yousif's eye, not for her good looks and fanciful ways but because she looked out of place in this impoverished neighborhood. Her walk and talk spelled trouble.

Over several weeks Yousif noticed that Leena was never seen casually dressed or without heavy makeup. Her wardrobe was extremely limited, yet the few pieces she owned were of good quality and in good taste, and she never wore the same outfit on the consecutive days. Her knack was to combine and switch sweaters, blouses, and skirts that gave her the look of a relatively well-to-do woman. On her own she was attractive; among the other women in the neighborhood she was stunning. The most noticeable quality about her was her moodiness. Not blending with the others, she seemed to find comfort in Yousif's company. And vice versa, for in some odd way she reminded him of Salwa. And she indulged him in talking about how he could find her.

Whenever he arrived with her brother-in-law Hikmat, Leena would disengage from the women sitting in the shade, and would attach herself to the two young teachers. More and more, Yousif began to enjoy walking Hikmat home. And more often than not they tended to walk together in front of other women sitting in the shade or on doorsteps knitting or gossiping or nursing their babies. One particular phenomenon always overwhelmed him. A devout Muslim woman who covered her face with a black veil did not find it in the least peculiar to expose her ample breast to nurse her infant. To his utter shame and guilt toward Salwa whom he adored, he nurtured a secret wish that Leena had a baby so he could watch her pull out her magnificent breast and nurse it.

"I'd love to see Salwa's picture," she once told him as they strolled in their customary short walks together. "She must be gorgeous."

"The only picture I have of her is in my head," Yousif answered.

Leena was astonished. "You mean it?"

"Yes," he answered, nodding. "The enemy soldiers rushed us out of the house at gunpoint with only the clothes on our backs. They didn't give some of us time to get out of their pajamas. Besides, we thought we'd be back by Christmas."

As they strolled back and forth, reminiscing and commiserating with each other, Yousif told her about the rape of Hiyam, the bride of his friend Izzat who had rented a room in their house. He told her how the enemy soldiers even blasted many of the birds in his aviary, and how they threatened to blow his head off if he tried to resist.

Yousif exhaled deeply and allowed painful memories to flood his mind.

"One soldier put his gun to Mother's waist and shoved her out, saying, "Go to Abdullah . . . Go to Abdullah."

Yousif exhaled and remained as quiet as the other two.

"Well, here we all are," Leena finally said, "in King Abdullah's country."

"Indeed we are," Yousif said. "That soldier knew what he was saying."

"For sure," Hikmat concurred. "He was following orders . . ."

Before long Yousif concluded that Leena's relationship with her family was strained at best, for she seemed to get along well only with him and Hikmat. One afternoon she was in a rare good mood and Yousif asked how and where she had met her husband. Suddenly her mood changed. Her face became noticeably drawn, and she excused herself and went inside her apartment and did not come out. Another time she was joking and laughing with Yousif and Hikmat when her husband arrived. The poor slovenly one-eyed man felt the conviviality of the moment and tried to put his arm around her waist. She brushed it aside and walked away.

Yousif and Hikmat glanced at each other without saying a word.

MIDNIGHT OFTEN PASSED WITH Yousif lying wide awake thinking of Salwa and their whole dreary existence. Uncle Boulus and Salman were more accustomed than he was sleeping on the back patio. What would they do, he thought, when winter came? They would have to move inside no matter how congested their quarters became.

One night, Yousif was sleeping on the balcony when he heard a car stop on the street below and a door open and close. As the driver shifted gear and drove off, Yousif heard a knock at the door. He stood on the patio debating whether to wake one of the men. On the second knock he saw his mother already out of her bedroom and standing in the middle of the foyer clutching her robe.

"Who could it be at this hour?" she wondered in a low voice. "What time is it?"

Yousif did not know and did not answer. The third knock was louder, and the men and women stirred on their mattresses.

"Who's there?" Yousif asked, weaving his way around sleeping children.

"It's me, Basim."

The name had a magical ring and pulled the men onto their feet and Aunt Hilaneh and Maha out of their rooms. But Yousif beat them to the front door and was the first to see Basim in the doorway, his necktie loose, his white shirt open at the collar, and his jacket hooked over his shoulder. Yousif was also the first to embrace him. The last one to embrace him was Maha, his diffident wife.

"Go on," Yousif coaxed her. "Just once I'd like to see you two kiss."

"Never mind," Maha told him, putting her arms through the sleeves of her kimono.

"It's good to be home," Basim said, his soft eyes shining with happiness.

"You call this a home?" Yousif teased. "I'm shocked."

Basim paid him no attention, and knelt to kiss the children on the floor. He woke everyone up, shaking a slender shoulder here and pulling a tiny foot there. The children jumped on him, their eyes still half-closed.

Because electricity was often turned off at irregular hours during the night, they all sat on the patio. At one o'clock in the morning they snacked on oranges, white goat cheese, and taboon bread. The children went back to sleep, except Basim's youngest daughter, Reem. She wound herself around her father like a grapevine around a wooden post. Salman was tired and sleepy; Uncle Boulus was now in a talkative mood, full of opinions and questions. When he reached for his pocket and pulled out his *masbaha* and began clicking, Yousif headed inside to light a kerosene lamp, for he knew that his uncle was settling down to meet the dawn.

"Jordan's Arab Legion," Uncle Boulus began, reclining on his elbow and making himself comfortable, "is thoroughly trained by the British.

One can see it by the way they're occupying what's left of Palestine. People sense what's going on. The last time I went to Jerusalem, I saw with my own eyes how friendly the Bedouin soldiers were. They went around chatting and smiling so as not to antagonize anyone. Not heavy-handed, not obvious—just clever."

Basim lit a cigarette. "The king learned well from his masters," he commented under his breath. Then he seemed to stop listening to what the old man was saying.

The women, now fully awake, were noisily but happily busy peeling oranges and tiny cucumbers, slicing bread, and filling a small dish with black olives.

"Anyone up for coffee?" Maha asked

"Please," Basim told her.

"This late at night?" Yousif remarked, already aware of the answer. He watched Basim enjoy the food, without letting go of his daughter. He kissed her cheeks between bites, and she hugged him and kissed his forehead.

"There are rumors," Uncle Boulus continued, undaunted by the lack of attention, and clicking his worry beads, "that King Abdullah will soon annex what's left of Palestine to Jordan. Is it true?"

"I've heard the rumor," Basim said indifferently, wiping his mouth and pecking Reem on the cheek and purring in her ear: "That orange is sweet, but your kisses are sweeter. Much, much sweeter. How can that be? Let me kiss you once more to see if I have made a mistake."

"Oh, Baba," Reem said, giggling and nestling against his neck and letting him smother her with more affection.

Uncle Boulus's barrage of questions did not seem to interest Basim in the least, but they dragged Salman into the discussion.

"I've heard," Salman said his arms wrapped around his knees, "that they're courting prominent Palestinians for more surprises."

"Sure," Yousif said, "wantonness must seem justified."

For the first time that night Basim looked at Yousif with special regard. "Not bad," he told him, and went back to teasing his young daughter.

It seemed obvious to one and all that the seasoned revolutionary Basim was not about to divulge any news. He did not tell them where he had been or what he had been doing. All he said, with characteristic nonchalance, was that Palestine had been sold and delivered. He pitied the refugees who thought they would be going home for Christmas. Yousif paid attention to the tone as well as the words. Ultra secretive by nature and hardened by underground experience, Basim was hinting, not informing; happier to be with his family than with the discussion.

"Salman, where's your flute?" Basim asked. "I want to hear you play again."

"Flute . . .!!!!" several voices exclaimed.

"You're lucky to hear his voice," Abla said. "He's not the Salman we all knew. Just ask them."

They all agreed that Salman had changed most of all.

"I'm not so sure," Basim said, looking around. "From what I can tell there's been a significant change in Yousif . . ."

"That's because he still can't find Salwa," Maha said.

"Poor Yousif," Abla said, her eyes twinkling. "He's heartbroken."

"I should be," Yousif said, going along with the humor.

They all laughed.

"That can't be it," Basim said. "Look at the mustache. Listen to his political awareness. And I hear he's now a teacher. I'm impressed . . . But tonight I want to hear Salman play."

Silence descended upon them like an unseasonable mist. Basim ran his fingers through his daughter's long, soft, brown hair, humming a well-known folk song. The girl was now fast asleep on his chest, and her mother tried to carry her back to her room. But Basim shook his head and held onto her.

It was an unusual scene, Yousif reflected. Basim's low, hushed voice flowed like balsam, soothing and yet lifting the scabs off old wounds. The humming turned into melancholy singing, first by Basim alone, then by Yousif's mother. She matched him verse by verse, and they alternated in a duet of infinite sweetness. How enchanting and genuinely touching, Yousif felt, tears welling in his eyes. Scenes of Ardallah and fragments of his past, particularly those of the night before his wedding, flooded his mind. Salwa haunted him and would not leave him alone, nor would he let go of her image. He looked around and found the others rapt in their solitudes, their own memories. The two singers segued from song to song each emotion giving rise to a deeper one. The balmy night was quiet, except for two tormented voices, too fragile to take wings and soar.

Only after the coffee had been served was Basim willing to let them carry his daughter back to bed. The coffee seemed to wake him up and to shift his mood back to reality.

"Our Jordanian brethren have chosen the name," Basim told them, taking another sip from his demitasse cup. "The war is technically still on and they have already picked out a name for the new country. Soon the Arab parts of Palestine will be annexed to Jordan . . ."

"By popular demand, of course," Yousif commented.

". . . The new country will be known as the Hashemite Kingdom of Jordan. Very few people know this, but take my word, it's official. Only the signatures are still to be affixed."

The silence was deafening.

Yousif and Basim exchanged looks, while the others looked as if dynamite had been detonated in their midst.

"What if we leak the story to the newspapers?" Yousif suggested. "What if we circulate a rumor? Would that slow the last-minute negotiations?"

Yousif's mother was aghast. "The only thing it would do is lock you up in jail. Please, habibi. Please don't get involved. Please, Basim, don't listen to him. Sometimes . . . sometimes, I just don't know what to think. His ideas worry me."

Yousif concealed his anger and tried to lighten the deadly serious moment.

"Why, Mother!!!" he said. "I didn't realize how badly you want to be a Hashemite citizen. Well, I'll be . . ."

His mother would not be placated. "Stop fooling, will you?"

"Where did they get the name?" aunt Hilaneh wanted to know. "What's a Hashemite?"

"Named after the House of Hashem—descendants of the Prophet," her husband explained to him. "The king's ancestors."

Between the European Zionists and the Jordanian Bedouins, Palestine was lost, Yousif thought. A line from the New Testament struck his mind: "They parted my raiment among them, and for my vestments they did cast lots."

At that moment, as if the heavens had been listening, the electricity was turned off all over the city. Only a lamp was burning in a far corner of the house.

Yousif and Basim stared at each other, their eyes fixed and glowing in the dark.

~~~~~~

4

WHEN WINTER ARRIVED, YOUSIF was convinced that the heavens had no mercy. Over a hundred thousand homeless people were beaten down by stormy weather. The wind howled and played havoc with the tents: tearing many to shreds, and blowing more away. Day after day, night after night, with a few breaks in between, hailstorms, blizzards and strong winds pounded them. For a whole week, Yousif expected the spindly trees behind the house and in the field below to break or be uprooted. If human beings could be uprooted, he thought, why not trees? And there was no Salwa to share with him this new experience. Her absence made his life more calamitous.

In the midst of that ghastly weather, some refugees were on the run again, this time away from, not toward, the horrific camps. Some could find shelter, many more lived on the sidewalks, with few canopies over their heads. They remained pitted to the ground while the gods or demigods or the devils played their mischievous games. The camp on the other side of the road below Yousif's apartment became a huge puddle of mud. Most of its tents were trampled on, and those that were miraculously still intact, were circling and retreating from the wind like two ballerinas enacting a love-hate romance on the dance floor.

Next morning, as Yousif passed the camp, he counted dozens of legs sticking out from under the tents that were home to so many. Smoke billowed out of some, and the sound of children crying penetrated the sound of the wind. Yousif carried a black umbrella as a cane, but was ashamed to open it. He handed it to the first mother he met with a child in her arms.

The school building was teeming with families seeking shelter. The hallways and classrooms were filled with families. Desks were pushed against the walls, children and their parents were huddling to keep warm. Coal was burning in a brazier in the middle of the floor. Bedsheets were hung on a clothesline stretching from door to window to keep the wind and rain out. Soaking wet, Yousif stopped by the principal's office. Standing at the doorway, he wiped his neck and face with a handkerchief.

"Ah, Yousif," Ustaz Sa'adeh, smiling and wiping the mud off his own shoes. "This is just November. The best is yet to come."

December arrived with other shocks of greater magnitude. Yousif read about them in the newspapers and understood their dimensions. The ineptness, the sloppiness, of the Arab leaders infuriated him. He was getting restless by the day, wanting someone other than Hikmat with whom to share his thoughts. Uncle Boulus and Salman had enough worries eking out a living at the little grocery store to worry about his desire for greater comprehension of national politics. Salwa would understand, but she might as well be on the moon for all he knew. The couple of times he had stopped at the coffeehouse, Amin was too busy to talk. Basim would be best, but where the hell was he? Yousif glued himself to the radio whenever he could and entered lengthy discussion with fellow teachers as well as with his students, whom he now admired and trusted.

First, the war was dwindling down in most areas, except the south. There, it was escalating. In a final push, the enemy was launching a major offensive against Gaza from the sea and from the air. Initially, the Egyptians had put up a credible resistance and then began to crumble. What truly outraged Yousif was that while a fierce battle was raging,

Jordan's monarch was in the safety of his palace, watching his brethren getting smashed.

Not so, Yousif soon learned. The monarch had the spoils of war on his mind and was busy carving his share. His emissaries were already doing his bidding: rounding up Palestinian notables to a historic meeting in Jericho. The avowed purpose: "to appeal to him," "to plead with him," "to beg him," "to employ him," and "to entreat him" to let them be his loyal subjects.

To his credit, Uncle Boulus declined the invitation to join many from his hometown, such as the mayor and attorney Fouad Jubran, each of whom, no doubt, was angling for a position in the new government. Yousif was proud of his Uncle Boulus, and told him so. It was an act of patriotism which, in Yousif's eyes, absolved him from the sin of not having participated even in a miniscule capacity in the defense of their homeland. Young and old, they all should have sacrificed. He wished others had not scurried to Jericho to rubber-stamp their own death certificate. With raised hands or a loud outcry they had sealed their own fate and denied themselves the Right of Return—the right to be free and independent.

Out of "compassion," certainly, the monarch rose to the occasion and did not fail them. He "humbly accepted" to be their lord and master. Three days before Christmas he answered their entreaties: sending his new subjects a gift in the form of an official declaration, annexing the West Bank to the newly named Hashemite Kingdom of Jordan.

Young as he was, Yousif was enraged. Salwa, no doubt, would be fit to be tied. She was his girl and he knew how she felt. The unilateral action electrified the whole Arab world, especially the disinherited and displaced Palestinians. To understand the political ramifications of such a disastrous move, Yousif spent several hours with Hikmat, even a couple of times with Leena, trying to digest the present and dreadful future. Enough rumors and half-truths were circulating to fill a labyrinth with fog.

In the teachers' lounge, everyone was similarly preoccupied.

"It's laughable to think that states can be so instantly or easily created," teacher Imad said, grading some papers.

The fastidious teacher, Murad Allam, looked up, not in the least bit amused. "Who said it was created easily or instantly as you say?"

"Was it not?" Imad defended himself, glancing around for support. "The Zionists give more thought to blowing up a railroad station than we give to establishing a state."

"Not so fast," Yousif said. "What do you think they've been doing since the Balfour Declaration? How long has that been? Thirty years? And what do you think was the purpose of the British mandate? Was it not to fulfill Britain's promise to the Zionists and create a national home for the Jews in Palestine?"

Imad shook his head as if to put the pieces together. "What does that have to do with what we're talking about . . . ?"

"What kind of bargaining do you think was going on behind our backs? Both sides must've balked and it took years to satisfy them."

"You think so?"

Yousif eyed him with derision. "It's been cooking for a long time."

Suddenly grim-faced Ustaz Sa'adeh appeared at the door. "Walls have ears," he said. "I suggest dropping this kind of talk. Here and elsewhere. Unless you want the school to be shut down and some of you picked up."

WHEN YOUSIF RETURNED HOME in the early evening, he was amazed by an unfamiliar and unlikely sight. He saw a half-empty bottle of arak, two glasses relatively empty, and two men sitting at the kitchen table in an obviously jolly good mood.

"Just one more drink," Uncle Boulus insisted, trying to refill a resisting Salman's glass.

"What's the occasion?" Yousif asked. "Christmas is still a few days off."

"Christmas!" Uncle Boulus repeated, giggling. "What's the matter with you, boy? Where have you been? We Palestinians have two capitals . . ."

"Not one, t-w-o," Salman informed him, his tongue heavy.

". . . One in Amman and one in Gaza. What do you think of that? One ruled by Jordan, and one ruled by Egypt. Isn't this a good reason to celebrate?"

Yousif bit his lower lip and put his finger to his mouth. "Not so loud,

Uncle. Not so loud," he said, peering outside to make sure that they were not being overheard.

His mother met him at the kitchen door. "Yousif, I'm glad you're here."

"Glad!" he told her. "Why are you letting these two get drunk? Do you want the police to ring the house tonight?"

The word *police* brought the other three women out of the inner rooms, each holding her breath.

"Why the police?" Maha asked anxiously.

"What's wrong with them having a drink in their own home to drown their despair?" Aunt Hilaneh said.

Yousif shot her a sharp glance. "Talking politics? And opposing annexation?"

Abla's face clouded with apprehension. "I'll make coffee."

"Make it strong and bitter," Yousif told her. "We need to sober them up before they get us in trouble."

Yousif turned to the kitchen table and reached for the drink in his uncle's hand. "Come on, Uncle. Let's have a chat."

"What kind of a chat?" Uncle Boulus asked, trying to hold on to his glass. "Pull up a chair. It's time we had a drink together."

Yousif tried to coax him. "Not now. Please, Uncle, don't give me a hard time. I want your opinion on something that can't wait."

Yousif's serious tone seemed to revitalize the sixty-five-year-old man. "You think I'm drunk?" he asked. "Don't worry, I'm not. Tipsy maybe, but not drunk. But look at poor Salman—he's falling asleep. That's what happens to those who never touch the stuff—one drink and they're out."

A pot of coffee later, Uncle Boulus was weary but coherent. He clicked his yellow worry beads and stared at the fogged window pane. Yousif and the women sat around him, huddling together uncharacteristically. The children played on the floor in one corner. Salman was slumped in his chair and beginning to snore, his head resting on his shoulder and his neck so bent and taut it seemed about to snap. Every time his wife tried to wake him, he would sit up, rub his face, and again doze off.

"I just couldn't do it," Uncle Boulus explained, referring to the trip to

Jericho to pledge allegiance to royalty. "I said to myself: this is one circus I refuse to join. I'm not the head of a clan, or a *mukhtar* or a city councilman as they tried to flatter me. Nor am I a doctor or an attorney or an exporter of Jaffa oranges to the whole world. Who am I to be dragged into that show?"

"Stop that kind of talk," his wife said, trying to pull him out of his doldrums. "Our house was always full of government officials and town dignitaries who came to wish you happy holidays. They all held you with deep respect, and you know it. I can't stand hearing you talk like this."

"Like it or not, it's the truth and you know it," he answered. "Look at us now: if they come now we can't even offer them a chair to sit on. And not a glass of arak or cognac. Not even a decent cup of coffee or a piece of *baklawa*. Who's kidding whom? Now I'm a simple shopkeeper who sells candy and gum and a pocketful of sunflower seeds to children. And every now and then half a pound of coffee or sugar to a poor housewife. Dignitary my foot. Pathetic, if you ask me."

It hurt Yousif deeply to hear the pain in his uncle's voice. He should stop this proud, dignified, and respected man from belittling his own stature or mocking his old self with liquor or in any other fashion. Yousif understood that Uncle Boulus was bemoaning more than the loss of stature. He was wrestling with the guilt of his generation. Not having done his share to prevent the catastrophe was now gnawing at him. One way to save face or retain a modicum of dignity, he must have realized, was his refusal to be stampeded into total submission. That was his way of upholding his *izzit nafs*—his self-respect. Yet shadowboxing guilt was no way to live. And for that realization alone Yousif was glad to see this basically honorable human being striving to rid himself of those phantoms.

Appraising the king in retrospect, Yousif said: "Not bad for a desert emir who first ascends a throne and then becomes the king of Jerusalem—one of the oldest cities on earth and certainly the world's holiest."

Uncle Boulus put the *masbaha* down and lit a cigarette. "Nor is it bad for a young teacher like you, barely out of high school, to be so insightful. Hey, sister, you should be very proud of your son. I know I am."

"If only his father could hear him," she said.

"And you, Maha. Tell your husband Yousif is following in his footsteps."

"He'd like that," Maha said.

Yousif would have none of it. "Truly, Uncle," he said, "ruling over the sophisticated Palestinians is quite a feat."

"Even for someone as ambitious as His Majesty," Uncle Boulus said, draining the last drop in his glass.

Despite the lightheartedness, the conversation did not placate Yousif's mother.

"What's the use," she said, sighing. "This is our fate."

Yousif looked shocked. "Mother!!!"

"And if I were you, Boulus, I would've gone to Jericho and joined that chorus."

Uncle Boulus smiled for the first time. "I said circus, not chorus."

"Circus . . . chorus . . . what's the difference."

"Mother!!!"

"Listen, son," she said, glaring at him. "Now that they know where your uncle stands they'll be watching his every move. Listening to his every word. In their eyes he's now a suspect—not a subject. Understand? *Suspect* not *subject*. Keep it in mind."

During the silence that followed, Yousif heard an alarm bell ring in his ears. He could envisage himself surrounded by spies and informers lurking in an environment full of rumors, suspicions, deceptions and unrest. The prospect of living in such a shadowy and dangerous world put him on edge.

"Your mother is right," Uncle Boulus said. "I'm not against the royal family, I just don't want to be anybody's subject. My only dream is to go home. Between now and then . . ."

". . . You don't care," Yousif again humored him.

"Not really. I don't care who's watching . . . who's listening . . . who's . . ."

Again Aunt Hilaneh was upset with him. "Boulus, what's happening to you? Since when you don't care how the wind blows? Get hold of yourself."

The change in this prudent and guarded family patriarch was so pronounced—a concoction of guilt, angst and alcohol—that Maha made the sign of the cross as if to exorcise the evil spirit in the room.

After a long, anguished pause, Uncle Boulus seemed to emerge from his cocoon. Calm was in his eyes; serenity covered his face. No longer disillusionment; no more quiet desperation.

"Egypt controls the Gaza strip," he said, draining the last drop of his coffee. "Jordan annexes the West Bank, Israel occupies four-fifths of Palestine. What's left for us to do? Nothing but fight."

Curious looks were exchanged at his sudden change of heart. Like everyone else. Yousif waited for the rest of his uncle's assessment.

"Armed struggle is the one and only solution," Uncle finally said, as resolved as any militant Yousif had ever known.

Picking up the coffee cups off the table, Maha looked more amused than stunned. "I can hardly believe my ears."

"For a minute you thought Basim was in the room," Yousif said, winking.

"I most certainly did," she admitted.

Twittering lasted only a moment, to be replaced again by Uncle's unmitigated depression.

"Our real pain has just begun," he predicted, like a prophet of doom.

The lingering silence was so deep it woke up Salman.

WITH JANUARY CAME AN armistice, a return to school, and a worsening of already horrendous weather. New tents had to be put up and the refugees who had settled in the classrooms had to be moved back to their camps. Some had to be hauled in Army trucks to the distant camps of Irbid and Jerash, even back to the winter resort of Jericho in the West Bank.

One morning Yousif was unnerved when he woke to find a thin layer of snow covering Amman.

"Snow in the desert!" he mused. "Mother, come and see!"

She walked next to him and could not believe her eyes. "Lord have mercy," she prayed, making the sign of the cross. "Lord, You know what you're doing, but we mortals are having a hard time trying to figure you out. Why this now? Why Lord?"

She wrung her hands and stared out the window. The children got excited and wanted to go out and play. But the adults, now gathering at the window to gawk at the scene below them, were too flabbergasted to move.

"What next?" Yousif's mother asked, still questioning her indifferent God. "Exile and misery aren't enough. You had to top it with snow? What will the refugees in the camps do now? What can they do?"

Two days later, the sky cleared, snow began to melt, and Yousif was able to slosh his way back to school. There he came upon another tragedy. Several people were gathered under a tree in the schoolyard. The body of a man from a nearby refugee camp was hanging. Yousif recognized him as one of the demonstrators who had protested the opening of the school. The wretched scene was as frightening as anything Yousif had seen in the war. It was not a horror film he was watching, he kept reminding himself; not a dream or even a nightmare. A man had actually taken his own life. Yousif could see the rope cutting into the middle-aged man's neck; snow outlined his head and shoulders. Some in the crowd moved close, but not Yousif. He could not stomach seeing a human being's tongue hanging out.

"The poor man couldn't take it," a weather-beaten refugee said. "It was too much for him."

Yousif turned to him and asked, "Does he have a family?"

"That's why he did it," the man replied, nodding his head. "He just walked out of the tent while they were asleep and hanged himself."

The shocking news of the hanging spread throughout Amman. Yousif heard people describe the victim as a good man who simply could not cope with his children going to sleep hungry. A few were less charitable, calling him a coward. Two nights later a ten-year-old girl on the other side of town followed suit. She had seen her father break down and cry for lack of food to feed his family, and she in turn could not take it. She imitated the man who had hanged himself. People were now worried about a rash of suicides. Conditions, they all knew, were conducive to such behavior. But all agreed on one thing: suicides had to be stopped. They criticized any open discussion of it, especially in front of children. Many threatened to boycott any newspaper which would cover such tragic incidents.

However, the next morning newspapers reported another violent act of different nature but of wider implications. An Egyptian had whipped out his pistol and fired its bullets into the heart of the prime minister. It was the first political assassination since the catastrophic war, and it charged Yousif and the whole Arab world with excitement. Who did it? What was his motive? Yousif followed the news with consuming interest, as did his colleagues and anyone else he met. He wished he could discuss it with Salwa.

Soon the suspicions were confirmed. The assassin was a member of the Muslim Brotherhood which blamed the prime minister for the Arab defeat. "He surrendered Palestine to the Zionists," the killer explained. Most people agreed, knowing that Egypt, the strongest and most populous Arab country, could have performed a lot better. But the felled prime minister had not been the only culprit. Corrupt King Farouk and his cronies, Yousif heard people talk, had been equally responsible.

"Who's the next target?" was the one question that echoed throughout the region.

AFTER SPENDING ANOTHER DAY out of town looking for Salwa, Yousif stopped at Basman coffeehouse to see Amin. Luckily the place was not as crowded as usual, and he was able to tell his friend about the endless and fruitless search for Salwa.

"You're gong to be more despondent when you hear what I have to tell you," Amin said, on his way to serve other customers.

When Amin returned with the empty brass tray in his hand, Yousif waited eagerly for him to unload on him the other bit of unhappy news.

"I have accepted the offer from Kuwait," Amin said.

Yousif stared dejectedly at him. "When are you leaving?"

"This afternoon."

"Now you tell me?"

"If you had not stopped today I would have come to your house to say goodbye," Amin said, biting his lower lip in apology.

Yousif could not be more glum. "I'll miss you, you know that. But I know it will be a good move for you. There's no future here."

"There may be a future for both of us. I'll stay in touch with you."

During breaks between serving new customers, Amin filled Yousif in on the particulars of his adventure. A customer had a good friend in Kuwait who was doing extremely well in the construction business. "He recommended me to him and this fellow, whom I have never met in my life, sent me a ticket to fly there as soon as possible. Can you believe it?"

Yousif had mixed emotions. "I'm happy for you. Really I am." And trying to inject a bit of humor, he added: "Who knows, you might find Salwa there. And if you do, I'm sure you'll let me know."

Amin laughed. "And if you find another girl like Salwa, you let me know. I'll marry her sight unseen. That's how much I trust you—and your taste in women."

Amin set the brass tray on the next table and hugged his friend. Yousif hugged him back, and the two didn't have to utter another word. Their eyes communicated a friendship from the cradle to the grave.

At the bottom of the stairway as Yousif left, he ran into some acquaintances who were with others he did not know. Soon they were approached by a Gaza woman named Rabha. The tall, slender, attractive villager was dressed in black and cradled a baby in her arms. She was a familiar figure around town. Men at the coffeehouses and in their shops liked her and joked with her, for, ironically, she was always in good cheer. Many considered her a good omen in that dreary landscape and looked forward to her coaxing a smile out of them every day.

"It's been a bad day, *shabaab*," she prodded them, stretching her hand. "Start digging in your pockets."

Yousif gave her a couple of piasters. Hikmat said he'd pass this time. Ustaz Murad stiffly shook his head.

"As ancient as you are," she told him, "you ought to be glad I included you among the *shabaab*."

That did not sit well with the curmudgeonly teacher. She mumbled under her breath and moved on. Others contributed as much as they could.

"Come on, *shabaab*," she urged them on with her open hand. "When I say I need help, it means I need help. Come on now."

"Why don't you work for a living?" a stranger among them asked unexpectedly. "Most people do."

The smile on her face faded. His tone obviously offended her. "Work doing what?" she asked, glaring at him.

"Anything," the stranger replied.

"Are you working?"

"No, I'm not."

"Then why do you expect me to find work?"

"It's easier for a woman."

"How?"

"It just is."

"Maybe your mother has some dirty linen she needs washed and ironed. Maybe she's too fat and lazy to clean the dishes and make the beds. Is this what you'd like for me to do?

"Why not?" the stranger persisted.

"Because I'm not a maid. I need help, but I'll be a servant to no woman."

"Why? Are you too good?"

As the discussion began to heat up, Yousif stepped forward and stretched his arms between the two. "Enough," he said.

"No, I'm not too good to work," Rabha replied, pulling down Yousif's arm. "Give me a decent job, and I'll take it, although I never worked a single day outside my home. But no man or woman should be a slave for the rich and lazy who won't do their own dirty work."

Her temper was rising, yet Yousif thought she looked beautiful in her anger. She reminded him of a nun: her flushed iconic face draped by the silky black shawl. Other men turned their heads in her direction. It was a tense moment, and Rabha never took her eyes off her tormentor.

"Some say the baby is just a pillow or a rag doll you cover under your shawl."

"Don't be ridiculous," Yousif told him. He and Hikmat and others had enough of the stranger and tried to stop his harangue, but the doubter ignored them.

"Who is this man?" Yousif asked Hikmat. Shrugging, Hikmat said he did not know. Perhaps he was a friend of Ustaz Murad. The sour-faced teacher shot them an irritable look, pursed his lips, looked at his gold-chain watch and walked away.

"It's fake, I tell you," the tormentor insisted. "Has anyone here ever seen the face of her baby?"

"No, I haven't," Yousif replied. "But I'd take her word before yours."

Yousif had always disliked men with leathery faces or narrow eyes or thick necks as much as he disliked those who smacked their lips when they ate or chewed gum in public. He decided on the spot that Rabha's obnoxious accuser had such offensive qualities.

With her eyes fixed on the stranger, Rabha unveiled her baby's face. It was a nine-month-old boy, she told them. His black hair was uncovered, and his eyes were closed. The tense silence was interrupted with words such as "lovely" and "beautiful" and "*ismallah*," uttered by everyone around. Except the accuser.

"It's not yours," the accuser said, sounding more and more belligerent.

"Whose is it then?" Rabha shot back in furious calm.

"You must've borrowed him to make people feel sorry for you. It's a cheap trick. And you shouldn't get away with it."

Now Yousif was truly infuriated by the unending insolence. But before he could take the stranger on, the man himself clenched his fist. "I'm sick and tired of your insults . . . your scowls . . . and your intrusion," he snarled at Yousif.

Hikmat was quick enough to stop a blow from landing on Yousif's face. But the scuffling was ended by the arrival of a Bedouin soldier making the rounds on the street,

"Is someone bothering you, *ya okht*?" the soldier kindly asked. "Why the commotion?"

Rabha wanted no trouble. She thanked the soldier and flashed him a beguiling smile.

"Just a friendly dispute," she pretended. "I tell them it's a boy and this one keeps insisting it's a girl."

The short, pleasant-looking soldier had a shaggy goatee and wore his hair long underneath his red-and-white checked desert *hatta*. He looked around for confirmation of what he had just heard.

"Here," Rabha said, "look for yourself."

Slowly, a big grin burst on the soldier's dark face. "*Tabarak Allah!*" he said, almost touching the baby's cheek with his bony forefinger. "*Tabarak Allah*. Not dark enough to be a Bedouin, but he'll make a fine warrior."

The nimble soldier left them in good cheer, but Rabha was still piqued. Some in the group began to walk away, taking the scoundrel with them, and she followed. Yousif was a couple of steps behind her.

"I should've let that soldier handcuff you," she accosted her accuser. "But I wanted you to see that I'm more decent than you are."

"Let it go, Rabha," Hikmat advised, gently trying to block her. "You don't have to listen to his nonsense."

Yousif appreciated her justifiable outrage and stayed right behind her as she pushed her way through the congested sidewalk to catch up with the jerk who seemed sheepishly trying to get away. But she cornered him.

"What makes you say such lies?" she asked him, aware that a small circle of pedestrians was forming around her.

"Those who know you say you've never been married," the offender replied, "and that you're not a mother."

"And you believe them?" Yousif said, his tone hostile.

"I do," the stranger said, giving Yousif a dirty look.

Suddenly, and right on one of the busiest sidewalks in Amman, Rabha calmly and methodically pulled out her ample breast and squirted her motherly milk into her accuser's astonished face.

Eyes bulged. Words froze in onlookers' mouths.

How ironic, Yousif thought, for a woman born and raised in a conservative society to abandon her cultural modesty in order to defend her personal honor. The fragility of principles, he rationalized, must be another tragic outcome of war. His reverie ended when he realized that the new commotion had brought the Bedouin soldier back.

He arrived on the scene: unhurried, grinning, and still murmuring his blessings: "*Tabarak Allah . . . Tabarak Allah*."

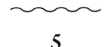

5

WITH ALL THE SOUL-SEARCHING and the anguish that had sent Uncle Boulus to the bottle, driven parents and children to suicide, made men like Tariq depend on sedition as a way of life, and compelled Rabha to bare her breast in public; with all the interminable talk about politics—at home, at school, at work, at coffeehouses, and, presumably, in bed; and with all the accusations and counter-accusations which flew around and which saw the Palestinian point his finger of suspicion at himself, at Arab kings and presidents, at the Ottoman Empire, at the West in general and Britain in particular, Yousif was a young man who could not swim across his troubled ocean.

And what a stormy ocean it was. Every time he attempted to float, the high waves crashed over him. To make bad things worse, the futile search for Salwa wrapped him in a shroud of despair.

Uncle Boulus, whose penchant to foretell was now spiked with liquor, once observed, "One day children will grow up and spit in their fathers' faces." Yousif thought often about that statement and wondered just how far off that day was. The night Uncle Boulus made that prediction Yousif had a dream. He saw himself straying into a room full of switchboard operators. Hundreds of hands were plugging and unplugging wires in and out of tiny sockets, and hundreds of foreign-sounding voices were overlapping each other into hundreds of microphones. Lost and helpless, he could not understand a word. He desperately needed someone who could talk to him in his tongue, someone who could guide him out of the maze.

It was revolutionary Basim who in the spring once again returned home, this time from Syria and Lebanon. And for the first time he seemed in no hurry to rush back out. Basim brought with him all his worldly possessions: two battered suitcases full of dirty laundry, two pairs of shoes, two belts, and a shaving kit. His suits and shirts, all in solid colors, were in an equally scuffed garment bag. That, to Yousif, was a clear indication that his cousin was home to stay. For how long he had no idea, and Basim would not tell. What Yousif did know was that Basim's appearance made life at home quite interesting. The children clustered around Basim who showered them with hugs and kisses and never failed to pull out of his pockets two or three packs of gum or a handful of English toffee.

Uncle Boulus and Salman welcomed Basim's return as a tonic for an existence that had grown stale and monotonous. Many close friends began to visit, although Basim did not yet want it widely known that he was back. As to the women of the house, they were beyond themselves trying to stretch their meager means to prepare him a favorite dish, although Yousif suspected the ambivalent Basim was like the enchanting hedonist who preferred "a loaf of bread, a jug of wine and thou beside me," the "thou" here being a political animal like him or an embittered soul. On the other hand, his visit created vexing sleeping arrangements. In furtive looks and hushed voices the family members tried discreetly to give Basim and Maha some privacy. To avoid embarrassment and quell any concern, Basim would be the first to lie on the mattress laid out on the patio or the balcony, often with one of his children sleeping on his chest, leaving the opportunity to be alone with his wife to a remote chance.

One late evening, when Uncle Boulus had had one drink too many and Salman was already fast asleep, Basim was not only fully awake but seemed eager to have a private talk with Yousif.

"What time does the coffeehouse downstairs close?" Basim asked, glancing at his watch.

"It depends on business, I guess," Yousif answered.

"Let's go down for a smoke," Basim said. "It can't be too crowded at ten o'clock."

They sat alone at the little coffeehouse below their apartment and ordered two nergilehs and two cups of coffee. A few men were playing cards or dominoes and arguing over who should pay. The radio was broadcasting a reading from the Qur'an, and the young waiter with suspenders and a soiled apron was bringing in straw chairs from outside and stacking them up against the walls. Yousif and Basim sat close to the door and watched refugees come in and out of the rows of tents on the other side of the street.

"I can't imagine how they live," Yousif said, expelling a deep breath. "Open sewage. No toilets or any place to bathe. I can't imagine living like that."

"All thanks to Israel."

"The stories Mother tells about her visits to so many refugee camps are simply horrifying. You should hear her."

Basim nodded, pulling on his water pipe. "I've been to too many of them and I know exactly what you're talking about. That's why I'm starting a political organization. And I want you to be part of it."

Yousif listened and waited for more information.

"At first I hesitated to ask you because I knew your mother wouldn't want you to follow in my footsteps. In a way, I don't blame her. Look where all those years have gotten me. Besides, when you find Salwa, your mother will expect you to settle down and give her grandchildren."

"That's natural. After all, I'm her only son."

Basim nodded his head. "But if we don't all sacrifice, we might as well bid Palestine farewell."

"You can't possibly mean that."

"Not forever, for sure. But for at least a generation or two. I can tell you this: if we want to liberate it, and we all do, each of us must be willing to face the challenge. To put his neck and pocketbook on the line. No other way."

Yousif was in total agreement. "Palestine is worth it."

"Damn right Palestine is worth it. And a lot more. That's why I want you to join me."

A five-year-old boy appeared out of the dark and approached them with an open hand. Both Yousif and Basim handed him a few coins, feeling sorry for him.

"Go home, son," Basim told the young beggar. "You ought to be in bed."

The boy did not answer, and made the rounds to other tables. Soon another destitute followed, this time a middle-aged woman. She did not ask them to give her anything, and did not thank them when they did. She just moved before them like an apparition.

"There's nothing a mother won't do to feed her children," Basim said, motioning to the waiter for another piece of charcoal.

There was a long pause during which the garcon pushed the ashes of the nergileh aside and placed blazing pieces of charcoal atop the tobacco.

"Why me?" Yousif asked, his voice deliberate and even.

Basim took time to read his thoughts. "I need you. As simple as that." The water in the nergileh gurgled.

The garcon returned with another pot of coffee, refilled their cups and left.

"I've watched you grow and mature politically far beyond your years," Basim told him. "I saw in you leadership potential."

Though disinclined to flattery, Yousif appreciated the compliment and said so. "High praise coming from you."

"However I must warn you," Basim told him, holding his demitasse cup in mid-air. "Politics is a serious—even dangerous—business. If you have any reservation, back off right now. But, if you do join the organization, I'm going to lean heavily on you and give you a lot of responsibilities."

"Doing what?"

"To start with, I'd like for you to be our recording secretary."

Yousif looked disappointed. "I'd like for you to think of me differently. A spokesperson for my unlucky generation would be more like it."

"What?"

"I'm not a stenographer. If I join, I'd like to be an activist."

"You're jesting."

"No, I'm not."

Basim uncrossed his legs, pleased. "That's one of the things I like about you. You know your mind and you stick to it."

"How else would I have been able to marry Salwa?" Yousif reminded him.

"Stopping her wedding in church was quite a coup."

"It's the best thing I've done," Yousif said. "I've been looking for her everywhere. I even left a message for her on radio. On the program for people trying to reunite. Still can't find her. Any ideas?"

Basim assured him that in time he would find her. And that he would, of course, help him in his search. However, for the time being Basim was not to be distracted from his main mission: to build a liberation organization.

"Will it be strictly political or diplomatic?" Yousif inquired. "Electing candidates to the Parliament and influencing policies?"

Seconds after he had uttered the words, Yousif felt he had misspoken. He did not show sufficient grasp of what his cousin was contemplating.

Their long stare at each other was poignant.

"It would be both," Basim assured him. "Political and military. With emphasis on the latter."

"I thought so," Yousif said.

"Mind you," Basim continued, "we can't possibly be the only ones planning to start a resistance or liberation movement. Others are doing just that right now. I'm sure of it. I only hope they won't try to lure you away from us."

"You have nothing to worry about, unless . . ."

"Unless what?" Basim said, amused.

". . . you insist on my being a recording secretary."

Basim's face relaxed. "Do you prefer carrying a gun?"

"Eventually I may have to. But not yet. Right now I want to prepare myself for the period of transition we'll be facing. On the one hand I see Uncle Boulus and cousin Salman and thousands like them who, for reasons of their own, did one big zero to save our country. They are what I call the losing generation. On the other hand, I see the students in my class who have gone through hell. Each has lost a father or a brother or a sister. You should see the pain in the stories they tell. We're the unlucky generation. We were ambushed and expelled before we had a chance to grow up. In my opinion, we're your hope, the main force you can count on. We're the future generation that will lead us to victory."

"And to *al-awda* to our homeland."

"*Inshallah*."

Basim seemed impressed. "Quite a visionary, I must admit."

"If that's the organization you have in mind, I'm ready."

"Welcome," Basim said, shaking his hand. "I'll have more faith in you when you find Salwa."

Yousif smiled. "I have a new strategy for finding her. So far I've been looking for her in refugee camps on every Friday, my day off from school. But apparently not many Christians live there. I guess because they had a little more money on them when they were kicked out."

Basim nodded. "And in exile they could afford to rent an apartment. As we did. Or build a shack."

"Now I'm going to start looking for her on Sundays in churches. She's not a churchgoer but somebody might know where she is."

"Good idea," Basim said, wrapping the cord of his nergileh around its neck and getting ready to call it a night. "Have you gotten used to the idea of not having school on Friday?"

"Not really. But it's the Muslims' Sunday. And I respect that. Say, Basim, next time you go to Beirut or Damascus will you please bring me some books to read? I'm starving for information."

"What kind of books? Romantic comedies?" Basim asked, winking.

"You know exactly what I need. Arab history. Jewish history. Biographies. Anything on colonialism or whatever the West calls their evil empires."

The garcon appeared and Basim paid the bill and tipped him.

"How about *The Arab Awakening*? Would you like that?"

"I didn't know there was an awakening."

Basim put an arm around Yousif's shoulder and squeezed. "It's okay to be skeptical, but not cynical. You hear?"

"I'll try."

TO YOUSIF'S SURPRISE, THE first organizational meeting was held at Ustaz Sa'adeh's apartment on the third floor of a building just off the business district, facing the post office and the telephone and telegraph buildings. It was small but considerably more comfortable than his and Basim's dingy and crammed dwelling. Two or three families, according to Ustaz Sa'adeh, were squeezed in each apartment, and children were constantly running up and down the stairway. Their noise, coupled with the sound of traffic on the street below, made it rather safe for the conspirators to debate the issues with relative ease.

Yousif was immensely surprised to discover that his first cousin and his principal were so close. He had not been aware that the two were in cahoots for months. When he confronted them with his disbelief, they laughed and told him that they had kept him in the dark on purpose. They wanted to impress upon him that the essential quality in revolutionary work was secrecy.

"Never trust anyone," Basim told him.

"Not even your shadow," Ustaz Sa'adeh concurred.

Soon the attendees began to arrive. The first was Hanna Azar, who had worked at Haifa's seaport. Basim embraced him, led him inside and made the proper introductions. Yousif judged him to be around forty, although his hair was almost completely gray. He was nervous, sitting first on a chair with his back to the door, then getting up to look out the window, then sitting back down, this time facing the door. His handshake with Ustaz Sa'adeh, however, was long and friendly. The link between the two, obviously, was Basim, who was also the link between these two and the tall balding young man who arrived ten minutes later. This was Ali Bakri, the youngest of the guests—and only six or seven years older than Yousif. Ali still had that college exuberance even though he had graduated from law school several years earlier. He sat on the edge of the seat with his hands clasped between his legs, ready to immerse himself in whatever activity they were about to undertake. Yousif liked him instantly.

Within minutes, the room grew conspicuously quiet.

"Let's get started," Hanna said to Basim. "We're all here, are we not?"

Basim shook his head and took out a pack of cigarettes and passed it around. "One more is coming," he said, placing an ashtray between him and Hanna.

"Who might that be?" Hanna asked, leaning on his elbow.

"You'll see," Basim said, smiling. "While waiting, let me tell you the latest political joke I've heard. A Bedouin soldier in Jerusalem was ordered by his lieutenant to take down the numbers off the cars involved in traffic violations. Guess what he did? He went out and literally pulled down the tags off those cars until he had a sack full."

Some laughed, some rolled their eyes, the rest shook their heads.

"Hard to believe," Ali said, still laughing.

"It's absolutely true," Basim told him, chuckling.

"May God help us," Hanna said, his fingers tapping the armrest.

"These are our liberators no less," Basim added, walking toward the window to look out.

"What do you expect from a camel rider who had never been out of the desert?" Ustaz Sa'adeh asked,

Still standing by the window, his hands locked together behind his back, Basim turned and spoke to Ali. "Haven't you heard one lately? You always have a political joke tucked away."

"As a matter of fact I have," Ali said. Then facing the others he began: "Have you heard about the Lebanese who asked a Palestinian refugee to describe what happens in war?"

They all shook their heads and waited.

"Well," Ali continued, "the Palestinian refugee could see that this particular Lebanese was naive, so he told him: 'It's like this. You take a gun and I take a gun. You stand there and I stand here. You aim at me and I aim at you. Then we both shoot.' The Lebanese was shocked. 'You mean we shoot for real?' he asked. 'Yes,' the Palestinian told him. 'Mon Dieu,' the Lebanese shrieked in his affected French, 'to hell with that game.'"

Amidst the laughter they heard another knock on the door. This time Yousif was seated closer to the door than anyone else, so he was the one to open it. To his surprise, Raja Ballout was standing outside. Basim rushed to greet the mournful-looking, emaciated and famous journalist from Jaffa whose popular editorials often stung readers and authorities alike. His buttoned-up gray jacket with his left hand thrust in his pocket made him look sickly and in pain. The tightness of his lips and the sour expression on his face more than hinted at his derision of the world.

Yousif knew a lot about Raja for reasons other than his journalistic skills.

It was said that Raja had suffered brutally at the hands of the invading army.

Before the forced exodus, the stories went, Raja was visiting his sick sister in their hometown, when suddenly the house was surrounded by military jeeps. Five or six soldiers jumped out and demanded that Raja and the rest of the family evacuate the house. Raja told them that his sister was bedridden and desperately needed medical attention. Her two young teenagers could testify to that. The soldiers could come in and see for themselves. She had a gallbladder attack and ought to be hospitalized, he repeated. He even led them to her bedroom to prove his point. Her face was pale and contorted, and her hands were clutching her right side.

"It will be most kind of you if you would help us move her to the hospital in one of your jeeps," Raja appealed to the soldier, with his nephew and niece moving closer to their mother's bed. Other soldiers, also with guns at the ready, were standing behind him and to the side of the room.

"You must be crazy," replied the first soldier, his gun pointed at him and his finger on the trigger. "Hurry up and take her with you."

"How am I going to take her?" Raja pleaded. "I don't have a car. I can't call a taxi. And look for yourself, she simply can't walk,"

"Then I'll help you out," the soldier said

With mystifying nonchalance, the soldier pulled out his bayonet and walked toward the bed. With one master stroke, he slit her throat. It was like a flash, so electrifying, and so particularly wild, that the poor woman didn't have a moment to blink her eye or make a peep.

A blast of horror filled the house. The children howled. Raja froze in place, his eyes glazed.

"Now you don't have to worry about taking her to the hospital. Get out."

Between looking at his dead sister with the blood oozing on the bed sheet, and with her hysterical children throwing themselves on her feet and chest, Raja felt utterly helpless. What could he do with the killer giving him a murderous look? Raja blamed himself for not having defended her. But he couldn't have, he told himself. Defend her with what? With his bare hands? His impotence, anger, despair, and indescribable shame consumed him. The world was closing in on him. Suffocating him. Suddenly he pictured the room as Hades, with a huge monster at the gate licking its chops, ready to swallow them.

"Church . . . simple funeral," Raja blurted, his well-known eloquence escaping him. ". . . cemetery . . . burial."

"No problem," the soldier assured him. "We'll bury her for you here and now."

"You'll do what?" Raja screamed, his eyes bulging.

"Just take the kids with you and get out before I kill all of you. Out, I said. Out, out."

Raja couldn't fathom how a human being could be so cruel, so cold-blooded. Traumatized, he led his niece and nephew out of the house onto the main street, and the boy and girl never stopped sobbing and clinging to him. After walking less than fifty yards, they heard an explosion. Their hearts sank. With sheer terror gripping their heart and soul, they slowly turned around to look. What they saw engulfed them in a higher level of panic. Their house was tumbling down. The body of their slain mother/sister was literally buried beneath the rubble.

"The bastard kept his word," Raja muttered, over and over again, enfolding the orphaned niece and nephew in his arms and leaning against a lemon tree. As the youngsters sobbed uncontrollably and kicked whatever was before them, Raja found himself too outraged to even cry. Dry-eyed and with all the solemnity he could muster, he made a silent vow to whomever or whatever or whichever was listening that the death of his slain sister would be avenged. So help him God, her death would be—most emphatically must be—avenged.

All of this Yousif had known already not only from stories that circulated about the famed journalist, but mainly from an article he himself had published under the title "Slain Mother / Slain Sister." Yousif still recalled the power of his words and the chilling effect it had on him and the multitudes of readers. Now he was in the presence of that same man, that same chronicler of Palestinian pain and suffering. He felt fortunate, even proud, to be associated with any group that included Raja.

"We all know why we are here," Basim began. "And I trust we are in agreement on what needs to be done. For the sake of clarity, let me repeat what I have told each of you in private, so that there will be no misunderstanding or secrets among us. What we're planning to do is build a political and military organization for the sole purpose of liberating our homeland. The real war is on the horizon, and we must be ready to fight on many fronts. Our organization and many other organizations like it, that are being established as we speak, will be the new factor in the equation. The winning difference. There's no other way left for us to redeem ourselves. I'm convinced, as all of you are, that our forced exile is meant to be permanent. Many of us thought we were going to be allowed to return home before last Christmas. We all know how naïve that expectation was. Many Christmases and many Easters and many Ramadans will come and go and our refugees will still be rotting in camps."

Yousif looked around and found everyone rapt in silence.

"The Zionists," Basim continued, lighting a cigarette, "did not work for the last fifty years to walk away from a victory that must've surpassed their wildest dreams. Not a chance. What they occupied they want to keep, make no mistake about it."

Raja was the first to offer an opinion, "The first president of so-called Israel reportedly cried when the conflict ended before they could occupy the whole country."

"For sure," Hanna added. "The head of their underground wants Palestine and Trans-Jordan for a start. The boundaries of his Eretz Israel stretch from Iraq to Egypt. His record is clear on that."

Basim returned to his interrupted introduction. "You are both correct. But how many of our so-called leaders have taken all these questions seriously? If the leaders are a lost cause, it is our job to awaken the masses to the enemy's grand design. Ours is a monumental job—no question about it. But start we must."

The discussion began and Yousif felt the urge to make his views known, if only to justify his youth among older men. But he considered it sensible to bide his time.

"The first thing we need to do," Ali said, "is to forget once and for all that there are Arab regimes and Arab leaders. They are all a sorry bunch."

Raja eyed Ali with a smile that seemed to attribute his sweeping generalization to immaturity. "I understand what you're saying," he said, "but governments and rulers have armies. They have tanks and planes and rockets and all kinds of armaments. And we don't have a single hand grenade—not yet, anyway."

Suddenly Ali was on the defensive. "But they hardly committed themselves or much of the equipment they did have. What's the use of having it if you don't use it?"

"Some did, maybe not as well as we had hoped, but they did. There's no denying that there were some heroes in those battles."

"And a lot of traitors in high places, if you ask me."

"That's the reason we are refugees," Basim said, eager to stop the early and unsuspected wrangling. "That's the reason we are meeting today. That's the reason we need to form this organization. To address all these issues."

"There are millions of good and patriotic people in those countries who are as angry and bewildered as we are over what happened," Ustaz Sa'adeh volunteered. "One of the aims of this organization is to keep an eye on all of our leaders, and to sort out the trustworthy from the corrupt. To support those who share our agenda and oppose those who don't."

"And when will we defeat and expel the enemy?"

"Patience, Ali, patience," Hanna counseled. "That day will come sooner than you think."

In an effort to shift from the argument that teetered on becoming heated, Yousif posed a question to the famed journalist, hoping to engage him. "What should our first priority be now: the pen or the gun?"

"What do you think?" Raja responded.

"Both," Yousif said. "It depends on the situation. From what I hear most of our real battles were fought in the halls and chambers of governments here and abroad. Congresses, senates, parliaments, palaces, embassies, and the rest. The military outbreaks were an aftermath."

When Yousif finished, he was surprised to find all eyes were focusing on him, as if they had not expected such analysis from an upstart. A moment of silence lingered, which threw Yousif in deeper thought. Maybe he should not have been so presumptuous as to speak so readily to people who supposedly knew a lot more than he did. Maybe they thought he was too young to speak of warfare as a result of failed diplomacy. Or to say that diplomacy or the failure of diplomacy was a precursor to the clash of arms.

Abide your time, he chastised himself, and don't be so rash. So pompous. You would alienate potential friends. To his relief, he heard Hanna say to the principal, "Ustaz Sa'adeh, I congratulate you for having taught Yousif so well. I wish more adults knew half of what he knows."

"The credit is all his," Ustaz Sa'adeh said. "He's always been our top student, and now one of our best teachers."

"He was also raised well," Basim added. "His father, Dr. Jamil Safi, who was also my uncle, was a rarity: a healer, not just a physician. And his private library was the best I've seen."

It was Yousif's turn to deflect the attention away from himself. "I didn't mean to be a distraction. I truly apologize."

With that, the meeting proceeded as Basim had planned. He divided the priorities under different headings: fundraising, recruiting, training within the country or abroad, buying or smuggling arms, buying a printer to publish their own newspaper and occasional leaflets. Then he asked those gathered to express their opinions on each heading, one by one. The money issue was the most dominant, and everyone wondered where it would come from. Basim mentioned Palestinians who still had money stashed in foreign banks, Arab states already awash with oil revenues, the millions of Arabs living in the Diaspora: South America, United Sates, Canada and countries as far away as Australia. Not to mention Muslim countries (stretching from Morocco to Indonesia) that were chafing at the loss of Al-Aqsa Mosque, one of the three holiest shrines in Islam. The possibilities were limitless, he said, and moved on to the subject of recruiting.

Here he emphasized and everyone agreed that a small force of a thousand men and women who were well-chosen, well-recruited, well-motivated, well-trained, and well-equipped could deliver more than a blow to their sworn enemy. Over the years, of course, they could double or even triple the size of that force. By that time they would have most likely merged with other liberation groups to make their sworn enemy realize that hijacking a whole country would never be tolerated.

After directing Hanna to the bathroom, Ustaz Sa'adeh motioned to Yousif to follow him to the kitchen. Yousif marveled at the preparation that had been done much earlier. On the spotless counter was a tray of six tall glasses and a pitcher of iced water. Next to it were a kerosene burner with a box of matches, another tray of demitasse cups, a large brass coffee pot, a small sugar container, a jar of coffee—even a small spoon with which to scoop the grinds.

"Do you know how to make coffee?" Ustaz asked. "Frankly I don't. I'll take the tray of water to the other room and I'd appreciate your making the coffee."

While waiting for the coffee to percolate, Yousif could see from the small undraped window over the sink the mud huts and the rows of tents in which some of the refugees lived. He could also hear the sound of a truck groaning and screeching from old age, and the voices of children playing in the dusty street. If only the truck driver and the children knew, Yousif thought, that Basim and fellow patriots were at that moment conspiring to change their destiny.

Watching the coffee boil, Yousif reflected on the proceedings in the other room. He was struck by the challenge facing them. Defeating a sworn enemy that had been scheming and plotting for half a century—backed by America and the major powers of Europe—was like a child trying to climb the highest Giza pyramid. He had once heard his pacifist father say that evil begat evil, and wondered what he would say to him now. "Son," he would probably say, "it's a daunting task indeed, but what's the alternative? Injustice must be confronted." Basim, of course, was intent on answering thunder with thunder. Considering the tremendous odds against them, Yousif thought, a tooth for a tooth and an eye for an eye was more like it. If only they could, he told himself; if only they could.

"Tell me something about Ali," Yousif asked when Ustaz Sa'adeh returned to the kitchen. "He's itching to fight."

"His father and Basim were together during the 1936 revolt," Ustaz Sa'adeh explained. "They fought the British and the Jewish underground and finally went into hiding in Iraq. They didn't return until after World War II, when the British Mandate exacted promises from them to lay down their arms. You should know all this from Basim's own history."

"Where's Ali's father?"

"Apparently either the Irgun or the Hagana had a special grudge against him," Ustaz continued. "Soon after they entered Lydda, they waited for him to come out of the mosque after the Friday prayer. When Ali's father saw a dozen soldiers with guns at the ready, he knew what to expect. He raised his hands above his head and tried to negotiate with them. He said he'd be willing to leave town with all the people they were expelling. In answer, they riddled his head and chest with bullets. The casualties around him were countless. How Ali escaped unharmed was a miracle. Now he's out for revenge."

"Wow," Yousif said. "I didn't know that."

When both rejoined the rest, the discussion underway was about what to call their fledgling organization. Many words were bandied about, including "movement" or "revolution" or "liberation" or "institution" or "institute"—or even "jihad." The last word was unanimously rejected because of religious connotations. The conflict was complex enough, they all thought, and there was no need to broaden it. Finally they settled on something simpler and catchier.

"At least for now," Basim suggested, "let's call it *Amana*. Amana as a vow. Amana as a sacred trust to keep Palestine alive in our hearts. Let's test it on the people. I have a feeling it will resonate with them."

A new debate arose as to whether or not they should go public with the creation of the organization.

"The less we say about it the better," Yousif argued.

"I agree," Hanna added. "No sense in alerting the authorities to our existence. God knows they'll be infiltrating us soon enough."

Ali nodded. "Also, new recruits would be intrigued by belonging to an organization that operated in total darkness."

"In secrecy," Raja suggested instead. "In total darkness might be mis-construed. They might think of us as the blind leading the blind."

After agreeing that initially it would serve them best to run their affairs clandestinely, they began to address the important question of recruiting. This issue occupied them past lunchtime. They went round and round trying to identify the characteristics of the thousand-member force they wished to recruit.

The idea of recruitment led to another subject that was unanimously agreed on: to open up several youth clubs in the major cities. Ostensibly that was to keep the idle youth off the streets, but in reality it was to keep an eye on those who might one day qualify for membership.

"We need all types of men," Basim said, "and not just freedom fight-ers ready to shoot or throw bombs. Before we admit anyone, he or she must have two qualifications. One, they should come from families that lost more than just property. They must've been injured in their guts. They must've lost someone dear to them at the hands of our sworn en-emy. They will be the ones itching to get even. Two, not a single one of them would be officially admitted into this organization until they have been meticulously scrutinized by a reviewing committee. Checking the recruits' backgrounds diligently is a must. We need to make sure that they are not lying. This might take weeks, even months. Which is as it should be. The important thing is to guard against having a mole working on somebody else's behalf. If one manages to slip in, he's mine. I'll deal with him personally."

Switching the conversation, Yousif wanted to know about the political aspect of Amana. How would it be organized? And, what would it entail?

It was the signal for Raja to rise, ready to leave. "That's another story for another day," he said. "If it took God seven days to create this wicked world, how long do you think it should take us to plan the liberation of beautiful Palestine? A few hours?"

On that note, the meeting was adjourned. On his way out, Yousif found himself walking with Hanna Azar. Hanna was the only enigma among the group. Yousif wished to ask about his background but did not want

to seem too inquisitive. Luckily it was Hanna who wanted to hear about
Yousif's background.

"I know you're Basim's first cousin," Hanna began. "But tell me, are
you one of those injured souls Basim wants to recruit? What have you
lost beside your home?"

Yousif tried to be evasive. "I lost most of Palestine, isn't that enough?"

"We all did. But what in particular did you lose to qualify you to be a
member of Amana? Your kinship to Basim notwithstanding."

On the sidewalk, they ran into Rabha, her palm forever open. She
flashed Yousif a smile of recognition and gratitude. Yousif smiled back,
gave her a coin and introduced her to his companion. By reflex, Hanna
reached in his pocket and handed her whatever he could afford.

As they continued their walk, Yousif told Hanna about the incident
with the jerk who had doubted that the poor woman was carrying her
own baby. And how she had pulled out her breast on the sidewalk and, in
front of many onlookers, squirted her motherly milk in her accuser's face.

"Good for her," Hanna said, incredulous.

"He was so outrageous I wanted to punch him in the nose."

"I would've. But tell me, what did you lose in the war?"

Yousif did not know where to begin. He told him how his father had
been killed during an incursion by the enemy on top of a hill in Ardallah.
He had gone there to treat Basim who was wounded but would not leave
the battle scene. He also told him about Salwa's father's death in the open
desert during the treacherous journey on foot to Jordan. The sun was
merciless on that day and they had to leave his body prey to wild animals.
One couldn't imagine the pain the family had to endure. Furthermore,
he told him how he and Salwa got separated, and what agony it had been
looking for her.

"What else would you like to know?" Yousif asked, "Oh, yes. I also lost
one of my dearest friends, a Jewish boy I grew up with and went to school
with from first grade through high school. His name was Isaac Sha'lan."

The circumstances of Isaac's killing clouded Hanna's face.

"We seem to have much in common," Hanna began, weaving his way

around the congested sidewalk. "One of my distant uncles was an Orthodox priest. His oldest son was married to Raheel, a Jewish woman. In
those days marriage between faiths was not uncommon in the big cities."

"I know," Yousif said. "Nablus has a number of such marriages."

"When the hostilities intensified, the Zionists who had emigrated from
Europe wanted Raheel to end her friendship with the natives. That's what
they used to call us. But Raheel refused. As the situation heated up, and
our neighborhood was being bombarded, my mother sought refuge at her
friend's house. She called her up and Raheel told her to come over, she
would be waiting for her. My mother did exactly that. She went straight
to Raheel's house, but apparently terrorists from the Jewish Stern Gang
were waiting for her arrival. When Raheel opened the door, they plastered
her and my mother with a hail of bullets."

Numbed by hearing so many such horror stories, Yousif remained
visibly unperturbed.

"If you didn't witness the killing, how did you come to know the details?"

"The Stern Gang claimed responsibility and bragged about it that same
night on their underground radio. They meant it as a warning to any Jew
who might harbor any sympathy with an Arab."

Yousif nodded knowingly. "My mother used to tell me that in Jerusalem, where she was born, new immigrants always discouraged Jews from
mixing with so-called 'natives.' But I've never heard of Jews killing Jews."

"Your mother was talking about the 1920s. I'm talking about 1948.
Things became a lot rougher. Jews killed Jews in Iraq to force them to leave
and fight in the upcoming war. And to settle in the land of milk and honey."

After a long pause, Hanna added: "Our experiences qualify us to be
legitimate members in Basim's Amana," Hanna said.

"Our Amana," Yousif said.

"I stand corrected."

Hanna bought a pack of cigarettes from a young refugee with a badly
damaged eye, perhaps from a sniper's bullet. His tray of trinkets was
strapped around his neck. They lit their cigarettes and jostled their way
through the crowd in silence. When they were about to go their separate

ways, they looked at each other, their eyes full of gloom.

"What plans do you have for the future?" Yousif asked.

The unexpected question gave Hanna a pause. "To live without shame. And you?"

"To live with honor."

As if to gloss over the subtle difference or to rectify the imbalance in their perceptions, they sealed their newly formed bond with a warm handshake.

Both walked away with heavy hearts—but determined not to veer from the huge struggle ahead.

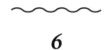

6

THE ORGANIZATION OPENED ITS first youth club, Nadi Al-Amana, in an old converted warehouse on the edge of the Amman business district. On one side of the lobby was a reading room of sorts, where patrons sat and read newspapers or magazines. Next to it was a kitchen and mini-coffeehouse, where a couple of boys worked as waiters. The three rooms on the other side provided ample space for physical activities. One room was for ping-pong, a second one for gymnastics, and the third one, the largest, was designated for boxing. In the middle of the room a ring built on a makeshift platform was bordered with heavy ropes on four sides. And in one corner, space was secluded to serve as a dressing room.

The stretch of rooms on the mezzanine was basically for the Amana organization. One office was for Basim, who would use it whenever he happened to be in town. Another was Raja's office, the editor of the yet-to-be-launched *Amana Daily*, which was to be a modest four-page newspaper. And one room was for a secretary and two part-time reporters, yet to be hired.

With a couple of sheets in hand, Yousif entered Basim's office and found him busy reviewing some of the articles to be published in the first edition of the newspaper.

"What have you got?" Basim asked, barely looking up.

"The article you asked me to write."

"That's quick. Put it down and I'll take a look at it."

Unobtrusively, Yousif did as he was told and went downstairs to wait for the verdict on his maiden journalistic effort. He did not have to wait long. Ten minutes later, he heard Basim calling from the mezzanine. He put down the magazine he was leafing through and dashed upstairs.

"Raja is going to love it," Basim told him as he entered the office. "Let's show it to him."

Together they found Raja pecking at the typewriter with two fingers and waited for him to finish recording his thoughts. Basim handed him the article and waited for his reaction. A few minutes later, Raja's face brightened.

Not known for his humility, Yousif had chosen to chastise the entire Arab nation. "Where among us are the leaders in the arts, literature, and science? Where is the Arab scientist worthy to be the descendent of our forebears who made undeniable contributions to medicine, astronomy, and mathematics? Where is the new Ibn Sina? Or Ibn Rushd who was the first to advocate, before the Renaissance, the separation between faith and reason?"

As he watched Raja read and re-read what he had submitted, Yousif wondered whether they would consider him full of himself or talking above his head. But he did not care. What he had written expressed exactly how he felt. He knew that Salwa would agree with him.

"Listen to this," Raja said, reading aloud. "'A nation incapable of producing such giants is equally incapable of true independence and is ultimately destined to be embroiled in future battles. There is an inescapable correlation between culture and freedom.'"

Motioning for Basim and Yousif to sit, Raja continued reading. "So long as we Arabs remain in a state of political chaos, we will always be in danger of more and more defeats. So long as we continue to flounder in a state of incompetence, delusion and, above all, disunity, our countries will be ripe for the vultures to devour. So long as we allow selfishness and bickering among ourselves to continue we will be condemned to remain on the fringe of modern civilization. Our new generation must rid itself of the consciousness of shame and replace it with consciousness of pride— pride in our heritage, pride in our future."

Raja looked at Basim, astonished. "Who helped you write it?"

"Who me? This is Yousif's paper. Not mine."

Both Raja and Yousif looked equally baffled. All along Yousif thought Raja knew that he had written it. And all along Raja was under the impression that Basim had penned what he handed him to read. A few embarrassed glances across the room finally put the matter aright.

"Apologies, Yousif," Raja said, extending his hand. "Young man, I predict a bright future for you as a writer."

"Right now we need warriors not writers," Basim said, laughing. "Unless they're brilliant like the two of you, of course."

"The pen and the gun, remember?" Yousif said, his confidence restored.

Basim grabbed the article and began to read. "Listen to this, will you? 'We must discard the shackles of ignorance and ill-directed passion and face the twentieth century. The abyss between us and the civilized world must be bridged in haste or we shall be doomed to remain forever colonized.'"

Yousif was elated by Raja's praise and Basim's enthusiasm.

Next morning the first issue of *Amana Daily* hit the streets. Seething with nationalist indignation and desperate for a flicker of hope, the readers of the first edition were equally impressed as they flooded the editor with calls.

Yousif could not be happier. His words, thoughts, and ideas were being read and discussed in offices, homes, barber shops, coffeehouses, and even in refugee camps. His colleagues and students congratulated him. Friends slapped him on the back, and girls pointed him out. Learning that the first issue was a complete sell-out, he was so happy, he hugged Basim around the waist, lifted him up and whirled him around. If only Salwa, he thought, could have read the article. Surely she would have located him then. Where in the world was she?

But happiness for Yousif that day was short-lived. On his way home, he stopped at Hikmat's house to make sure he had seen the first issue. Hikmat had gone home to lunch that day and had not returned to school. It was past four o'clock when Yousif stopped to check on him, and neighbors were milling in the street, gloom on their faces. They reminded him of the days in Ardallah before the expulsion.

"What's wrong?" he asked Jawdat, one of Hikmat's friends.

"It's his sister-in-law," Jawdat answered.

"Leena? What about her?"

"She's been gone for over twelve hours," another man said, "and no one knows where she is. It's not like her."

"Where's Hikmat?" Yousif asked.

"Inside. With the police."

"Police?"

"What do you expect? They have to investigate."

Yousif attempted to go in and see for himself, but with one look and a slight head movement Jawdat restrained him.

Yousif stood with the rest of the neighbors milling around, and waited for Hikmat to emerge. Meanwhile, he heard all kinds of speculation: Leena was extremely unhappy; Leena wanted a divorce; Leena was kidnapped; Leena was probably in love and ran off with her lover.

For two days the neighborhood hummed with questions. When Hikmat finally showed up at school, he was surrounded by many.

"According to the police," Hikmat told Yousif and a few others, "she crossed Ramtha on her way to Lebanon."

That only fueled more rumors: When did she cross the border? When did she have the passport photographs taken? Who helped her obtain the documents necessary to obtain a passport? Where did she get the travel money?

Three days later, her husband Fareed received a brief note from her in the mail, blunt and rude. She was gone, she had written, and there was no use looking for her. Under no circumstances would she ever consider returning. In truth, she had added, she was on her way to Brazil where she would start the divorce proceedings. And quite sharply, she added, save yourself the money and the agony. She would never ever come back.

The husband read the letter sitting by himself at a congested coffee-house. Eyewitnesses said he simply crumbled the letter and began to sob.

Only after Leena's disappearance, Yousif noticed, did Hikmat's family show genuine signs of distress. Only then, and for the first time, did Hikmat open up and talk to Yousif about his brother's personal life. They were alone in the reading section at the Nadi when the unloading of grief began.

"Fareed and Leena got married a few months before the war," Hikmat confided. "She was considered one of the prettiest girls in town and Fareed handsome and quite a catch. And, without bragging, we were relatively comfortable. Many said we were rich, but that's a matter of opinion. Everybody thought the couple were well suited for each other. For the first few months after the wedding they were extremely happy. You could see it in their eyes, and hear it their giggles. Then the war came, and everything changed. Fareed lost his right eye, and was no longer handsome. We, as a family, lost our riches. Everything we owned—home, rental properties, orange grove, two cars, bank accounts—suddenly vanished. Leena couldn't cope with her misfortune and became intolerable."

"As if it were Fareed's fault," Yousif said.

"Exactly," Hikmat continued. "Even as an impoverished refugee she demanded the same style of living as before. She bought fine clothes, slept until noon, and spent endless hours in front of the mirror. You saw how she presented herself in public."

"Yes, I did," Yousif said, nodding.

"The catastrophe—or *al-nakba* as it is now called—the loss of our homeland, the forced exile, didn't make a dent in her attitude. I saw how selfish she was and felt sorry for my brother. I also felt sorry for her, too. A vain and shallow woman like her, who cared about her own pleasure and nothing else, ought to be pitied."

"No doubt," Yousif agreed.

"I watched her tantrums, and heard her bitching, but I kept quiet to prevent things from getting out of hand. But . . ."

Hikmat's gloom was as thick as syrup. Yousif listened to him and let him unload. He also began to consider him an excellent recruit for Amana. He should recommend him to Basim and Ustaz Sa'adeh.

"How did Fareed lose his left eye?"

Hikmat took a deep breath and tried to collect his thoughts. "As I said, my father was considered a rich man. He built a six-bedroom house between Ramleh and Jaffa and finished it shortly before the outbreak of the war. I spent only one year in it, before we were expelled at gunpoint."

Yousif nodded his head, similar memories flooding his mind,

"On the outskirts of town," Hikmat continued, "they frisked every-one of us and got angry whenever they couldn't find anything of value. The soldier who searched my mother was a female who wanted to know where she had hidden her jewelry. 'We know you're rich,' the soldier said. 'Where is your diamond wedding ring? Where are your gold bracelets?' Father, who was standing by, explained that they had to sell all she had in order to finish building the house. 'Liar . . . liar,' another male soldier barked, slapping his face. Fareed and I were mortified but helpless in the presence of all that weaponry. To appease the soldiers, Fareed offered them his wife's wedding ring, which they pocketed in a hurry. This was another thing Leena held against him."

"Poor Fareed was trying to save lives," Yousif said.

"Exactly. But that's not the way she saw it. Anyway, they took the ring and all the money that father had on him and then shot him because they said he had lied to them."

"How heartless."

"They shot him again. Yousif, as long as I live I'll never forget how his body, already flat on the street, made a couple of jumps, or jerks if you will, before he took his last breath."

"Is that when a stray bullet hit Fareed's eye?"

"Whether it was stray or not I couldn't tell. I was too busy crying over my father's body and trying to stop mother from screaming any louder. I was afraid the soldiers would go wild and start shooting again. Strangely, the very opposite happened. The sudden burst of violence seemed to shock them and to bring some kind of sanity to their heads. They stopped firing and began pushing us out."

Yousif took a deep breath. "There was nothing you could've done but comply. The same thing happened to us."

Hikmat stared at Yousif. "Believe it or not," he added, "we still resisted. Father was already dead, and Fareed's face was a mess and blood was all over him, so why leave? They began to fire again, this time in the air and on the ground around our feet. Just to scare us. And they did."

"They were determined to get all of us out."

Hikmat lit a cigarette and took a long drag. "I swear to you, Yousif, during that whole ordeal we saw bodies of friends and neighbors strewn all over town. I couldn't help but puke."

"I believe you," Yousif said, the muscles of his jaws tightening.

A young waiter approached them with a small pot of coffee and two demitasse cups. Ironically, the noise from the billiard and ping-pong sections filled their isolation with a sense of peace.

"Was your father telling the truth when he said he had sold your mother's jewelry to finish building the house?" Yousif asked.

Hikmat shook his head. "Father thought he could outsmart them. He knew from the start that the invading soldiers were robbing people. So one night he went out and hid the jewelry in a small cave on our grounds. Right after the war, he thought, he'd come back and get it out. Besides, carrying the jewelry was too risky. It would surely be taken from us at the checkpoints."

How well he knew the feeling, Yousif thought. His mind traveled to Ardallah, and to the night he had lifted the tile and dug under it to make room for his own mother's and Salwa's gold and diamonds. But he was not ready to divulge that information to anyone. Not yet.

"Many people are sneaking back to dig up their buried valuables," Hikmat said, spilling hot coffee on his leg. "They claim it's that easy."

"I've heard that," Yousif replied, thinking.

"I can see why," Hikmat continued. "The borders are long and still unprotected. One refugee managed to go back and come out with his two cows."

Yousif's reaction was a blend of shock and amazement. "Are you serious?"

"It's true. They were his family's only source of income and he felt he had to take a chance. Don't ask me how he did it, but he did."

"Wow. Sneaking in and digging under a tree I can understand. But coming out with two cows is astonishing."

For the first time Hikmat smiled. "I agree," he said.

"But these crossings to our own homes are headlined all over the world as violations of truce or armistice or whatever . . ."

"We're called marauders. And a threat to Israel's security."

"Sure. They occupy our homes and we don't have the decency to let them sleep in peace."

"Imagine that!"

"We even have the audacity to trespass on our own front yards."

"What kind of barbarians are we?"

"Shame on us."

"We don't even have a sense of charity."

"How ungrateful of us."

"The UN divides our country and gives each of us a measly piaster to live on, and we don't kneel down and kiss the ground. How ungrateful, indeed."

"What kind of weird people are we?"

"Shame on us."

"After all, they're our cousins."

"Shame, shame, indeed."

The satire provided them with a dose of relief they both needed. And it gave Yousif an idea for another column. Yet, he wondered, would a humiliated and dispossessed people appreciate acid humor?

AFTER SPENDING EACH AFTERNOON looking for Salwa, Yousif went to school on Thursday morning, only to find Hikmat in a worse mood than his. Apparently Hikmat had been waiting for his arrival, for no sooner had he stepped in the teachers' lounge than Hikmat motioned for him to join him outside. They had roughly ten minutes before the start of the first period. Hikmat looked anxious and Yousif couldn't wait to hear him out.

"I'm going back home," Hikmat confided as they began the stroll around the schoolyard.

"You mean home . . . home?" Yousif asked, staring at him.

"Yes, Ramleh," Hikmat replied. "I've got to, Yousif. Mother told me several times where father hid the jewelry. I know exactly where to find it. I'm going with someone who has made such trips many times. He even brought back with him his mother's utensils from her own kitchen."

Yousif was impressed though skeptical. "It can't be that easy."

"It still is. For how long I don't know."

"How would you do it?"

"We'd wait until it's dark and make sure everyone is asleep. Then I'd steal my way to the cave near the blackberry tree, dig the jewels out and run. It would take only a few minutes."

Yousif was still skeptical. It was a dangerous operation, and Hikmat did not strike him as the adventurous type. He would have to reconsider his qualification for recruitment.

"Mother had lots of jewelry," Hikmat went on, "and if I don't get it soon, the 'new residents' would eventually find it. I bet by now the occupiers all over the country have removed every tile in every Palestinian home looking for money and jewelry our people might have left behind. If I'm lucky, they haven't looked inside the cave. I've got to find out."

The reference to the removal of tiles in every room made Yousif wince. He tried to discourage his friend, yet his mind was traveling afar.

"If I pull it off," Hikmat said, "I might dispel the tension and gloom around the house."

"That's a big if."

"To be honest with you, our money is dwindling. You know we can't live on my salary. Nor can we buy a cheap dress for my mother. The one she left Ramleh wearing is becoming shabby and it brings tears to her eyes. She can't sleep and is losing weight. I'm hoping this venture might, just might, restore some kind of life to the house."

It was a predicament not unlike the one Yousif was facing. "I know what you mean," he said.

"Fareed is even more pathetic. He sells vegetables in the souk and hides his face every time an old acquaintance passes by. He's too ashamed, what with the damaged eye and the fact that his wife has deserted him. Like my mother, he's haunted by the past. Someone told him he'd be crazy to even think of looking for her. But he thinks he can talk her into coming back. Mother tells him she's unworthy of him, that he'd be better off without her. But he won't listen. To him she represents the past—the rich, beautiful, happy days of Ramleh and swimming in the Mediterranean Sea. What he doesn't realize, and what no one has the heart to tell him, is that to her he stands for the ugly present, from which she wants to escape."

When the bell rang and the students hurried to go inside, the two turned to go to their respective classes.

"When are you planning to make the trip? Yousif asked.

"This afternoon."

"This afternoon?"

"Yes. Someone will drive me as close to the border as it is safe, and from there I will go on foot. If things go well we should be back Sunday."

"Saturday is a school day," Yousif reminded him.

"I plan to tell the principal that I won't be coming to school that day, but I won't tell him the reason."

"Why not? You'll find him very understanding."

Hikmat was hesitant. "Would you tell him if you were me?"

Yousif nodded. He planned to recommend Hikmat to Amana, anyway. Why not have the principal on his side from the beginning?

"Frankly," Yousif added as they walked through the narrow corridor, "I'm dubious about your companion. What if he robs you of all that jewelry?"

"Have no fear. I have checked him out. He's okay."

"You can't be too sure. With all that jewelry in your possession he'd be tempted to knock you off and blame it on the Israeli or Jordanian border patrol."

Hikmat reached for the door knob. "I plan to tell him that you know, and if I get in trouble you'd get him in trouble."

"I'm talking about him killing you . . . not just getting you in trouble,"

"Relax, Yousif, he's made the trip many times," Hikmat said, as he opened the door and went into his classroom. "I'll introduce you to him after school."

"You will?"

"Meet me here."

Instead of heading toward his own classroom, Yousif veered to the principal's office. He found him conferring with a student, whom he dismissed upon seeing Yousif in an agitated mood.

"You look nervous," the principal began.

"I certainly am. May I close the door?"

The principal nodded and Yousif walked closer to the cluttered desk. In less than a minute he told Ustaz Sa'adeh all he knew. He said he was concerned that Hikmat was making a hasty decision. He had not thought out the plan well enough.

"I hope you don't think I'm betraying my friend's confidence," Yousif added. "I was thinking of recommending him as a recruit."

"Let's see what he does. It will be one way to test his resolve. Ali would be delighted if he succeeds. He knows how to check him out. We need to know whom to call on for future operations within the occupied territories."

Trying hard not to sound feckless, Yousif said: "What if he does not succeed?"

Ustaz Sa'adeh did not respond and his callousness shocked Yousif. For the first time he was seeing a side to this gentle man he did not know.

Ustaz Sa'adeh reached for a yellow pencil and started to sharpen it. "Tell me, Yousif. How do we expect to liberate Palestine without sacrifice? For Hikmat's sake, and for your sake, I hope he makes it back safe. If he doesn't—so be it. We could learn from his experience."

Obviously, Yousif thought, he himself had no aptitude for the military aspect of the liberation movement he had joined. Stark grim reality was undermining the exuberance he had felt only a few weeks earlier. In a sense he was already at war: with the enemy, with his friends, and with himself. And he was not happy about it. Militant revolutionaries had basic instincts that he obviously lacked. It crossed his mind that if he were to stay in the movement he would have to either steel his nerves or find another cross to bear.

"If the companion turns to be trustworthy," Ustaz Sa'adeh said, getting up and watering the plant on the window sill, "you might have found two potential recruits instead of one."

"I wish he had given me time to report to Ali about his traveling companion. Ali has a lot of information about shady characters. But they are leaving this afternoon. Right after school."

The principal turned around and looked Yousif in the eye. "Then let's wish them both a successful and safe journey."

IMMEDIATELY AFTER SCHOOL, YOUSIF walked with Hikmat to the coffeehouse where the traveling companion, Maher Radwan, was waiting.

"He's the only one who knows about the trip," Hikmat said to Maher by way of introducing Yousif.

"*ahlan . . . ahlan*," Maher said, rising and extending his hand. Then he sat down and resumed puffing on his nergileh.

The excessive greeting and the clammy handshake did not endear the man to Yousif. The man's looks matched the image Yousif had of him: tall, muscular, and swarthy. Only his natural hoarseness surprised him. His white short-sleeved shirt was open at the collar, revealing a thicket of black and white hair on his burly chest. He wore his shoes like house slippers, bending down the back ends and showing heels that were chafed but not dirty. His whole demeanor was open and relaxed, a trifle too relaxed to suit Yousif.

Then there was Hikmat's reference to Yousif being the only one who knew about the trip. That gave him a slight pause. Had Hikmat not spoken to Ustaz Sa'adeh about the trip? Or about missing school on Saturday?

Yousif looked at Hikmat as if to remind him that he should have informed the principal. Hikmat bit his lip as if to apologize.

The three sat on small straw chairs on the sidewalk of a third-class coffeehouse that was usually overcrowded, but not today on account of the stifling heat. The congestion was on the other side of the street where the shade and a small canopy were more inviting.

"We ought to be going," Hikmat said, looking at his watch.

"What's the hurry?" Maher asked in a dialect that sounded more like Jaffa than Ramleh. If he were to wear the typically baggy and bizarre-looking pants of the fishermen from that town, he would pass for one of them.

A waiter came and both Yousif and Hikmat asked for a glass of lemonade. Both also turned down Maher's offer to order for each of them a nergileh.

Sensing that Hikmat was a bit tense, Maher stopped smoking, and stared at him. "If you have any doubts about the trip, you can back out now. No one is forcing you. Either way you decide is fine with me." Without waiting for Hikmat to give him an answer, he turned to Yousif and said: "But if he decides to go I hope you'd wish us good luck and keep us in your prayers. I'm a superstitious man, and I don't like negative vibrations. They jinx me."

A big diesel truck was churning slowly and blocking the view and Maher had to wait a moment for it to pass. Then Yousif saw Maher stand and waive his arms and call for Rabha who, clad in her usual black, was still clutching her baby to her bosom and entreating pedestrians with her open right hand. The urgency in Maher's voice made her collect the last offering and risk her life dodging and navigating her way through the heavy traffic. When she approached them Maher had a purplish half-a-pound out ready to slip in her hand.

"*shukran*," she repeated several times and stuffed it in her bosom.

"May Allah protect you and your whole family," she prayed. "May Allah grant you all your wishes. May good luck be with you all the way."

Only then did Maher feel satisfied enough to sit down. "I don't deserve all of Allah's blessings. But somehow the two words 'good luck' do the trick for me always. What can I tell you. 'Good luck' is my good omen."

"Good luck and good fortune and good health be with you wherever you go," Rabha said almost like a chant. Then upon seeing Yousif she started. Slowly her features softened and a smile of recognition flashed on her face.

"You were there . . ." she said, delighted to see him.

". . . at the christening with milk," he reminded her. "How are you, Rabha?" he asked, reaching for his pocket. Both laughed at their own private secret.

She shook her head and put a restraining hand on his arm. "No need. You were kind enough to defend me. I hope one day I'll be able to pay you back in kind."

Her voice was sincere and Yousif was touched.

"Pay him now," Maher's rough voice interrupted.

"Pay him how?" she asked, puzzled.

"Tell him to encourage his friend here about making the trip with me." Maher drew so hard on his nergileh that the gurgling water could be heard in the middle of the street.

Momentarily a dusty black Mercedes pulled in front of them and a man resembling Maher but much younger and less stocky was behind the steering wheel and peering at them through the open window. Upon seeing him, Maher coiled the long tube around the neck of the nergileh and scrutinized Hikmat's face one more time.

"Here's your last chance to make up your mind," Maher told him.

Hikmat's answer was spontaneous. "Let's go."

"Good," Maher said, standing up. "Yousif, why don't you come with us. It's a lot of fun."

Yousif shook his head.

"Then have no fear. *Inshallah* we'll be back in time for Hikmat's eight o'clock class Monday morning. You teach too, don't you?"

"Yes, I do," Yousif answered, not knowing what to expect.

"Wonderful," Maher said, walking toward his brother's car and opening the door. "Three types of people always impressed me: teachers, nurses, and pregnant women. They are the most caring people. But the ones that truly tug at my heart are . . ."

Suddenly the man spread his arms wide open and shouted, ". . . our homeless refugees."

The gesture was so melodramatic, so bizarre, so unexpected, yet it failed to register on Hikmat's face. But it stunned Yousif. In a sense it made the man seem human, capable of deep feelings.

Yousif watched the car carrying Hikmat and Maher disappear around the corner of a long narrow street, wondering if he would see his friend again.

"Don't worry," Rabha reassured him. "I'll keep them in my prayers."

As she walked away, Yousif had a hunch that she knew all along what those two were up to. Yet she was discreet enough not to mention it. And he appreciated that in her. Suddenly a thought crossed his mind. Amana Forever could probably benefit from her contacts. She was constantly on the move around Amman, befriending people wherever she went. He must tell Ustaz Sa'adeh and Ali Bakrii about her. She might turn out to be a source of invaluable background information on possible recruits.

7

ON FRIDAY, THE DAY after Hikmat began his adventure to retrieve his mother's jewels, Yousif resumed his search for Salwa—she was the jewel for which he would be willing to risk his life.

He now realized that for all these months he had been looking for her in the wrong places. He agreed with Basim that Christian Palestinians most likely did not live in refugee camps. He would do better to start visiting churches where someone might be able to give him a lead. Like him, Salwa was not a regular churchgoer, yet it was only prudent of him to explore all avenues. How religious her mother was, he was not sure. But there was always the possibility that in these dark days she might have sought refuge in the house of God instead of depending on kings and presidents. When leaders fail you, the saying went, it couldn't hurt to start praying.

He rode the bus to the town of Irbid north of Amman where a sizable community of Christians lived. Though the trip yielded him no useful information regarding Salwa's whereabouts, it made him aware of a new obstacle that was hindering his searh: Now that he was a teacher, he had no normal weekends. The two off-days were interrupted by a school day. In Muslim countries such as Jordan, schools closed on Friday and opened on Saturday. This meant he could not go to the West Bank and look for Salwa on two consecutive days. To visit the well-known Christian towns of Ramallah, Bethlehem, and Beit Jala, he would need time to travel and canvass the entire area. To make a separate trip to each town would be costly and time consuming.

Crossing the Allenby Bridge, over the Jordan River, on his way to what was left of Palestine, was an agony in itself. He felt tormented by the memories of the exodus more than a year earlier. The short span of time surprised him, for it seemed he had been a refugee for decades. His eyes grew moist upon seeing Jericho itself. That winter resort which used to be called a sleepy town was now dotted with refugee camps and teeming with people sitting along the sidewalks or walking aimlessly. He was sad as he remembered the good winters he had spent with his parents here. The banana fields and the orchards of citrus fruit were on both sides of the road. How well he could still smell the aromas of mangos and tangerines! How well he could still recall floating in the Dead Sea, a few miles away. How could a Zionist teenager—who had been born and raised in Budapest or Amsterdam and had never enjoyed the incredible sensation of floating in the sea's salty water—claim the land to be his and not Yousif's? The sight of the Mountain of Temptation towering before him was too cruel in its intensity. Were the Palestinians being tempted? Tempted to do what? To remain loyal to their motherland or to accept the indignity of forced exile? None of it made sense.

The climb to Jerusalem on the narrow and twisting road provoked in him religious angst. On that very road Jesus had healed the Samaritan and performed one of his miracles. Justice, he thought, must have been crucified on the same cross with Jesus. Jesus had risen, trampling death with death; justice, alas, was still rotting in a deeper tomb.

On top of the road Yousif passed the Garden of Gethsemane where Jesus had been betrayed and sold for thirteen pieces of silver. What kind of exchange was being performed now, he wondered, and who was paying whom? And how much? Immediately adjacent to the Garden was the Church of Virgin Mary, on the spacious grounds of which Yousif had enjoyed many a picnic with his family. He could visualize his mother and aunts spreading blankets under an olive tree to lay out dishes of baked kibbeh, rolled grape leaves, and meat pies they had brought in straw baskets. Some of his fondest childhood memories were of those annual celebrations in honor of the Virgin's burial. After attending the Mass and taking communion he and his cousins and playmates, young boys and girls, had a wonderful time running amongst the hundreds of families like his, camping under acres of olive trees, and playing games till sunset. The taste of hard-boiled eggs, white goat cheese, crusty circles of sesame bread, homemade baklawa and date-filled cookies was palpable.

The religious sights were incredible. To his right, he could see Mount Olive, which he had climbed, often wondering how cars could be driven on its very steep road. To his left he could see the walls of the old city of Jerusalem and the Dome of the Rock, which he had visited many a time with Amin and other Muslim friends. Again, the panoramic view startled him. What some nations foolishly if not unconscionably wanted him to do now, he thought, was to forsake his ancient roots in this Holy Land to make room for immigrants born and raised overseas and whose ancestors had not set foot on it for two millennia. Some dreams were big; some, even huge. Some truly bizarre.

After visiting four churches in Ramallah (two Catholic, one Orthodox, and one Protestant), Yousif still had no trace of his wife. He made the rounds to beauty salons and nouveaute shops asking for anybody who ever heard of the names Salwa or Safi or Taweel, names that, strangely enough, sounded to those he encountered as alien as Rabindranath Tagore. The three priests and one Anglican minister, when he finally located them, were equally of no help, though the four offered to keep him and Salwa in their thoughts and prayers. Yousif wished he had money to make a contribution, but he barely had enough to get back to Amman. In a couple of churches he did light a candle and drop a few coins in the wooden box placed at the entrance.

As it turned out, his visit to Bethlehem and Beit Jala had to be postponed. Unable to share a taxi with other passengers, he bought a falafel sandwich and waited in a long line for the next bus. With luck he would arrive in time to attend the Amana meeting scheduled for seven o'clock that evening.

THE MEETING AT USTAZ Sa'adeh's apartment was already in progress when he got there twenty minutes late. The room was packed with familiar faces, and Basim was on a roll. Yousif nodded to some and took the first seat he could find without saying a word.

". . . South America is full of wealthy Palestinians," Basim was saying. "What we need is to form a delegation to Brazil, Colombia, Chile. Argentina and Peru are definitely worth considering. The Palestinians over there are just as heartbroken as we all are and I believe they'd be generous with their contributions."

Raja curled his lips with satisfaction. Others simply nodded.

"What kind of a delegation do you have in mind?" Ali asked.

"We'd start with mayors, priests, sheikhs, bankers. Even poets."

"How interesting," Yousif said.

"My contact, who shall be nameless at the moment, said they were familiar with the poetry of Elias Farhat, Ibrahim Toukan, Abu Salma, Elia Abu Madi. They even know the poetry of contemporary ones such as Kamal Nassir and Fadwa Toukan."

"I'm not surprised," Ustaz Sa'adeh said, crossing his legs. "An Arab is an Arab, wherever he may be. Poetry is in his blood."

"You mean his emotions are stirred more by poetry than by empty rhetoric," Raja said, his smile forced.

Yousif recalled the skeptic who not long ago had complained that the enemy fought them with guns and bullets while they, the Arabs, retaliated with a thousand lines of poetry.

"Did your nameless contact give you a check?" Hanna inquired.

"A generous one," Basim answered, sensing sarcasm. "And, for your information, it didn't bounce."

After assigning Raja the task of selecting a delegation of three or four men, they moved on to the subject of recruits. Glancing at Ustaz Sa'adeh and Ali Bakrii in particular, Yousif told them that he had a couple of men and one woman in mind, but would need more time to check them out. All agreed, hoping that the number of recruits would increase. Suddenly Basim introduced a name that sent Yousif into a minor shock.

"I wholeheartedly recommend recruiting Adel Farhat as quickly as possible," he said without glancing at Yousif.

"He'd make an excellent choice," Ali said. "If he'd only accept."

"He'd accept all right," Basim added. "His experience in the RAF under the British in Jordan would be invaluable. Also, he could attract other Palestinians who served with him."

Yousif was still smarting. Adel Farhat! Of all people, he thought. And to be recommended by none other than Basim himself. They would have to have a talk about that. A serious talk. Soon.

"From what he tells me," Basim continued, "more than a thousand of our young refugees have already joined the Jordanian Army, or the Arab Legion, as they call it. Most of them did so out of desperation or strictly for income during these dark days. Some may end up choosing the army as a career. Others would eventually prefer to join our resistance movement. And we certainly could use them."

The next topic revolved around the issue of passports. They debated whether it was advisable for the refugees to apply for a Jordanian citizenship. Yousif was still chafing at the idea of having to work directly or indirectly with his former rival, Adel Farhat. But everyone else agreed that a passport was only an expedience.

Yousif disagreed. "It might establish the wrong precedent," he said. "Little by little, they'll demolish our identity and we'll end up with nothing to fight for."

Unexpected silence filled the room.

"I admire your idealism," Raja said. "But a Jordanian passport is only tactical. Just a cover. But for us to come out in the open and oppose the concept would be tantamount to rejecting the annexation of the West Bank. His Majesty would not be pleased in the least. Overnight our office will be ransacked and we will all be hunted. None of us is ready for that."

Basim's pragmatism was of a different shade. "If we don't have a country, and right now we don't, a piece of paper would make no difference. If need be, I'll carry five or six passports at the same time to reach my goal."

Yousif did not flinch. "Would the man on the street agree?"

"The man on the street may be homeless now, but don't sell him short," Basim said. "He knows the score. Listen, Yousif, any passport that will get me through gates and secure a seat for me on airplanes is immaterial. It's just a convenience. I grant you, I don't like it anymore than you do. But remember this: we're fighting for our homes, our future, our lives and the future and lives of our children. Toward that end I'm willing to learn how to forge passports."

HIKMAT WAS ALREADY IN the teachers' lounge when Yousif arrived on Monday morning. With books under his arm, Yousif squeezed himself between teachers and chairs to reach his friend.

"You must've fallen in love over the weekend to be grinning like this on Monday morning."

"Fell in love and bought a wedding ring," Hikmat answered and winked. When the other teachers looked up and began to congratulate him he quickly assured them that he was only jesting.

The eight o'clock bell rang and all the teachers except Yousif and Hikmat gathered their books and papers and hurried out to their classes. Now by themselves, the two friends slapped each other's backs, their eyes brimming with joy.

"How was it? . . . Was it dangerous? . . . Did you get what you went after?" Yousif blurted.

"It was a great success," Hikmat admitted. "I might do it again just for the thrill of going back home one more time."

"Maher must've been okay then."

"Beyond suspicion." To emphasize his point, Hikmat reached in his pocket and pulled out a handful of sparkling rings and broaches. "Look, Yousif," he said, beaming. "Aren't they beautiful?"

"And valuable," Yousif replied, remembering his own mother's equally precious jewelry.

"Thank God you didn't talk me out of making that trip," Hikmat said, opening the door to his classroom. "You almost did, you know."

"I was being cautious."

At the ten o'clock recess, the two resumed their conversation as they circled the football field. That Hikmat had encountered no difficulties during the trip struck Yousif as incredible. He had entered enemy territory and yet came out smiling?

"What made it so easy," Hikmat said, reading his friend's mind, "is that the enemy is still securing the borders. I only saw one army jeep from afar, and it could've been a patrol car. I just don't know. Also, don't forget that some of our towns still have some of our people in them. I don't know why, but there are pockets of Arabs in most places. I guess the Israelis need some workers—some hard labor and such—for the time being. Once they are settled they'll get rid of them the way they got rid of us."

Still Yousif was unable to comprehend a journey so free of danger.

"Don't forget," Hikmat added, "one of my best friends is my neighbor back in Ramleh. His name is Nader. We were very close. Why and how he managed to stay behind escapes me. All our friends in Amman want to know why wasn't he kicked out like the rest of us. Some people think he might've been a collaborator, but I seriously doubt it. He certainly was a great help to me, though."

Glancing at his watch to make sure they had enough time to give more details, Yousif wanted to know how Hikmat had managed to pull off his adventure.

"Quickly, how did you do it? I mean digging out the jewelry."

"Before I get to that let me tell you who lives in our house. When I saw the lights on, I headed for my friend's house, a couple of doors away. I knocked on his door, and when he opened it he couldn't believe his eyes. They bulged at seeing me. I told him what I was after and he led me in, still not believing that I was there. My conversation with him was surreal.

"He said our house was occupied by an old German couple—'sweet people,' he described them—in their late seventies or early eighties. Nader told me that one day he saw the old man stumble and fall in the middle of the street and he rushed and helped him get up then walked him to 'their house.' I had to correct him that it was not 'their' house. 'I'm sorry, your house,' Nader said. Then he went on to say that he has become good friends with them although they don't speak a word of Arabic or English. According to Nader, they just nod their heads and smile at each other."

Yousif urged him to go on.

"Nader said that one day they brought him and his wife a plate full of berries from 'their' tree. I told him, 'Dammit, Nader. The berries came from our tree. *Our* tree. What's wrong with you?' He apologized again. Anyway, there's a tiny cave in our yard—maybe a burial place from ancient times," Hikmat continued. "The workers discovered a skull in it when they were digging around to build our house. When things got really hot before our expulsion, mother wrapped her jewels in a handkerchief and told me to crawl into that cave and hide them. I did and found a hole in the wall which was a perfect hiding place. For extra protection my father handed me a couple of rocks and told me to cover the hole. That's where I had left them."

The school bell rang and the faculty and students began to file inside the building. Hikmat started to follow, but Yousif grabbed his arm. "And you found them where you had left them?"

Hikmat took a deep breath and continued. "Nader and I waited until the lights in our house were turned off and we knew that the German couple had gone to bed. We walked to the front yard and I slipped inside the cave and found the jewelry exactly where I had left it. Anything else you want to know will have to wait."

The rush Yousif felt at hearing Hikmat's account made up his mind.

He must make a similar visit to his home in Ardallah. The dissimilarities did not faze him. His mother's jewelry was buried under the floor of his bedroom, not outside in a cave. And "his tenants" might not be as old or unthreatening as those in Hikmat's house. Still, he yearned for the experience. He must not hesitate. The sooner the better, for the enemy would not leave the borders unguarded for long. Also, the Jordanian army in the West Bank might start strengthening their border patrol to avoid clashes with the mighty occupiers.

Yousif tossed and turned in his bed weighing the possible dangers. What if the house were not occupied? How could that be? His house was substantial, and modern, and in the last year hundreds of thousands of Jewish immigrants from around the globe had arrived to settle in his usurped homeland. Surely some strangers must have bought it from the state, moved in, and were now calling his home theirs. Unlike so many refugees who had left with the keys to their homes, he had no key to his home. He could still remember the face of the soldier who had evicted his family from their own home. Though in a hurry, he made sure to take his father's car key. But he forgot to slip the house key out of the inside of the door and pocket it. Could he now get inside? The iron gate and the wrought iron bars at the windows made the house safe from thieves. Thieves!! What irony! Going back to his own home would be viewed as a crime by the enemy. One day they would be taught the real meaning of thievery. Right now he must concentrate on what to do, should he not be able to get inside.

In spite of his trepidations, Yousif resolved not to weaken. But it was clear to him now that taking a companion with him was not only wise but imperative. Should the occasion arise, an ally could help him tie up the strangers in his home, allowing him to go about digging for the treasure underneath his bedroom floor. Or simply to stand outside as a sentry.

During the next two days, Yousif queried Hikmat at length, and passed the information about Hikmat and the driver Maher on to Ustaz Sa'adeh and Ali, the only two he had confided to about Hikmat's trip. They were in the principal's office and the two were pleased to hear of its success.

"These two would make good recruits," Ali offered. "We need daring men like them."

Yousif nodded. "I was hoping you'd say that. I also have a woman I'd like to tell you about."

"Tell us now. Who is she?"

Yousif told them about Rabha and both told him to keep an eye on her. She might be of use, indeed. Ali expressed interest in meeting her and Yousif promised to wait for a suitable time and place.

Leaning back in his swivel chair, Ustaz Sa'adeh returned to asking about Maher.

"Does he know what Amana is all about?"

"I doubt it," Yousif said. "Even if Hikmat is aware of it, he didn't hear it from me."

"Perhaps you and I should start clueing him in. After that Ali should interrogate him further."

"Let's wait until I make my trip."

"What trip?" Ustaz asked.

"I intend to pay Ardallah a visit myself," Yousif confessed.

His listeners looked at each other and then at him. Encouragement was written all over their faces.

A WEEK LATER, YOUSIF was traveling with Ali and Hanna to the West Bank to help establish youth clubs in the major cities. Nablus was to be their first stop. They were driving on the back road which Yousif had traveled by foot during the infamous march out of Ardallah. While still in Jericho, they passed the Mount of Temptation and plush green fields on the left, and the Ain el-Sultan water fountain and the ruins of Hisham Palace on the right before reaching the rugged mountains and desolate terrain. As the white cottages and small huts zipped by, Yousif relived that earlier torturous exodus. The death of Salwa's father and leaving his body in the wide open desert invaded his mind. Salwa's fury afterwards was understandable and definitely unforgettable. She must also be furious at him for not having located her by now.

Sitting alone on the back seat, Yousif occupied himself by reading his favorite newspaper, *Amana Daily*. For the last couple of weeks Raja had been publishing a series of articles under the heading, "Know Thy Enemy," in which he explained that the catastrophe (now referred to as *al-nakba*) that had befallen them was hatched and plotted decades before 1948. In one of those articles he had written,

> From St. Petersburg to London—via Istanbul and Rome—they were meeting with the highest officials and testing their grounds. When the Ottoman Empire was considered the sick man of Europe, and its collapse was deemed imminent, the Zionists offered to purchase—yes, purchase—Palestine from Turkey. The price: paying off the debts of the dying Empire. Just imagine! Their effrontery to think our country was up for sale was no less insufferable—no less shameless—than Britain's promise to establish a national home for the Jews in our midst. On our land—land we were born on, we worked on, and we died on for more than a millennium. All of this devilishness was conducted behind our backs. As if Palestine were empty. As if we literally did not exist.

Reclining in his seat and making himself comfortable for the ride, Yousif began to read aloud.

"Listen to this," he said to his fellow travelers. "If it took those well-armed, well-financed, well-placed and well-connected diehard Zionists over fifty years to scheme, conspire, and conquer most of Palestine, it might take us just as long to liberate it."

"But liberate it we shall," Ali proclaimed.

Yousif read further:

> If they could turn the wheels of history two thousand years, our leaders could turn them back a mere few years. But they cannot do it alone. They need our help. The help of the masses. That is our Amana. We had better roll up ourselves, activate our minds, and start preparing for the inevitable hurricane. Each must do his share. In schools,

in offices, in clinics, in shops. While plowing the fields or herding the sheep. Or harvesting our crops. Or making financial contributions to worthy causes. Wherever. Whenever. Whatever. The focus of all our efforts must be the liberation of our country. Each must find his way. Each must bear his responsibility. Mobilizing our masses is essential. Turning that ill-directed and ill-fated wheel of history around and setting it on its right course is our duty. Our ultimate *amana*.

"Our Sacred Trust," Ali echoed, almost chuckling.

Yousif set the newspaper aside and waited for Hanna and Ali to respond. Both remained silent. All Yousif could hear was the sound of tires swallowing the road. Ali was driving through a cut in a mountain known for its hazardous mudslides during winter. A curve in the road was in sight and an oncoming truck was hurtling toward them. Ali had to slow down and pull to the side of the road.

Ali looked at him in the rear mirror, grinning. "Who are the wise leaders Raja hand in mind?"

Hanna snickered. "That's his way of appeasing the censors."

"But it could be misconstrued," Yousif said.

"How?" Hanna asked, lifting his eyebrows.

"They might accuse him of sarcasm. And what about the reference to 'mobilizing the masses'?"

"You're right there," Hanna said. "It's a wonder the censors haven't bothered him so far."

"They're waiting for him to cross the red line," Ali said, pressing on the accelerator to pass another pick-up truck.

"All they have to do is come to his office and find him reading *Das Kapital*," Hanna said, cracking the window and lighting up a cigarette. "They'd accuse him of being a communist."

"Which he's not," Ali said.

Yousif nodded. "I know I'll never be a communist, yet I'd like to read that book myself."

"Just don't let them catch you," Ali cautioned.

"Books are read for knowledge. Not commitment."

"You can argue that point behind bars."

While listening to Ali and Hanna consider the ramifications of pockets of communist cells among young people, Yousif's mind shifted around Raja's series on the roots of Zionism. He wished he knew more about their mortal enemies. He also wished he knew the history of colonialism in the Arab world. How devastated he felt when he first learned that, except for the Arabian peninsula, the entire Arab world was under colonialism. Maybe Egypt was not technically a British colony, yet it was under occupation nevertheless. It was widely acknowledged that British control of Egypt far exceeded that of King Farouk and his government. How absurd, Yousif thought. His mind swirled with questions. Why were the Arabs so feckless as to allow themselves to be the target of western exploitation or direct domination? Why were empires bent on subjugating and robbing other peoples? Why was Britain in India and Canada? France in Algeria and Vietnam? Italy in Libya and Ethiopia? The United States in Cuba and the Philippines? Even little Holland, why was it in South Africa? And now the newest victim: Palestine. Was it intended to be an outpost for western powers determined to control the oceans of oil in Arab lands?

The more he reflected on such dilemmas the more he was convinced that his role with Amana would be ineffective until he became better informed. Better educated. The scope and scale of the looming problems would require of him nothing less.

He rolled the newspaper in his lap, crossed his legs at the ankles, and viewed the passing terrain. Stretches of green fields and orchards of olive trees were interspersed with acres and acres of rust-colored earth. The ravages of countless conquests across the centuries were visible to him now. Or so he surmised. He could envision the waves of storming invaders leaving the skulls of their dead and the hooves of their horses on every inch of this sacred land. The more he concentrated on the wars and what might still be in store for his homeland the more he seemed to agree with Shakespeare who deemed the world "full of sound and fury," but he failed to comprehend the rest of the line. "Signifying nothing" did not reflect the grim reality, nor the devastation, of the innocents. Any widow or orphan in any refugee camp could refute that. He was more inclined to agree with Kahlil Gibran who, in his quiet lamentation on the world's hypocrisy, had written: "He who steals the flowers is a vilified villain / he who steals the whole field is a celebrated hero."

In moments like this, Yousif missed his late father. He was more than a parent: he was his mentor and friend. The old doctor would have been able to guide him into his future. Yousif wanted to serve, of course, but in what capacity? He certainly had no aptitude for military action. His father was dead, but supposedly Salwa was still alive. Where in the world was she? He wanted to share with her his anguish, for she was his only comfort.

He could see her teasing him. "Oh, really! So you don't think you can fight?"

What if he told her that he compared the world to Egypt's pyramids, full of narrow and steep stairways leading to steeper and lengthier stairways at the top of which there were doors leading to other doors and then to a maze of doors—without revealing any of its dark secrets! As a burial place for the Pharaohs, its tombs concealed much more than just the incredibly preserved mummies. Or, what would Salwa say if he told her he saw the world as a web of geometric shapes: circles tumbling over circles, triangles overlapping triangles, and straight arrows crashing into each other?

Salwa would probably stare at him in puzzlement as she had done years earlier when he confided in her alone that he had once seen a huge vision of an old and weary-looking Jesus, spreading his long arms like wings across a sky bathed with the solemn color of dusk. It was like yesterday, he now recalled. He would go to his grave believing that it was a real vision, not an apparition, not a figment of his imagination. How he remembered with acute vividness that very moment in his early teens, when those large dark eyes peered down at him from the sky, looking at him neither tenderly nor angrily, but, for lingering moments, had mesmerized him and touched his soul.

Suddenly a voice snapped him out of his reverie.

"What are you daydreaming about?" Hanna asked.

Yousif shook his head for a second to gather his thoughts. "I've never been to Nablus before," he said. "What does it have other than a soap factory and a great poet?"

"Thousands of bitter refugees," Hanna replied.

"In other words," Ali added, "fertile ground for Amana."

Still overwhelmed by the enormous challenge ahead, Yousif asked: "This attorney Khaled Suwwan we're going to meet—does he know the real purpose of Nadi Amana? That it's just a cover for recruiting?"

"Of course, he does," Hanna assured him. "He's no fool. Besides, Basim knows and trusts him . . ."

". . . well enough to hand him five thousand pounds in cash to get him started," Ali added.

NABLUS WAS AN OLD city and one of the biggest in Palestine. As they entered its old district, Yousif could see that it was bursting at the seams with pedestrians and pushcarts. What struck him most was the number of Muslim women draped in black from head to toe. Many peered at the world through slits in the black *hijabs* covering their faces; others wore *hijabs* made of thin veils that covered even the eyes. It was not an unfamiliar scene in some Arab quarters, but its predominance in this city made on him an indelible—and unfavorable—impression.

Khaled Suwwan shared his offices with another attorney who was in court that morning. A young male secretary rose from behind his typewriter and ushered them to the right office.

Khaled was a big man just under fifty, with a wide smile and a shock of prematurely graying hair. He had large hands and his grip was as flinty as his surname implied in Arabic. Yousif's first impression of Khaled was positive, and it grew more so over the next couple of hours. Unlike professional Arabs who worked hard at looking westernized, this one eschewed suit-and-tie formality and sat behind his desk with an open collar. He reminded Yousif of those Israeli cabinet ministers, even Prime Minister Ben Gurion, who never bothered with silly ties as if to present themselves as men of action. In that respect, Khaled was true to form.

"The problem we have," Khaled said, "is not lack of recruits. We have enough young men seething with anger to form a private army. I promise you I can fill up five or six trucks—right now—with young men ready to do battle. Ready to kill and be killed."

"That's hardly what we need," Yousif said. "Not now, anyway."

"You're absolutely right," Khaled continued, "What we need is a select group of daring men ready to fight not to die, but to live."

"There's a big difference," Ali said.

The secretary walked in with a tray of coffee, which they began to sip without missing a beat in their conversation.

"What's quite encouraging," Ali offered, "is the number of organizations, more or less like Amana, which are sprouting all over the place. You've heard of the Storm, the Awakening, Tomorrow's Youth . . ."

". . . and the New Generation, and Black Ayyar . . ." Hanna added.

"Black what?" Yousif asked.

"You know, Black Ayyar. Black May. The month of the *nakba*."

"I see. How stupid of me," Yousif said. "But these are mere *nawadi*—or clubs—in the real sense of the word. From what I can tell, none is a movement like ours. Am I right?"

"Well, I can't believe they're founded just to get young men off the streets," Khaled said. "There's more to them than ping-pong tables and boxing rings."

"No doubt," Ali said. "The whole population is itching for revenge. There's more to these clubs than staging plays and providing the public with reading rooms."

Suddenly they heard a thundering noise in the street that seemed to get louder and louder. Khaled moved in his swivel chair and looked out the window.

"Here's what we're talking about," he said. "Come and see."

They all rose from their seats and stood behind and around Khaled. A demonstration of no less than five hundred young men and women was headed toward the government building. Fluttering white-black-green-red Palestinian flags and banners with Arabic and English slogans were hoisted with pride. An inciter with a booming voice was being carried on a couple of shoulders and the crowd behind him was repeating his chants with equally powerful voices. Stabbing and jabbing the air with his fist and sinewy arms, he redoubled his forceful exhortation.

"Free, Free Palestine."

"FREE, FREE PALESTINE."

"No, no *issti'maar*."

"NO, NO *ISSTI'MAAR*."

Yousif felt an extraordinary affinity with the marchers. He could easily imagine Salwa marching with them and acting as a cheerleader. What surprised him was the sight of the local police and some Bedouin soldiers standing by and watching on both sidewalks. They seemed nonchalant to the robust parade passing before their eyes.

"I presume the demonstration is legal," Yousif inquired.

"For sure," Khaled replied. "The authorities are smart on that score. Why not give these frustrated youngsters a chance to vent their anger?"

"As long as they're kept in check," Ali said. "I won't be surprised if there are secret agents milling in their midst, looking out for real troublemakers."

"For sure," Khaled repeated, his elbow resting on the window frame.

Hanna seemed more pleased than the others. "Here you have it," he said. "Any organization can recruit all it needs in one afternoon."

"But are they hard-boiled enough for us?" Khaled asked.

"If they're handpicked with care," Yousif mused.

They returned to their seats. The subject of the birth of other organizations surfaced again. After a long discussion, they generally agreed to wait and see how they would develop and what direction they would pursue. Above all, Amana's secret agenda must not be exposed.

As they all got up to leave, Yousif could not help but turn and face Khaled with a burning question on his mind.

"Have you happened to hear the name Salwa Safi or Salwa Taweel?"

Khaled looked at him, unblinking. "Isn't Safi your family name?"

"Yes it is. Salwa is my wife and we've been separated since our forced exile."

"I'm sorry. No, I haven't."

At the end of a productive day, and on their way back to Amman, Yousif caught himself humming "Free, Free Palestine." And the others echoed his chanting. Encouraged, Yousif went on to declare, "No, no, *issti'maar.*" And the others followed suit: "No, no *issti'maar.*" Then they all laughed, because they too had a need to vent their anger.

"I'm so glad they emphasized the rejection of *issti'maaar,*" Yousif said. "Colonialism is the biggest problem we face. And my generation senses it better than our fathers did."

Though gratified by the enthusiasm he had witnessed, Yousif remained skeptical if not cynical of what the future held for his homeland. Considering the colonial powers' grand design to divide and rule the Middle East, all the patriotic efforts of tiny groups such as Amana Forever were comparable to a bird trying to peck through a marble wall stretched from Palestine all the way to China. The awareness gnawed at his heart. In the absence of Arab unity, which was not on the horizon, and with no renewal of miracles since the days of Jesus, he felt that the Arab world was in a desperate need for another giant like Saladin who had ended the shameful Crusades and liberated holy Jerusalem.

But he could not voice his doubts lest the others begin to question his commitment to the immediate struggle.

"All I heard today was encouraging," Yousif said, weighing his words. "Especially the fact other groups like Amana are getting organized."

"You didn't think we'd be the only ones, did you?" Ali asked.

"No, but a widespread revolt will have an impact."

"The hurricane is imminent," Hanna said. "Have no fear."

"I'm not as worried about the occupiers of our land as I am about the big powers behind them."

"Who's using whom is the real question," Ali said.

After a pause, Yousif finally said, "What we really need is another Saladin."

"Amen to that," Ali said. "But men like him don't come around except once in a thousand years."

"Which means we're due to have one before too long."

"Another couple of hundred years. That's all."

"He'll come. I assure you, he'll come. But what blessed womb is there to give birth to such a giant?"

"Saladin could've expelled the Jews out of Jerusalem when he expelled the Crusaders, but he didn't." Hanna said.

"He was magnanimous," Ali said. "Even his defeated enemies acknowledge that. And respect him for it."

"That's what my father used to say about him," Yousif said. "Even today the West still refers to him as the noble warrior."

THE ORGANIZATIONAL MEETING IN Nablus was overshadowed by events in far-away Rhodes where the armistice talks were being held. The Arabs had once again proven as inept at negotiating for peace as they had been at fighting a war. There had been a border line, a slightly crooked line on the map, and the glib Zionists only wished to straighten it out. Surely the Arabs too would prefer a straight line to a crooked line. Certainly, the flattered, naïve Arabs replied, they did not mind at all. A straight line was certainly neater and more preferable than a crooked line. But when the agreement was implemented on the ground, the pencil adjustment on the map turned out to be a colossal loss of thousands of acres. The forfeited land around Tulkarm and Jenin (twenty odd miles from Nablus) became known as the Triangle. Arabs everywhere were distressed to learn not only of the major loss but with the reckless manner in which it had been lost.

Every newspaper Yousif read from around the Arab world called it another mockery. *Amana Daily* minced no words and labeled it a treason. It was this charge that brought the censor to Raja's office, demanding a retraction.

Raja stood fast. "It was more than stupidity."

"Call it a mistake, call it an oversight, but not treason," the censor objected.

"How can you say that?" Yousif asked. "Every man on the street knows it was treason."

The tall thin censor glared at him. "What do you know about treason?"

"A whole lot," Yousif said, not afraid of being defiant.

"One more word from you . . ."

Deep silence followed. But the man with the red pencil had the upper hand. The next issue of *Amana Daily* appeared with a quarter of its front page blank. The reason for the deletions was not lost on most readers. The word "treason" was no longer whispered, but chewed and regurgitated on everyone's tongue. From then on it was a constant battle between *Amana Daily* and the authorities. Another time Raja was questioned, in Yousif's presence, for holding the Arab leaders responsible for the tragedy in Palestine.

"What did you mean by that remark?" a Bedouin soldier asked, his rifle several inches taller than he was.

Both Yousif and Raja knew what the soldier alluded to. Any reference to His Majesty, implied or not, would be considered criminal.

"You think I was referring to Sayyedna? God forbid. But, in essence we are all to blame. I'm responsible for writing instead of shooting."

Yousif shook his head. "The public needs to be informed."

The soldier eyed both with derision. "Be careful what you write," he said, ambling out.

After the door was closed, Raja and Yousif sat down, rather amused. "Harassment is the order of the day," Raja said, steepling the tips of his fingers. "I think we should relocate in Beirut. It's a far more refined city anyway. I loved the four years I spent at the American University of Beirut. That was long go, when we still thought the Americans were fair and honest people."

The idea of him leaving surprised Yousif. "What would Basim say?"

"He'll understand. If we ever catch up with him. From week to week we never know which continent he's on."

Yousif managed a faint smile. "But we do know he's either raising money or buying arms."

Raja nodded, thoughtfully. "There's more to be done abroad than here."

"At least he's not facing Bedouin rifles."

Raja suppressed a chuckle. "Did Ustaz Sa'adeh go with him?"

"You mean to Chile? Oh, yes. Ustaz knows many rich Palestinians who live there. They won't come back empty-handed."

Yousif had deep admiration for Raja and felt comfortable in his company. They were like father and son and seemed to share the same disillusionment. It was Raja who brought up the subject of Adel Farhat's recruitment.

"I saw you cringe when his name was mentioned," Raja said. "You don't like him, do you?"

Before Yousif could answer Raja said that he had heard about the personal drama that had erupted between them over Salwa.

"But in this organization," Raja added, "we need to put personal grudges aside. Adel can be most useful to us. He's a military man and has good contacts with men who served in the British forces both in Palestine and Trans-Jordan. He knows all about training camps and could be of great help setting them up for us. Besides, Amana will soon grow bigger and spread out. You two don't even have to see each other, much less be in contact."

"I hope not," Yousif said. "He almost took Salwa from me."

"The way I understand it, you took her from him. You busted his wedding in church, did you not?"

Yousif grinned. "I did."

"See there! Who should be holding a grudge against whom? Be cordial to him. After all, he may be the one to help you find her."

Yousif exhaled. "I wish somebody could."

Raja toyed with a pencil and grinned coyly. "The irony is that he knows exactly where she is."

Yousif gasped. "What?"

"He told me she works . . ."

"Where . . . where . . . ?" Yousif interrupted.

". . . at the hospital in Salt. How he knew that I don't know. But that's exactly where you'll find her."

"And now you tell me?" Yousif asked, leaping from his chair. "How long have you known this?"

Raja laughed. "Only last night. I knew I'd be seeing you . . ."

Without hesitation, without waiting for further details and without even saying goodbye, Yousif bolted out of the office. His heart was throbbing with finding Salwa.

The busy street was full of cars but no taxis. The minute he spotted one crawling toward him, he jumped in and told the driver to head for the town of Salt. The driver hesitated saying he would have to wait for other passengers headed that way. Negotiating ensued and finally Yousif promised him a triple fare so that he would not waste any time. Luckily he had cashed his monthly check that day and could afford to pay the exorbitant charge. He reached for his wallet and pulled out three one-dinar bills and handed them to the driver, urging him to step on the accelerator and keep moving.

"Wow!" said the driver, taking the money and shaking his head with amusement. "The bus would have cost you a fraction of this. You must be in an awful hurry."

"I'm on my way to reunite with my wife."

"How long have you been separated?"

"Since we were kicked out."

"I hope you'll find her."

"And if I do find her, I'll tip you even more."

"Find her and that will be good enough for me. Best of luck to you."

Left alone to his thoughts, Yousif wallowed in nostalgia. Considering the menacingly dark recent past, he looked back in sorrow at all the traumas that had preceded their separation. Nothing compared to the their having been driven out of their ancestral homeland, but the personal dramas were equally painful. The chilling circumstances of their fathers' deaths, for instance. His father died on a hilltop trying to attend the injured Basim who was battling to defend Ardallah against the invaders. The agony of those thoughts plagued him. His father was killed a week before he crashed Salwa's wedding to Adel Farhat to save her for himself. Incredibly, he had been triumphant, but at a price. Salwa's outraged father had promised Man and God, right on the doorsteps of the church, that if Yousif did not marry his daughter that same week he would never ever hope to marry her. And so, he had to rush into marrying her—without giving his poor mother the chance to mourn her husband properly. Was this the kind of wedding she had hoped for her only son? She begged for the minimum forty-day period, but he would not listen because he had no choice. He could not afford to scandalize Salwa's father twice. The man would have gone berserk and made good on his promise. And the unprecedented wedding was forced upon them. It broke Yousif's heart to see his mother shuffle her feet pretending to dance on the same floor where two weeks earlier her husband's coffin had lain.

Horrific as those circumstances were, Yousif thought, they paled in comparison to the death of Salwa's father. Anton Taweel had a fatal heart attack during the arduous march out of Palestine. His collapse shocked his family and his wife began to scream. Hysterical Salwa threw herself on his body before his eyes closed, begging him for forgiveness. Yousif knelt beside her, held the dying man's hand, and both were lucky enough to hear him forgive them before expelling his last breath. The worst part was what followed. The ground was impossibly hard and there were no instruments to dig a grave, so they had to leave him unburied. The marchers kept moving, nodding their heads in sympathy and murmuring a few words of sorrow but they too had suffered casualties who could be seen strewn around. As his cruel fate would have it, Anton Taweel lay unburied, not even covered from the infernal sun. Salwa shrieked and Yousif put his arm around her waist and let her sob on his shoulder. Then she rushed and hugged her mother and two brothers, and all of them, including Yousif, huddled together and cried with her in unison. As they began to slowly move away from the body Salwa was struck by a new realization and burst anew with fierce crying. What would the wild animals do to him in this wilderness?

Her sheer despair was contagious and Yousif struggled to console her. How could he? Biting his lip, and trying to hold her from rushing to throw herself on her father's corpse, he let her pour out her emotions. Before long, he thought to himself with overwhelming sadness, the wolves would feast on the poor man's body.

As his taxi began to climb up the steep mountain, Yousif felt jarred by other memories. Eighteen-year-old boys and girls should not have that much pain so early in life. The last time he felt this excruciatingly anxious was on his way to crash a wedding ceremony and save Salwa. He had made a vow to himself and to God that that inglorious wedding would never take place but he had no idea whether he could stop it. Such audacity was unheard of in Ardallah, and the odds against him seemed insurmountable. Would the priest allow it? Would her father smash his face? Could the community, linked by blood and marriage, and proud of its customs and traditions, accept such flagrant infringement? Arranged marriages were the norm, and the lovelorn youngsters were cutting against the grain. What nonsense. What trend would that start among the young generation? Yousif sighed deeply as he remembered the story of a young handsome man in his early twenties, from a nearby village, who had committed suicide because he was denied the opportunity to marry the girl he loved. And the poor girl spent the rest of her life as a spinster. That would not be his and Salwa's fate. Confident that he and Salwa were ordained for each other, Yousif confronted the priest, the father, and a church full of guests. And he was triumphant. Only because Salwa backed him up, and declared right at the altar, and with tears in her eyes, that they were truly in love.

What a historic moment, Yousif thought. What anxiety and what thrill! He smiled as he remembered the middle-aged women who squeezed his hand and whispered in his ears their gratitude for his groundbreaking stand. Those poor souls must have endured, nay suffered, through years of loveless marriages. But would the anxiety he was now feeling be similarly resolved? Here he was again chasing another rainbow: suppose Adel Farhat had lied to Raja about where Salwa could be found. Suppose it was only another wicked ploy to torment him. He would have to wait and see.

Yet he felt his heart racing and found himself relishing the agony of hope. Let the dream of reuniting with his beloved wife tantalize him.

8

YOUSIF PRESENTED HIMSELF TO a dowdy receptionist at the Government Hospital in Salt. She was busy with paperwork and while waiting for her to acknowledge his presence he lit a cigarette. When she looked up he was struck by her large open face and the deep dark wrinkles under her eyes. But her smile was warm and her eyes sparkled.

"I'd like to see Nurse Salwa," he said.

"No smoking, please," she told him.

"I'm sorry," he apologized, looking around for an ashtray. Not finding one he stubbed out the cigarette on the sole of his shoe and put it and the lighter in his pocket.

"We have two Salwas. Which one do you wish to see?"

To him there was only one Salwa in the whole world. "Salwa Safi," he told her. He could barely breathe.

"She's on duty. You can't see her now."

"It's urgent."

"I wish I could help you."

A young woman in a native dress approached the counter holding the hand of a toddler. She asked to visit a patient, but the nurse informed her that hospital rules did not allow visitors under twelve. Yousif was beside himself.

"I can't leave him in the lobby," the visitor pleaded. "He's only three."

"You should've known better than to bring him with you."

"I've never been to a hospital before. He's well-mannered, and I'll hold his hand all the time."

"Manners have nothing to do with it. I'm sure he's well-behaved. It's for his own protection. He might catch some germ."

"But we're already here. What am I supposed to do with him? I came a long way."

"I'm sorry. But I'd lose my job if I let him in."

Yousif offered to keep the young boy while his mother visited her patient, but the boy would not cooperate. He whimpered and clung to his mother. The disappointed visitor thanked Yousif for his kindness and walked listlessly across the sparkling marble floor and sat in the waiting room. Yousif remained standing before the information station, wondering what to do next.

"Young lady . . .," he said, trying his luck again.

"I appreciate flattery," the receptionist said, smiling. "Go on."

"Salwa's mother is very ill. She needs to go home now. But I need to see her first."

The receptionist cradled the headset on the telephone base, staring at him. "You're persistent, but lying doesn't become you."

"I beg your pardon!"

"You heard me. Salwa's mother isn't sick. She's a midwife who happens to have delivered twin boys about an hour ago."

Yousif was bewildered. That could not be. She must have spoken of a different Salwa. Or was this a case of mistaken identity? His heart sank in fear that he was about to be traumatized all over again.

"Her mother is not a midwife," he said emphatically.

"She became one after the exile. Tell me, please. Does your name happen to be Yousif Safi? And are you from Ardallah?"

"Yes," he said, and his heart soared again.

She extended her hand toward him. "Then you owe me."

"Owe you for what . . .?" he asked, shaking her hand as time seemed to slow to a crawl.

". . . for all the times I spent reading her fortune in coffee cups."

"Looking for . . .?"

". . . a sign of when your highness would show up."

Yousif beamed. "I feel like coming around to give you a hug."

"Don't you dare. But tell me if you don't mind—if you love her as much as she loves you, how could you stay away from her for so long?"

"Not by choice," he cried, clasping his hands. "It was not by choice! I could not find her! I have looked everywhere!"

The telephone rang and she picked it up. Sensing that the conversation was not going to be brief, Yousif took a few steps toward the large window, his eyes darting back and forth between the nurse's station and the landscape outside. In his ebullience, the panoramic view of the outside world was vivid with hope. The old hospital was on top of a high mountain, and magnificent pine trees reached as high as the balcony. The valley below and the slopes of the opposite mountain were forests dotted with homes built of chiseled stones. The landscape reminded him of Ardallah, except the gabled-rooftops in his hometown were covered with reddish Spanish tiles which were especially attractive in their surroundings of leafy green trees. Here the rooftops were simply flat and less scenic. But never mind scenery. It was at the ceremony of having the rooftop raised at his family's villa that he first saw Salwa in her yellow dress. How many blissful moments had he had in that house dreaming over her and—after he had won her—enjoying living together as husband and wife? And now he was about to be reunited with her after the dreadful separation. He simply could not wait.

As he turned around he imagined Salwa walking toward him on the long shiny marble corridor. He saw her in a crisp white uniform and cap, looking like a beautiful bride parading toward the altar. He wondered if she had gained or lost weight. Was her hair long or short? She could only have become more glamorous.

Suddenly he was jolted out of his daydream as the receptionist finished her call and turned her attention back to him. What she had told him earlier was true: Salwa was on duty. Except not at the hospital, but somewhere else, she now informed him.

"For God's sake where is she?" he cried out to her, his nerves frayed.

"Calm down, calm down. She's with Dr. Rashad at a local elementary school where he's giving the students typhoid shots." She looked at her watch, then added, "They ought to be finished within the hour. After that I don't know whether she'll come back to the hospital or go back home. If you hurry, you could find her at the school. Go on now, she'll be happy to see you."

Fifteen minutes later, Yousif stood in a dim narrow corridor full of students waiting in a queue, presumably for the typhoid injections. Twenty or thirty students stretched out before him and many others were on the stairs coming up from the lower floor. Too anxious to wait any longer, he pushed to the head of the queue, right outside a classroom which had been converted into a temporary clinic.

Just before entering the room he heard her voice. Her unmistakable voice. And he rushed inside. Despite the hot weather, the cheerful middle-aged doctor was wearing a striped brown suit, a gold watch with a long chain strung across his vest. He was sitting on a chair in the middle of the room with a stethoscope plugged in both ears. Behind him was none other than Yousif's beloved, turned with her back toward him.

He tried to call out, but he could not make sounds come out of his mouth. He pushed his way between students and desks, catching the doctor by surprise. He looked blankly at Yousif, who finally managed to croak, "Salwa! Salwa! At long last you're here."

"Yes, she's here," the good-natured doctor responded. "And this youngster needs a shot. If you don't get out of our way I'll make her give it to you."

Yousif moved forward. "Oh, doctor. You have no idea what I've been through. She can give it to me any time."

She heard him then, and turned toward him. He thought she was even more ravishing than on the day of their wedding. His sudden appearance lit up her face with blazing joy.

Time now stood still. Then, in perfect harmony they flew into each other's arms. As he held Salwa, Yousif understood that he had not fully realized how much he had missed her nor had he really remembered how delicious her embrace was.

"Oh, *habibti,*" Yousif said, planting small kisses all over her face.

"I missed you, darling," Salwa whispered, reciprocating his endearments.

The confused doctor was flabbergasted yet impressed by their audacity. His eyes widened as the students cheered them on with spontaneous applause.

"Look what you've done," the doctor told Yousif. "It's getting late and we have a lot to do." Then looking straight at Salwa, he added, "But when you two get married I expect to be invited to the wedding."

"We are married," Yousif blurted. "She's my wife."

The doctor's eyebrows shot up. "What in the world. . .? Salwa, is it true?"

She nodded and clung to Yousif's neck, laughing. The students were beyond themselves.

"Okay, you're married, but all the boys still need to be injected."

"Oh, doctor," Yousif said, "you've given me the best medicine any patient could ever hope for. I'll never forget you."

Despite his effort to maintain a professional air, the doctor couldn't hide his happiness at Yousif's joyful reunion with Salwa. He and all the students watched and clapped as Salwa and Yousif tried to convince themselves that they were not dreaming, that the long ordeal of their separation was finally over.

"So don't forget me," the doctor said. "But will you kindly step outside until we finish our work?"

"It'll be all right, darling," Salwa said to Yousif as she dried the tears of joy that had been coursing down her cheeks. "We have waited for more than a year; a few more minutes will not kill us."

"Speak for yourself," Yousif teased. But he reluctantly released her and moved aside so she could get back to work, one eye on the syringes she was filling and the other eye still on Yousif, her husband who had finally found her, as she had known he would.

Resuming his job, the doctor motioned for a sickly boy in his early teens who seemed to need more than a typhoid shot. The doctor asked him to pull up his shirt and bare his chest.

"Inhale," the doctor said, placing the metallic end of his stethoscope to the boy's right side. "Now exhale. Turn around."

The boy turned and smiled shyly as he saw the others now gazing at him, especially at seeing a much older Yousif among them. The doctor shifted his instrument.

"Take a deep breath . . . exhale . . . you're fine," he declared. "Next."

BACK IN THE CROWDED corridor Yousif ruffled the heads of a few admiring students. Elated by the glee in their eyes, he played along with them. A tall clownish boy with a mass of dark hair clutched his hands over his heart and swooned, mimicking someone in love. Undaunted, Yousif replicated the mock gesture and swayed his body, adding, for an extra measure, a deep sigh. The students burst out laughing.

A muscular but pale-looking boy they called Fahd did not share the fun. Noticing Yousif's concern, the other boys around said that Fahd was epileptic and was traumatized by the sight of a needle. He was known to faint before a doctor or a nurse could give him an injection. True to form, Fahd dropped to the floor and began writhing when it was his turn to be injected. The froth forming around the boy's mouth did not faze Yousif. Quickly he bent over the prostrate body, took out a pen from his pocket, and stuck it between the boy's clenched teeth to prevent his tongue from being swallowed.

Drawn by the commotion, the doctor quickly moved to Fahd's side. "Who taught you how to do this?" the doctor asked. "I'm impressed."

He knelt beside Yousif and took charge. The ring of students was getting tight and Yousif took it upon himself to clear a space around the boy on the floor, whose eyes were rolling.

"Give him a chance to breathe," he said. "Move away. *Yalla. Yalla.*"

Soon Fahd was revived, but he was still flat on his back and was embarrassed. The doctor began to lift him and motioned for Yousif to help.

"You did well," the doctor told Yousif. "Salwa, you've got yourself a fine young man."

"The best," Salwa said, her face glowing.

Before long the injections were finished. After helping the doctor get settled in his small black sedan, they watched him drive away. Standing alone at last in the schoolyard, Yousif leaned Salwa back against a pine tree and took her face in his hands.

"That's the last time I'll ever let you get away from me. You might as well know it from now."

"Is that so?" she demurred, circling her arms around his waist.

"Absolutely."

"I have no say in the matter?"

"You certainly have—as long as you agree with me."

She giggled and shook her head, revealing an adoring heart that was more than willing to submit to the unreasonableness of the man she loved. Salwa and Yousif savored the sweet moment, so long awaited, and so eagerly wanted. They hugged and kissed and by their joyful embrace told anyone witnessing their rekindled passion—as well as all those reactionary people who frowned on public affection—to go and drown in darkness.

SALWA AND HER FAMILY lived on the second floor of a two-story house in the old section of town. She and her mother slept in one bedroom and her two brothers, Zuhair and Akram, slept in another. It was a far cry from where they had lived in Ardallah, but there was no sense now comparing standards of living. What standards? What lifestyle? That was then and now was now.

There were no family pictures on the walls, and that struck a familiar note of sadness in Yousif's heart. He did not have a single picture of his late father, as Salwa's mother had not a single picture of her husband. All she had was the memory of him lying dead in the wilderness and the horror of having left him unburied and prey to wild animals.

The mother had new creases in her face and gray was overtaking her black hair. Her inquiries about his mother and how they were coping were often interrupted by deep sighs.

"I understand you're now a midwife," Yousif said. "How did this come about?"

"The times . . ." she said, her voice wistful. "I never worked outside the house a day in my life. But . . . the times."

Yousif was extremely fond of the mother who had sided with him during the agonizing ordeal prior to marrying her daughter. He crossed his legs and watched her, his eyes full of genuine sympathy.

"How did you choose . . .?" he asked.

"I didn't choose anything but it chose me," she said, then turning around to ask Salwa to make them a pot of coffee. "I'm sure Yousif would like a cup."

"Yes, I would, thank you," he said.

"My three children were born in the hospital," she explained. "So I have no training whatsoever in a midwife's line of work. But I did know the Armenian lady who delivered most of the children in Ardallah. Everyone in Ardallah loved her. She was bow-legged and five-foot tall—or short, I should say. People, especially children, used to stand by and watch her wobble her way up and down the streets. So confident and so much in control. We all just loved her. I happened to run into her in Zarqa . . ."

". . . Zarqa? I went there looking for all of you. And I never saw anyone from back home."

"I don't know when you came, but at one time there were a number of us there. Anyway, the midwife . . ."

". . . You're talking about Nazeera, I'm sure. I remember her."

The mother seemed to come out of a fog. "Of course you do. Oh, my God. Anyway, Nazeera told me she was overwhelmed with work and asked if I would consider assisting her. 'Doing what?' I asked, shocked. 'Delivering babies,' she answered. To make a long story short, I followed her around, boiling water. Holding the pregnant women down when they start screaming. Cutting the umbilical cord. And bathing the babies afterwards. Before too long she let me take over several times. Well, here I am. I have more deliveries than I can handle. When Salwa got the job at the hospital here in Salt, I found sweet Nazeera a new replacement and came to be with her."

Yousif was intrigued by the shifting fortunes. "It's a good job," he said.

"Listen, Yousif, there are two kinds of pain in life: bad pain and good pain. Losing a loved one to death is a bad pain . . ."

". . . losing a country is the worst pain."

"We all know that. I'm talking about ordinary living. The good pain is in giving birth to a new life. I enjoyed giving birth myself. And I'm enjoying assisting other women to do it."

"I can see that," Yousif said, smiling. "Salwa, have you been listening."

"Yes, I have," Salwa answered from the tiny kitchen.

"Husbands and wives nowadays are keeping me busy," the mother continued. "Either out of boredom or out of frustration, they are hard at work making babies."

Now laughing, Yousif rose from his seat and walked to the adjacent kitchen, telling Salwa he had not laughed so hard in a long time. It was a perfect diversion from what else was on his mind.

"But listen, you two," the mother said, her voice loud enough for both to hear. "When Salwa starts having babies, don't you expect me to be her midwife. I just won't do it."

"Mother!!!!" Salwa exclaimed, either from embarrassment or dismay.

"Don't you 'Mother' me, I will not do it."

The coffee was percolating. As Salwa turned around to laugh with Yousif, it boiled over and spilled over her hand.

"Ouch!" she said, removing the brass pot quickly off the stove and kissing the painful spots.

Yousif held her two hands and looked into her eyes. "Maybe when you become a medical doctor, you'd specialize in obstetrics."

"Pediatrics is more like it," she answered, kissing his forehead.

"Practice begins at home," he said, planting on her lips a lustful kiss.

Holding Salwa in a tight embrace, Yousif set aside his political concerns. At least while they were savoring the joy of their reunion.

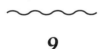

9

B Y THE END of the first week after their reunion, Yousif and Salwa chafed against life in the congested apartment. With four women and three men bumping into each other, in addition to five children romping in and out of the house, they had no time or place for privacy. They had not even had a single opportunity for a heart-to-heart talk.

Next morning, over breakfast, Yousif gave his wife a meaningful stare and told her that he would be taking her out to lunch. Sharing his frustrations, she winked at him with full understanding. "Where?" she asked.

"A surprise," he answered, rising to leave for school.

He returned at noon and found her waiting at the front door. She was wearing a blue skirt and a white blouse and, in her simple attire, looked alluring as usual. But instead of a handbag strapped on her shoulder, she only had a hanky she twirled in her hand. They said goodbye to the women of the house, descended the outdoor steps, and hailed a taxi. Yousif told the driver to take them to Swayleh. The street was noisy and the driver craned his neck and asked him to repeat his destination.

"Swayleh," Yousif said.

"I've never been there," Salwa said.

"You'll like it. Trust me."

They sat in the back seat close to each other with their hands intertwined. Their silence was meant to conceal their yearning—a company of three was one too many.

Twenty minutes later the driver dropped them off at a small countryside restaurant shaded by grapevines climbing on wood-framed arbors. The garden was enhanced by strips of roses and a variety of flowers. The covered tables under the leafy trees reminded Yousif and Salwa of home and their pre-exile lives. Well-dressed ladies were dining with their men, some of whom were in traditional robes while others wore western suits. They were either bare-headed or wearing maroon fezzes. Some puffed on their nergilehs and stared into the distance. But here no background music enlivened the scene, and no joy flickered on the customers' faces. They all seemed listless and absorbed in their own thoughts, as if guilty for enjoying an outing in these dire days. The only sound Yousif and Salwa could hear was the gurgling in the water pipes.

Despite the eerie atmosphere, the natural beauty of the unexpected oasis in the desert lifted their spirits and flooded them with memories. As they sat at a table across from each other, they held hands and sighed tenderly.

"Can you believe it?" Yousif said. "From the beginning of our relationship we had one interruption after another. And after a long and agonizing separation we can't even give each other a proper kiss."

"How well I know," she said.

As soon as the waiter took their orders and left for the kitchen, Yousif held Salwa's hand more firmly and looked her in the eyes. "I looked for you everywhere. Were you trying to find me, too?"

"Why, you know I was! I chased every clue I could get looking for your highness. I went to Jarash. I went to Shuneh. I went to Jericho. I went to Ramallah. I even rode in the back of a truck piled up with refugees and headed to south Lebanon. Oh, Yousif. I cried many times because no one knew where on earth you were—and because of the misery I saw in all those refugee camps. I must've toured ten or twelve of them. And each one was more of an eye-sore than the last."

Yousif was bemused. "Quite a journey, I must say. Please forgive me."

"Oh, Yousif. It was awful. Just awful."

"I thought sure you might see what I had written in the *Amana Daily*. Everyone I know read it, and one of the reasons I had it published was to attract your attention. If you had only read it and contacted *Amana Daily* our search would've ended. Then, when weeks went by and I didn't hear from you, I listed my name on the radio broadcast that promoted family reunions."

Again, Salwa took a deep breath and shook her head. "Your article must have appeared during my travels. As to the radio broadcast, how could I have heard it? We couldn't afford a radio set, and my brothers are too young to sit at coffeehouses for hours listening to the broadcasts."

His expression softened. "At least you tried."

"Tried? Are you kidding me? I was miserable."

They ate their hummus, tabbouleh, stuffed green squash, and stuffed grape leaves with the appetites of those who were either famished or had never savored such delicacies. As they enjoyed their meal and the novelty of being alone together, Yousif insisted that the next thing for them to do was to rent an apartment and get the hell out of the hole in which they were living. It was too small. Too crowded. A cave was preferable.

Salwa paused her fork in midair and stared at him. "But we can't afford to move."

"And we can't afford to stay."

"Agreed. But how—"

He outlined the possibilities. With what was left of the money they had left Palestine with, his mother's salary from UNRWA, his teacher's salary, and his regular allowance from Amana, they should be able to manage. And before long she would find a new job and whatever she made would help. But they should hurry. For the last couple of years there had been a lot of construction on Jabal Amman and other areas. Apartments were being snapped up before they were even finished. They should waste no time to lease one.

Salwa was amazed. "You can't be serious."

"Dead serious."

"The living expenses and the rent will be beyond our means."

"Then there are two alternatives, both of which are unacceptable. One, to stay where we are—which is hellish. Two, you and I will have to check into hotels three or four times a month. And that's costly."

Her eyes widened. "Will have to check into hotels?"

"To be able to live as husband and wife. Or shall I draw you a picture?"

Salwa smiled but did not blush.

Over coffee he continued acting like the man of the house and told Salwa that she and his mother should look for a new place to rent, adding that whatever suited them would be fine with him.

"I know you better," Salwa said, shaking her head. "You are so convinced of your plans—and so strong-headed, I must say—nothing we pick will please you."

Yousif grinned. "I'll be on my best behavior and will agree to whatever you decide on. Provided—"

"Here we go again. Provided what?"

"Provided you choose a three-bedroom apartment. One room for you and me. One room for my mother. One room for your mother and brothers when they come to visit. Or for any friend who happens to be stranded."

Salwa shook her head, bemused. "You're already talking like someone who has forgotten that he is still a refugee. Your hospitality . . ."

"Hospitality has nothing to do with it. Practicality is more like it. If the expenses become a burden, we can always sublease the third room to a friend in need."

Salwa laughed. "Oh, how I missed your sense of humor."

"Only my sense of humor?"

"And your self-confidence. And your arrogance. And your—"

"Stop it and let's go. There's someone else I want you to meet."

While they waited at the curb for a taxi, Yousif told her that he was taking her to the office of *Amana Daily*. The famed journalist and ardent nationalist, Raja Ballout, was one of his mentors. Salwa was delighted. She knew who Raja was and looked forward to meeting him in person and shaking his hand.

"He's the one whose sick sister was slain in bed—"

"While he and her children were watching," she recalled.

"Do you remember his article, 'Slain Sister / Slain Mother'?"

"Who can forget it?"

"Now he's the editor of *Amana Daily*. And I respect him a lot."

"As you should," she said, wrapping her arm around his waist.

On the mezzanine of *Nadi Amana*, Yousif ushered her into Raja's office. As usual, the editor was pecking with two fingers on his typewriter. When he saw them standing at the door, not only did he stop typing but he walked around his desk to greet Salwa.

"No wonder two good men fought fiercely over you," he told her, extending his hand. "You're more beautiful than I was led to believe."

Never did Yousif see or hear Raja gush about anything or anyone. He certainly appreciated his warm welcome. Salwa, of course, simply thought she was in the presence of a national hero,

"I'm honored to meet you," she said, beaming. "I have admired you even before I was old enough to read your column."

They sat down, and Raja buzzed his assistant for coffee. While Raja and Salwa were getting better acquainted, Yousif reflected remorsefully that he had misjudged her during their long separation. Then turning to Salwa, he asked her to tell Raja how long she had traveled to find him.

"Thousands of people like us did the same thing," she said, understating her effort. "We're lucky that we finally found each other. There's no telling how many are still looking."

"Don't be modest," Yousif said. "Tell him about the refugee camps."

Salwa took a deep breath and hesitated, waiting for further encouragement. When Raja urged her with a nod she felt more at ease.

"I have seen several refugee camps in Jordan and the West Bank," she began, "but not as many and not as crowded. Three or four hundred thousand of us must've ended up in south Lebanon." Suddenly embarrassed, she stopped. "Why am I telling you this? You're the expert on the subject. It's presumptuous of me—"

Raja knew that the last remark was meant for him and with a hand gesture he urged her to continue.

After regaining her composure, she obliged him.

"Everything I saw brought tears to my eyes. Women washing clothes and dumping the dirty water in open sewers. Men and women running to the fields to relieve themselves. Trash everywhere. Sick babies dying from lack of care. Children crying from hunger and thirst. Husbands and wives quarrelling for no reason other than frustration. It got to me. I kept thinking: these are landowners, homeowners, farmers, and merchants who were minding their own business when tragedy struck them with a mighty force. I kept asking myself what they had done to be uprooted and disinherited. They had done no harm to anyone, and look at them. They were like sheep ready to be slaughtered. Walking between rows and rows of tents, and witnessing all this misery, I felt enraged. And spontaneously, I found myself lifting up my arms toward the sky and screaming: 'Hey, God, where are you? Why are you letting this happen to us. Why? Why? Why?' Baffled men and women rushed out of their tents and looked at me as though I had lost my mind. But I didn't care. I kept on screaming, 'Why, God? Why? Why?'"

After a charged pause, Yousif asked, "Well, did He answer you?"

Salwa shook her head and pursed her lips.

"Maybe He has grown too old and lost his hearing."

"Or maybe He's tongue-tied."

The tall, laconic Raja cleared his throat and stared at them, his sour look returning to his face. "I'm usually averse to blasphemy or any kind of cursing or profanity, but in view of our ungodly tragedy I'm willing to wager that Jesus himself is so disheartened that he wishes he had never set foot on this unholy holy ground."

Yousif and Salwa were stunned by Raja's own irreverence.

"As to you, young lady, I must say your inner strength, your sense of morality, your sense of justice, and, I might add, your feistiness are not only justifiable but endearing. May you never lose them." Then turning to Yousif, he added. "Here's an idea for another column you should start writing. It will be entitled: Why, Why, Why???"

Yousif and Salwa were overwhelmed by his high praise. "As soon as we settle in our new apartment, you'll be our first dinner guest," Yousif declared, as Salwa nodded approval.

"I simply cannot wait," Raja assured them.

SOON AFTER HAVING MOVED into the three-bedroom apartment, Yousif was determined to retrieve the jewelry hidden under a tile in his bedroom in Ardallah. Maher drove him and Hikmat to the closest point near Ardallah, telling them he would be waiting for them around midnight. If they did not find him waiting, not to worry. He would be cruising around until he picked them up.

They walked briskly on a serious mission, well-prepared and well-motivated. Three valleys and two mountains lay between them and Ardallah. Yousif worried that the barren grain fields they were passing through would make them more easily spotted. The thick olive orchards which could shield them were to the south and east, and they were headed west. Right now he could see the sun, like the proverbial ball of fire, rapidly sinking behind the far horizon. But before darkness fell, he could tell that parts of the landscape had been altered. Three yellowish bulldozers were squatting in the fields, having cut two roads which looked like long fresh gashes on the earth's fertile belly.

When they reached the carob tree by the pond, Yousif was filled with memory. His sigh was loud enough for Hikmat to inquire about it. Yousif related how he and his friends Amin and Isaac spent many hours at the spot, trying to catch live birds for his aviary.

"Do you remember what Cleopatra told Mark Antony as she bid him farewell?" Yousif asked Hikmat, as they sat for a brief rest.

"Excuse me?" Hikmat asked.

"Once Antony was on his way to do battle. Do you know what the famous queen, his mistress, told him?"

"I have no idea," Hikmat said.

"She charged him with: 'Stride like a lion / Soar like an eagle / Come back triumphant / Or, never come back.'"

Hikmat gazed at him in the moonlight. "In our case, who's the lion and who's the eagle?"

"It doesn't matter," Yousif laughed. "We shall both return triumphant."

"And you see yourself as returning triumphant to your Salwa."

"My dazzling queen."

They drank a few sips of water out of a bottle and lay flat on the ground, exhausted. Yousif rolled onto his side and felt the hammer in his handbag press into his hip.

When they stood to resume their journey, Yousif was stiff and fatigued. Mountain climbing was not his forte. But as they walked on he felt rejuvenated. As they continued down the last valley, Yousif knew that they only had one more slope to descend and one more to climb. It was already past seven o'clock. With luck they would make it as pedestrian traffic began to lessen. To Yousif's surprise, Hikmat was curious about Amana.

"What's behind the Amana Forever and the Nadi Amana youth clubs," Hikmat asked. "What can you tell me?"

"Let's start with the word *amana*. What does it mean?"

"Don't play games with me, Yousif. I know what it means. A sacred trust. Something to hold and protect. But what does it mean politically to men like Basim and Raja? Be serious, and tell me who's behind it? And what does it aim to do?"

"Nobody has asked me that before."

"Everybody wants to know."

Yousif smiled. "I've been waiting for the right time to tell you. *Amana Daily* is to give our readers our own slant on the news. Amana Forever is a resistance movement, if you will. On a small scale, it aims to confront our tragedy. How do we face the challenge ahead of us? What do we do next—sit on our butts and wait for our kings and presidents to restore our rights? That's like waiting for the sun and the moon to switch places."

Hikmat looked disappointed. "And now you tell me about it. We've been friends for a long time, and I shared with you my family's problems, and you never bothered to clue me in?"

"Actually, it's because you've had so much going on with Leena that I preferred to wait. I was going to recommend you and Maher to join us. Will you be interested?"

"Absolutely. So would Maher, for that matter."

Yousif was pleased by the enthusiasm on Hikmat's face. "I even considered recommending Rabha, the woman in black—the one who makes rounds at shops and coffeehouses—"

"Yeah, carrying her baby. She'd make a good one."

"What makes you say that?"

"That woman knows a lot of people. And everyone likes her."

They talked more about it, and Yousif promised Hikmat to submit their names to the selection committee. What surprised Yousif was Hikmat's willingness to become a commando from the start.

"Your trips back home—the one a couple of weeks ago and now this one—must've whetted your appetite for adventure," Yousif said.

"Revenge, not adventure. Revenge," Hikmat corrected him.

THEN THERE IT WAS. Glittering across several hilltops was Ardallah, the love of which was seared into Yousif's brain and which he now was forbidden to enter. His heartbeat quickened. He felt gripped by a sensation similar to what he had felt when he at long last reunited with Salwa. Intense emotion clung to him like his own shadow.

Only a mile or so separated him from the town. A few hundred yards past the carob tree and the nearby pond, they took the cemetery route as Yousif had planned. But first they had to eat, drink, rest, and wait. The traffic noise was still loud.

"Really amazing," Yousif said, almost to himself.

"What?"

"We've crossed the West Bank into no-man's land and now we're in enemy territory. Yet we have encountered no sentries and no soldiers patrolling the divided country."

"Let's not jinx our luck," Hikmat said, unwrapping his falafel sandwich.

"These rolling hills and connected valleys declare natural unity in defiance of votes and resolutions."

Hikmat took a bite and chased it with a sip of water. "Don't go philosophical on me, please. The test is yet to come."

Ardallah's gentle breeze enveloped them and calmed Yousif's mood. He recalled a song describing a man in a similar predicament. He wanted to sing it and other nostalgic songs until the lyrics thundered and echoed to the farthest hill. But this was not the time. They ate in silence. Afterwards, they refreshed themselves by splashing handfuls of water on their faces.

Yousif turned on the cigar-sized flashlight and was extra careful to mask its narrow beam between his knees to avoid detection. His watch read 7:45.

"It's time to continue," he said. "Within half an hour we should be knocking on the front door."

A peculiar feeling ran through him for not saying "our door," but he dismissed it lest stray emotions distract him. He led the way, and Hikmat followed. Except for a short stretch of paved road and about fifteen houses they would have to pass, the route they were now taking went through the surrounding countryside.

A fox wailed deep in the wadi, and an airplane zoomed above their heads. From its roaring sound and low altitude he thought it was military rather than commercial. He wondered about its target and destination. The sky was studded with brilliant stars, and God's nocturnal eye—the moon—was wide open and watchful.

"I don't think we need the flashlight," Yousif said.

"I'm glad you brought it. You never know what to expect."

As a child Yousif had been terrified of darkness, but tonight he felt one with it. When they reached the cemetery, he wanted to visit his father's grave but knew he could not take the time. Suddenly he thought of Isaac's killing on the other side of town and of Salwa's father's death during their exodus. And he wondered why these thoughts had sprung to his mind at that very moment. He realized more than ever that the dead might be buried in the ground for decades, but they were alive in the consciousness of those who still loved them.

As they circled the cemetery and were approaching the final drop to the urban part of the city, they heard the sound of a vehicle. By instinct they knew what to do. They flattened themselves against the closest stone wall and held their breath. The headlights came closer, toward them, bright like the eyes of a wild cat. It had to be a patrol car, they whispered to each other, for this was not a residential area. They were at the very edge of town and the street was a dead end.

"They could be lovers seeking privacy," Yousif again whispered.

"Let's wait and see," Hikmat whispered back.

The vehicle came closer and closer. Yousif knew they would be apprehended unless the driver turned off at the intersection or they managed to jump into the field below before the headlights fell directly on them.

"Are we safe?" Hikmat asked, his voice steady.

"Let's take a chance and jump," Yousif answered.

"It's too risky."

But there was no room for debate, no options left. In a split second they jumped and flattened themselves against the retaining wall as the car stopped right above them. Yousif could almost feel the bumper hit the four-foot stone wall above the road. If the driver got out and stood at that spot and looked down, he would easily see them. To his surprise, Yousif did not feel fearful. Only anxious. His mission was on his mind, not just their safety. He felt for the pistol taped to his right thigh. He had only fired it twice in practice but was prepared to use it now. The hammer inside his handbag was again poking his side and was hurting him. He pressed his rib cage with both hands and looked at Hikmat, who was already pointing his own pistol upward toward the parked car, ready to blast anyone who looked in their direction.

They heard the car doors open and close and the sound of a woman giggling. Yousif's heart raced faster. Quickly but very stealthily he loosened his belt, unbuttoned his pants, and reached for the pistol. He had planned to do this closer to town, but now he had no choice. What if the couple decided to spread out a blanket in the field and make love outdoors in the moonlight? Would that not be the ultimate absurdity—his careful plan fouled up by two lovers eager to get laid? More opening and closing of the car doors assured him that they had opted for the more comfortable back seat. He held the pistol in his hand, but did not risk making a noise by cocking the hammer. But when the love sounds rose to an orgasmic height, he cocked it without fear.

Half an interminable hour later, the lovers drove off. Instead of rising, he and Hikmat threw themselves on the ground from utter exhaustion. They were behind schedule already and their legs ached from crouching motionless beneath the retaining wall. But Yousif knew that they must not weaken. God was looking after them, otherwise they would not have had such a narrow escape. The moon winked at him as he looked to the heavens for guidance. He rolled on the ground, and kicked his legs up in the air to relieve the cramps behind his knees and to loosen the tightness in his muscles. Hikmat was doing the same. They looked at each other, unhinged by the ordeal but grateful for their good fortune.

Then they were up and walking again, the dry leaves and overgrowth crackling underneath their feet. Then there was another climb, along a short dirt road. Yousif could see cars zipping by on the main road and could hear music coming through the Srouji family's window. He felt absurd for thinking of the window as the Srouji family's. The rightful owners of the house were now refugees in some distant camp and strangers were living in their home. His mind flooded with unanswerable questions: who were those strangers, what were their names, where did they come from?

They passed an old house with an open stairway to the attic. It had belonged to the Qurbaan family, and again Yousif was relieved that no one was sitting on the balcony. What would they do if someone was suspicious enough to call after them? He had no answer and did not try to elicit one from Hikmat. They could pretend to be new Jewish immigrants from Morocco or Yemen who spoke Arabic but no Hebrew. That was the only notion he could muster and he let it go at that.

In his original plan he had decided not to act like a thief, stealing from yard to yard. That would surely draw attention should someone spot them. Taking a deep breath, he crossed the road with Hikmat at his side. They walked as normally as possible. Yousif began whistling as men were wont to do walking at night, but Hikmat looked at him as though he had lost his mind. Anything he whistled would be a giveaway, he admonished, for every tune in Yousif's head was bound to be Arabic. Again and again Yousif had a rueful time trying to remind himself that he was, alas, in an occupied country.

At the start of his driveway, Yousif found the bottom part of the wrought iron gate smeared with dark paint or charcoal, he could not tell which. One side of the heavy gate was bolted to the ground, but the other side was half open. As he touched it, the gate swung more open and its hinges squeaked. Hikmat held it in place to stop it from making noise and they looked around to make sure no one had heard. Luckily no one had.

Under the apple tree in the front yard, Yousif paused to catch his breath. He was panting not from fatigue but from the trauma he was feeling. He leaned against the thin tree trunk, and looked around, quietly describing to Hikmat what glorious times he had living in that house. He could remember his mother fussing at the craftsmen who were building the house, and later on his father in his bathrobe early in the morning bending forward to prune roses, and the maid Fatima entering the side door, by the cistern pump, bearing a basket of groceries on her head.

"The ceremony of raising the roof of this house seems like yesterday," he whispered to Hikmat. "What a festive day that was. I can still see and hear the women singing and bringing trays of stuffed lambs, and big bowls of *manasef*. Not to mention the trays of *kinafeh*, a welcome gift from Isaac's parents, brought all the way from Nablus. Then there were the laborers chanting and carrying buckets of mortar up the ladder to the roof. Dozens of relatives and friends, even some British judges and high officials, clerics and local dignitaries, basking under the trees, drinking *arak*, eating *maza*, and joining my parents' celebration."

"Even in the dark," Hikmat said, "I can see that it's beautiful."

Swept by melancholy, Yousif recalled the forced exile. What had they done to deserve this fate? Why, why had total strangers turned their happy life into a nightmare?

"Mother would wail," he said, "if she saw all this neglect to her garden. Look at the weeds, the empty soda bottles on the ground. Look at the trash where the lilacs used to bloom. She took so much pride in them."

Hikmat touched his elbow and urged him on. "Let's not waste any time."

THEN YOUSIF FOUND HIMSELF standing at his own front door, the handbag under his left arm, his other hand clutching the pistol, and Hikmat right behind him. Every smell in the garden, every inch of that beautiful villa evoked strong and painful memories. There in the middle of the driveway, his father used to park his blue Chrysler. From that tree he and Salwa used to pick green almonds. Stop it, Yousif told himself. His concentration had to be as sharp and focused as a beam of light. Sentiment was not permissible; curiosity, forbidden. He knocked on the door with the butt of his pistol. He heard voices and the Jewish announcer on Kol Yisrael. Ah, the radio, he reminded himself; he must not forget to turn the volume high while he dug for his mother's jewelry.

They could hear someone coming to the door and Yousif's heart fluttered like one of the birds in his aviary of old. The latch was lifted, the door opened a crack, and Yousif and Hikmat burst inside the house, pushing back the man who had opened it and pointing their pistols at his head. A thoroughly frightened middle-aged man stood in the foyer, his face as white as an eggshell, his hands above his head. A freckle-faced middle-aged woman and a boy of about ten stood rooted in the living room to the left, their mouths gaping. Yousif heard feet running in the hallway and knew that he and Hikmat were vulnerable.

"Tell whoever that is to come out," Yousif ordered the man, his pistol still pointed. The running in the hallway stopped. Tension hung in the air. "I must understand every word you say. So speak in Arabic or English. For your own good, do as I tell you."

What if the man did not know either language? Yousif thought. What if he only knew Hebrew or Yiddish?

"Deborah," the man called in English in a thick foreign accent. "Come here. He'll kill me if you don't. Come out."

The man's voice was full of fear. So was Yousif's silence.

A blonde girl in her mid teens nervously appeared at the opening between the foyer and the inner corridor. She was wearing house slippers, and her hands were raised in submission. Yousif motioned for her to join her mother and brother in the living room.

"Do as you're told and none of you will get hurt," Yousif impressed upon them, surveying their eyes one by one. "Is there anyone else in the house? Tell the truth. Your fate is in your hands."

They shook their heads and he believed them. They looked too frightened to lie.

"Is this the only telephone you have in the house?"

The man nodded, as did the rest of his family. Again, Yousif believed them, for in all his days he had never known any house in Palestine that had more than one telephone. If any. That was the norm and probably it had not changed since the occupation.

"*Yalla . . . yalla,*" Hikmat whispered, urging him to hurry up.

Hikmat stood behind him like a personal bodyguard, his finger on the trigger. Yousif withdrew a pair of scissors from his handbag and crossed the foyer to the table on which the black telephone had been placed below a mirror. As he reached to cut the wire, he saw that the telephone number in the center of the dial was the same one his family had when they were living there. It was another reminder of where he was.

He knew what to do next and did not glance at Hikmat for consent. He bent down and pulled colored scarves from the handbag and handed one to each of their captives, ordering them to stuff them into their mouths. They grimaced but obeyed for they feared provoking him.

Hikmat then took over. He cut several pieces of duck tape and taped their mouths. He cut pieces of rope and hobbled their ankles and tied their wrists behind their backs. Meantime, Yousif realized that there was too much light in the living room and walked in to turn off the switch. His finger froze as he noticed that his parents' wedding photograph, which had been a permanent icon in that corner, was missing. It hurt him to see that it had been removed and probably trashed.

Full of anger, he returned to the man and with one swift movement pulled the tape off his mouth. Yousif noticed the man wince in pain but he didn't care. He yanked the gag from the man's mouth and demanded, "What did you do with my parents' photograph?"

The man shrugged his shoulders, his eyes bulging.

"Where is it? This is my house, damn it. My house. What did you do with the photograph?"

The man stared, the children whimpered, and the mother's face was twisted in terror. The disappearance of his parents' photograph—in fact, of all the family photographs that hung on the walls—was a tipping point. He no longer had a single photograph of his father and he wanted to find one in the worst way. Now he was truly on the verge of losing his temper.

"Where did you come from?" Yousif cried.

"Bulgaria."

"Is that so! You were born and raised there?"

"Yes."

"I was born and raised here. My parents and grandparents and their great, great, great, great, great, great, great grandparents and generations before them were born and raised here. And now all of you have the audacity to come from Bulgaria or Romania or Poland and, with a flick of a finger, take our houses from us? This house is mine, damn it. It's mine.'"

"I bought it from the State."

"I see. You bought it from the State. Well, well. For your information, your State never paid us a lousy dinar for it. Nor did they pay anything to the million homeowners and property owners like me. Do you think that's fair? Do you think that's right? Answer me."

But the man would say nothing else, so Yousif roughly stuffed the scarf back into his mouth and motioned to Hikmat to retape him.

Hikmat did as he was told but was troubled by Yousif's flash of outrage. "*Haddi . . . haddi,*" he whispered, telling him to calm down. "Let's get your mother's things first."

Hikmat was right, Yousif knew, but he could not resist casting another look around the room. He saw his mother's crocheted tablecloth and framed tapestries on the walls; even his father's curved pipe was still on the rack. He reached for it and caressed it in his hands, wondering if someone had defiled it with his lips. He stuffed it in his pocket. If need be he would have the stem replaced. Or he would have it buffed so that no part of the original pipe would be missing. He wanted to smoke it just the way his father did.

"Have you smoked my father's pipe?"

The man shook his head, and Hikmat again had to remind Yousif to speed it up. They had no time for tantrums.

Yousif crossed the room to the large mahogany radio console in one of the corners and turned up the volume. He catalogued in his mind's eye every piece of furniture. This, he said to himself, was his father's favorite chair; that flower vase was always full of his mother's hand-picked flowers. How many happy and sad events had taken place in the middle of that salon. He remembered the body of his father reposing there in his coffin after he was murdered by a sniper's bullet. The sight and sound of his weeping mother and the wailing of relatives and neighbors were echoing in his heart. Then there was the celebration the night before his wedding to Salwa. He could still see his mother gamely moving her feet on the dance floor even while she was still in mourning over her husband's tragic death.

Though anguished by his memories, Yousif tried to move on. But where, where was the bookcase with all the volumes of his father's collection of classics. He was hoping to take back with him at least a couple to leaf through and read the very same pages that his father had touched and read. He wanted to grab the stranger in the house by his throat and demand an explanation.

"Where are my father's books?" he screamed.

Widened eyes stared at him but no one answered.

Despite Hikmat's admonition, emotion surged within him. He wanted to run through the house: to the balcony, to the aviary, to the three adjacent bedrooms on the other side of the corridor, and to the bathroom, kitchen, and dining room on his right. Drenched with passion, he wanted to howl: this was his house, the house his parents had saved and labored to build. Who were these strangers now living in it?

He took a deep breath. What was the use of all that anger, he finally concluded, returning to his senses.

"*Yalla . . . yalla,*" he said, herding the family of strangers as he and his family had been herded by the invading soldiers.

His captives, their ankles hobbled, hopped before him like rabbits and he had to warn the man to stop jumping so loudly because his hard-soled shoes were making too much racket. When they reached the bathroom, he pushed them all in, turned on the faucet and the shower, removed the door key from inside and locked the room from outside.

When Yousif reached his parents' old bedroom, Hikmat had another plan.

"I'm going outside to look around. Okay?" Hikmat said.

"Don't go too far," Yousif told him.

"I won't. I just want to check the gardens and the surrounding area."

Opening the door to his bedroom where the jewels were hidden, Yousif was dismayed to see that its furniture had been rearranged and more added, leaving him little room to maneuver. To a great extent the whole house was as his family had left it except for the missing photographs and bookcase and now this cluttered room for which he had specifically risked coming. The chifferobe was directly over the tile he sought, and it looked too cumbersome for him to handle alone. He put his shoulder to the chifferobe and pushed, to no avail. He decided to empty it, but its door was locked and the key not in sight. In his frustration, he threw his handbag on the bed, cursing his luck. He had not anticipated this obstacle, and Hikmat was outside checking to make sure no one had noticed them.

He ran back to the bathroom to get the man of the house to help him, something he was loathe to do but under the circumstances was necessary. He found the whole family huddling together and growling like a bunch of drunks. At first he thought they were commiserating with each other by looks and rubbing of each other's cheeks, but then he realized that they were trying to loosen their gags. Yousif put the mother in the adjacent lavatory, tied the boy to the hot water tank and the girl to the pipe under the wash basin, and then told the father to follow him. The disgruntled man obeyed, and hobbled behind him all the way to the bedroom.

"I'm going to untie your hands and ankles," Yousif explained, his tone menacing, "I want you to help me move that chifferobe. Do you understand?"

The stranger nodded, his eyes glazed with fear.

"If you try anything stupid, I'll finish you off with one bullet. Keep this in mind," Yousif said. For emphasis, he grabbed the man's bushy hair, which reminded him of his own, except for the prevalent gray. "Help me and none of you will be hurt."

The stranger seemed to acquiesce. His droopy eyes made him look pathetic, and strangely enough Yousif felt a tinge of sympathy for him.

Suddenly Yousif had second thoughts about untying the man. That could be foolish, he told himself; what was wrong with his thinking? Instead he cleared the room of the two small chairs, a small desk, and a clothes basket, moving them into the hallway. He then told the stranger to squeeze himself between the wall and the chifferobe. The stranger looked either reluctant or confused, and Yousif found himself demonstrating what he expected him to do.

"Watch me," Yousif said. "Put your back to the closet, and the palms of your hands against the wall. Then push with all your strength. You push from one end, and I'll pull from the other end. We both push and pull, understand?"

As they got ready, Yousif was seized by a new anxiety. Since the furniture had been moved around, it was possible that the strangers who were living in the house might have noticed something peculiar about one particular tile and become curious. The coloring of its grout might have struck them as fresher, or cleaner, or rougher than the rest, and they might have suspected something under it and removed it to find out. What a calamity that would be, he thought. The hidden jewelry had once sparkled in his mind's eye; now he envisioned the hole under that tile to be dark and empty. But digging under it was a chance he had to take.

"Push," Yousif ordered the man with a new fervor, himself stooping to pull from the bottom of the other end.

At first the chifferobe felt as immovable as the Rock of Gibraltar, but then it moved slightly. Yousif stood and tried to pull it away from the wall, hoping to turn it aside instead of pushing it all the way to the door. He knew exactly where the tile was, and he wanted to get at it quickly. As he crouched to pull again, the man shoved the chifferobe with extraordinary power and without warning, tilting it and catching Yousif off guard.

"Stop, stop," Yousif protested, trying to keep the cabinet from falling on him. The man was undeterred and seemed intent on pushing it over. It was obvious that he was trying to pin Yousif under the chifferobe.

"Stop!" Yousif repeated, this time angrily, but the cabinet continued to tilt. Yousif summoned every ounce of his strength and pushed back, the muscles in his legs and shoulders straining. Like a heavyweight lifter competing for a world championship, he rose slowly from his crouching position and slid his arms upward, distributing his energy on a larger surface. He continued to slide upward until his knees began to straighten and the veins of his neck to bulge. A muffled growl came from the stranger's throat. Yousif was now standing, capable of counterbalancing one more angry push by the stranger, a push that brought the cabinet back to its feet. The stranger's anger was now working in Yousif's favor. If he could push that hard, he could clear the tile Yousif was after. And if the two of them pushed together, the tile would be freed that much sooner. It was the sixth tile from either wall, and the lower right leg of the cabinet was in its center. Yousif walked around and stood near the stranger, putting his back to the cabinet and his own palms on the wall. The stranger was in the corner now, with Yousif on the outside. Both were panting.

"One more push will do it," Yousif said to the stranger whose sweaty face was only inches from his. The stranger was about three inches taller than Yousif with a bleached complexion and four tiny black warts around the right eye. How ugly these warts will look, Yousif caught himself thinking, as they grow larger with age.

"Come on . . ." Yousif said, ready to push. "One . . . two . . . three . . ."

Yousif pushed with all his strength, but the man didn't move. When Yousif turned around to see why, the man lowered his head to Yousif's face, butting him with a forceful blow. Blood spurted from Yousif's nose, and he felt dizzy. He tilted his head back to stop the flow of blood, and reached for his handkerchief, then picked up the gun from the bed and pointed it at the stranger.

For the life of him he could not understand why the man was acting that way. What was he up to? He and his family were tied up and gagged by two armed men revisiting their home, demanding justice and ready to kill if provoked. Why was he acting so irrationally? Was he expecting company that might come in any minute to rescue them? Or was he hoping that the unusual racket in the house would alert the neighbors to call the police?

"Push it by yourself, you bastard," Yousif demanded, for lack of something else to say.

The stranger only glared at him. Yousif cocked the pistol and brought it closer to the man's temple.

"If I don't get what I came after—what's mine, mine!—I'll kill you. So help me, God, I'll kill you."

Silence fell between them like a block of ice. The stranger seemed to relent. They resumed their earlier positions and began to push. One, two, three . . . and the desired tile was in the clear. By that time, Hikmat appeared at the bedroom door. Yousif was relieved to see him.

"What took you so long?" he asked, exasperated. "Keep an eye on the son-of-a-bitch. He busted my nose."

Yousif opened his handbag of tools and took out a hammer and a chisel. The general condition of the tile reassured him that it had not been detected or removed by the usurpers in his house. He dug feverishly, glancing occasionally at Hikmat and the stranger, and feeling drops of blood fall on his hands. He wiped the blood off his nose with his shirt sleeve and continued to dig and to remove the grout. When the tile was loosened, he pried it up with the chisel. His eyes fell on his mother's green-and-white scarf in which she had wrapped her jewelry. His eyes closed involuntarily to savor the moment. He then lifted the bundle as if it were the Holy Grail and untied it, his joy suffused with apprehension. There they were, the gold bracelets, the earrings, the gold crosses and chains, the diamond rings, the watches and brooches. He looked at the two men with him in the room: Hikmat was grinning; the stranger was glum.

Yousif stood and brought the treasure closer to the stranger's face. "This is my mother's scarf," he told him. "And these are her and my wife's jewels. My mother wrapped them with her own hands. They belong to us. Us . . . us . . . do you understand? This villa is ours, too. It took my parents ten years of saving before they could afford building it the way they wanted. We lived in it for less than a year. Then strangers like you descended upon us like *jaraad*—like waves of locusts—and didn't give us time to enjoy it."

The man would not have been able to say a word even if he were miraculously ungagged. Which he was not. His eyes bulged with terror.

"One day you'll have to give it back, I promise you. So don't get too comfortable in it. Understand? Don't get too comfortable living in my house."

More blood was dripping from his nostrils and Yousif became conscious of the blood splattered on his arms, face, and shirt. He could not venture outside like this—what if someone saw him! Not eager to see the children in the bathroom, he headed toward the kitchen. The smell of food was unappetizing but he would not have touched it anyway even if he were famished. After scrubbing his face and arms, he went to look for a towel and a new shirt. He remembered the basket of clothes he had moved into the hallway, and he dried himself with one of the wife's cotton slips. At the bottom of the heap, he found a florid shirt which he normally would never wear but which he took out of necessity.

"This shirt is yours and I'm taking it," Yousif told the stranger while changing shirts. "Cheap rent, don't you think?"

Hikmat snickered; the stranger growled.

With the jewelry stowed in his handbag, which he now carried as the most valuable possession he had ever had, they were ready to leave. But Yousif had one more thing to do—he locked the front door.

This time he took the house key with him.

STANDING ON THE BALCONY, Yousif stopped for a moment to reflect on a conversation he once had on that very spot. And he wished to share it with Hikmat, his faithful companion.

"Right here," Yousif remembered, "Basim once questioned my plan to study abroad. I can still see his stare and hear his words. He more or less accused me of being afraid of joining the fight for Palestine. His castigation still rings in my ears: 'Could you live with yourself if we lost the war and you hadn't done your share?'"

Hikmat nodded. "Well, you never left. The struggle is still on and now you're doing your share."

Yousif's guilt was not assuaged. "We should've all done more, much more."

"They caught us asleep. The good news—"

"Good news?"

"—is that we've only lost one battle. The decisive wars are yet to come."

Yousif was wary of the future. The longer they waited the harder it was going to be to end the occupation. He recalled what Basim had done on that memorable night.

With Hikmat at his side, Yousif walked down the steps and disappeared into the darkness. His spine was straight and his head was unbowed.

10

Y OUSIF DROPPED THE JEWELRY on the dining room table and told
his mother and Salwa to share them as they pleased. He watched
them try on each diamond ring and gold bracelet as if they had
never seen them before. But the ecstasy on their faces faded as he told
them about the ordeal of the last couple of days.

"First, thank God for your safety," Salwa said.

"Amen," his mother added. "Now start from the beginning. I want to
hear everything."

And so he did, skipping only the journey through the countryside. That
was less interesting to them for now, and some other night he would give
them a full report of walking up and down the mountains.

The two women sat in rapt but apprehensive attention as he related
the journey step by step from the moment he had opened the squeaky
iron gate until he descended the doorsteps and left the iron gate gaped
open behind him. The anguish on their faces reflected what he had felt
going back to Ardallah and entering their home. His mother clutched his
wrist and her eyes moistened. Slowly and with great care he described the
ruined garden, the knock on their door, bursting in, and coming face to
face with the strangers occupying their home.

"Where did they come from? Who are they?" tumbled simultaneously
out of their mouths.

"Bulgarian Jews," he told them, watching their eyes widen.

He went on to tell how he and Hikmat had tied up the strangers' hands
and gagged their mouths. Salwa and his mother were dumbfounded by
his account, but they gave him an admiring look and again thanked God
for his safety.

Looking at Salwa, Yousif said, "Do you remember how you lost your
temper while touring the refugee camps in Lebanon? That was what happened to me when I discovered my parents' wedding picture missing. Yes,

mother, it is gone. Gone. And we don't have a single picture of my father. I nearly lost my mind and began screaming at the aliens in our house wanting to know what they did to it. Or with it. Did they destroy it? Did they trash it? Damn it, what did they do to it? The more the man glared at me and shrugged his shoulders, the crazier I got. If it weren't for Hikmat telling me *haddi, haddi*, I don't know what I would've done."

His listeners remained dumbstruck, though tears filled their eyes. That strangers from distant lands were occupying their home and scattering them to the wind was more than they could comprehend.

Finally Salwa spoke, wiping the tears from her cheeks. "Did you pass by my parents' home?"

"There was no time. It was getting late and we didn't want to push our luck."

"I understand. What about this ugly shirt you're wearing?"

"Oh, this is the cheap rent I charged them for living in our home."

"Cheap rent? What do you mean?"

Again he related to them how he had solicited the assistance of the man of the house to help him move the chifferobe off the tile under which the jewels were hidden.

"The bastard tried to topple it over on me and he ended up busting my nose. I wiped my bloody nose with one of his wife's silk slips and I swapped my bloodied shirt with one of his. 'Cheap rent, don't you think?' I said to that stranger and walked away."

Mother and Salwa were too drained and weary even to smile. They just stared at the floor or the blank walls. But when he reminded them to set aside a portion of the jewelry for sale, they woke up.

"I'm sorry," he said. "After all, that was the main reason for the risky trip. We needed the money. And still do."

"Oh, really?" Salwa huffed. "Then why did you insist on renting this three-bedroom apartment before we could afford it?"

"Because the two alternatives were totally unacceptable. Remember?"

Mother and wife nodded, as they tried to change the gloom by slipping the necklaces and crosses from around their necks. The silence that followed was poignant, but Yousif would not let it linger.

"Now what?" his mother asked, trying to read his mind.

"Nothing," he said. "I was just thinking—"

"Dare we ask about what?" Salwa asked.

"The apartment looks half empty. Buy a few more pieces of furniture . . . a few more pieces of clothes . . . but don't splurge."

Salwa and mother looked at each other, unsure whether to laugh at him or themselves. Or to reproach him for his high-handedness.

"Like Hikmat told you: *haddi, haddi,*" his mother said, gesturing for him to calm down. "We're not the Bulgarian Jews you're still fighting."

"I'm not fighting. I just don't want people to start asking where the money came from all of a sudden."

"You've got a point there," Salwa admitted.

With that tentative approval and muted snickers behind him, he told them he trusted their judgment and started toward the bathroom to take a shower. Then he remembered something, stopped, and turned around.

"Oh, Mother. I forgot to give you something very special." He fished in his handbag and took out a four-inch metal object. "Look, it's the key to our house in Ardallah."

"Oh, my God," she shrieked, reaching for it. "Oh, my God."

"I locked the door and brought the key with me. Just for you."

"I'll treasure it. Bless you, *habibi,*" she said, rising to kiss him.

He was struck by how much that key meant to her. More, perhaps, than the jewelry he had brought back. Could symbols unlock memories and be just as powerful as valuable objects? They connote hopes and dreams, no doubt. But was his mother seriously entertaining the thought . . . and anticipating the day when she would return home and use that key to open the door of the house she and her husband had built?

For her sake he hoped so. As well as for the sake of the multitudes of homeowners like her who were now languishing in refugee camps. One day the occupation will end, but will it be in her lifetime? With a heavy heart, he wondered.

When he finally went to bed Salwa was waiting and ready to give him the proper kiss they had for so long been denied. He kissed her back with equal passion and enfolded her in his arms. But he was emotionally and physically exhausted, and he soon drifted into deep sleep, shadowboxing the demons in his head.

THE NEXT DAY HE met with Ustaz Sa'adeh in his office and told him about the trip and of his conversation with Hikmat concerning Amana.

"He wants to be a commando on day one," Yousif said.

Ustaz Sa'adeh feigned a smile, and chewed on his tiny piece of gum in his most imperceptible way. "The last thing we need is a hot head. Though Hikmat doesn't strike me to be that kind."

"He's a lot calmer than I am."

Yousif went on to explain how he had lost his temper after being slapped in the face by the traumatic reality of finding his house in Ardallah occupied by Bulgarian immigrants. Not to mention his anguish on entering the familiar space but now with his parents' photograph missing and his father's library gone. And how Hikmat had kept whispering in his ear that there was no time for tantrums, reminding him to focus on the purpose of the trip.

That account seemed to reassure Ustaz Sa'adeh.

"I have another possible recruit for you," Yousif added, then told him about Rabha.

"Interesting," Ustaz Sa'adeh said, raising his brows.

"It's really sad," Yousif said. "Right now the arrogant West is supplying our enemy with intelligence, tanks, mortars, guns, and tons of money. And we are turning to a homeless woman to help us recruit fighters."

The principal looked at him soberly. "It's a shame, indeed. But we must not despair. Besides, we're doing rather well, considering the circumstances. Hey, Yousif, cheer up."

With each passing day, Yousif found himself willingly slipping further into the Amana movement. And with each step, new perceptions flashed before his eyes like emeralds that had been dusted and buffed.

Little had he known that there were men like Dr. Khaled Hassanain, better known as Abu Thabit, who were more hawkish than Basim. Little had he known that even the frail, kindly priest who had once come to his neighborhood to recruit young boys for the priesthood was now a pastor in Ajloun, urging men in his congregation to join the patriotic doctor. Little had he known that even a homely, innocuous baker's daughter was a dedicated saboteur, running messages and disrupting the office work of those whom her handlers considered suspicious. Little had he known that the tall thin man, who was always dressed in black and always carried a small box on which the word "CIRCUMCISER" was printed, was more than a frightful sight to all the young boys in the neighborhood. In reality he was a political agitator—even a recruiter. How pleased Yousif was to realize that the fire in his belly was burning in the bellies of others. The web of liberation, like a river with a hundred eddies, was pouring into one river: resistance.

On a summer day, Yousif accompanied Basim on a rare visit to Abu Thabit who was recovering at home from gallbladder surgery. Rumors had it that the doctor had suffered a heart attack or a severe stroke. And Basim wanted to check on his friend and fellow rebel from the thirties.

They found Abu Thabit going through a stack of newspapers under a tree in his backyard. He was glad to see them. Wearing a blue cotton robe over his checkered pajamas, he attempted to rise from his chair to greet them but Basim was quick to shake his hand and urge him to keep his seat. Yousif was delighted to meet the famed patriot and to find him in good spirits. Abu Thabit assured them that his overall health was fine.

To Yousif's surprise, the two old comrades did not talk politics or strategies. Instead, they launched into a discussion of the "theology of revolution," the meaning of which simply escaped him. To his mind theology meant the study of religion. Not revolution. Before long they moved on to discuss the difference between evolution or revolution. They agreed that both were essential to achieve a turnaround in the Arab world but disagreed in terms of priorities. What should come first, was the ultimate question. Yousif was even amused to hear the chicken-and-the-egg argument. Without evolution society would not be ready for revolution. And without revolution society would not undergo evolution on its own accord.

The maid arrived with a platter of fruit which she placed on a small table. In the pause from her arrival, Yousif reached for an apricot—one of his favorite fruits—and asked, "Why can't revolution and evolution go on simultaneously?"

The two older men looked at him and then at each other. Wide-shouldered Abu Thabit seemed willing to indulge his young visitor. "In tandem, you mean?" he asked. "The two phases could slow each other down, don't you think?""

"Perhaps," Yousif agreed. "But not necessarily."

Basim glanced at Abu Thabit, smiling. His look seemed to say, *What did I tell you? He's more mature than his age.*

Abu Thabit nodded. Then turning to Yousif, he said, "Before one starts a credible revolution, conditions on the ground have to be made ready. For a nation to correct its course and chart a new destiny, all the elements necessary for success would have to be put in place. Otherwise, the revolution would be doomed to failure."

Yousif did not shrink from the challenge. Basim's silence was tacit encouragement for him to plow ahead.

"If by revolution," Yousif argued, "you mean that our society would have to be radically reformed to rise to the occasion, I agree with you wholeheartedly. But let me ask: What time span are we talking about? Are we talking about years, decades? I suspect it will take a generation or two. In that case I beg to differ. We simply cannot wait."

Abu Thabit lit a cigarette, amused. "No one expects you to."

"How strong would Israel be if we gave her all that time to grow and prosper?"

Basim was delighted. "It's about time someone stood up to Abu Thabit. And you, doctor. Will you explain to him what you mean by evolution? He called it radical reform, and he may not be off the mark. Tell him that you want a sweeping change in our way of life all across the Arab world."

Over the next half hour Abu Thabit briefed Yousif on what he had in mind. The Arab world was vast, he said. And most people in its twenty-two countries scarcely knew each other or could name the capital of each country. In most cases they used French or English instead of Arabic to communicate. That was one of the evils of colonialism. The Arab world needed education that would unite and not divide it.

"More important," Abu Thabit went on, "we need to learn how to become an industrial nation. We need to make things instead of buying them from others. We cannot manufacture a tricycle, much less a gun or a tank. Can you imagine us building a helicopter?"

There was silence, and Basim goaded Abu Thabit to get on with his real vision. "Don't stop there. Why don't you tell him the rest?"

"I'll tell him. He's a bright young man and I'd love for him to join my group."

"Go ahead, tell him."

"Look, Yousif. We're saddled with a variety of rulers: kings, presidents, emirs, tyrants, dictators, despots, and what have you. They're all corrupt. They all must go. Every sorry one of them. Or be thrown out. We need regime changes in the worst way. Unless and until we get rid of all these bums, we'll suffer one defeat after another. What happened in Palestine will only be a dress rehearsal for what they have in store for us. There you have it. A clean slate, and nothing else. Have another apricot. They're delicious."

"But this will take forever," Yousif protested.

Basim cut in to help his young cousin. "No one can wait."

"Of course not," Abu Thabit said, slicing an apple. "In fact, organizations such as Amana are desperately needed. Many have already sprung up and more will follow. But, frankly, the best they can do is needle the enemy. By themselves they will not liberate a single inch of our homeland or stop the enemy from expanding. For that to happen and for us to get rid of—once and for all—the greedy and arrogant western powers, who have been treating us like pawns on a chessboard—"

"Or kicking us around like a soccer ball," Basim added,

"—we need a genuine, sweeping revolution. On the scale of the French, American, and Russian revolutions that ended long periods of tyranny and suffering. And, I might add, changed history."

"For that to happen," Basim suggested, "we need someone like Kemal Ataturk, the founder of modern Turkey."

"Exactly," Abu Thabit said. "He is my role model. After the collapse of the Ottoman Empire after World War I, he achieved miracles in his country. It took him ten or fifteen years but he turned Turkish society upside down. He proclaimed Turkey as a republic and abolished the caliphate succession. He changed the Turkish alphabet. Most significantly he liberated women. He reformed their dress code and got rid of the *hijab*. Sent them abroad to study at the universities. Helped elect them to the parliament. In other words, his far-reaching reforms plucked Turkey out of the Middle Ages and thrust it into the twentieth century."

Yousif was jubilant. "That's what we need."

"We need a Kemal Ataturk of our own," Abu Thabit said. "Then let the Zionists go on dreaming of robbing us of our land."

"Too bad you can't be him," Basim said.

"Nor can you."

"That's for sure," Basim grinned. "Our own Kemal Ataturk, if we are so lucky, would have to be Muslim and come from our largest and most populous and strongest Arab country. In other words: Egypt. No one from anywhere else could pull it off. Or be accepted by the masses."

The maid appeared again, carrying, appropriately enough, a tray of Turkish coffee. They sipped on their demitasse cups and refilled them from the large brass pot more than once while Abu Thabit ventilated over his Turkish hero. It was an enlightening visit for Yousif who had always heard nothing but derision of the Ottoman Turks who dominated the Arab world for four hundred yeas and set them backward in almost every sphere. They, he had come to understand, had been indirectly responsible for the loss of Palestine. Now an Ottoman Turk was being hailed as a paradigm by none other than Abu Thabit, the steadfast Arab patriot.

Basim stood to leave and Yousif rose with him. "I'm glad you're feeling better," Basim said, extending his hand to his recuperating friend. "Yousif has had an earful and I hope he'll forgive me for having subjected him to your tirade."

They all laughed and shook hands and promised to resume the discussion on better occasions.

"You'll make a great revolutionary," Abu Thabit said to Yousif, giving him a firm handshake. "I'd love to have you as a comrade."

"Comrade, hell," Basim said, then turning to Yousif, he added, "Don't you dare listen to him."

TWO WEEKS LATER, BASIM called for a special meeting for the youth club directors and sent Yousif to assess the situation in person. On Wednesday Yousif went to Nablus and Ramallah. On Thursday he went to Bethlehem, Beit Jala, and al-Khalil. On Friday he went to Jerusalem. During the rides from one town to the next, he re-read the letter he was carrying in his pocket from Amin who apparently was enjoying himself in thriving Kuwait.

At Bab El-Amood, Yousif descended the short incline which led to the enormous iron gate of the old city. He entered and began to weave his way through the congested crowd in the dim, cobblestoned, labyrinth of passageways. Hordes of people in diverse attire were bumping into each other, their cacophonous chatter filling his ears. Restaurants, sidewalk cafes, fruit stands, and perfumed tourists lent the scene an exotic amalgam of scents, evoking Yousif's memory of an earlier walk through the same place when he and his mother had come to visit Aunt Widad at the French Hospital when she had a gallbladder operation. That was a particularly awful time, and he hoped this trip would be less stressful.

It was not to be. Suddenly there was panic that turned into a mayhem. Men and women began to run, screaming. Shop owners tried desperately to close their stores. Yousif began to run too, not knowing why or where he was going. It just seemed a mass rush to safety—with no one willing to divulge the reason. Several angry Bedouin soldiers beat their way through the crowd, clubbing people on the head and firing aimlessly. Yousif could not see anyone wounded, but from the loudness of the screams it was obvious there were casualties. The stampede gained momentum. A tall woman running by him broke one of her high heels, stopped to take off her shoes, and then screamed as her feet were trampled in the melee.

Pushing and shoving, Yousif reached the end of the street leading to the Holy Sepulcher. He and the crowd around him ran into a bigger crowd headed in the opposite direction. For a fraction of a second he considered hiding inside the church. He recalled how his mother had wanted to go in and pray for her sister and how he talked her out of that notion. He quickly dismissed both thoughts and turned to his right. The street was rather empty, but soon another big crowd appeared at the other end, headed toward him. He turned around again and slammed into a man turning the corner.

"Why is everyone running?" Yousif asked, panting.

"Hide anywhere you can fit," the man said, himself breathless.

Luckily, Yousif thought, he was not carrying a pistol in his clothing. Something awful must have happened, and any weapon, even a pocket knife, would be incriminating. He wished he knew the old city better. There was a dark narrow street on which a lame aunt had once lived, but where it was he could not remember. A large arched wooden door reminded him of the one on which he had once knocked, looking for a brothel for him and his classmates, including Amin and their late friend Isaac. How odd, he thought, that he would remember such juvenile experience at a time when he was running away from certain danger. The recent past seemed galaxies away. At twenty, he felt like an old man.

People began to disappear through little doors on both sides of the street. Yousif wanted to get out of town altogether, and he ran toward the end of the street looking for an exit.

"Stop!" he heard a man call, but Yousif paid him no attention.

"Stop or I'll shoot," the man again shouted.

Yousif was alarmed. Instinctively, he stopped and raised his hands above his head. Turning around, he saw a Bedouin soldier coming at him on foot, his gun at the ready. They were alone on the street, and the soldier's face was dark and sinister.

"Who are you? What are you doing here? Show me your *hawiyya*," the soldier asked sharply, not stopping for a reply. "*Jawib, ya kalb.*"

Yousif fumbled in his pocket and stammered his name. But he did not think the soldier was listening. Nor did he have an ID card.

"I'm going to kill you," the soldier said, stepping back to take a better aim.

Yousif could not believe his ears. "What have I done?" he cried, trying hard to be brave. As the soldier stepped backward, Yousif stepped forward, not allowing the space between them to increase. The soldier kicked him and hit him with the butt of his gun and said he was determined to kill him.

"But why? You're mistaking me for someone else."

The soldier hit him again in the face. The edge of the gun almost broke his jaw. Sharp pain shot through his neck and head, but he would not show any sign of weakness. If that raging maniac was intent on killing him, he would try to defend himself. But he would not grovel.

"What have I done?" he asked in genuine sincerity.

"*Tha'r . . . tha'r,*" the soldier snapped back, holding the gun horizontally in both hands and shoving it in Yousif's face. It cut his lips and blood began to ooze.

"Revenge for what?" Yousif insisted, still moving closer and closer to the soldier. "I don't understand."

"One of you *klaab* killed my king," the berserk soldier shouted.

Yousif froze. "Sayyedna!!! King Abdullah? God forbid!"

"Don't tell me you're sorry, *ya kalb.*"

"As much as you are. May God cut off the hands that killed him."

The shock filled Yousif with black despair. The tall brownish walls of the old city and the patch of blue sky between them began to swirl around him. To a Bedouin, revenge was a way of life; revenge for a king's murder, only God could stop.

"Sayyedna!!!" he murmured, as a way of expressing his horror.

"I must kill you," the angry Bedouin said, pushing him away.

"Would you kill an innocent man because he happened to cross your path? *La, ya akh.* The Prophet, peace be upon him, wouldn't want you to have my blood on your conscience."

"How dare you mention the Prophet—"

"*Salla allahu alaihi wa sallam.*"

The wiry, craggy-chinned soldier looked threatening, but, Yousif thought, as long as he was talking and not shooting there was hope. If only the crowds would show up and distract him. If only other soldiers could pass by and intervene. The emptiness of the shadowy street was ominous.

A pause gave Yousif some encouragement. "The criminal will soon be caught. And he'll pay for his heinous crime. Allah will punish him."

"The dirty *kalb* has already been killed. The king's bodyguards shot him dead inside the mosque."

"*Allahu akbar*! Is that where the crime was committed?"

"*Al-kalb* fired at the king as he entered to pray."

"*Allahu akbar*," Yousif repeated, sensing a sliver of hope. "Revenge has already taken place. Blood called for blood and *al-kalb* has paid for it with his."

Yousif could detect a relaxation of the Bedouin's facial muscles. The white heat of his rage seemed to be passing. There was a short pause. Then the soldier involuntarily lowered his gun.

"As a lover of the desert and the ways of the *bedu*," Yousif began, "may I have your word of honor that you will not kill me?"

A second passed. Then another. Finally the soldier relented. "You can go," he said, slinging his gun on his shoulder. "I will not kill you."

The soldier's face looked even more creased by the anger that had engulfed him. Their eyes met for a second, and Yousif felt truly sorry for him.

Yousif walked away as if shackled. He looked straight ahead, afraid to turn to see what the soldier was doing. He heard footsteps receding behind him and his heart still pounded, despite knowing that a Bedouin would not go back on his word of honor.

Suddenly Abu Thabit's words echoed in his head. One ruler had already been felled. In fact, the Lebanese prime minister had been shot and killed a couple of weeks earlier while on an official visit to Jordan. Was this what Abu Thabit had predicted? Was this a partial fulfillment of a much wider plan? Did he have any part in it?

An excruciating headache added to his disorientation.

He did not know where he was or where he could hide. Suddenly a bullet whistled by his ear. He felt it whiz behind his neck, and heard it bounce off the opposite wall. He glanced back to see another Bedouin soldier on the loose, in brown ankle-length desert uniform and more crazed than the first. Yousif slowed to avoid suspicion and because he could not stand the sound of his footsteps echoing like drum beats. He turned at the bend of the road and crashed into a wall. The road had been blocked long ago by a high wall on which Arabic graffiti had been scrawled and where many men must have relieved themselves. He flattened himself against the wall, side-stepping a puddle of urine, smelling the awful stench, yet grateful for the bend of the road that had given him a niche to hide in. But the running footsteps assured him that the second soldier was on his heels. He was certain that this time he would be killed. Logically the Bedouin would follow the same bend, thinking it would lead to an open street. Prepared to meet his fate, yet determined to defend himself, he murmured a short prayer and bade his mother and Salwa farewell.

As the Bedouin appeared, Yousif jumped him like a ferocious tiger and twisted the gun out of his hands. The gun fired, the bullet hitting the ground. The crazed Bedouin pulled a dagger off his waist belt and plunged at him, but Yousif swung the butt of the gun and knocked his attacker down. Looking stunned, the soldier attempted to rise but Yousif hesitated to shoot. He moved backward to deny the soldier the chance to grab his legs and pull him down. Up on his feet, he did not know what the soldier would do. Should he scare him with a shot over his shoulder before the soldier managed to overpower him? Should he appeal to Bedouin sense of honor and try to reason with him as he had done a few minutes earlier with the first soldier? While debating within himself, he saw the humiliated soldier standing before him ready to exact *tha'r* from him: one, for the assassination of Sayyedna; two, for letting a despicable *madani*, a city dweller, challenge a desert hawk and knock him down. How dare he!

Seeing the fire in the soldier's eyes, and bracing himself for the fight of his life, Yousif slammed the soldier on the right side of his face with the butt of the gun, knocking him once more to the ground. He stood over him ready to do it again, but not to fire and kill. Moments ticked by and Yousif could tell that the soldier was unconscious but still breathing.

He felt relieved that he had not killed him, pitched the gun over the wall, and walked away as calmly and as collected as if he were on his way to a rendezvous with Salwa.

But inwardly he was on edge. What if he ran into yet another vengeful soldier? The city must be full of them. He watched a crowd disappearing into small doors on both sides of the narrow street. Obviously people were still hiding, probably totally unaware of what caused the havoc. He himself was in no mood to divulge anything to anybody. The less he talked, the safer he would feel.

He sought refuge through the first door he encountered. The entrance led to a small courtyard, around which there were two-story apartments clustered under one roof. The bedlam had begun around ten o'clock, and by noon most people were still looking for a place to hide. The commotion continued on the street and Yousif could hear sporadic firing. But the suspense, the fear, the unawareness of what really had happened kept the tension high.

From the vantage point of the second-floor window, Yousif could see soldiers patrolling the narrow street and the clearing at the end of it, beating up anyone who had the misfortune of coming their way. He saw one man hurrying along when he ran into two soldiers. The man stopped for a moment, turned around and began to run. The soldiers ordered him to stop, but the man continued running, unable to find shelter. The soldiers chased him. Yousif empathized with the man and watched him dash across the clearing, running in his direction, with the two soldiers on his heels. He entered the street below and Yousif gripped the window's iron bars and lifted himself up in an effort not to lose sight of him. The runner disappeared, and the soldiers disappeared after him. The sound of their feet on the cobblestone began to fade. A couple of shots later, Yousif knew the runner's fate was sealed.

"We'll probably spend the night here," a chic young lady said to a woman standing close to her, her native dress heavily embroidered.

"God forbid."

"I just have a feeling."

"If we only knew what happened."

The air in the packed room was suffocating. People were sweating. An old man in his mid seventies was dabbing a knot on his forehead. A young mother's blouse was wet with milk seeping from her full breasts. Men and women alike were wiping their faces and fanning themselves with their handkerchiefs. Yousif needed to use the bathroom, but knowing it would be impossible to go through the congested room and the rest of the house, forced himself to endure the agony.

Like Yousif, most of his fellow sufferers were from out of town. There were a thousand reasons why one came to Jerusalem, and precisely for these reasons thousands of people were caught today in the drift of history. Some were from Jerusalem, and they too were unable to go home—be it around the corner or just outside the ancient walls of the holy city. Some wanted to call their families but did not know how since most people did not have telephones in their homes.

One frail old woman standing next to Yousif was beginning to look weak. She asked him what time it was and when he told her it was quarter past twelve she seemed to panic. "I'm a heart patient and I'm supposed to be on strict medication," she faltered, her right hand rising indecisively to her chest. "My pills are with me but I can't take them on an empty stomach. They'll make me sicker."

"I'm sorry," he told her, wondering how he could help.

Those around her looked at each other, equally concerned.

"We have a sweet old lady here who's a heart patient," Yousif said, his voice loud enough for everyone in the room to hear. "She can't take her medicine until she eats. Does anyone have some food he could share with her. It's very critical. An apple, a banana, a piece of bread will do. Anything, please."

His message was repeated and shouted throughout the cluster of apartments. The old lady thanked him and blessed him and would not let go of his arm. The announcement created a commotion and Yousif could hear some of the soldiers in the street respond by barking orders and threats. A few minutes later someone in the hallway raised his two hands and passed the old lady something to eat: a circle of sesame bread, two hardboiled eggs, and a shiny yellow apple. Another man handed her a glass of water. People were so delighted that some forgot where they were and began to applaud.

All eyes in the room focused on the poor old woman as she ate and wiped her mouth after every bite. What a tidy woman, Yousif thought. She was embarrassed and began to apologize for all the trouble she had caused.

On the other side of Yousif was a man with pigmentation on his chin and neck and large circles of sweat under his armpits. In the close heat, most people were wiping their faces, but this man sweated profusely and had to mop his face, all around his neck, and the upper part of his hairy chest. He seemed eager to talk, but Yousif would not encourage him.

"I bet there's a coup d'état," the man whispered. "You know. *Inqilaab.*"

Yousif pretended not to hear. He feigned abstraction because he did not trust anyone. Especially a stranger. Especially at a time like this. He did not answer because there was no need to speculate; he already knew the score. He also knew what Abu Thabit had envisioned only two weeks earlier. Could that day's calamity have been plotted by that mysterious, angry, volatile doctor who desired to have the entire Arab world freed from its despicable regimes?

Again, Yousif's mind traveled to Abu Thabit's backyard. Could it be a coincidence? In all fairness, Yousif had to concede, Abu Thabit might not have done it. Someone else might have had the same idea. The Arab world was seething with disenchantment and rife with disillusion, if not sheer disgust. Still, what happened that day aggravated him. A national tragedy, his own near death, the tension in general, the pervasive guilt, and the uncertain ramifications had robbed him of the dubious pleasure of savoring the unsavory news.

The man with the pigmentation and bulging eyes cleared his throat and mumbled again. "*Inqilaab*, I tell you," he said, his voice conspiratorial.

"Let's hope not," Yousif said, feigning shock.

"You wait and see," the man whispered, wiping his face and wrapping his sodden handkerchief around his fat neck.

AT MID-AFTERNOON, THE QUIET outside became so intense that the slightest movement could be discerned. Suddenly there was reaction among the crowd, as if a signal had been passed from somewhere else. One by one they evacuated the building, forming a long line in the dim street. Apparently the situation was now under control, Yousif thought: the regime itself was no longer in danger. Now people could return to their homes. But the soldiers in the streets were still angry. They cocked their guns and herded the masses out the old city's arcades and out of Bab El-Amood gate, where many army trucks were parked. There people were grouped and told to wait. No one dared open his mouth. Yousif had not eaten all day and his stomach growled. A fat ten-year-old boy and his mother were separated. A soldier passed by, and the boy tried to explain that he and his mother needed to be together.

"Shut up," the Bedouin soldier snapped at him.

"She's right there," the boy complained, pointing to a woman a few yards away. "I need to be with her."

"Don't move," the soldier ordered him.

"There's no reason to keep them apart," Yousif entreated.

"*Sakkir tummak*," the soldier shot back, his eyes inflamed.

The boy was grief-stricken. Yousif watched the mother biting her knuckles. People were being loaded, their protestations ignored. The mother begged the soldier to no avail. A minute later she was hauled off and driven away, both she and her young son crying and waving their hands to each other.

Half an hour later, when it was time for Yousif to get on one of the trucks, he wanted to take the boy with him in hopes of uniting him with his mother. But his wishes were brusquely brushed off by the soldier. Yousif was stunned by such meanness.

"What on earth—" he said to those around him, his eyes searching for a clue to the soldier's excessive cruelty.

All seemed equally shocked but chose to remain mum.

Passing the museum on the right and St. George's School on the left, Yousif could see thousands of people still stranded and waiting. A kilometer beyond, they arrived at an open field at Shaikh Jarrah. Again they were told to wait. Crowds were already there like sheep just outside the slaughterhouse.

What surprised Yousif till then was how reticent people were on anything political. They all talked about getting home. About missing their children and sick relatives. No one dared to suggest that there might have been an Israeli attack. Or a Palestinian revolt. Everybody knew that something of horrific magnitude must have happened but no one, except Yousif (or so he assumed) knew what it was. They were too scared to even speculate among themselves. The absence of gossip and the conspicuous silence were by themselves worrisome. The situation was so tense, and the ill-tempered soldiers were so threatening, that all must have been worried that even their thoughts might be transparent. Like the rest, instead of engaging others in a meaningful conversation, Yousif found himself preoccupied with thought of his family and friends. Uppermost on his mind were Salwa and his mother. And what about Basim, Raja, Ali, Ustaz Sa'adeh, and the rest of the Amana members? What were they all doing? What were they thinking? More important, what were the immediate ramifications of the tragedy?

Finally, the shocking news was out in the open. And it went through the crowd like brush fire. Sayyedna had been assassinated. The assassin had been gunned down on the spot. Some shrieked. Others flailed their arms and shook their fists. Most were simply aghast. Yousif surveyed the faces around him. He sensed jubilation camouflaged as sadness. He could read their sentiment: one down and more to go. He himself was not one of those. Yousif feigned deep sorrow at the death of Sayyedna, and expressed profound shock as he mingled around the crowd. Then he spotted the man with pigmentations wobbling toward him, and he could predict his first words.

"You didn't believe me, did you?" the man asked, the bags under his eyes looking darker in the sun.

"I was hoping you were wrong," Yousif said. "It's awful."

"I knew it. I just knew it."

"Let's hope and pray for no more trouble," Yousif said.

The man's eyes seemed to dance. "No more trouble?"

"Yes, we've had enough trouble already."

The man guffawed.

"Why not?" Yousif said. "We all should."

"That's a laugh."

Yousif did not know what to make of the man. All he wanted was to get away from him. He oozed trouble.

Eventually a caravan of buses arrived and began shuttling people to different destinations.

Yousif and a few others managed to grab the first taxi that could take them to Amman. The fare of three pounds was a lot more than he could afford, but it was no time for haggling. He paid in advance, as did the others, and about eight o'clock that evening they took off, with him sitting in the back seat with two other men—strangers to each other and each keeping to himself.

The half-hour drive to Allenby Bridge took two hours. Roadblocks had been set up everywhere and passengers were frisked several times. At the bridge itself, the wait was long, reminding Yousif of the first crossing after the expulsion from Palestine, and making him wonder if the Jordan River had a special meaning in his life. It had in the life of Jesus, he mused; why not in his?

When Yousif finally reached his apartment close to midnight, he could see that flickering light of the kerosene lamp in the sitting room. He barely knocked on the door when it was flung open and both Salwa and his mother appeared in their bathrobes. Apparently they had been waiting for him all night, sleeping on the sofas instead of their beds. Their frightened faces made him imagine how Martha and her sister must have looked at seeing Lazarus's empty tomb.

"It's you . . . it's you," Salwa said, pulling him inside, kissing him and giving him a tight embrace.

"Thank God you're here," his mother added, hugging him and kissing him on both cheeks. "What a night!"

"What a fright is more like it," Salwa said. "But why do you have a bruise on your face?"

"Oh, it's nothing," he said, putting his arms around them and kissing the tops of their heads. "You can't imagine what I've been through!"

"You must be starving," his mother said. "I'll get you something to eat."

"Please do, while I run to the bathroom."

Salwa giggled as she watched him rush to relieve himself, his hand clutching his groin.

In the next hour, and in the dimness of the night, he related what he had experienced in Jerusalem. At several points he could see that they, silhouetted against the window, were on the verge of tears. His encounters with the two Bedouin soldiers rattled them, and he himself felt lucky he was still alive.

"Thank God you're safe," his mother said, crossing herself. "Is that why you have the bruise?"

"It's nothing," he said, touching the bruise next to his right ear. "I came very close to killing the second soldier. He was bent on ending my life."

"But you left him breathing, and his blood isn't on your hands," Salwa consoled him, softly touching the bruise with her lips.

After watching him enjoy two big helpings of rice and *yakhni fassoulia* (one of his favorite dishes), his mother retired to bed, again and again thanking God for his safety. Yousif and Salwa remained in the sitting room, talking. Had he been a drinking man, he would have drunk half a bottle of whiskey and still remained sober.

The remorse, the shame that had plagued him that night forced him to reflect on his shortcomings as a freedom fighter. That certainly was a pivotal day in his life. Could he continue his active involvement with Amana if he was unwilling or incapable of pulling the trigger? Could he in all consciousness expect others to lay their necks on the line while he sat in an office somewhere passing judgment and planning strategy? There was no honor in doing less than one demanded of subordinates.

"Leadership comes at different levels," Salwa argued. "Your role is still being defined. You'll find the right way to serve."

"What about you?" he asked, squeezing her hand.

"I know I want to be a doctor. Right now let's go to bed."

He remained fully awake, too agitated and exhausted to fall asleep. He remembered her prodding him in the past, and exacting from him a promise to redeem himself. She had told him to join the struggle or forget all about finding her should they get separated. Even after a daunting day, she was still the same spirited Salwa, forever committed to the Cause. And he loved her *iltizam*—as he would always.

She settled next to him and let him question her about her mother, two brothers, and the rest of his family. She told him all she knew. Right after the news of the assassination was announced, martial law was immediately declared. Troops roamed the city enforcing it. She had seen with her own eyes men beaten up or lashed at for no provocation. They gave everybody an hour to return home and clear the streets. For the first ten hours Amman had become a ghost town. Except for the military, not a soul . . . not a car moved anywhere.

"I wonder if that soldier actually survived," he said, the tragic event of the day weighing on him. "I wonder if he was married or had children . . ."

Salwa began to lose patience. "Will you stop it? You can't go on like this. That man was a raging maniac—I can just imagine him. What you did was in self-defense."

"Still . . ."

"What do you mean still? The assassin was Palestinian and that soldier was out for revenge."

Yousif's blood froze. "The assassin was what??"

Salwa looked surprised. "Palestinian. I thought you knew."

Yousif shook his head in complete silence. For the first time that day, he wanted to take the tobacco pouch and fill his father's pipe and smoke. He needed to absorb the awful new revelation.

Realizing that the real brooding had just commenced, Salwa went to the kitchen, brewed a pot of tea with mint leaves and returned to find him still gazing out the window, as though the uncertain future lay smack on his shoulders. She sipped her own cup and swam in her own thoughts.

They stared at each other without saying a word.

Instead of turning outward to speculate on what was to become of Jordan and who might be the successor, Yousif turned inward to see if he could find peace in himself. The impact of reality seemed to expand his consciousness, to alter his psyche. The reprisals against his people, he knew, would be ruthless, and the guarded freedom they had at Amana headquarters and the youth clubs would soon be curtailed. Some might be shuttered altogether. Al-Jafr prison, the medieval dungeon in the heart of the desert, would soon become a permanent residence for many of his friends and acquaintances. And possibly for himself. As of tomorrow, he thought, every false accusation or trumped-up charge would be tantamount to an indictment, even conviction, and the poor innocent would end up locked behind bars. Even if the suspect were not imprisoned, he would be forever marked.

Half an hour later they turned off the lights and went to bed.

"The retaliation against our people is going to be severe," he predicted, tormented by all kinds of visions.

"We're used to upheavals," Salwa reminded him. "Aren't we?"

"We haven't yet learned to endure expulsion."

"And I hope we never do."

Their lips touched as if they were too ashamed to indulge in a proper kiss. Before drifting to sleep in each other's arms, they felt comforted and reassured by the warmth of their bodies.

"How lucky we are to have each other," he said, momentarily relishing the smell of her luxuriant hair.

"Blessed is the word," she said, snuggling against the curve of his neck.

Just before closing his eyes, Yousif involuntarily glanced at the window. The bright stars were inexplicably closer than usual and serenely untouched by the evil on earth. As to the gray, pucker-faced, full moon—it looked cheerless, if not morose.

HE AWOKE TO FIND Amman a city in deep mourning.

There were as many black flags in windows and on lamp posts as there were troops on the streets. As expected, foreboding gripped the capital and commerce was at a standstill. Radio broadcasts could be heard in all coffeehouses, in some shops, and in the windows of many homes and apartments were blaring verses from the Qur'an, turning the entire city into one huge mosque.

According to news broadcasts, all schools were closed that day. And he had no idea when they would be opened. On his way to the Amana office, Yousif stopped at his Uncle's and Salman's shop to inquire about them and their families. They were glad to see each other, yet gloom clutched them like a boa constrictor. He knew that inwardly Salman was not in the least grieved at the demise of one Arab ruler, though his face did not show it. He wore solemnity as a shroud, at least in public.

"Have you seen or heard from Basim?" Yousif inquired.

Both men shook their heads. "God knows where he is," Uncle volunteered.

As Yousif started to leave, his uncle stopped him. "Be careful," he whispered. "That emaciated boy, the son of a tailor, couldn't have killed the king all by himself. He must've had others with him. Until they catch them we're all going to be suspects. For your mother's and wife's sake, be careful. Yousif, listen to me, these are awful, awful times. Be extra careful, will you?"

Yousif looked his uncle in the eye, thanked him for his genuine concern, nodded his head, and continued on his way. A few streets away, he stopped at the store of their old neighbor, Abu Mamdouh. The situation there reminded him of cousin Salman: relief, uniquely veiled as sadness.

Abu Mamdouh folded the newspaper he was reading and placed it on top of another on his desk. Yousif noticed that the front pages of both papers were bordered in black. And both had a large photograph of the slain monarch. Yousif hoped that the afternoon issue of the *Amana Daily* newspaper would be similarly mournful, lest they be criticized, even condemned, by the authorities.

"You haven't been to see me in a long time," Abu Mamdouh said, almost joyfully. "And I haven't seen any articles by you lately. What's going on?

By the way, have you ever located your wife?"

"At long last, I did. Thank you for asking."

"Bring her over to the house. Imm Mamdouh and I would love to meet her. And bring your mother with you. She's a fine lady."

What struck Yousif profoundly was the casualness in Abu Mamdouh's tone. The seismic earthquake of the day before did not seem to faze him, and he, Yousif, did not want to pry. Were there many people that indifferent, or timid to express an opinion? Were they masking their inner satisfaction by pretending that the tragedy never happened?

Nadi Amana was open, but less crowded than usual. Yousif surveyed the scene: no one was playing games. No ping-pong balls bouncing across the green table. No chips shuffling on backgammon boards. Instead, the customers were sitting in the reading section, leafing through magazines or having quiet conversations.

Yousif waved to those he knew and ascended the steps to Raja's office. The door was open and the radio was softly broadcasting Qur'anic verses. Upon seeing each other, both avoided morning greetings, dispensed with the usual amenities, and communicated by lifting eyebrows, locking eyes, and nodding heads. The less said the better seemed to be the tenor of the day.

They spoke in shortcuts or in codes. Soon Yousif learned that Basim and Ali were out of the country. Where exactly? East, he was told. By this he understood that the two had gone to Eastern Europe, to procure arms. And Ustaz Sa'adeh? The answer: UNRWA. Meaning: he was holding more talks with the United Nations Relief Welfare Agency about financial assistance for his school.

At that point Yousif felt obligated to tell Raja all about his experience the day before.

"I was there," Yousif began, motioning to Raja to raise the radio volume.

"Where?"

"In the old city. Near the Holy Sepulcher. Almost got killed by a crazed soldier."

Raja's eyes widened and his tight features became even more pinched. He reached for the dial on the radio and raised the volume. For more than ten minutes Yousif whispered to him the chilling experience. Both sat in silence, wondering how many others had gone through similar encounters. No wonder people were so hesitant to open their mouths. Fear pervaded the whole country.

A young reporter suddenly appeared with some bad news. A Palestinian shop, on the outskirts of downtown, had been set on fire half an hour earlier. First it was drenched with gasoline and then torched by a couple of young men. The firefighters were still trying to stop if from spreading to other stores. The police were dispersing the awe-stricken crowd. So far there were no injuries.

The reporter made a quick exit, leaving Raja and Yousif to themselves.

"Another example of why people are so uptight," Raja said. "Anything they say would be deliberately misconstrued."

For the next thirty minutes they talked in generalities if not in circles, as if the room's four walls were planted with ears. Then a delivery boy arrived with a stack of the afternoon issue of their own newspaper, *Amana Daily*. One look at it, and Yousif felt disappointed. Even concerned. The front page was not bordered by the black color of mourning, like the other newspapers. Also, the size of the slain monarch's photograph was conspicuously small. The bold headline, "Tragedy Strikes Jordan," was accurate enough, yet tame. Would it satisfy their detractors who would expect nothing short of outpouring of sympathy? How would it compare with another headline that screamed "Revenge! Revenge!"

Aware that Raja's eyes were focused on him, Yousif held his breath and began to read. The lead article was typically well-crafted but a bit too restrained. It contained no splashes of indignation, patriotism or emotion. The violent act was surely condemned, but the tone lacked the outrage the man on the street demanded. The last sentence caught Yousif's eye. "Let those who stopped believing in miracles ponder the fact that the late king's sixteen-year-old grandson, Hussein, who was standing next to him at that fatal moment, had been saved by a medal on the military uniform he was wearing at the insistence of an intuitive and loving grandfather."

Was it a miracle or simple fate? Yousif did not know. What he did know was that the young man who narrowly escaped murder would soon succeed to the throne and would have to carry a large load of the region's problems on his tender shoulders. What a formidable challenge that would be for any grown man, not to mention a teenager. Yousif's heart went out to that youngster who seemed to have been predestined to assume responsibilities beyond his age.

"I'd hate to be in that young man's shoes," Yousif said. "He's four years younger than I am. Imagine that."

"He'd do well if he's half as smart as you are," Raja said.

Yousif smiled. "Compliment appreciated but declined."

Raja's eyes were still scrutinizing Yousif's face. He seemed to gauge in it the public's response to his article.

"I can tell you're disappointed," Raja said.

Yousif put the newspaper in his lap and took a deep breath. "I just hope they don't accuse us of not being shocked—or tormented—enough."

Raja nodded his head. "You've got a point. However . . . no matter what we say or do, the native Jordanians, especially the Bedouins, are going to blame all Palestinians. In their eyes we are all culprits to the crime."

"That's all we need," Yousif said, worried. "To be targeted by Zionists on one side and Bedouins on the other."

"We could very well be," Raja said, rotating the radio dial from one station to another in search of a news broadcast.

"Perhaps it's time for us to open other Amana offices in other cities . . . in other Arab countries. To recruit members if nothing else."

Raja nodded. "We need to organize on a much, much bigger scale and to expand our horizon."

"Either that or we'll fold up. People will not put up with talk and more talk. They want action. Today, not tomorrow."

"That's why I'd like to start publishing *Amana Daily* in Beirut. Six or seven newspapers are already being published there."

"In three different languages, no less."

"*Akeed.* I don't think they'd mind one more."

Yousif had doubts. "For how long, I wonder. Look how they treat our refugees. They confine them to a dozen camps and won't grant citizenship to any—"

"Except the very wealthy businessmen."

"It's true, is it not?"

"Of course it's true," Raja agreed. "Haven't you heard: the wealthy are a special breed . . . a special class. They look after each other. They're privileged wherever they go." Then raising the radio volume and lowering his voice simultaneously, he confided, "Listen, Yousif, Lebanon is not Jordan—"

"I know that."

"Lebanon is a tiny country . . . and had no army to speak of to commit to battle. That's why she didn't enter the war. Not really. Only by name. That's why no one holds her responsible for our defeat. Jordan, on the hand, is in the thick of it. It's the hub of many rumors. As we all know, it's the chief beneficiary of what's left of our homeland. Rumors swirl, and will continue to swirl about her behind-the-scene shenanigans. Why am I telling you all this? I guess I'm inviting you to join me in Beirut. Would you come?"

Yousif had no ready response and remained silent. He had other things on his mind, and he leaned forward and exhaled.

"A scrawny son of a tailor couldn't have committed that heinous crime all by himself," Yousif said, his voice barely audible. "What if it took days, or even weeks, before his conspirators were apprehended and brought to justice?"

Raja chewed on his lower lip, thinking. "What of it?"

"How will it affect your plans to move to Beirut? Wouldn't the timing raise suspicions?"

"Yes, it would," Raja replied. "But we have nothing to worry about. We're absolutely in the clear. We had nothing whatsoever to do with that heinous crime."

Both emphasized "heinous crime" by raising their voices. Both wanted to declare their innocence just in case the walls were listening.

"I'd like for you to join me in Beirut," Raja said.

Yousif looked surprised. "I'd love to, but—"

"—You have your mother and Salwa to consider."

"You understand."

"Yes and no. When duty beckons one must be ready. Anyway, you don't have to decide now. The move would have to be approved by the executive board."

11

TWO MONTHS AFTER THE king's assassination, Yousif was in Beirut, holding a bundle of *Amana Daily* under his left arm and handing a free copy to anyone willing to take it. He figured he must have passed out a hundred copies that afternoon, for he had covered Sahat el-Borj at least three times, jostling and cajoling pedestrians on the busy sidewalk. It was a cool and pleasant autumn day and he did not mind the tedious work. Until the newspaper became credible they could neither charge for it nor hire anyone to sell it. Besides, it was an opportunity for him to come in contact with the Lebanese people for whom he had a deep affection, not least because his favorite modern poet, Kahlil Gibran, was born, raised, and buried in Lebanon. Thanks to his father's tutoring, Yousif could recite Gibran's poetry from memory.

The *Amana Daily* readership was rapidly increasing, but not rapidly enough to please Raja. The numbers had to be multiplied, the message spread, recruits found. The organization needed to change people's mindsets. Otherwise, why exist?

"Communist!" an old man with a thick gray mustache and haughty black eyes snarled at Yousif when offered a free newspaper. The man froze defiantly in his tracks, pursed his lips, and crossed his arms behind his hunched back as if to ward off contamination.

"Didn't mean to bother you," Yousif smiled in reply, moving on to other potential takers.

The shoppers were in a hurry yet many accepted the free handout. It was one of Yousif's better days, and he felt good about himself. He recalled many skirmishes with obdurate Lebanese who resented the Palestinian presence in their country. To some extent he could understand their feelings. By now he had grown accustomed to their indifference and had learned to take their brusque manners in stride. But the condescending effete who answered him in French—those were intolerable.

Crossing the streets, he heard a chorus of horns blast all around him. His month-long stay in Beirut had convinced him of the hazards of driving and walking through the bottlenecked streets of this westernized, glittering, and often charming city. With agility and fancy footwork he zigzagged around the heavy traffic, patting the hoods of a few slow-moving cars which were coming at him from all directions, and listening to the shrill whistle of the traffic officer who put his life on the line by standing, spinning and gesturing with his arms and coming face to face with danger a hundred times more than he would have encountered in the war to save Palestine.

Not even at a moment like this could Yousif forget the sorry performance of all the Arab regimes. They betrayed us, he reminded himself; and, without realizing it, they destabilized their own countries. Look at all the prostitutes in the legalized red district, he thought. Every apartment must be packed with girls who should not be there. Look at them crowding in the windows with their bosoms hanging out. Look at them in their skimpy and garish costumes on balconies and doorsteps. You would think you were in gay Paree, with every harlot showing off her curves. Soon the neon signs would light up and flicker names such as Lido, Miami, and Kit Kat, and every horny man with a few dollars or liras in his pocket would be scampering inside. Someone was getting rich off the war. War? Did these decadent fools realize that there actually had been a war?

"Watch where you're going," shouted a confectionary peddler carrying a large tray of pastries on his head.

"I'm sorry," Yousif apologized, but the man gave him the finger and shouted after him with a vulgar expression.

Yousif was undeterred, and kept passing the newspaper to those who cared to read it. There were a few takers, and one impeccably dressed young man with hair parted in the middle and groomed with too much Brylcreem shook his head and curled his lips.

"*Je n'ai pas besoin de ton* Amana. *J'emploi le tissu pour m'essuyer le cul,*" the young man told Yousif.

Yousif did not understand a word of French, but the man's tone and demeanor were venomous.

"What did you say?" Yousif demanded, pushing the dandy against the stone wall. "I dare you to repeat it."

The gathering crowd seemed to give the offender courage.

"*Je n'ai pas besoin de ton* Amana. *J'emploi le tissu pour m'essuyer le cul,*" the dandy spat at him again.

"What does it mean, you French ass-kisser?"

The offender refused to interpret what he said. The crowd grew bigger and Yousif could see their images reflected in the dandy's sunglasses and could feel their bodies press against his. Many were giggling and muttering in French.

"I'll tell you what he said," a middle-aged man standing behind Yousif volunteered. "He said that he doesn't need your *Amana*. He uses tissue paper to wipe his ass."

Yousif's anger flashed, and once again he found himself debating whether to ignore the insult or to hit back. Most likely, he figured, the crowd consisted of Lebanese. How many shared the offender's opinion, he did not know. They could all gang up on him. It was more prudent to choose his battles, and the one at hand was not worth fighting. Besides, would he hit a possible relative of Gibran's?

"I could wipe your filthy mouth with one of these newspapers," Yousif finally said, "but you're not worth it."

As the men and women began to argue, Yousif slipped away. A couple of blocks down the road, an electric tram approached. As it rolled past him he reached for the post by the back door and leapt on the side step. He felt lucky to have a spot big enough for his feet to land on, for the tram was bursting with passengers. For a moment he tottered and was afraid he would lose his grip or be accidentally pushed off. After securing his handhold on the post, he turned his head to view the receding scene. The crowd he had just left had apparently dispersed. He was again struck by the variegated costumes and dresses of the pedestrians: from Parisian-looking women attired in chic dresses and fancy hats or coiffured hair, to shapeless women in pitch-black veils, to men in tailored gray flannel suits, to men in ankle-length robes and red fezzes or desert headdresses, to crippled beggars with outstretched hands. Who among those, he mused, were the decent or the wicked? Who could tell the elegant poets from the staunch patriots or from the miserable creatures like the one who offended him earlier?

As the tram wound its way past the fenced campus of the American University of Beirut, Yousif glanced at a pedestrian on the sidewalk who looked awfully familiar. He got lost in the crowd before Yousif could get a good look at him. Yousif shook his head trying to recall that gait, that profile. Frustration lodged in his throat.

The sight of young men and women of his and Salwa's age walking together with books under their arms made him forget for a moment that he was now an underground revolutionary. He wished he had the opportunity to complete his studies. But normal life was now denied to him and many of his generation. Salwa would love to attend classes rather than work as a medical assistant in refugee camps. In his mind's eye he could see the two of them strolling together on the grounds of the shaded, awe-inspiring, century-old campus: reading books, listening to lectures, exchanging ideas, laughing with professors, enjoying life. One day, he hoped, she would be able to pursue a career in medicine. Nursing was honorable, but it was not enough for her. She had the mind, the desire, and the burning wish to do good for her people. She belonged to this university or any other university that would open doors for her. One day he would help her realize her dream, as she would help him realize his. Together they would keep the sacred trust alive until they returned home and did not have to put up with idiots like the recent offender.

The daydreaming distressed him, and the lump in his throat grew as solid as a large walnut.

HE GOT OFF ON the fashionable Alhamra Street and walked toward the
Café Al-Hayat which faced the Rosheh Rock—better known as Suicide
Rock. The contrast between this elegant section of town and the one
he had just come from never failed to impress him. The boulevard was
extremely wide; the hotels had marble fronts and uniformed concierges
ready to serve; the traffic was less hectic, the noise less deafening, and the
people more relaxed. Sidewalk cafes with multitudes of colored umbrellas
were everywhere, with the rich and beautiful patrons as part of the décor.

He walked by a few cafes until he reached a haven frequented by many
political exiles. Familiar people greeted him with a nod, a raised hand,
or an offer to join them. But he thanked them and continued on. Basim
was not to be seen, and he wondered if his maverick cousin was in town
or even in the country. Regardless of how well you knew Basim, Yousif
thought, you could never consider him a close friend. You could share an
apartment with him and exchange many confidences, but he would never
let you in on all he knew. That was Basim's nature and Yousif had taught
himself to accept it. Nevertheless, it often amused him.

Yousif was looking for a particular group and he found them at the
usual place—a large round table close to the building and at the outer
edge of the open-air terrace. A stout man with a Syrian accent was telling
an obviously riveting story, but he stopped when Yousif approached. Even
after they were properly introduced the man, Sari Abu Reesh, kept quiet
until he felt comfortable that Yousif was not an informer. "After all," he
said with a self-directed smile, "I'm wanted not by just one country but
by both Syria and Iraq."

"No one can blame you," Hanna said. "But go on with your story."

"One has to be extra careful," Abu Reesh said, nodding apologetically
toward Yousif. "Anyway, I don't know how I managed to get on the wrong
plane, but as soon we began to taxi the man next to me asked me how long
was our flight to Baghdad going to be. I nearly froze."

The group snickered and Abu Reesh prolonged the merriment at his
own expense by taking out and lighting a cigarette.

"Here I was," he continued, "trying desperately to escape from Syria and

Iraq—and where was I headed? Straight to the lion's den. But I tried my best to be cool and not let the man know I was nervous, which I definitely was. I smiled and pretended I didn't know. I saw the stewardess walking down the aisle and I intuitively knew that I should not ask her. Instead, I turned around and asked the man sitting behind me. He was an elderly man with a heavy Iraqi accent. He said we should get there in less than three hours. Something like that. I can't remember exactly because I didn't really care. The distance was not important. What I really wanted to know was where the hell were we flying to? I made it a point to let him know that I was asking about Baghdad, and the man said he was, too."

Abu Reesh's turning what could have been a tragedy into a comedy of errors fascinated Yousif and the rest of his rapt listeners.

"When my worst suspicions were confirmed," Abu Reesh added, "I suddenly had a headache bigger than the plane itself. And I got really, really sick. My first impulse was to press my right side as if I were suffering from appendicitis. But that wasn't serious enough to grab anyone's attention. I decided to have severe chest pain. Really, really severe. Seeing the convulsions I was going through, the man next to me was alarmed. He asked me what was wrong. 'Help! Help! I need help,' I faked it as best as I could. 'Please call the stewardess. Tell her I'm having a heart attack.' The poor man wasted no time. He pushed the emergency button and then stood up and waved both hands. In few seconds the stewardess arrived. I saw her staring at me along with all the men and women nearby on both sides of the aisle. I told her of the pressure across my chest. Luckily the plane was still on the tarmac. My face must've turned white. I pretended that sharp pain was shooting down my left arm like an electric shock. With my right hand I massaged the top of my chest."

"What a clown," a bespectacled listener said, laughing.

"The poor stewardess rushed to the cockpit and alerted the pilot. She must've been quite persuasive, because he didn't bother to check her story. He took her word for it and turned the plane around and taxied close to the airport building. All the passengers were so helpful and so concerned, especially the stewardess, I felt guilty pulling a hoax like that."

"You had no choice," Yousif replied. "Your life was at stake."

"Exactly. The Iraqis would've locked me up the minute my feet hit the ground."

Yousif thought of the man's narrow escape and recalled his own predicament when he had bludgeoned that Bedouin soldier in Jerusalem.

"And you weren't asked too many questions afterwards?" Yousif probed. "They simply let you go?"

Abu Reesh nodded, pleased with himself.

"If you were going to Cairo and ended up on a plane en route to Baghdad, may God help us," Hanna Azar chided him.

They all laughed, including Yousif, and then the conversation turned to other topics and coffees were drunk and pastries eaten. Gradually, the group began to dwindle as one by one they got up and left. Yousif was preparing to leave, too, but his relaxed afternoon came to a sudden and brutal end as the sound of gunfire exploded the tranquil scene. A burst of bullets hit a woman at a nearby table. Yousif watched in horror as her body was thrown back in her chair and blood began oozing from her chest and throat. Customers screamed and fled in all directions. Killing in broad daylight? Was the political exile Abu Reesh the real target? Did his enemies miss him by a couple of minutes?

Yousif fled with the rest, his head throbbing with worry.

ON HIS WAY HOME, Yousif bought four newspapers (each from a different Arab country), a falafel sandwich sprinkled with tahini dip, and two bunches of roasted chickpeas on the vine. Then he boarded the tram to the Basta section of Beirut, where he got off. He ambled along to Musaybteh Street where his decrepit four-story "hotel" looked like a building awaiting demolition.

He stopped at the desk and asked the clerk for a couple of sheets of paper so he could write to Salwa. The sour-faced clerk had an ugly black mole next to his nose. He shuffled his feet and handed Yousif the paper, growling as he did that this was not Palestine and that if Yousif needed something to write on he had better go out and buy it; charity was not a hotel specialty. Swallowing his anger, Yousif slapped a few coins on the desk, exaggerated his thanks, and hastened up the dim stairway to his small room with its window facing a stone wall across a narrow alley.

He sat at the room's rickety table and ate his sandwich while reviewing the tribulations of the day: from the encounter with the insolent dandy to the raconteur Abu Reesh and, of course, to the horrific violence at the sidewalk café. Each incident was a square inch in the mental mosaic he was developing about his unhappy part of the world. Lastly he puzzled over the stranger he had glimpsed from the tram's window. The man's height and physique—even his walk—evoked memories, but not having seen his face Yousif could not place him.

He lit his father's cherished pipe and began to gather his thoughts. Before writing, he decided not to mention anything about the killing he had just witnessed lest the censors in Amman read too much into it.

Dear Salwa,

Life without you is hell. And you, only you, can make it bearable.

Lebanon is beautiful. The first time I came here I was thirteen. When I finished elementary school, my father had a strange notion of sending me—his only child—to a boarding school here and brought me and my mother to select one from those in Marj Eyoun, Hammana, Alayh, and Bhamdoun. The settings were equally spectacular—which explains why the Lebanese have so many poets—but mother and I were adamantly opposed to my leaving home at such an early age.

I regret to say it, but Lebanon of yesterday is not the Lebanon of today. As far as our refugees are concerned. Here the Palestinians are resented and abhorred. They are not welcomed as they used to be when our rich brought their children to school here and when they brought their families to spend summer vacations on its mountains, and were ready to empty their pocket in Lebanon's coffers. They were welcomed then, as were their young men and women who attended their universities. Some kinfolks we have, don't you think? When the political tide turned against us, they turned against us too. What our dear Lebanese brethren don't seem to understand is that we Palestinians did not come here as refugees by choice. We love our country as much as they love theirs. And Palestine is just as beautiful as Lebanon. We would have been more than happy to stay where we belonged. But we were cast out of paradise. Expelled. Driven out. Thrown out. Kicked out. Terrorized.

Wake up, Lebanon, I want to shout and tell them, what the enemies did to us they will do to you. The enemies' ambition is bigger than Palestine or Mount Lebanon. Today Palestine, tomorrow the rest.

Deep in my heart I don't know which is worse: defeat by strangers, or rejection by one's own kin. Without genuine and total Arab unity, we stand no chance.

Well, sweetheart, I'd better stop fuming. Write and tell me—and repeat telling me—how much you love and miss me.

Instead of signing the letter with his own name, he wrote "Who Else?" He then leafed through the several newspapers he had with him. And he turned on the radio and switched from one station to another in hopes of catching something about the killing he had witnessed. He fell asleep without hearing anything. The newspapers crumpled under him as he turned on his stomach and dozed off.

IN THE MORNING, YOUSIF made up his mind about two things. He felt it was unwise to mail the letter to Salwa, for it might fall in the wrong hands and he did not need anyone to snoop on him or to start misinterpreting every word he had written. He should stop writing her or sending such letters until he found a safe way of getting them to her without incriminating himself. He wished he could arrange for her to visit him for a couple of weeks. Two, he must try to find that stranger who had looked so familiar the day before. His intuition told him that the man would bring him solace.

Three days later, he spotted the mystery man, again in profile and from the back. This time, however, Yousif quickened his pace on the crowded sidewalk, murmuring apologies to the passers-by he bumped until he got to where the man was standing. He did not know what it was about the man's posture that jarred his memory, but he was about to find out.

The mystery man was none other than Izzat Hankash, who had been a tenant in Yousif's home in Ardallah just before the forced exile. Yousif was so excited that he had thrown his arm around Izzat before Izzat recognized him.

"Watch it, fellow," Izzat said, while handing a piece of pastry to a young customer.

"Izzat, it's me—Yousif!" he said, grabbing Izzat's round tray with both hands to get his attention.

Once his eyes focused on his former landlord and good friend, Izzat dropped the piece of pastry back on the tray and embraced Yousif. They pounded each other's backs as though they were lost brothers reunited. They were oblivious to the pedestrians, some cursing as they dodged around them. Izzat's young customer became disgruntled, snatched the wrapped pastry, and left without paying. Izzat did not seem to notice.

"What are you doing selling hareeseh?" Yousif asked.

"No complaints," Izzat said, "now that you're here."

"It's been a long time."

"Much too long. I wrote you once when I saw your article . . ."

". . . I received it. But you didn't send a return address. I didn't know how to reach you."

In the next few minutes, still standing on the sidewalk, the grief–stricken Izzat explained a lot. His eyes moist, he summed up to Yousif what had happened to him and Hiyam, whose rape by the Jewish soldier they and Yousif's mother and wife, had been forced to witness. Yousif knew he would never forget that horrific moment.

"Life has been rough on us," Izzat concluded.

Yousif could see that. Izzat was under thirty but he looked ten years older. His hair was flecked with gray as if it had been sprinkled with ashes. One of his upper teeth was missing, his mustache needed trimming, and his white shirt and brown pants were tattered and rumpled. His once broad smile was anguished, and his friendly happiness at seeing Yousif was tinged with embarrassment.

"How stupid of me," Izzat said, "I haven't even offered you a piece of hareeseh. See what time has done to me. It made me forget my manners."

Yousif took a pastry from Izzat's hand and tasted it. It was delicious. As he chewed, he watched his friend with wonderment. This was a job for the destitute, not for a university graduate with a degree in chemistry.

Izzat could read in Yousif's eyes his reaction to his appearance. "If you think I look bad," he said sadly, "you should see Hiyam. You won't recognize her."

"It's that bad?" Yousif asked.

"Her health has suffered ever since . . ."

"Like the rest of us, she finds it hard to cope," Yousif said sympathetically.

Izzat remained quiet until he had sold the last two pieces. Then he removed the tray from its wooden tripod and tucked one item under each arm and they started to walk. Yousif offered to carry the wooden tripod or the tray, but Izzat was too proud to let him.

They walked in silence, passing restaurants with multi-colored awnings. Both were in deep thought, but Izzat finally spoke. "You'll lift Hiyam's spirits," Izzat said. "Our apartment is small and run-down but it's much better than the wind-blown tent in the refugee camp. Come on. You'll see for yourself. On second thought, let's sit for a while so I can prepare you."

"Prepare me for what?" Yousif asked.

They walked glumly on until they reached a rundown sidewalk coffeehouse and took a table. With his gear propped against the wall, Izzat continued his story.

"A few weeks after we were forced out of Ardallah, Hiyam discovered that she was pregnant. In most marriages this would be cause for celebration. In our case, we thought the roof has fallen on our heads."

Yousif could think of two or three reasons why such a discovery would be a joyless event to a couple of young refugees. He held his breath and waited.

"It was as if it wasn't bad enough that we had no home, no income, and nothing in the world to depend on. Hiyam and I stared at each other, reading the horror of such a prospect on each other's mind. How in the world could we feed or care for a new baby? It was obvious that a child at this time was a burden, not a blessing. How lucky and unlucky we were. Couples hope and pray and seek medical help for years to be able to have a child, and there we were feeling ashamed of ourselves for her pregnancy."

The waiter arrived and they asked for two cups of coffee.

"It's understandable," Yousif consoled him.

"But that's not all," Izzat continued. "Hiyam was struck by a new alarming thought. She said it was impossible to tell who's the baby's father. I could be the father . . ."

". . . and the soldier who raped her could be the father."

"Exactly. Hiyam became hysterical and began to cry. From that moment on she was determined to have an abortion. Even that posed a problem. One, we may never find a doctor willing to do it. Two, if we did find him and he agreed to do it, how would we pay him?"

First sipping on his cup of coffee and then lighting a cigarette from the butt of another, Izzat proceeded to tell Yousif of the nightmare that had followed.

"I'm all ears," Yousif said. "And one day I'll tell you my tale of horror."

Hiyam had thought she could induce the miscarriage on her own, simply by jumping up and down every chance she got. When that did not work, she started running around the refugee camp at night and going up and down any hill she could find. When that did not work either, she began drinking all kinds of concoctions. One time she drank nearly half a bottle of vinegar, two glasses of salt water, and a small bottle of cough syrup. Izzat thought she was going to have a nervous breakdown. Especially when she realized that her pregnancy was beginning to show. One day he came to the tent, only to find her beating up on her stomach ten or fifteen minutes at a time. A few days later she started to bleed, and the bleeding became a hemorrhage. They did not have enough sheets or towels to stop it. The sight of the fresh blood and messy clots all over the bed, made them panic. Izzat went out looking for a doctor or a telephone or at least a midwife. As luck would have it, something like an elongated piece of meat came out of her body when they were both together at the house. Hiyam closed her eyes, traumatized. Izzat freaked out and felt like vomiting. He went out again calling on other women in the refugee camp. Many came carrying with them clean towels and the next door neighbor brought with her a pot of hot water. By the time they did locate a midwife in the nearest camp, Hiyam looked like a wet dishrag. Izzat could not decide whether she stopped breathing or had just fainted. For the third time he ran out yelling for anyone to call or flag down the police car for help. The police finally came and because there were no ambulances in Amman they rushed her to the nearest hospital. She stayed there on a critical list for over a week.

Yousif exhaled a couple of times before he could respond. "How is she now?" he asked.

"I never saw anyone who aged so much. Let's go and see her."

Yousif was not sure whether or not to accept his friend's invitation. Hiyam was not bearing the indignities of life very well, and he did not wish to embarrass her. Yet she and Izzat were a fresh breeze from home and he had many questions to ask them. Besides, Izzat would probably make a good recruit for Amana and she would be a companion to Salwa. The struggle ahead needed the brightest people—especially those wounded in the gut.

Reluctantly, Yousif again followed.

As IT TURNED OUT, Izzat was true to his word. Hiyam was a gaunt shadow of her old beautiful self. Her flowering youth of three years earlier had wilted. She was roughly the same age as Salwa, yet she now looked like a sickly older sister.

"How is Salwa?" she asked, offering him a glass of water. When she sat down and covered her knees with a kitchen towel she reminded him of old women from back home

Yousif told them of the drudgery and the length of time it had taken him to find her. And he told them about sneaking back to Ardallah to retrieve his mother's jewelry. Hiyam was shocked, but Izzat was impressed.

"Who is occupying your house?" Izzat asked, lighting another cigarette from the butt of the one he was just smoking,

"A European family from Bulgaria."

"Really? From Bulgaria. How did it feel to find total strangers enjoying life in a house your parents built?" Izzat asked.

"I nearly lost my composure."

"Composure?"

"I meant temper."

"Temper? I would've put a bullet in each of their heads."

After a long tense pause, Izzat was full of inquiry. He wanted to hear about Amana Forever, the *Amana Daily* and the Amana Youth Clubs. His curiosity, and the rapidity of his questioning, endeared him more to Yousif. He told him as much as he could, revealing that Amana Forever was basically an underground resistance organization in the process of being born. One day they hoped to have it comparable to the Jewish Haganah and Irgun underground during the British mandate. He planned to recommend him as a recruit. Someone psychologically wounded, and with that level of anger, could be an asset to the movement, if only they could control his temper. A revolutionary, Yousif was quickly learning, should be resolute but not a hothead.

"One day I'd like to join such a movement," Izzat said.

"One day we'd love to have you," Yousif told him.

For the first time, Yousif saw a faint smile brightening Hiyam's face. It reflected her total approval of her husband's obsessions. In that regard, she and Salwa seemed to be cut out of the same cloth.

12

THE OIL BOOM SENT many, including Yousif, to the nearest embassy willing to issue them visas. After exchanging several letters with Amin, and after visiting the Kuwaiti Embassy two or three times, Yousif found himself boarding a plane headed for the tiny desert sheikdom. It was several months since he had come to Lebanon and here he was on another trip to a third Arab country, not as a tourist, not as a student, but as a refugee. Would he ever return to his homeland? He had no idea, and he could only look out the window and wonder.

His thoughts were interrupted when a neatly dressed man with dark eyes and a pencil-thin mustache sat down next to him. The dapper stranger introduced himself as attorney Rashad Hamza and asked, "Have you heard the news?"

Yousif shook his head.

"King Farouk has been overthrown," Hamza said with a flourish, and loudly enough for others to hear. Commotion erupted as everyone within earshot clamored to learn more.

"That's all I heard on the radio, just before I got on the plane," Hamza answered, his eyes glowing with excitement.

"Do they know who did it?" a man up front asked, half-turned in his seat.

"No," Hamza said. "A bloodless coup, according to the news bulletin."

Yousif absorbed the comments without speaking. He was in a solitary mood, and the news took him to his last meeting with Basim and Abu Thabit when they had predicted that the new Saladin would have to emerge out of Egypt. Playboy Farouk was gone. Good riddance. Who was the new leader? Had the long march toward an era of hope begun? He leaned against the window and swam in optimistic thoughts.

Soon they were airborne.

As they flew eastward, over the hilly landscape of the Littani river and the flat Bekaa valley, Yousif could see hamlets and villages built on rich slopes that had once been a part of the fertile crescent. To his left was the picturesque Zahleh, overlooking the Bardoni River and famous for its riverbank cafes and for its arak and maza—and above all for the pride and valor of its men. More than any other setting in picturesque Lebanon, Zahleh reminded him of Ardallah. The people of both had a zest for life and for poetry and chivalry—and both cities had been praised in song as beautiful brides. Yousif sighed as the stewardess announced over her hand-held microphone that off the plane's right side was historic Baalabeck with its Ashtar temple and colossal monuments.

The brown carpet of the Syrian terrain, colored here and there with green stripes, reminded Yousif of how he first took an interest in history. He remembered being in the sixth and seventh grades when Ustaz Mahfouz brought history alive to his students. Ustaz Mahfouz was a smallish man, modestly educated by any standards, but a born raconteur, the male Scheherazade of his age. He approached history as a long narrative, an adventure, a complicated drama of endless conflicts, and, above all, as sheer entertainment. He entranced his students, even those who could not be bothered with the centuries-old past. He would move about the classroom flailing his long pointer, or would sit atop his desk with his short legs folded under him, and would reenact in comical fashion how the Trojans had waited and waited in ambush for the Persians in the battle of Salamis, surprising them and inflicting upon them the wrath of God. With modulating voice and grand gestures, he would clown through the whole battle, jumping occasionally off the desk to sketch a diagram or scrawl on the blackboard a date or a name. Those were the days of his innocence, Yousif recalled.

Of particular interest to him now were the lessons on ancient Syria. He could still see his green notebook and could still smell the ink with which he had written, in his fanciest style, the name of the invaders who had conquered and ruled Syria. He smiled as he remembered that Ustaz Mahfouz had often selected his notebook to pass from student to student and from classroom to classroom as a model of excellence. The names of the Assyrians, Babylonians, Hittites, Canaanites and Aramaeans sprang to his mind, soon to be replaced, in memory as in reality, by the Persians, Macedonians, Romans, and Ottomans. Then he recalled, with deep pleasure, there was the Umayyad Dynasty in the seventh and eighth centuries A. D., when Damascus had become the center of Islamic culture, heralding a period of glory never to be forgotten, and never, perhaps, to be equaled—a period when Arab warriors had literally stormed the known world from the Pyrenees Mountains in France all the way to China.

"Would you like coffee or tea?" the stewardess said, retrieving him from across the centuries.

"Do we have time?" he replied, first looking at his wristwatch and then at the attractive young woman standing in the aisle with a tray in her hand. She too reminded him of Salwa, as did most lovely young women with luxuriant black hair.

"Yes, we have time," she answered. "What would you like?"

"Coffee, please."

"*Tikram ainak*," she obliged in her charming and gracious Lebanese accent.

Sipping his coffee, he returned to gazing out the window. Syria was rich with archaeological sites, he thought, but not nearly as modern as Lebanon. No more than thirty-odd years ago, Lebanon had been an integral part of Syria, but France, the colonial power, had separated the two. How often had the invader, by whatever name, not only impeded Arab unity but pursued its fragmentation. A thousand years earlier, the Arabs were on the verge of conquering France, and now France was splitting Arab from Arab in his own land. Was that revenge? Probably not. Nothing was forever, Yousif mused in his father's fashion, except the firmament and this gorgeous . . . this battered . . . this wicked world.

As the plane began to descend, the stewardess announced the approach to Damascus, and Yousif could see out the window across the aisle to his right the peak of Mount Harmon. There was a flurry of activity as passengers readied their belongings for the landing, but Yousif sat still in his seat and watched below as the plane circled above the world's oldest city—famous for its fragrant orchards, plush hillsides, exotic arcades, throbbing bazaars, and, yes, its fair maidens. Soon he could see the spectacular Umayyad Mosque. Inside it, his father had told him, was the shrine of St. John the Baptist. One day, he vowed, he and Salwa would visit it.

THE HALF-HOUR LAYOVER AT the busy Damascus airport was long enough for new passengers to board with more news of the coup in Cairo. A group calling itself Free Officers had engineered a perfect takeover. Negotiations were being held at Abdin Palace for King Farouk to abdicate in return for his safe and orderly exit from the country he had misruled from the age of sixteen.

"If he takes with him all his mistresses and concubines," one cynic said, "all the cabarets in Cairo will have to shut down."

Yousif saw heads nodding and heard murmurs of agreement.

For the past hour, attorney Hamza had been quietly attentive to a stack of paperwork, but now he rejoined the discussion. "That playboy isn't even an Egyptian—much less an Arab," he said, as he lit a cigarette.

Yousif was stunned. "What are you saying? He's not an Egyptian?" From the looks of others, Yousif was not alone in his ignorance of that incredible piece of information. Yet it blistered his ego to have been caught not knowing.

"Of course not," Hamza continued, now again the center of attention. "He's of Albanian heritage. To be exact, he's a direct descendant of Muhammad Ali who was brought in by the Ottoman Empire to govern Egypt for them. Ten years after Napoleon's disastrous three-year invasion of Egypt in 1798, he saw a vacuum of leadership and made his move."

Most of the listeners settled back in their seats, apparently satisfied with that unexpected bit of history. Not Yousif. "What do you mean he made his move?" he asked.

Hamza seemed to appreciate Yousif's curiosity. "After Napoleon hurried back to France," he continued, "Muhammad Ali was so entrenched in Egypt that he revolted against the Ottomans, his masters, grabbed power for himself and declared Egypt's independence."

"And they let him get away with it?" Yousif said.

Hamza took a long drag on his cigarette. "Muhammad Ali was a man. A strong man. And he fought like one. Why, he almost overthrew the Sultan himself in Constantinople."

Yousif's interest intensified. Especially when Hamza praised Muhammad Ali for his hunger for progress in agriculture, education, economics, military, and bureaucracy.

"Though he himself was illiterate," Hamza said, "he sent droves of bright students to France to study all kinds of disciplines. In truth, he and his children accomplished a lot to benefit their adopted country. One of them even declared that Egypt was more in Europe than in Africa. And he went on to build the Suez Canal and the famous Opera House, both of which ended up causing Egypt major problems. But that's another story."

"Don't stop, please. You remind me a lot of my father."

"Get some books and learn more. It will be good for you," he encouraged. "As to Farouk, he was pathetic. What happened to him was inevitable."

A lovely song reverberated in Yousif's head as he remembered his mother's voice singing it in celebration of the young monarch's wedding to his bride, Queen Fareedeh. What hopes the Egyptians must have had for their new king; what promise he must have held for them. Images of slender and handsome Farouk flashed in Yousif's mind and were juxtaposed with images of a decadent man in his later years. He had ballooned like a buffalo, and he had failed his people and himself.

"Can you imagine ascending a throne at the age of sixteen?" Hamza said. "All that wealth, all that power. He literally owned nearly half of Egypt—and acted as if the rest should've been his too."

"Royalty fell in his lap absolutely—"

"—and the miserable creature couldn't handle it. That's why we have here a bloodless coup. He was probably glad to get rid of the responsibility—even if he only had it by name. Like that weakling King Edward of England. The one who abdicated to marry a stern-looking divorcee."

"They say Edward gave up his throne for love."

"Nonsense. He gave it up because he was unfit to rule. Same thing with Farouk. He'd be a lot happier chasing whores."

Hamza leaned closer and whispered, "Rumors have it that Farouk ate monkey's testicles for breakfast as an aphrodisiac. Fried them with eggs. Balls & Eggs, you might say."

Yousif smiled but did not reply. He found Rashad Hamza fascinating and began to think of him as a possible recruit for Amana Forever. As an attorney and a student of history, Hamza could become a recruiter or a fundraiser. The organization would need more than just those who could tote guns and throw hand grenades. Yousif made a mental note to bring his name to Basim's attention. On the other hand, what Hamza said about Farouk ascending to the throne at the tender age of sixteen depressed him. Was Farouk the king of the most populous Arab country on which the Palestinians had pinned most of their hopes? What about the two new kings who had recently emerged on the scene: King Hussein of Jordan and his cousin King Faisal of Iraq were also sixteen or seventeen years old, just like Farouk when he had succeeded his father. Was sixteen a magical age? Was it an accident that the three were teenagers? He suspected the imperialists had a hand in their ascendancy to each throne so they could manipulate them like pawns on a chessboard.

THE PLANE TOOK OFF again and circled above beautiful Damascus which Yousif knew was the home of many Arab nationalists. He remembered visiting Martyrs Square where scores of patriots had been executed by the Ottoman Turks and left hanging for days as a warning. Yousif thought of them, and of all those who had preceded them, in grief and gratitude. He paused as the word "wasted" crossed his mind. Blood, Basim would chide him, was never wasted in the cause of freedom. Many had died well; many had been betrayed. Like his beloved Salwa, he condemned all those who had sacrificed them and dishonored their nation.

Yousif focused his gaze out the window. The July sky was blue without a blemish, and the flat brown land below was stretched as far the eye could see. They were rapidly approaching the twin rivers, Tigris and Euphrates, where in historic Mesopotamia (now Iraq) man's earliest civilization had flourished. Remnants of that glory still existed, but not where Yousif was looking. There were no archaeological ruins here; probably not even a shepherd to graze his herd. The empty landscape made Yousif recall the opening line of an epic poem in which the pre-Islamic poet had compared the deserted house of his beloved to the remnants of a tattoo on a hand.

Circling above Baghdad and the short stopover there evoked in Yousif a sense of pride—despite the dismal performance of the Iraqi army in the recent war. "*Ako slah, mako awamer*," rang in his ears and he pitied the frustrated Iraqi soldiers who had the weaponry but not the orders to use them. This was the city of opulent Haroun al-Rashid whose fame and extravagance in the eighth century surpassed Charlemagne's. This was the city of the wily and seductive Scheherazade who had spun Arabian tales for a thousand and one nights to spare her life from the perverted whims of her husband, King Shahrayar. This was the city of enlightenment— where Arab scholars had translated Greek philosophy and introduced them to the West. This was the seat of the Abbasid power and grace—and the center of the ancient Arab glory. What would the forefathers think, Yousif now wondered, if they knew that the Zionists had crushed seven Arab so-called armies—they would disavow their cowardly descendents as unworthy to be called Arabs.

Flying again, they passed over an endless expanse of monotonous brown terrain on which ancient civilization had flourished. Yousif's mind buzzed with reflections, undisturbed by the passengers' jabbering or the droning of the plane's engines. Who would believe, he asked himself, that they were actually flying over the Babylon which had been one of the seven wonders of the world. Where were its hanging gardens and gilded chariots full of harems? Where was Mesopotamia's Hammurabi, the ancient law giver who decreed, "A tooth for a tooth, an eye for an eye." What sins—nay what crimes—had the Palestinians committed for the scales of justice to be turned on them so mercilessly?

As if Yousif had not had enough history for one day, the flight brought them closer and closer to the land of Ur. They were heading southeast, and approaching the southernmost tip of Iraq. Below was the land on which the Sumerians were the first to learn how to write, the very spot from which Abouna Ibrahim, the patriarch of both Arabs and Jews, had journeyed in search of God. Here it all had begun. Had Abouna Ibrahim gone north instead of south, had he turned left instead of right or right instead of left, Yousif would not be a refugee. Arabs and Jews would not have had a Holy Land over which to quarrel. Yousif could trace all his troubles to that moment, that first step in search of God. And where did Abouna Ibrahim, blessed be his name, discover the idea of one God? In

Baiteen—an obscure, rocky, sun-bathed village between Ramallah and Ardallah, Yousif's hometown.

Young Ibrahim, then known as Ibram, had led his family and herded his sheep a thousand miles—maybe twice that distance, if one considered the trips to Turkey in the north and Egypt in the south—before it had occurred to him that there were not many Gods—only one. How he arrived at that conclusion, and why was he compelled to think it through, Yousif did not know. But the umbilical cord had started here—and wound itself throughout the Levant—and ended up in Ardallah. Why? Why not? From Ur to Syria, to Turkey, then all the way down to Egypt, then back up again all the way up to Palestine—to father Izhaq and the Jews, and to father Isma'il and the Arabs. And in Jerusalem—less than ten miles from Ramallah—Abouna Ibrahim, wanting to obey his God, had poised his sharp knife to slay Izhaq and sacrifice him on a burning bush. What fright that little child must have suffered. But then God intervened, and Izhaq was saved. Thousands of years later, another Izhaq, now called Isaac, one of Yousif's dearest friends, had no one, not even God, to intervene on his behalf and snatch him from harm's way. Two innocent Izhaqs—why had one been spared and the other sacrificed? Had God grown too weary to look after all his children? Had he grown too old and too feeble to care?

Quickly, Yousif repented. Confused as he was, he still had faith. But unlike in his younger days, he did not reflexively cross himself.

As the plane flew onward above the remaining ziggurats of ancient Ur, he felt a stronger gravitation toward God than toward Man. Hung in space, he felt the presence of an indelible power far superior to anything on earth. Pity, he thought, he could not chart progress in man's travails—only the invisible cobweb in the midst of shifting tides.

THE BLAZING KUWAIT SUN forced Yousif to shed his jacket and drape it on his arm. During the last three years Amin had gained some weight, and his luminous skin was a shade darker. His smile, however, was as infectious as ever. He seemed little bothered by his amputation, which, despite all those years flooded Yousif with sad memories when he noticed the empty sleeve tucked under the stump of Amin's left arm. Perhaps the greatest change Yousif could detect in Amin was in his clothing and hair style. To Yousif's immense delight, Amin had become a nifty dresser. He cut a handsome figure even though, due to the desert temperature, he wore no jacket or tie. His long hair overlapped his ears and touched his collar. The general impression was that Amin exuded health and prosperity.

They met at an airport so small it belied the wealth of oil-rich Kuwait, where men in flowing white robes were more prevalent than anywhere else. The plane on which Yousif had flown sat alone in the hot sun, and the blue observation tower above the terminal appeared useless for lack of anything to observe. The building itself was of mud brick reminiscent of the mud huts in Jericho and Amman. Missing were the hustle and bustle of the Beirut airport and its crowded sky and tarmac; the beautiful stewardesses in smart uniforms with handbags strapped over their shoulders; the endless and sparkling ticket counters with hundreds of passengers waiting in line, and many more rushing to catch their flights; the frequent announcements over the public-address system in varied languages that only a few could understand. In comparison, this Kuwait airport was no more than an outpost in the wilderness, and Yousif's empathy was with those who had been assigned to run it.

"You look surprised," Amin told Yousif as they waited with other passengers in a small room with dusty floor and windows badly in need of washing.

"It's even smaller than Kalandia," Yousif answered, "and I thought that was the tiniest airport in the world."

Amin laughed, his bright teeth contrasting well with his skin. He explained that the Kuwaiti government was planning to build an ultramodern airport, but it had not been a priority; the real wealth had yet to start gushing.

"No doubt," Yousif said.

"Don't forget you're in the desert," Amin added, "and the population here is entirely Bedouin. The influx of manpower and foreign businessmen and technical experts is a recent phenomenon."

Riding a taxi to town and already feeling uncomfortable in the blistering sun, Yousif was reminded of the humiliating march from Ardallah to Jericho and the forced entry into Trans-Jordan. Such memories often taunted him, and he could not suppress them now. He breathed hard and involuntarily wet his lips with his tongue as if the thirst that had plagued him during that unfortunate journey was threatening again. He thought of his mother's sickness from the heat, and of Salwa's father's tragic death in the open wilderness. Imperceptibly he shook his head as if to drive the ghosts away. The asphalt road ahead glistened in the burning sun; he could almost see vapor rising out of it and anticipate the melting of the car's tires. The sandy sides of the road were like the floor of a vast open local oven without a loaf of bread or a tray of spaghetti in it to bake.

"That's why many of our teachers and accountants went to Libya to work," Yousif said. "There the oil industry is much older."

"For sure," Amin said, "Libya's capital, Tripoli, is relatively modern because of the Italian rule and its proximity to Europe—but the rest of the country is just as neglected as here. Which is unforgivable. The Libyans have been flush with money for decades, but here the tremendous fortune is yet to come. Kuwaiti leadership seems more responsible."

"And let's hope more progressive," Yousif said, wiping his forehead with his handkerchief.

"I truly believe it will be," Amin said. "Not like Saudi Arabia for instance. There the sudden riches made many heads dizzy and they squandered tons and tons of it. You remember the stories about their custom-made foreign cars with gold handles and hubcaps, the jewelry on the women's shoes, the mistresses flown in from European capitals, and all that gambling. There's nothing like this here."

"Not yet," Yousif said under his breath lest the driver hear.

Amin noticed Yousif's reticence and understood. "Oh, meet our driver, Hassan; he's a Palestinian, too." Then Amin proceeded with his analysis. "Maybe it will happen here, too," he conceded. "But so far the ruling family is willing to share the wealth with their people. It's a small country, even smaller than Palestine—and there's plenty of money for everyone to be comfortable. I'm glad you came; you need to get your share."

"I don't know how long I'll stay, but I'm glad I came."

"I don't brag," Amin confided, "you know that, but before long I'm going to be well off. You may say even rich. Can you believe that? Amin, the stonecutter's son—a rich man? We never had enough to eat, and look at me now. I paid more for a couple of suits than my father ever made in a whole year."

Yousif smiled. "I'm happy for you."

"Say, what's this with the mustache? I grew one once but then I said the hell with it. I was shaving one morning and I thought I should trim it. I clipped it on the right and I clipped it on the left. Soon one side was drooping and the other side was pointing up. The more I trimmed the more ridiculous it looked. So I shaved it off."

Yousif nodded, realizing for the first time that the new Amin was quite talkative.

Everywhere he looked, Yousif could see construction men at work. The sweltering brown desert was being transformed. The mud huts were being pushed down by gigantic bulldozers, making way for progress. New modern buildings lined both sides of the wide boulevard whose median was planted with spindly palm trees that had not had time to grow. The few new buildings were as tall or as clustered as those in Lebanon or Palestine. They were built of cement brick and covered with stucco that was painted blue, yellow and orange. The new structures with stretches of desert between them reminded Yousif of colored blocks he had played with as a child. Kuwait did not strike him as a regular city, as Jerusalem or Haifa or Beirut, but as a wasteland some men were trying to reclaim.

Amin pulled a thin slim silver cigarette case out of his pocket and offered a cigarette to Yousif who declined.

"You still smoke a pipe?" Amin asked, producing out of another pocket an expensive-looking silver lighter.

"I gave it up," Yousif answered. "I couldn't afford it."

"Couldn't afford it?" Amin said, laughing. "I haven't heard that expression in a long time. Here one can afford anything, don't you agree, Hassan?"

"Yes, I do," the driver said.

Amin crossed his legs and turned around in his seat. "The Kuwaitis are building their country from the bottom up. Believe me, one day it will be considered a utopia—not just a modern country."

"How so?" Yousif asked.

Without sounding quite like an official spokesman for the chamber of commerce, Amin explained that the intent of the regime was to make every citizen happy. Before long they would be taking care of all the needs of their people, literally from the cradle to the grave. Education was already free. They even sent buses to pick up children and return them home. They provided school uniforms. They provided books. They provided free meals. Soon they would have free health care. No taxes. Interest-free loans, etc.

Yousif had his own opinions but said only, "They certainly have the means. A population of less than half a million and oil income in the billions."

Amin had a different take. "What's more important is their willingness to share their wealth."

Perhaps, Yousif thought. But this was no time for polemics. There would be other times to further Amin's political awareness. "They're certainly wiser than the other oil-rich countries," he said.

When the taxi dropped them off at their final destination, Yousif was flabbergasted. There were no homes in sight—only rows upon rows of tents. Bigger and sturdier than the tents in the refugee camps—but tents nevertheless.

"Welcome home," Amin said.

"Here?" Yousif asked. "You live in a tent?"

"Why not?" Amin jested, waiting for the driver to open the trunk. "Am I not a Palestinian?"

"Don't be facetious."

"Hassan, tell him I'm telling the truth."

The driver, whose forehead was as wide as his cheek, considered his answer. "I hate to disagree with you," he told Amin. "No Palestinian should live in a tent. Here it's okay because we're working. It's part of our job. But a tent is never a Palestinian home."

"Bravo," Yousif said, tipping Hassan a few extra Lebanese pounds. "Where are you from?"

"Gaza."

"Long live Gaza."

"And you?" Hassan asked in return.

"From Ardallah. Same as Amin."

"Long live Ardallah."

"Long live Palestine," Yousif added, quite happy.

Hassan carried Yousif's suitcase into the tent, followed by the two friends.

"Long live Kuwait," Amin said. "And on with the flow."

"On with the flow," Yousif concurred, fully understanding the reference to the ocean of oil Kuwait was perched on and the beneficial effect it could have on the national problem.

The tent was spacious and livable. It had electricity, an electric fan, a small refrigerator placed on a narrow bench, two flap doors, and a concrete floor to make the room look ordinary.

"Why can't the refugees back home have tents like this?" Yousif wondered. "It would make their lives a lot less harsh."

Amin picked up Yousif's battered suitcase off the floor and placed it on a nearby bench, turned on the electric fan and positioned it in Yousif's direction. The cool air was refreshing, and Yousif wanted to inhale as much of it as he could.

"You keep a clean tent for a bachelor," Yousif said, wiping his forehead and placing his jacket on the arm of a canvas chair before sitting down.

"A couple of Asian women work this camp six days a week," Amin said. "This is a Muslim country, remember, and they give them Fridays off. I tell you, this is a wonderful country. They even give the Christian workers Sundays off, and are allowing them to build a church of their own. Unimaginable in Saudi Arabia or the Arab Emirates."

Amin opened the refrigerator and produced two ice-cold bottles of beer.

Uncapping both and in anticipation of Yousif's queries, he said: "This is a progressive and tolerant Muslim country. Just like the Palestine we knew."

They touched bottles and said "*kasak*" to each other, happy to be reunited. They drank in silence as if each needed time to absorb the moment. Yousif was touched by Amin's friendliness and warmth, finding it impossible to imagine a better reception even by an immediate relative.

Yousif remembered the adage that money corrupted, and was glad to see that it had not gone to Amin's head. With his support, his parents and many siblings had moved out of Swayleh refugee camp, near Amman, and he was still dutifully sending them a check every couple of months His wish was for them to relocate in any part of the West Bank, just to be on Palestinian soil. Maybe one day he would send them enough money to buy a house—or have one built, provided he could keep his father away from building it himself.

"He's a good builder," Yousif commented. "Father was always impressed by his work."

"No matter," Amin said. "That man's back is literally bent from bending over the rocks he chiseled. I won't let him do it anymore. Not if I can help it. He and my mother earned their rest."

Eventually the conversation turned to Yousif's own affairs. It began by both recalling Yousif's derring-do at stopping Salwa's wedding in the church, marrying her at a wedding which Amin himself had attended, and then getting separated from her during the forced exile. Over two more beers, Yousif summarized his search to find her and his adventure to retrieve his mother's valuables from their home in Ardallah. Throughout the telling, Amin found himself both understanding and admiring.

"You haven't said a thing about Amana Forever," Amin finally said.

"That by itself requires a whole evening."

Amin rose from his seat and drained the last drop of beer. "We'll set aside a special night then. For now let's shower and get ready. Wear your finest suit. We've been invited to a special dinner party."

Yousif laughed, and threw his arm across the back of the settee.

"Why are you laughing?" Amin asked.

"I don't own a suit. That jacket, a couple of pants and a few shirts are all I have."

Amin sat down again, startled. "I ought to be ashamed of myself."

"No need. You've been away . . ."

"That's no excuse. I shouldn't forget the hardships back home. How could I . . ."

". . . you left shortly after our expulsion . . ."

". . . I'm truly sorry."

The genuine remorse was followed by a lingering period of silence. During the entire ride to the party, no matter how hard Yousif tried to explain to Amin that a momentary lapse of memory was no reason for him to feel so guilty.

Not until they reached a house in Ahmadi, a small town a short distance from Kuwait City, did Amin perk up a little.

YOUSIF WAS NOT PREPARED for the surprise within the surprise that had been awaiting him. As the door opened he was met by none other than Dr. Selim Afifi and his wife, Jihan, from Ardallah. For a second Yousif was stunned, unable to cross the threshold. The last time he had seen them was in Jericho, at the end of the long march out of their own homeland. God, he thought, how they had changed. Dr. Afifi's hair had gone metallic-white, and Jihan had lost so much weight, he hardly recognized them.

"Welcome to Kuwait," Dr. Afifi said, his arms stretched out to receive him.

Yousif rushed to embrace him and they pounded each other's backs feverishly. He could not help but tear up, yet managed to shake hands with Jihan who seemed less restrained. She hugged and kissed him, and he could feel the tears on her cheeks. For a minute none of them could speak. The two men bit their lips and their chins trembled, but Jihan let her tears fall freely. The rest of the guests, including Amin, stared in awe, their own breath suspended.

Yousif had always loved Jihan, but his affection for her deepened when she defended his father at a large public meeting at a hotel garden in Ardallah. In a flashback, he recalled that unforgettable event. His father, a prominent doctor had been raising funds to build a hospital which the town badly needed. But when the hostilities were about to break out between the natives and the outsiders, the citizens of Ardallah wanted the doctor to turn over the money to them to buy arms and defend themselves. A reasonable request, one would think, but not necessarily. One, the doctor was conscientious and a genuine pacifist who opposed all violence—especially upon the heels of a harrowing world war. Two, he was a realist. He thought the outcome was predictable. His leaderless and totally unarmed countrymen were in no way ready to face a highly trained and well-funded and sufficiently equipped opponent. The money he had been raising for years would simply go to waste, and the desperately needed hospital would remain a dream unfulfilled. The well-attended gathering in the hotel garden was meant to resolve the dispute. But when some men began to vilify the doctor, maligning his motives and impugning his integrity, the refined and generally restrained Jihan was incensed. She sprang up and lashed back at them for casting aspersions on his father's character or integrity. What short memory did they all have? How rude of them to accuse him of anything short of utter patriotism and decency? How dare they criticize the noblest man in town? Have they forgotten all his good deeds and his long service to their welfare and the welfare of the city. Shame on them. Shame on them, indeed.

Yousif shook off his memories and returned to the present. His chin wrinkled and his eyes misty, he hugged Jihan again. "It's so good to see you, Auntie. So good, indeed."

There were over twenty people in the house. Introductions followed, but the doctor and Jihan hovered around Yousif as if to monopolize him. Dr. Afifi kept his arm around his waist, calling him his best friend's son. The guests, all Palestinians, were also demonstrative in their spontaneous affection. They received him as a long lost son or brother whose reappearance had been least expected. Someone handed Yousif a drink, and Dr. Afifi raised a toast in his honor. Jihan clung to his arm, trying hard to hold back her tears.

Between introductions she showered him with questions. How was his mother? How was Salwa? She had no idea about the long separation but was delighted that they had finally found each other. The large house was congested and they weaved their way from room to balcony and back again. This man was from Jerusalem. This one from Nazareth. They were all men—other than Jihan and three nurses. One man, Yousif was told, had brought his young bride but the government officials at the airport had denied her entry. They had even made her spend the night on the airplane itself to go back on the first flight next morning. Yousif was appalled. Someone attributed it to the housing shortage, but Yousif could not follow the rationale.

The gathering of all those strangers from back home had turned into a family reunion. If appearances were to be trusted, everybody seemed to be doing rather well; some even prosperous. From Yousif's perspective it was an impressive group of architects, engineers, developers, accountants, teachers and nurses: the kind of manpower needed to build an emerging society. More importantly, each was a potential donor to Amana Forever. And for this reason alone, Yousif was determined to get to know all of them personally. But a glance at the hostess would change his mood.

Jihan had aged considerably, and her pale complexion worried him. Traces of her beauty were still there, for sure, but in a deathly sort of way. She looked like a woman who had been put in a pressure cooker and whose voluptuousness had almost melted. Her delicate bone structure was now slightly misshapen; her lips precisely stretched. Gone was the hefty bosom; her hand was constantly clutching her chest, either to look for it or to prevent her heart from stopping.

The dining room table was laden with a variety of dishes. Everything Yousif liked or enjoyed was on display: sliced leg-of-lamb roast, jaj mashwi, baked kibbeh, raw kibbeh, kiftah with potatoes, kifta with tahini, baked snapper with tahini, open-face meat pies, fattayer with spinach, stuffed squash and tiny eggplants, grape leaves and cabbage rolls, large platter with hashweh heaped with fried pine nuts and thin noodles, baba ghannouj and a medley of dips and spreads, kmaj and shrak and an assortments of breads.

"Looking at this magnificent table, no one can tell we're refugees," Yousif said to Amin, his astonishment surpassing his hunger.

"They're the most generous couple," Amin said, sampling a pickled cauliflower. "And she's always looking for an excuse to throw a party. Every time a Palestinian arrives we have something like this. This time she outdid herself."

The guests enjoyed themselves filling their plates. Yousif did the same, his appetite quite awakened. He and Amin stood in a corner, each remembering home cooking.

When Jihan asked them if there was anything else she could get them, the two looked at each other and laughed.

"Auntie," Yousif said, "I don't know how to thank you."

"Enjoy yourself, that's how," she said. "You too, Amin."

They certainly did. So did the others, whether sitting or standing. Whether in the dinning room, or on the balcony.

"Only the Egyptians number more than we do here," said Khalil Shalabi, a sandy-haired attorney from Haifa. "Kuwait imports all her workers. Even the laborers are from Iran or the refugee camps. Some are even from the Philippines."

The word "imports" triggered a barrage of examples of how much Kuwait relied on outsiders for help.

"Up until recently . . ." a woman with sharp features started to say.

". . . how recently?" the man next to her interrupted.

"Up until they built a kitchen in every school," she continued, "they were flying lunches for school children from England. Imagine that."

Khalil Shalabi looked skeptical. "Who told you such nonsense?"

"It's true. I even heard that every day a charter plane still flies in ice-cream for the Royal Family."

Shalabi stared at her reproachfully. "We're guests here, remember?"

Met with general disapproval, the woman murmured an apology and slipped away.

As the night progressed and the crowd thinned, the topic of conversation revolved around their core problem. The convivial atmosphere, it turned out, was simply an escape from the troubling reality. They were hurting inside just as much as he was, Yousif realized. And he was right. As soon as someone spoke of "back home" a curtain of gloom descended on everyone in the house. Men lit their cigarettes or squashed them in the nearest ashtray.

Eager to hear something new from "back home" all eyes turned to Yousif as if he were the messenger of hope.

"Cheer us up," an engineer from Akka said, addressing Yousif.

"You were published twice in *Amana Daily* . . ."

Yousif looked around, surprised.

". . . yes, we've read you. Calm our nerves, if you will."

Yousif took his time to formulate his thoughts. He debated within himself how much to tell them and how much to save for other times.

"First let me thank all of you, especially our hosts Dr. and Mrs. Afifi, for such a wonderful Palestinian evening. I haven't had such a good time since our forced exile. We all know things are awful, but they could be worse. Amana Forever, in all its outlets, intends to keep the hope alive. And to point the way . . ."

". . . to what?" a man from West Jerusalem wanted to know. "Liberation? Redemption? What?"

"All of the above," Jihan said.

The man from Jerusalem was persistent. "I want to hear it from Yousif. He's a bright young man who seems to be well connected. Amana seeks what?"

Yousif nodded to Jihan, an implicit thank-you for her support.

"Like all normal people who find themselves in our predicament, we need to find a way to restore our rights. It's as simple as that. It is inconceivable that we would let the aggressor get away with his aggression. As victimized and angry people, we can't sit still and let our enemy turn the clock two thousand years at our expense. The whole world expects us to revolt. What on earth did we ever do to them to deserve occupation, expulsion, pillaging, and dispossession? We're innocent people. And innocent people must rise and resist until justice is done. It's our duty, no more and no less."

The resonating silence implied, to Yousif, that these embittered countrymen had heard enough of such bravado. If the combined Arab armies
could not stand up to the Zionist invasion, what could a few hundred
unarmed, untrained and ill-equipped men do?

Reading pessimism, if not hopelessness, on their faces, Yousif tried to
inject some encouragement.

"Amana Forever is not alone," he said. "Many such organizations are
sprouting everywhere. We're all itching to do something no matter how
small. Collectively we might be able to do something big. At least have
an impact. At least give something of ourselves for the sake of beloved
Palestine."

"How can we help?" someone in the back of the room asked.

Yousif hesitated, then said, "You can start by helping us raise some
money."

Laughter erupted, and Yousif wondered if he had already committed
a gaffe. He did not know these people, and he was too young to be so
presumptuous.

"You asked the right man," Amin said, laughing. "Rameh is an ac-
countant and knows everybody. But first he should be a donor himself,
don't you think?"

The merriment that followed assured Yousif that he was among friends
and he had done nothing wrong. "I'm sure he will. And I trust the rest of
you will do the same."

They broke up into small groups and began discussing what they had
just heard. More at ease now, Yousif studied their demeanor, their facial
expressions, and tried to remember the names of those who struck him
as potential supporters. He would certainly call on them. Or have Amin
call on them after he had left Kuwait.

At the end of the evening they were all on their way out. Many made
their way to where Yousif was standing, shook his hand, and invited him
and Amin to dinner at their homes.

"Just for dinner?" Amin asked, feigning surprise.

"And dessert, of course. And maybe some donation."

~~~~~

13

YOUSIF COULD not sleep. He sat on a chair outside his tent, next to Amin's, long after Amin had gone to bed. The meaning of the whole trip to Kuwait—and last night's dinner party in particular—preoccupied him. Dr. Afifi and Jihan were quintessential Palestinians, but that had not surprised him. What touched him most was the whole group's sentiment and longing. He went inside and wrote his wife a letter.

Darling Salwa,

Needless to say, I miss you. I'm nearly a thousand miles away from you—in Kuwait, to be exact—yet I feel you're so close I can almost touch you. The longer we stay apart the more I agonize.

I wished you were with me on the plane from Beirut to Kuwait. I traveled over four countries: Lebanon, Syria, Iraq and Kuwait itself. Intellectually I crossed a millennium, flowing back and forth in time. How I wish I could describe to you my emotions when I recalled the great contributions our region had given the world and which are now either forgotten or mere footnotes to history. As my father, rest his soul, used to say, the passage of time seems to have taught man nothing, or almost nothing. One part of me cries for revenge against the heartless enemy which robbed us of everything we cherish; another part of me agrees with that part of Ecclesiastes which says: "Vanity, Vanity, said the Preacher." Victims and victimizers are to be pitied, for they switch roles as easily as nature changes its seasons.

Amin is wonderful. He looks and acts as a man of means. He deserves everything good that has come his way. How kind and generous he has been to me. One day you'll get to know him better and you'll realize this for yourself. We are like brothers.

Last night I met a group of fine people at a lavish dinner party, and how I wished you were with me. There's a big Palestinian community in Kuwait which includes none other than our own Dr. Selim Afifi and his wife, Jihan. Surely you remember them. Oh, Salwa, how they have aged. She looks gravely ill. They say that her health began to deteriorate soon after their arrival in Kuwait. Dr. Afifi's hair is almost completely gray, but it's becoming. He's coping much better than his wife.

I can't live in Kuwait for too long, even if I were free to do so. The government has strict rules on who can enter and work in the country. And I don't blame them—up to a point. The only women they would allow in this country are nurses, female teachers to teach in girls' schools, and the wives of professionals they deem vital, such as doctors. They fear, I suppose, that foreigners who bring their wives with them would start raising children and sooner or later begin claiming residency. This could cause them problems in the future. (Oh, yes, they do import domestic help, and those are always women.)

How miserable my life would be if I were to live anywhere without you beside me. One long separation in a lifetime is horrendous enough. This is a troubling thought which we must address thoroughly, but not tonight. My mind is in a fog and I'm getting sleepy. Goodnight, sweetheart.

With all my love,
Who Else?

The job Amin had arranged for Yousif was that of a foreman with a construction company specializing in commercial and residential buildings. The fact that Yousif was only twenty-two and knew zilch about construction and the crafts entailed did not seem to worry Amin.

"Yours is basically a managerial job," Amin said, dismissing his concerns. "The two things required of you are a sense of responsibility and common sense. And of these you have plenty."

Kuwait was embarking on an ambitious program of erecting many hospitals and almost a school a day and there was plenty of work to keep Yousif and his thirty-six-man crew busy. The salary was eighty-five sterling pounds a month, a whopping increase over the eight Jordanian dinars he had received as a teacher in Amman. He certainly had no complaint to make on that account. Not to mention the free tent and free food. And free access to a nice car and a chauffeur.

As it was customary in Kuwait, work started in the morning and came to a standstill at two o'clock in the afternoon. By then the searing heat numbed the body and dulled the senses. Yousif spent the first afternoon lying on his bed in his shorts, with the fan turned on high. He read local newspapers, wrote letters to his mother and to Raja in Beirut, but mostly calculated how much he would have to save to attend a university or go to law school. Preferably in Cairo.

On the third day, he returned to his tent to find a package awaiting him. He opened it eagerly. It contained two Dunhill pipes (one black with a curved stem, the other brown with a long straight stem), two cans of English tobacco (Capstain and Three Nuns), a package of colored pipe cleaners, and an attractive tamper. He was thrilled and could not wait to see and thank the sender: the thoughtful Amin, no doubt. He rushed to Amin's tent and found him sprawled on his bed, fast asleep. The two fans, aimed at his bare back, were blasting full speed.

That evening Yousif met many Palestinians at a quad in the middle of the tent compound. Chairs had been set out and a long table was laden with drinks, alcoholic or otherwise, and a bucket of ice. These were Yousif's neighbors during his stay in Kuwait. Mingling with them were two surveyors, an Italian and a Maltese. Like the group of few nights earlier, they were all gracious in welcoming him. Some drank beer, but most preferred gin or rum, believing it would lower the bodily heat. Many, he was told, had rarely touched liquor prior to coming to the desert, but the isolation imposed a change on their way of life.

Yousif relaxed in his chair, watched the star-studded sky, puffed leisurely on his pipe, and listened to the men rationalize their newly acquired habits. There were no cinemas, no social clubs, no real homes with families—not even girls to dance with or romance—only plenty of free time with nothing to do or fret about except sit around and drink, play cards or backgammon, smoke nergilehs, play the ʿoud and occasionally sing, but mostly argue or simply talk politics. It was monotonous living, but far more lucrative than any alternative job anywhere else.

"An engineer friend of ours had a reason to return home," a man from Bethlehem told Yousif. "He ended up working for his municipality at a very low salary, but with the promise by the mayor and the city council that he would be paid more in happier days."

"This is like saying never," Khaled Ayyash said, smirking and pouring himself another gin and tonic. "For Palestinians, happier days are gone. Over. Bye-bye."

Yousif looked disappointed. "Only if we lack the will . . ." he said, lighting his pipe with a match.

"Damn," Amin interrupted. "I forgot to buy you a lighter."

"You bought me plenty," Yousif said, smiling.

"Take this," said a man sitting to Yousif's right. "I have three."

Yousif's gentle protest was overridden. Khaled Ayyash told him to take it and go on with the conversation. "Tell us what you meant by 'unless we lack the will.' I'm fifty-two and I value the opinion of the younger generation. My generation failed you—let's hope yours will redeem us."

A hush followed. Yousif glanced at Amin, as if to ask how much to tell them. Without mentioning Basim and Raja or any of Amana's board of directors, and without hinting at their political or military agenda, Yousif said that the turmoil within each Palestinian family, within each Palestinian individual—even within each Arab no matter where he lived—was bound to have repercussions.

"What kind of repercussions?" Khaled inquired.

"An uprising of sorts—an insurgency if you will—" Yousif obfuscated. "It's the duty of all oppressed and disinherited people to try to change the outcome. Some will falter, some will fail, others will sacrifice and bring credit to themselves. Whatever we do will be just the beginning of a long, long struggle."

"Will it have a happy ending?" Khaled persisted, rather amused.

"I'm no prophet . . ."

"But you're smart and well-informed. What do you think?"

Yousif wished to speak in generalities but decided to lighten up the exchange. "It will depend on how well educated, motivated, and prepared we are, or will be, to finish writing that long, long drama."

"In other words, we'll need to start using our heads," Khaled said.

". . . and opening our wallets . . ." someone added.

There was muted giggling. Khaled clinked his glass to Yousif's bottle, winking back at him.

For the third time since his arrival Yousif felt truly welcome. First by Amin. Then by Dr. Afifi and Jihan. And now.

One young man seemed not to share the repartee. His name was Ramzi, the son of a goldsmith from Haifa, and only two or three years older than Yousif. Ramzi stood slightly apart from the crowd, his lips curled into a sneer.

"Wishful thinking," Ramzi said, ambling closer to Yousif.

Yousif was taken aback. "I don't understand."

"Yes, you do," Ramzi said, puffing on a cigarette. "We couldn't stop a small band of our enemy when we were in our homes—you think we can stop them now from our tents, when they're already a hundred times stronger than we are?"

Yousif could not tell whether Ramzi was sincere in his skepticism or simply enjoyed being contradictory.

"The whole Arab world is restless," Yousif finally said. "Look what happened in Jordan and Egypt."

"And don't forget the murder of the Lebanese prime minister in Amman before that," Ramzi reminded, sarcasm all over his face. "And before that the big fire in Cairo, if I'm not mistaken."

Yousif studied him seriously. "Then we have a choice: lie down and die, or rise and resist. What will it be?"

Welcoming a debate, Ramzi offered to bring Yousif another beer. Yousif declined but waited for him to refill his glass and continue.

"As King Farouk's great ancestor, Muhammad Ali, used to say: 'There's only one power greater than God's . . . and that's Britain's.'"

"Meaning?"

"Like a puppeteer, Britain pulls the strings . . ."

". . . and our leaders would jump up and salute."

"Not only salute, but prostrate themselves. And obey. You don't think so?"

"No, I don't," Yousif said.

"If Churchill could twirl Roosevelt around his finger and thrust him into World War II, a war he did not wish to enter, you don't think *lingleez* can manipulate our so-called leaders?"

"That was yesterday. Not today."

"Look," Ramzi said, suddenly emboldened. "We stand zero chance until Britain goes under. And waiting for that to happen is like waiting for the trees to start walking."

"Oh, really. Look what the Egyptian mob did to their embassy."

"They burned Cairo, not London. Remember?"

Ramzi was incorrigible, Yousif decided. To avoid acrimony so soon after his arrival, he let the conversation end and walked away.

Another surprise awaited him as the gathering began to disperse. He watched several men hose down their tents with water until they were fully drenched. He recalled reading that the desert heat could be extremely high in the daytime, but freezing at night. That was true in Kuwait, but apparently not for all men. Especially non-Arabs. The proof was before Yousif's eyes. He watched the Italian and Maltese surveyors prepare themselves to sleep by wrapping their naked bodies with soaking-wet sheets. The scene was so comical, so bizarre, that he began to chuckle. He stood and observed these two men looking like ghosts and creeping into their separate tents, each dripping all the way to bed.

He headed toward Amin's tent and they shared a laugh at the uncommon scene Yousif just watched. Neither was sleepy, but ready for a private talk. The exchange with cynical Ramzi prompted Amin to question Yousif about Amana and its long-range intentions.

"The liberation of Palestine, what else?" Yousif said, settling down and pulling out his pipe. "Amana would be just a cog in a great wheel. But it has to exist."

They talked past midnight, and Yousif laid down his immediate goals for being in Kuwait: to discreetly organize a fundraising system in support of Amana's aims and ideals among the Palestinian workers in oil-rich Kuwait. There were close to a thousand there already, and their numbers were increasing every month.

On a personal level, he wished to save enough money to at least start his university education. To meet his family's needs and to serve the national cause at a higher level, he needed a profession. He was leaning toward a law degree but that could change. History and political science were appealing, but they did not offer much of a career. He needed to be practical and be able to provide for his mother in her old age and for himself and Salwa and their future children.

"*Inshallah*," Amin said.

"There's so much to do, so much to learn, so much to absorb," Yousif said, ready to stay up all night talking.

"And no time to waste," Amin said.

Suddenly Yousif's mood changed. "Our enemy is far ahead of us on all fronts."

"And they're spread all over the world."

"More important, they seem to excel at everything," Yousif added, his voice full of lamentation. "Except at one thing: telling the truth about us."

YOUSIF THREW HIMSELF INTO his work, making sure that the property owners and developers were equally satisfied. Most of the laborers were Palestinian refugees for whom he had genuine compassion. To them he was exceptionally kind. If a man was sick he would replace him without deducting his wages. If a man was late, he would never reprimand him harshly. Some were bricklayers or plumbers or housepainters by trade; others were civil servants who had taken manual or menial jobs out of desperation. He was the youngest among them, but he gave them no reason to resent his youth. He treated them like family, and they appreciated his friendliness and sense of fairness.

After two months on the job, his boss was so pleased with his work that he raised his salary to a hundred pounds a month. A generous vote of confidence, Yousif thought. He renewed calculations of how much he would need to go to the University of Cairo. Salwa with him, of course. She wanted to become a doctor. Could they afford two tuitions? What about accommodations and living expenses? He had to locate Rashad Hamza whom he had met on the plane coming to Kuwait, and who was jubilant in telling him and other passengers about the end of monarchy in Egypt. An attorney, in his mid-thirties, Hamza could tell him what to expect.

But first there was something else he needed to do. After work, he went to the business district and bought Salwa a gift from one of the stylish boutiques that were being opened throughout the city by Lebanese and Palestinian women entrepreneurs. He scribbled a note and tucked it in the gift box before mailing it at a new post office with a marble floor.

> Darling Salwa,
>
> I have never thought of being jealous of inanimate objects. But of this silky, lacy nightgown, I must admit, I'm extremely jealous. I trust you'll think of me when you try it on in front of the mirror . . . and go to bed wearing it.
>
> The inimitable Nizar Qabbani, our sensual and sensuous (and I must say audacious) poet, got it just right when he wrote:
> Your breasts are not meant
> To be kissed by garments,
> But only by mouth.
>
> > Warmest kisses,
> > Who Else?

His spirits high after mailing the package, he stopped at a modern department store and purchased three expensive shirts in different colors, three sets of underwear, and six pairs of brown and black socks. Amazing, he thought, as he ambled his way back to his compound, with the box of his purchases under his arm. Fine homes, ten-story office buildings, and shopping malls were sprouting every where. Holes and ditches were being dug around each corner for lamp posts and telephone lines. But, alas, no one thought of opening a bookstore, or bothered to establish a public library. That too would have to change. No liberation without education became his motto. He should arrange with a newspaper seller to distribute the *Amana Daily*. He wondered what kind of red tape he would have to go through to obtain permission. First, he should ask Raja to send him a parcel.

Post-haste he received from Salwa a figurative but loving slap on the wrist.

My Audacious Hero,

How could you!!! You've been gone long enough to lose your tact, if not your senses. Or your gentlemanly manners.

In the future, please make your gifts less intimate and your endearments less passionate. What if your mother (not to say my mother) happened to see your note? But have no fear, dear, I tore it up as soon as I finished reading it. I'm even planning to hide the negligee from her until after your return. And this alone bothers me, for she and I are so close I hate to keep your gifts a secret from her. (No girl could ever hope for a better *hamah*, let me tell you.)

Also, I'm now worried about my weekly visits to the post-office, which I routinely make every Saturday morning, for I'm sure the censor (who must've entertained himself on your risqué note) would be waiting to give me one of his leering looks. Why do some men embarrass women and make them feel uncomfortable?

Reserve your "affection" for display—only at home.

"Warm" hugs & "tender" kisses,

Who Else, Indeed

Yousif chuckled at Salwa's rebuke but knew she was secretly delighted.

JIHAN'S WORSENING HEALTH GNAWED at Yousif's heart. How many times had she and Dr. Afifi invited him, and how many times he wished she had not bothered herself with so much preparation. Although she had domestic help, she supervised all the cooking. Each meal in her house was a feast, and she always dismissed his protestation with a shrug and a smile.

One late afternoon, while waiting for the doctor to come home, Yousif was sitting in the living room with Jihan drinking coffee. During the ten minutes, she went back and forth to the kitchen to tell Madeeha, the housekeeper, what to do. Jihan's nervous energy belied her frail body.

"What else is there in this desert for me to do?" she confessed as she sat down. "It's a prison without walls."

Yousif nodded with empathy. "If they'd only allow more women to enter."

"I wish," she said, exhaling. "Selim goes to his clinic and I stay bored at home. How many dinner parties can you give or go to? How many magazines can you read? And how many books can you wish for and can't find?"

"I understand," he said, inwardly thanking Amin for the pipe he was lighting. How well he could relax at moments like this, smelling aroma and watching smoke swirl around him.

"Can a woman enjoy herself without a group of gossipy women to cheer her up?" she said, forcing a wan smile. "Say, why doesn't Salwa come and teach here? Teachers are considered essential and are given top priority. I'm sure a visa and a permit for her could be arranged. As they say: It's not what you know, it's who you know. It works every time."

The thought buzzed in Yousif's head. "You think so?"

"I know so. We have many contacts."

"But I don't plan to stay here too long . . ."

"Stay as long as you like. Then both of you can go and pursue your education. You want to be an attorney, and she . . .?"

"A doctor."

"Wonderful. Then you can come back and practice law or go in the banking business, as so many do. And she can train under Selim and one day take over his clinic. By the time you both get your degrees, he'd be itching to retire."

"In fact, when I finally located her she was working at a hospital."

"Perfect. We must tell Selim. He'd be thrilled."

She then called out to Madeeha, in the kitchen, asking her to bring Yousif a bottle of ice-cold beer. The dark-skinned Sudanese housekeeper appeared with a beer bottle, a tall empty glass, and a napkin on a silver tray. She placed it on the glass table before him, and left the room, smiling. Well-trained, Yousif thought.

Jihan was still bubbly. Her enthusiasm equaled the rush Yousif was suddenly feeling. Salwa would inject a new life all around, and rejuvenate Jihan in particular. Besides, with two salaries they could probably save enough money to have a decent head start at the university. But he had better do all his private calculations before raising Salwa's and Jihan's hopes. These two women were both driven. Yet he had many angles to consider.

Then she threw him a twister.

"Take it from me, Yousif," Jihan added, her hand massaging her flat-tened chest. "You and Salwa should start having a family as soon as you can. They'll be your pals when they grow up."

His surprised look was unmistakably clear.

"I don't mean while you're in school," she added, sighing. "How we wished we had some. Our life would've been entirely different."

From that moment on, Yousif became even more sensitive to their feelings. He was particularly impressed by Dr. Afifi's attentiveness to his wife. He would see him put the hassock under her feet, bring her a glass of her favorite brandy, and walk across the room to light her cigarette, all the while chiding her about smoking. In most Arab households, especially of the older generation, it was customary for the woman to cater to her husband's needs. The reversal of roles in this case could only mean that Dr. Afifi had given up on her health. Obviously she was terminally ill and he became her primary caretaker. As far as Yousif could see he did everything in his power to make her last few months, or however long she lived, comfortable. But Yousif could never summon up the courage to probe into the nature of her ailment. They did not tell him and he did not pry into their private affairs.

One late afternoon he was sitting with Dr. Afifi and Jihan on the veranda watching the glorious sunset.

"What do you think is happening to your home in Ardallah? Is it empty? Or have you sold it?" Jihan suddenly asked. "It was so beautiful. Selim and I were hoping to build one just like it."

The two men were shocked. Had she lost her mind?

"We still can," her husband finally managed to say. "That's why we're in Kuwait. To make enough money to build your dream house."

A forlorn look crossed Yousif's face. She sounded as if the last four years had not happened. Had she not heard of occupation? What did the invaders usually do when they occupied the homes of those whom they kicked out? Kept them neat and tidy, mopped the floors, and waited for the owners to return?

"And the birds?" Jihan added, rubbing her chest under the blue cotton dress, oblivious of the uneasiness she had created. "They were so lovely. Do you think they're still in the aviary?"

What disturbed Yousif was the fact that he had told her and her husband all about his trip back to Ardallah and the tremendous pain he felt upon finding strangers from Eastern Europe living in his home. At the time she had been thrilled by the adventure and pressed him for details. She had specifically asked about his mother's and Salwa's reaction when they saw their rings and bracelets. Whatever happened to her? She was always clear-headed. And now, listen to her.

The phone rang and the doctor went inside the house to answer it. When he returned he told Yousif that there was an emergency at the hospital. Would he, Yousif, mind keeping Jihan's company until he returned? They exchanged meaningful looks and Yousif sat alone with Jihan, wishing he knew more about her ailment. He suspected she had cancer which must have metastasized to her brain. Or was she suffering from early dementia? He would not go home until he received an answer.

On two previous visits, Yousif and Jihan had sat together either on the veranda or on the sofa by the open window, waiting for the doctor to return from his clinic. On both occasions she asked him to sing for her . . . or with her. Both times he reminded her that singing was a talent he wished he had. Twice she persisted, her deep green eyes entreating. Once he succumbed to her wishes, finding it difficult to keep saying no to a lady whose months might be numbered. A tender feeling passed between them, but their eyes never met. She asked him to sing folkloric songs ("like those we sang at the *sahra* before your wedding.") He obliged her by singing a few lines from the melodious Andalusian songs that recalled the glory of Arab Spain and that of late had become extremely popular. To his surprise he moved on to singing old and new nationalistic songs that tugged at the hearts of his unlucky generation.

"You are a Palestinian thoroughbred," she told him that night, her eyes tearful.

He nodded, her apparent melancholy suppressing in him the words he might have spoken. His mouth suddenly dry, he watched her finish dabbing her tears.

"The only wish I have left," she confided, "is to be buried in Palestine."

"*La samah Allah*," he said, appealing to divine protection.

"But where?" she said, lighting a cigarette in defiance. "My preference of course is in Ardallah, my place of birth. Yet . . ."

She watched him struggle for an appropriate response.

"Any place will have to do," she said, "as long as it's on Palestinian soil."

That had been nearly a month earlier. Tonight she did not ask for singing or even conversation. She walked briskly and he followed her to the living room. She went straight to the piano and immersed herself playing some of her classical favorites. He watched her fondle and caress—with an occasional burst—the ivory keys before her, and saw peace and tranquility return to her milky face.

"Do you like classical music?" she asked him when she finished.

Finding all answers trite, he said: "As long as you play it."

"To tell you the truth my favorite instrument is not the piano. I play it because I enjoy it, but it's not my favorite. My favorites are the 'oud and flute."

Yousif looked surprised. "Really!"

"No music can wrench my heart as they do."

Soon after the doctor returned, the three of them sat on the veranda.

The night was majestic, with star-studded galaxies peering down on them like distant orchards with golden grapes hanging on their vines. Jihan got up and went inside. A few minutes later she reappeared with a bottle of cognac and two liqueur glasses on a silver tray. Was there anything else she could fetch them before she went to bed? Both wanted her to sit and have a shot of cognac with them. She apologized, said good night and withdrew, looking tired.

It was time to smoke—in contemplated silence. The doctor produced a Cuban cigar. He methodically unwrapped it, clipped its end, struck a match to its tip, rotated it and puffed on it before the match went out. Yousif went through a comparable ritual: he got out his pipe, scraped its bowl and dumped the crud in an ashtray, filled it with tobacco from his black pouch, lit it methodically, dangled it in the right side of his mouth, and began to puff on it. All the while, each brooded and waited for the other to speak.

"I'm sorry you had to witness her lapse of memory," the doctor said, pouring cognac in their glasses.

"Does it happen often?" Yousif asked.

"Not really. But I'm concerned. She asked me recently when are we going back to Ardallah. But most of the time she's one hundred per cent coherent."

"Early in the evening, before you came back from the hospital, she asked me why not bring Salwa to Kuwait. She said both of you have connections and Salwa could come as a teacher."

The doctor looked pleased. "See what I mean, most of the time she's like that. Lucid and clear-headed."

They smoked and sipped and sat in lingering silence.

"As I recall you said Salwa has been working in a hospital or with doctors ever since the forced exile."

"Yes, she has."

"Then why did Jihan say she could come and work as a teacher? She should come and work in my clinic. I'll train her to be the best nurse."

Yousif's attention was aroused. "One day she hopes to be a doctor."

"Better still. As soon as you both decide, I'll get her a visa and a permit to work here. You can depend on that."

The rapid exchange and the excitement it generated in Yousif was short-lived. The doctor returned to his pensive mood.

"Jihan hasn't told you about her last wish, has she?"

Yousif nodded. "Is she serious?"

"Very," the doctor answered. "Luckily I can afford to take time off for a year or longer. Looking after her will be my fulltime job. We'll settle in Ramallah. I don't know exactly where."

The housekeeper came with a platter of fruit and two small dishes of cheese and slices of home-baked bread.

"Let's hope it won't come to that," Yousif said, picking up a small piece of goat cheese.

"It's inevitable, I'm afraid," the doctor said, crossing his legs and leaning on his elbow. "I intend to take her to the AUB's hospital for comprehensive examination. And we'll see what they find out."

Yousif refilled their glasses with cognac.

"I'm a man of science," the doctor said, "and I shouldn't believe in anything that can't be scientifically proven. There's irrefutable evidence that she's dying from cancer. The blood count, the white cells, the platelets, the X-rays, the loss of weight, the jaundiced eyes, the lack of energy—everything points to one fact: her ailment is terminal. Yet, deep in my heart I believe she has brought death on herself. She willed herself to die the minute we were thrown out of our homes. It's been downhill for her ever since. Call me crazy, but I honestly believe it."

Yousif took the pipe out of his mouth and looked at the doctor as if to confirm his suspicions,

"Her lapse of memory seems to revolve around your home, my home, my birds. Everything about Ardallah."

"Clever observation, Yousif. She never mentions anything about our travels in Europe or South America or to the Pyramids and the Sphinx or Luxor in Egypt. It's always our home this, or our home that. Notice how she even dreamed of building a beautiful house like your parents.'"

Yousif was puzzled. "Does depression cause cancer?"

"I don't know. But depression can be deadly. It weakens the immune system and could—I say could—contribute to mental or physical illnesses. There are too many unknowns about the cause and cure of cancer. Everything is being researched and assessed. One day, we'll know. In Jihan's case, I suspect that her sickness is related to her depression after our exile."

"She's been devastated by it," Yousif said.

"I'll tell you something very few people know."

Yousif waited, wondering what it could be.

"Just before the Zionist soldiers who were already in our house threw us out, she was in the bedroom trying to vomit. Suddenly she heard an explosion just outside the window. She looked out, only to see our neighbor's house being blown up. Dynamited. Debris and smoke filling the air."

"I can imagine," Yousif said, recalling similar horrors.

"She became hysterical. By the time I reached her to find out why she was screaming, one of the soldiers was slapping her left and right. I guess to get her to shut up. I held him by the shoulders and he turned around and knocked me with his elbow, threatening to blow my head off."

Yousif did not know what to say. "What did you do?"

"The soldier threatened to rape her before my eyes unless she stopped screaming. She did and we both got the hell out before he changed his mind."

Two similar stories leapt into Yousif's mind: Hiyam's rape in his house and in front of the whole family, including Izzat her husband. The second was the slaying of Raja's sister because she was too sick to get out of her bed as they had ordered her. Taking a deep breath, Yousif mentioned these two episodes to Dr. Afifi, who nodded in total understanding.

Finally the doctor said: "Jihan knew that our next-door neighbors had a retarded and paraplegic son who could hardly move. You've seen him, I'm sure, lying in the middle of the street and holding up traffic. Well, the soldiers wanted the neighbors to take their son and get lost regardless. When the father tried to explain, they took it as a sign of resistance and blew the house over their heads. If you were Jihan, would you forget a scene like that?"

Yousif shook his head. "A crime totally unprovoked. How could anyone forget such a scene. That's why we're trying to organize Amana. To restore a semblance of our dignity, if not to regain our rights."

And for the first time, Dr. Afifi looked Yousif in the eyes and said: "I'm with you all the way. Tell Basim I said so. The older I get the worse I feel. And the more guilty."

That night Yousif went back to his tent and wrote two letters: one to Basim, inviting him to come to Kuwait where many patriots were ready to be enlisted; and the other to Salwa, telling her to pack and come to Kuwait to be Dr. Afifi's private nurse.

DURING THE MONTH OF waiting for Salwa's arrival, Dr. Afifi shared Yousif's excitement, but not nearly so much as Jihan did. Yousif had chosen a nearby apartment in a new high-rise building, which Jihan proceeded to furnish as if she were to live in it. Often she went out shopping by herself, but occasionally Yousif—knowing her lavish style—accompanied her to make sure she didn't overspend. After his first objection to an expensive sofa, she told him not to worry.

"Everything is on us," she said, stepping back to evaluate the size, the color and the texture. "It's lovely, don't you think?"

Yousif was astounded. "What do you mean it's on you?"

"You heard me. Selim and I agreed that we would furnish the apartment as a present to you and Salwa."

"Absolutely not," Yousif objected.

"Calm down, Yousif. Her coming here is a gift to both of us. She will do me a world of good. You see how lonely I am. Just having her around will cheer me up. And you know how crazy Selim is about you."

Yousif would have none of it. "But we won't be staying here. You know that. We plan to go to the University of Cairo to pursue our studies."

"All power to you. After you leave, we'll keep the apartment for our own visitors. We always wonder where to put them."

Witnessing a new side of Jihan, and convinced that she was not about to relent, Yousif decided to humor her.

"I presume. . ." he began.

"What?"

". . .that you'll be kind enough to let us at least pay the rent."

"Don't be silly. But if you insist I'm sure Selim will deduct the rent from Salwa's salary."

She was being delightfully impossible, Yousif realized, unable to suppress a giggle.

"Let me show you the dining room table I'm considering buying. . ."

Yousif followed her to another section of the large store. He was amazed at her sudden vitality. As thin and sickly as she was, she skipped and flitted around as if she had swallowed a handful of stimulants for breakfast.

"Lovely, don't you agree? Sit and see for yourself how comfortable the chairs are."

There was no arguing with her that morning. Yousif sat at one end of the table and she at the other. He nodded and watched her beaming.

THREE WEEKS LATER, YOUSIF embraced his beloved Salwa at the airport, much to the chagrin of some ladies decked in black from head to toe.

"Sooooo good to see you," he declared, squeezing her.

"I missed you terribly. But please don't try to kiss me. Not right here. The women are watching."

"I don't care. Let them feel jealousy."

As he leaned to kiss her she pulled her head away. But on the sidewalk he managed to sneak a kiss. While riding in the taxi to their apartment, they sat in the back seat and, out of respect for the Muslim driver who had several Qur'anic verses hanging on the dashboard and right under the rearview mirror, they were content to hold and caress hands. In the meantime she observed the panoramic view before her eyes. The tremendous construction going on all around her and far into the distance boggled her mind.

"Incredible," she said, looking at her husband. "Reading about it isn't like seeing it."

When they arrived home and shut the door behind them, he dropped her two suitcases on the black-and-white marble floor and she flung her purse on the recliner. They flew into each other's arms and kissed until they were breathless.

Finally she pulled away, eager to see the rest of the apartment.

She went from room to room, admiring the golden-brown sofa, colored pillows, tables, chairs, and the mirrors on the walls of the foyer and living room. She was particularly impressed with a large photograph of Jerusalem's Dome of the Rock, before which she stood for a moment and expelled a deep sigh. She continued on to the kitchen. She opened the drawers below the stove and found all the utensils one needed. The cabinet above the counter was stacked with cups and tall water glasses and short ones for alcoholic drinks, and plates of all sizes. The cabinet below was loaded with pots and pans and a couple of skillets.

"I'm very impressed," she said, "You did all this by yourself?"

"I wanted to please you," he lied with a straight face. "But you haven't seen the bathroom yet."

"More surprises?"

"Perhaps."

The bathroom cabinets were full of quality beige towels, soaps, toothpaste tubes, tooth brushes, shampoo and conditioner bottles, and different kinds of combs. On the counter next to the sink and below the beveled mirror was a vanity mirror upon which were vials of cologne and perfume as well as creams, for both genders.

She looked into the large mirror and pointed her accusatory finger at his image standing behind her.

"Did Jihan do all of this? Tell the truth."

Yousif smiled broadly. "All of it, except this room."

"Really?"

"I'll tell you all about it later. Now let's start the honeymoon we never had."

A flicker of sadness crossed her face. "Exactly. We never had a honeymoon."

He led her to the bedroom and tenderly undressed her. They made love on top of the multi-colored coverlet of their king-sized love nest until they fell asleep.

JIHAN'S DINNER TABLE WAS laden with the usual bounty. Salwa's eyes bulged at the variety of dishes that reminded her of the happy days in Ardallah.

"Thank you so much, Auntie," Salwa gushed, kissing Jihan on both cheeks. "It's fabulous. You didn't have to go to this much trouble."

"You're more than welcome, habibti," Jihan answered, refilling her glass of chardonnay.

"Just for you," Amin quipped, winking.

"Don't listen to him," Yousif told her. "She's the queen of all hostesses."

"Compliments appreciated," Jihan told them and headed toward the kitchen.

Dr. Afifi's toast and welcome of the beautiful Salwa only heightened the appetites of the eight diners around the table. At first the conversation was of general pleasantries, but the mood turned more intense when Salwa began answering their questions about the conditions back home. Terrible, she said. Everyone grew pensive. Forks and knives were held still. All eyes were on her.

"As you can imagine, life on both sides of the Jordan River is miserable," she said. "People are bewildered and seething with anger. Some are struggling to eke out a living. Half of the men who thought they'd be back home by now are unemployed and don't know how to care for their families. Yes, the refugee camps are still unsightly. Worst of all, the meager UN rations cannot stop hungry children from going to sleep crying. Or from dying for lack of proper nourishment, not to mention medical attention."

Her candor was searing. Suddenly she felt guilty for uttering so much bad news while they were about to indulge on an extraordinary feast.

"I'm sorry," she apologized, biting her lower lip. "I don't mean to ruin your meal and depress you."

"Don't worry," Jihan said. "Your mere presence lifts our spirits."

"You're very kind," Salwa told her, their eyes locking.

Silence lingered a few more seconds.

"God help us when the bottle is finally broken and the genies come out. . ." a pediatrician by the name of Sarri Allam lamented.

"Evil begets evil. . ." his wife Ramona added, sighing.

It was time for Yousif to dispel the gloom. "Don't forget, Amana Forever will come to the rescue," he said.

"Oh, yes," Dr. Afifi concurred, raising another toast. "Long live Amana Forever."

"And may her members multiply," Yousif said.

"And may her coffers be filled. . ." Salwa added.

". . . filled to the rim," Yousif expanded.

"Long live Palestine," Amin said.

All raised their glasses and repeated in unison, "Long live Palestine."

Soon the room was again filled with gaiety.

After dinner, Salwa insisted on helping Jihan clear the table. She felt among friends—almost at home—and no protestation on the part of the gracious hostess would deter her. After leaving the dishwashing to Hameeda, Salwa went around the room serving Arabic coffee.

Stuffing his pipe with tobacco, Yousif was on the wide veranda trying to get acquainted with Wassfi Shaheen, who was a senior vice president of one of the new banks. He was a tall man in his late forties, with graying sideburns that were becoming.

"I'm glad we now can buy and read *Amana Daily*." Wassfi said, lighting a cigarette. "It gives a slant on issues one doesn't find anywhere else."

"I'm glad you're enjoying it," Yousif responded.

"Can you tell me more about Amana Forever? It was founded by Basim. . .your cousin, am I right?"

"I'm proud to be his cousin. Yes, he is one of its founders."

"What can you tell me about it?"

"It's one of many underground organizations that are being formed all over. When Basim comes. . ."

"Is he coming here?" Wassfi asked,

"I hope so. But when and if he does, he'll be the one to tell you more about it."

Wassfi eyed him, smiling. "In general, is it political? Military? Both?"

What a question, Yousif thought. "Well, you know. To assist in the struggle to liberate our country."

His hesitancy did not go unnoticed by the banker. "Don't worry, I appreciate your reticence. By the way, one of our employees, Rashad Hamza, seems to know you. I mentioned that I would be dining with you and he said he met you on the plane to Kuwait."

"Oh," Yousif said, remembering the man who shared the news that decadent King Farouk had been deposed and banished. "I've been looking for him all over, but no one seemed to know where I can find him."

"He's been traveling for our bank quite a lot, but now he is settled. He's on our in-house legal team. And doing a superb job. Listen, why don't you come over to the bank and the three of us will have lunch at the presidential dining room."

"I'll be delighted," Yousif said.

"Rashad and I share one interest beyond the banking business. We're both admirers of your cousin Basim and the famous executive editor of *Amana Daily*."

"Raja Ballout."

"Yes, of course," Wassfi nodded "All Palestinians admire their patriotism. Basim for his sacrifices during the Revolt of 1936, and Raja for his stinging editorials throughout the 1940s. Anything these two men do is worthwhile. And we'd like to be part of it."

"They will be pleased to hear that," Yousif said. "As am I."

THE LUNCHEON TOOK PLACE three days later on the twelfth floor of the bank building. For more than an hour they explored how best to support Amana Forever. It boiled down to the basic issue of fund-raising. Money was needed from the Palestinian community at large. Especially here in Kuwait, as well as Saudi Arabia and other oil-rich countries.

"There are at least a thousand of us in Kuwait alone," Wassfi said.

"And more and more arrive every month," Khalid added.

"And everyone of them is eager to help," Yousif said. "I'm sure of that."

The bankers nodded and suggested that a finance board should regulate and monitor all financial transactions.

"Do you know if there's such a board?" Wassfi asked.

"I really don't," Yousif answered. "Of course I've been away for nearly a year now. They may have formed one."

Again, Yousif hesitated. He liked these two men and they sounded sincere, but he did not really know them. Trust no one, Ustaz Sa'adeh had warned. Yousif had no doubt that the region was crawling with agents or spies or collaborators. After all, Kuwait was still a British protectorate, and ruled by a monarchy, both of which might not allow any activity that smacked of danger. Then there were other underground organizations that could be competing for recruits or donations. The bankers he was lunching with could be trying to pry information out of him for their own benefit.

A voice snapped him out of his meditation.

"If you see Basim before he pays us a visit," Wassfi said, "do tell him that I would like to be part of Amana. So would Rashad."

Rashad nodded enthusiastically. "Absolutely," he said.

"As bankers," Wassfi continued, "we can help him set up a system to collect and transfer funds, if need be."

Yousif thanked them and promised to relay the message to Basim. Then a waiter approached to tell the bank's senior vice president that he was wanted on the phone. Wassfi excused himself and went indoors to take the call.

"What kind of a job do you have here in Kuwait?" Rashad asked. "It seems to me you ought to be helping Basim."

"I'm a foreman for a commercial developer. My friend Amin got me the job."

"Interesting. How long do you plan to stay?"

"Until my wife and I get accepted at the University of Cairo. She wants to be a pediatrician and I want to be a lawyer."

"Have you applied for admission?"

"Not yet. Salwa just arrived from Amman and Dr. Afifi is letting her work in his clinic. Training her to be a nurse, you might say. As soon as we have enough money to get a head start, we plan to apply."

"When you're ready to apply," Rashad continued, "I'll be more than happy to give you a recommendation."

"I would appreciate it."

"I attended the same university and graduated from its law school."

"Really?" Yousif asked, pleased. "How was it?"

"I enjoyed it, but to tell you the truth I wish I had studied in America instead. The two systems are quite different. Egyptian law schools admit you right out of high school and in three years you graduate as a lawyer. That's much too young, if you ask me. In America, you have to be an undergraduate for four years before entering law school for three more."

Yousif was disheartened. "But you certainly did well in spite of that inadequate schooling."

"True. I was lucky to get a lot of experience under good lawyers. The first five years I was with a reputable law firm in Haifa. Then I worked in the Attorney General's office for three years in Jerusalem. The next three years I was, believe it or not, a judge in Jenin. And since our forced exile in 1948, I was a bank counselor in Amman."

Yousif was impressed. "Not bad, not bad at all for someone—"

"True," Rashad interrupted him. "But I was most fortunate to find lawyers willing to take me under their wings. And I slaved all those years to make up for what I should've learned as a regular university student. I always regretted not having had the chance to take the many wonderful courses available to all undergraduates."

Yousif sighed, resigned to what was ahead of him. "Oh, well," he said. "There's no way I can afford seven years of schooling. Besides, I can't be away from Amana Forever for that long. Palestine might be liberated before I graduate. And I would have missed the pleasure of kicking the occupiers out of our country."

A sardonic look crossed Rashad's face. "I'm afraid it's going to take longer than that to achieve that goal."

"How well I know," Yousif admitted. "Anyway, I'm glad I'll be going to Egypt. It's the heart and soul of the Arab world and I need to experience it first-hand—not just read about it."

Rashad expelled a deep breath. "We can't win wars without Egypt, that's a fact."

THREE DAYS AFTER HER arrival, Salwa began working at Dr. Afifi's clinic. Every morning at eight o'clock the doctor would pick her up in his Chevrolet. And every late afternoon he would drop her off at her apartment, and she would exuberantly tell her husband everything she had seen or done. The two other nurses at the clinic were very kind to her as if they had been instructed by the doctor. On the first day they handed her a white uniform and began to teach her everything they were doing, from answering the telephone to studying and filing patients' charts. They showed her how to take blood pressure, draw blood samples, and give injections. Many of these procedures she already knew, but out of respect for their enthusiasm, she let them instruct her. Everything they showed her was repeated and elaborated on by Dr. Afifi. The first time he asked her to be with him in an examination room, she saw a woman remove her blouse and brassiere and expose her breasts; she felt embarrassed but did not flinch. She just hoped he would not let her watch him examine the men's private parts or probe a man with his finger to check his prostrate.

Before long she was coming home carrying books on biology and would spend most of the time poring over the color pictures and drawings of the human skeleton. She marvelled at the complexity of the human body—so many bones, so many nerves, so many blood vessels, so many arteries, so many organs, either intertwined or overlapping each other. And so many names and words of foreign origin to study and commit to memory. The details before her were eye-popping and mind-boggling, to be sure, but she was intrigued rather than intimidated. Enthused and challenged rather than discouraged. Deep in her heart and soul she wanted to be more than just a doctor. Above all, she wanted to be a healer.

"The best part," she told Yousif during dinner, "is having private tutorials from Dr. Afifi. He pours information into my head and opens my eyes to so many things, as if he were trying to turn me into a doctor, not just a nurse, in whatever short time I might have with him."

"Fantastic," Yousif said, truly happy for her.

"A dream come true," she said. "But how will we ever repay them? First Jihan and her extravagance on this apartment. Then him, for God's sake."

"Some parents don't do half as much for their own children."

"What are we going to do? How can we begin to repay them?"

"First by looking after Jihan," Yousif answered, rising from his chair and taking his dirty dish and utensils to the sink.

"Be serious, please."

"I am serious. Jihan is very lonely and terminally ill. They don't have any children, and they look at us as their adopted children. I don't know if they have any close relatives. Have you ever heard them mention anyone?"

"If you haven't, you know I haven't."

THEY TRIED TO VISIT the doctor and his wife at least a couple of times a week. Each time, they would be reproached for not having come more often. They could not do that, they would explain. Jihan did not give ordinary dinners, she specialized in throwing lavish parties. And these no one could reciprocate. Until Salwa learned how to cook reasonably well, they would have to limit their getting together to simple visits.

As Jihan pulled Salwa to another part of the house, laughing as they went along, Dr. Afifi and Yousif would end up on the veranda to smoke their cigar and pipe.

"I want to congratulate you on having Salwa as a wife," Dr. AFifi began. "I'm truly fond of her."

"That's very kind of you to say," Yousif answered. "Both of us are grateful for her opportunity to work with you."

"Don't be so modest. She's going to be a wonderful doctor."

"That's high praise coming from you."

"I'm impressed by her analytical mind, her curiosity, and by her ability to absorb difficult concepts. As for Jihan, you can see for yourself. I can't believe my eyes. In the few times she's been around Salwa, she seems rejuvenated. Look at the way she moves and talks. Salwa was not just fresh air. She was more like a shot of adrenalin. I thank both of you for entering our lives. And I mean it."

"It's the other way around, believe me," Yousif said.

Now they could hear Jihan playing the piano and listen to both women singing familiar folkloric Andalusian songs. Dr. Afifi puffed on his cigar and Yousif on his pipe. Shortly Madeeha arrived with a tray of drinks. The doctor poured two glasses of cognac, and they reclined in their chairs as the voices of their wives wafted over them like the gentle breeze of their beloved homeland.

MORE MEMORIES OF PALESTINE flooded Salwa's and Yousif's minds when Amin came home for dinner. They did not invite the doctor and his wife to join them because Salwa was still reluctant to display her rudimentary cooking before the master hostess.

While Yousif was on the apartment's small balcony grilling three skewers of kifta strung with wedges of onions and cherry tomatoes, Salwa was in the kitchen making tossed salad. When Amin rentered from the balcony with an empty beer bottle, she opened the refrigerator and handed him another one.

"Amin," Salwa told him, scooping spaghetti on a large platter, "Yousif can't stop bragging about you. And not just to me, either."

"Believe every word of it," Amin said, flashing his infectious smile.

"You've been a great friend to him and we both appreciate it."

"He has no brothers and I have only five sisters. So we're stuck with each other."

Salwa laughed. "When are you going to get married? I bet your parents think it's about time."

"I agree with them," Amin said, sipping on his beer.

"Why not then? God knows you've been blessed with success."

"That's part of it. I can't leave my job and go hunting for a wife. I want to marry a Palestinian girl, and there aren't many around here to choose from, not to mention to fall in love with. And I'm not going to leave it to my parents or siblings to choose one for me."

"I never thought you would."

"There you have it. My success has come at a price. I can't leave it long enough to get married, and I can't wait too long either."

Yousif brought in his tray of kifta, placed it in the middle of the dining room table, and came toward them wiping his hands with a towel.

"What are you two talking about?" he asked.

Salwa handed him a bottle of beer. "I asked him when is he going to get married, and he gave me a reasonable explanation."

"He's got a problem," Yousif said, leaning against the wall.

"But I have a solution," Amin said, raising a toast. "You two are hereby appointed to be in charge of finding me a suitable bride, and when you do I'll marry her sight unseen."

Yousif and Salwa looked at each other.

"If you will only find me a girl half as beautiful and good and smart as Salwa, I'll buy her the biggest diamond ring in Kuwait and fly back home tomorrow to marry her."

They all laughed. "You are full of it. Come on, let's eat," Yousif said, reaching for the chair at the head of the table.

"You haven't changed," Salwa told Amin, filling a platter with spicy-smelling spaghetti.

"But you two have changed," Amin said.

"Changed how?" she asked, ready for another quip.

"You have become closer and dearer to me than ever."

"You're so sweet."

"Don't listen to him," Yousif cautioned. "He's talking on an empty stomach. And—"

"—a hungry man will say anything," Amin finished the thought, laughing.

They tittered and began filling their plates.

The dinner conversation ranged from Yousif's luncheon with the two bankers, to Amin's new opportunity in Kuwait.

"The developer we both work for wants me to be his partner on the next project," Amin informed them.

Yousif's and Salwa's forks froze in mid air.

"When did this happen?" Yousif asked.

"This afternoon. And you are the first ones to know."

"Congratulations," Salwa said. "No wonder you are in such a good mood."

"Am I not always in a good mood?"

"You are, you are. I didn't mean it that way. I'm sorry."

While enjoying the highly flavored food before him, Amin went on to remind them that Kuwait was a virgin country. Any investment in it now would multiply in the near future. Many people stood to become millionaires—even multimillionaires—in a hurry, and he wanted to be one of them.

"*Inshallah,*" Salwa said.

"It can't happen to a better man," Yousif said. Then with all solemnity, he added: "Let's only hope that your partner is not setting you up to marry his daughter."

Amin looked baffled. "I didn't know he has a daughter."

"That's because she's homely and he keeps her hidden until you become beholden to him and can't escape from his clutches."

Yousif's eyes twinkled and both Salwa and Amin turned on him.

"For a minute you had me going. . ." Salwa chided him, threatening to toss her napkin in his direction.

"You devil," Amin said, smiling. "When did you become so suspicious?"

"Only when I think someone is trying to trap my best friend."

They finished the meal with Arabic coffee and large pieces of freshly-baked baklawa Salwa had bought from the marketplace. But the sweetest part of the evening was the camaraderie that was never in danger of diminishing.

THE NEXT SIX MONTHS were a whirlwind. When Amin embarked on building his and his partner's first shopping center, he hired none other than Yousif to be his foreman. He even doubled his salary. When Dr. Afifi decided to take his wife to the hospital at the American University of Beirut, Jihan insisted that Salwa accompany them.

"It will be good for both of you," Dr. Afifi told Salwa, who seemed reluctant because she did not want to be a burden on them. "You will continue to cheer Jihan during her series of examinations. And you will experience a high level of medical treatment. It will look good on your application to the University of Cairo."

The doctors in Beirut discovered susupicious spots on both of Jihan's lungs which made them question her whether she had tuber-culosis in her youth. When she said no, they decided she must have had come in contact with someone who did have that contagious and incurable disease and told her husband, Dr. Afifi, to keep an eye on those specks. But they also discovered a large benign colon polyp which they removed as a precaution. For the two nights after the operation, Salwa slept on a cot in Jihan's bedroom at the hospital. Even back in Kuwait, she insisted on staying with them at the house serving Jihan as a private nurse.

Eventually the time came for Yousif and Salwa to apply for admission to the University of Cairo. Dr. Afifi wrote a glowing recommendation for Salwa, which meant a lot to both of them. And Yousif received two recom-mendations: one from Ustaz Sa'adeh, the principal of his high-school, and one from Rashad Hamza, his new acquaintance at the bank and a graduate of the law school he was hoping to attend.

Stuffing the two applications and the three recommendations in a large envelope addressed to the University of Cairo, Yousif included a cover letter which said in part: "We apologize for not including any school transcripts, for those remain (we hope) in our occupied but soon-to be-liberated country."

The letters of acceptance arrived a month later. Yousif and Salwa im-mediately phoned Dr. Afifi and his wife Jihan who were excited but not surprised.

"Come for dinner and let us celebrate," John told Salwa.

"We'd love to come, but we have already had supper. We just want to be with you two."

After hugs and kisses and the usual congratulations, Jihan looked at Salwa, her eyes moist.

"We are going to miss both of you more than we can say," Jihan said. "Selim, don't you agree?"

"It goes without saying," Dr. Afifi answered, "You've been wonderful to have around and we look forward to your success in all your endeavors. Yousif, you will be a seeker of truth and a defender of justice; and you, Salwa, you will be one hell of a doctor."

"You think so?"

"I know damn well you will be."

Jihan's eyes were now brimming over.

"I don't know how much longer I will live," she said, "but I know one thing. Salwa, you have added a year or two to my life."

Salwa got out of her chair and moved next to Jihan.

"Auntie, don't say that. You look wonderful," she told her, draping her arm around her neck. "You'll live long enough to christen our children."

"Most unlikely, but thanks for the sentiment."

A week later, Yousif and Salwa departed for a stopover in Amman before heading to Egypt.

14

THEIR APARTMENT in Amman was nondescript compared to the one they had left in Kuwait. What it lacked in architectural design and fancy furnishings, it gained in the warmth of Yousif's mother and immediate relatives—Uncle Boulus, Aunt Hilaneh, cousin Salman, his wife Abla and their children were all there to welcome them back home. The gathering reminded Yousif of their first year as refugees, when they were all crammed in an even smaller apartment. Only then he was still agonized with longing to find Salwa, and the children were nearly six years younger. God bless them, he thought, now they are no longer toddlers. The boys had a smattering of black hair on their legs and the girls had grown prettier and several inches taller.

"Does anybody know if Basim is in town?" Yousif asked, opening a bottle of arak.

Uncle Boulus leaned on his left elbow and clicked his yellow worry beads. "We thought you might."

Yousif looked disappointed. "Is that why Maha and the children aren't here?"

"I called but couldn't find her," Yousif's mother said. "She's in town, though. You'll see her soon, I'm sure."

Salwa came out of the kitchen with a tray of glasses and small dishes of white cheese and an assortment of pickles. Yousif poured glasses for Uncle Boulus and Salman, and when the women opted for mint tea instead of a drink he poured one for himself and sat down.

"Welcome back," Salman said, smiling.

Uncle Boulus and Yousif joined him, and the women seemed delighted. What surprised Yousif the most that evening was Salman's profound change. The debilitating pain he had long endured after the forced exile seemed to have been lifted off his shoulders and out of his general demeanor. He was no longer sullen but rather ready to engage with those around him. His clothes, neater and less wrinkled, reflected his inner calm.

In turn, Yousif and Salwa described their experiences in Kuwait, painting a picture of the boom that the tiny desert kingdom was undergoing, and eventually describing the Palestinians in their Diaspora and, in particular, showering the highest praise on Dr. Afifi, Jihan, and Amin.

The women were eager to hear about their friend, Jihan.

"How does she like Kuwait?" his mother asked.

"Not as much as Ardallah, I'm sure," Abla said.

"She's the queen of hospitality there," Yousif told them. "Her house is always open to guests . . ."

". . . and her dinner tables are fit for magazines," Salwa added.

"Why am I not surprised," Aunt Hilaneh said.

The long pause that followed made the ladies curious.

"What's wrong? How is she, really?" Yousif mother asked.

"She has lost a lot of weight," Salwa said. "But there's no worry. She's under the best care in the world. Dr. Afifi can't be beat."

Yousif's mother was not satisfied with the answer. "What does he think is causing the weight loss?"

"A number of things," Salwa said. "Mainly the forced exile. Apparently she's still can't get over it. Also she doesn't feel the desert is right for her. But she's making the best of it."

"And how!" Yousif elaborated, changing the subject lest they reveal too much. "They and Amin are the best friends one could have. If all the Palestinians are half as good as those three, we'll be just fine."

"That's a big if," Uncle Boulus scoffed, lighting a cigarette, "Individual goodness is not the point. What matters now is collective effort to recapture our homeland. And this I don't see happening."

Salman was the first to disagree. "Come on, Uncle. Give us time."

"Listen to him," Uncle Boulus said, bemused. "He was more pessimistic than I am and yet . . ."

"Yousif, tell him how long it took the Zionists to realize their dream."

"Fifty years since Herzl established the modern Zionist movement in 1897."

"See," Salman said, placing his youngest daughter on his knee. "If it took them, with all their wealth and the support of colonial powers, fifty years, why should it take us less?"

"Because I'm sixty-five and I don't have fifty more years to live," Uncle Boulus retorted. "That's why."

Salwa returned from the kitchen with cups of mint tea for the women. "Don't let Basim hear you say that," she said.

"Basim is one of the very few I trust. The rest are all hollow."

"Hollow! What do you mean?"

"Empty. Talk. . .talk. . .talk. That's all they're good for. Why, look at the refugees still rotting in their dreadful camps and waiting for UN handouts to sustain their lives. Some lives, if you ask me."

Gloom descended.

"He's right," Salman said, eyeing Yousif. "We are twiddling our thumbs and Israel is getting stronger and stronger."

"I'll give you a very simple example," Uncle Boulus said to Yousif. "Try to sneak back to Ardallah as you did a couple of years ago. Since then five men have been killed at the border trying to do just that. In the meantime, we've been sitting at the coffeehouses playing cards or dominoes and doing nothing of course, except talk. . .talk. . .talk."

"And write angry poetry," Salman jested, but no one laughed.

Yousif turned over in his mind his uncle's darker and more dangerous viewpoint, but decided this was not the time for a family squabble, or for reminding the guilt-ridden curmudgeon of the hopeful signs of the assassination of one imperious monarch and the dethroning of another, not to mention the rise of a dynamic new leader in Egypt.

"There's a lot of truth in what you just said," he told his dear old uncle whom he had always admired for his astute observations. "But with all due respect let me assure you that my generation will redeem your generation."

"You think so?"

"I know so."

"May I ask how?"

Yousif was undecided whether to overlook the grilling or to indulge the old man. A wink from Salwa as all he needed.

"It's a timeless strategy," Yousif said, toying with him.

"In other words you don't have one."

"You're teasing me."

"No, I'm not. You don't have a real strategy."

"In fact we do," Yousif said, his tone respectful. "And it's a simple one: above all instill in the youth the love of freedom and the conviction that fighting for our legitimate rights is far more preferable to living in exile and humiliation. Energize the masses by giving them hope that if the enemy could turn the clock back two thousand years we should be able to turn it back a couple of decades. And definitely rattle our impotent regimes and move them to action."

"As simple as all that," Uncle said, smirking.

Salwa weighed in. "And prick the conscience of the world by reminding anyone who will listen that we are neither the Romans who threw the Jews out of Palestine in 70 A. D. nor the Nazis who committed the ungodly Holocaust against them."

Uncle's eyes widened. "You two are a perfect match."

Yousif's mother beamed. "Why do you think he defied her father publicly and stopped her wedding in church? They're the ideal couple."

Yousif draped his arm around Salwa's waist, smiling.

Uncle pondered Yousif's so-called strategy and several seconds passed while he clicked on his worry beads. "You realize of course what a horrendous job is ahead of you. You'll eventually need the total commitment of our regimes. Their armies, their air forces are essential. You can't do it all by yourselves, you know that. I don't care how many resistance movements there are. What if those regimes don't respond to your appeals . . . your demands . . . or threats, if you will? What then?"

"We'll topple them before going after the enemy with every fiber in us and for as long as it takes," Yousif said. "So help us God."

Uncle forced a smile for a few more seconds. "We'll need tons and tons of God's help. Plus all the human assistance we can muster."

Yousif was delighted. By uttering "we" instead of "you" the cynical uncle had endeared himself again to Yousif who lost no time thanking him for it.

Those in the room were pleased. Yousif winked at Salwa and she blew him a kiss.

"All power to you," Salman said.

"I drink to that," Uncle echoed, somewhat enthused.

"Long live Palestine," Yousif said, raising his drink.

The men tipped their glasses and the women invoked on them all their good wishes and blessings. Having won round one, Salwa hastened to the kitchen, light on her feet, to fetch some dessert.

NEXT MORNING YOUSIF WANTED to visit Amin's family. On his way to their house, he deliberately went through downtown Amman, only to find it just as congested as the first day after their expulsion from Palestine. The sidewalks were crowded, the shops all open, with hardly any customers inspecting or even looking at any merchandise. Except for grocery shoppers with bags in their hands, few buyers were walking out with goods under their arms. He inhaled the air and recalled earlier memories that left him appreciative of the sights and sounds and smells of the recent past—dreary as those tantalizers were. They reminded him of the narrow, congested and winding roads of the old Jerusalem, and any such traces were welcome to his senses. They were to his Palestinian mind far more heart-wrenching than the endless open space of the desert.

After wandering among perverse reminders for almost an hour, he boarded a taxi and headed for his desired destination. On his way he passed sprawling refugee camps that broke his heart. Children were playing in the fields while their mothers squatted between the tents washing clothes and dumping the dirty water into sewers that did not exist. The few men were walking on both sides of the road, their hands clasped behind their backs, or leaning against trees, or sitting and brooding over large rocks. What existence was that? They were more than watching the traffic go by, he reflected, they were watching their future and the future of their families dissipate before their eyes. What a shame! What a disaster! Who knew what they had lost before they were tossed out of their homes and what meager jobs they were willing to take but could not find!

AMIN'S FAMILY LIVED IN a small house that looked like a palace compared to the tents that had been turned into dingy brick dwellings. First they had lived in a refugee camp until Amin started sending them monthly allowances to live on and to rent a house. And the house they were living in now was the only one they could find or afford at the time. They admitted all this rather sheepishly but were grateful for all the help they were getting.

"Your wonderful son gave me this to give you," Yousif told them, handing the father a check for a thousand Jordanian pounds. "And believe me there are a lot more to come. He wants you to buy a nice piece of land and build yourself a house just as beautiful as the one you built for my parents."

Abu Amin held the check in his hand, his lips trembling. "God bless him. I didn't make this much in ten years."

The five sisters gathered around their father to look at the enormous check. They were used to getting fifty pounds a month, but this one boggled their minds.

"But," Yousif he told Abu Amin, "he insists that you should leave all the chiseling of stones and pouring of concrete to others. You worked hard enough in your life and he says it's about time that you just relax and enjoy watching others do it."

"God bless him," Abu Amin said, his lips pursed and eyes dewy.

Amin's mother took a deep sigh. "We want him to save and get married first," she said.

Yousif realized that they had no idea how rich their son had become.

"Trust me, he has more than enough to get married and build you a house," Yousif said, his voice joyful. "He wants to get married, believe me. The trouble is he's so busy. What he needs more than anything else is time to find the right one."

"We keep looking and looking," Abu Amin said. "So far we haven't seen or met anyone who deserves him."

"For sure," Yousif agreed. "But he's still relatively young. Before long he'll be swamped with beautiful women who will throw themselves at him."

The only married sister looked somewhat alarmed. "We don't want any girl who would throw herself at him."

"That's just a manner of speaking," Yousif explained.

The mother agreed with her daughter. "We want a girl from a good family. Someone as fine and beautiful as Salwa. He keeps writing us about how good you both are."

"You're very kind," Yousif said. "Listen, Amin is more than a friend to me. I consider him a brother. Salwa and I will keep looking and hoping . . ."

"And don't forget praying," the mother added.

"We won't, I promise."

After a congenial hour swapping stories while drinking the customary

Arabic coffee and enjoying the tasty date-filled cookies, Yousif rose to leave but the parents insisted that he should stay and have lunch with them.

"You can't leave without sharing a meal with us," the mother said, visibly concerned that he might consider them inhospitable.

"Amin won't like it," Abu Amin added, clutching his arm.

"Please stay," a teen-aged sibling entreated him.

"Some other time," he apologized, walking toward the door.

"Is this a promise?" the married sister asked.

"Actually we'll be leaving for Cairo before too long. But I'll do my best to come back and bring Salwa with me."

Reasonably satisfied, they all shook his hand and gave him a warm goodbye.

FROM THERE YOUSIF HEADED back to his former school where the principal, Ustaz Sa'adeh, was expecting him. He could not wait to catch up on the news of Amana Forever, to see his former students, and to reconnect with Hikmat, his good friend and former colleague. What stories they could tell each other!

Ustaz Sa'adeh rose from behind a desk that was not exactly cluttered but was heaped with books and papers, and they embraced as if reenacting the return of the prodigal son. They looked at each other at arms' length, then fell back into hugging.

"It's so good to see you," Ustaz said.

"Likewise, believe me."

"How long has it been?" Ustaz asked, leading him to the sofa.

"Almost two years," Yousif said, sitting down.

"It feels like ten," Ustaz said, sitting in an armed chair facing him. "You look terrific."

"So do you. How is the family? How is Amana? There are so many questions to ask."

"Too bad you missed Amana's monthly meeting a few days ago. We are up to our ears with work."

"I can imagine."

"Otherwise everyone is fine. I trust Salwa enjoyed her few months with you in Kuwait."

"Yes, she did. I'll tell her you asked about her."

"You were absolutely right fighting to marry that girl."

Yousif thanked him and went on to inquire about Hikmat. "Is he around? I can't wait to see him."

Ustaz pulled out a pack of cigarettes and lit one, smiling mischievously. "I guess you haven't heard."

"Heard what? Did he get married? Is he okay?"

"Hikmat and over fifty of our recruits are now fighting in the Algerian Revolution."

Yousif's eyes bulged.

"Guess who else is fighting with them? Your friend Izzat Hankash whom you ran into selling pastries on a Beirut sidewalk. Remember?"

Yousif's chin dropped. "When did all this happen?"

"Moreover, we now have eight military training camps in central Africa and we're planning to launch two more in Jordan and Lebanon."

Yousif began to feel fire in his belly. Perhaps he had wasted time in Kuwait and missed out on the expansion of Amana. Chewing on his lower lip, he thoughtfully pulled out his Dunhill pipe and black tobacco pouch and settled for a not-so-leisurely smoke. "No wonder Basim never came to Kuwait regardless of how many times I asked him to."

"He's been like a weaver's *makook*, shuttling from country to country all over the world not just the Middle East. You want to hear something else?"

"Please astonish me," Yousif answered, smoke billowing around him.

"Your friend Rabha, the one who squirted her breast milk . . ."

"I know . . . I know."

"She turned out to be one hell of an informer for us. She dug up information about applicants to join Amana that we couldn't believe. Guess what else she does now in her spare time!"

"No telling," Yousif said, ready for more surprises.

"She baby-sits for Basim and Maha. Even when they travel abroad together, they trust her with their house and children."

Yousif tamped the ashes in his pipe and grew wistful. "There I was trying to make enough money for me and Salwa to go to the university, while all of you were here building Amana from the ground up. How selfish of me . . ."

"Nonsense," Ustaz said, rising to pour two glasses of ice-cold water from the pitcher on a corner table. "You will be more useful—more effective—to Amana as an educated man than . . ."

". . . someone with a mere high school diploma?"

"True, is it not?" Ustaz said, handing him the glass of water. "Besides, I bet you didn't waste any time in Kuwait preaching our revolutionary 'gospel' so to speak."

"That I did as discreetly as possible. Yet, wouldn't I have been of more immediate benefit if I were with Hikmat and Izzat in Algeria tasting battle and learning how to fight?"

Ustaz took a sip on his glass of water and looked at him, a laugh gathering to erupt. "You'd be as good a gunfighter as I would be a brain surgeon. Your target enemy would be utterly safe but my poor patient would die the minute I touched his skull."

They laughed and smoked and exchanged anecdotes then Ustaz asked about his experiences in Kuwait.

"Where shall I begin?" Yousif started. "Dr. Afifi and Jihan are incomparable. They are so generous and so hospitable, their home is the unofficial Palestinian embassy in Kuwait. They live and breathe Palestine, and don't be surprised if one day they became great donors to Amana. Besides, Dr. Afifi gave Salwa during her few months of training in his clinic what amounted to a crash course in medicine. She should be starting as a second-year student in medical school, she is so qualified. And Amin was and remains the brother I never had. He is on his way to becoming wealthy and will be great asset to Amana."

"What are they waiting for? We need all the help we can get. Now."

"Have no fear, they'll do all they can—and more."

Ustaz was very pleased and said so. He looked at the clock on the wall and got up.

"Classes will end in few minutes, and you might be able to see some of the teachers you knew as well as some of your former students."

"I'd love that," Yousif said, rising.

They walked out of the office and began to circle around the schoolyard. The general improvements to the school building and its surroundings were modest but included new doors and windows, fresher coats of paint, cleaner footsteps, straighter stone walls between fields, and, Yousif could envision or at least hope for, nicer blackboards, world maps hung on the walls of the classrooms, and brighter corridors.

"How many students do you have now?" he asked.

"About fifty more than when you taught."

During the leisurely walk, Yousif alluded to the great number of Palestinians working in high places and making more money in Kuwait than they ever did, only for Ustaz Sa'adeh to knowingly nod his head.

"We know about that. And there are thousands more in the oil-rich countries of Saudi Arabia and Libya."

"But are we tapping them for monthly donations?" Yousif wanted to know. "I met two Palestinian senior bankers who are quite ready and willing to join Amana and help us set up a financial trust, at least in Kuwait. That could mean a yearly income of thousands and thousands of pounds."

Ustaz lit another cigarette. "Again we know all about it," he said. "But we need to be careful to set it up without antagonizing the local governments. It could be tricky. After all, we will need those governments."

"Exactly. But when you're ready to discuss Kuwait, Dr. Afifi and Amin could be great contacts."

Suddenly the school bell sounded and students and teachers began to come out of the building. Yousif was enthralled, trying to find those whom he had the pleasure of teaching. He spotted three or four and they hugged each other as old friends. Of the teachers he only saw the fastidious and pinch-faced old man whose hand he shook without being able to recall his name.

Before he left school, Yousif turned to Ustaz Sa'adeh, his face solemn.

"What's wrong?" Ustaz asked.

"In few days, Salwa and I will be going to Cairo to study."

There was a long pause.

"Yes?" Ustaz again asked.

"I never thought I was running away, but leaving Amana at a time like this essentially amounts to the same thing."

"Absolutely not. None of us thinks of you that way. The board of directors as well as Basim and I applaud you for it. You're getting ready for the huge fight ahead."

"Four years is a long time to be away."

"Long but not wasted. Stop worrying and just go. You'll come back highly educated and better prepared to be the leader you're destined to be."

They shook hands, again embraced, and stared at each other for a long time before parting.

IN MID-AUGUST, YOUSIF AND Salwa left for the University of Cairo, where they would enter law and medical schools in early September. Both were eager with anticipation. Yet Yousif's head throbbed with conflicting thoughts as he sat next to Salwa on the plane on their way out of Jordan. Turning the pages of Al-Ahram newspaper which he was listlessly scanning and obsessed with the fate of his victimized people, he could not mediate between the Arabs' glorious past and their abominable present. His emotions swung like a pendulum. He considered Kuwait's sudden riches welcome, yet worrisome. No one could predict whether it would lead to utopia or decadence. So far the ruling family was wise in dealing with the welfare of their citizens. As a rule, he knew, great fortunes often came accompanied with trouble. If not careful, the blessing the oil-rich countries were now experiencing could turn into a curse. His mind flipped to Hikmat and Izzat who were learning how to fight in Algeria, while the refugees back home were still rotting in an ocean of camps and not knowing what tomorrow would bring. True, Arab leadership had been changed to the better, at least in Jordan and Egypt; Amana Forever had come into being; and similar resistant movements were emerging and offering some hope. Above all, there was the Egyptian colossus whose every whisper—and he often thundered rather than whispered—mesmerized all his listeners, and echoed throughout the Arab world like God's new set of commandments.

Yet, on the personal level, other matters nagged at him that morning. Certainly the letters of acceptance he and Salwa had from the University of Cairo were a source of joy. But he had no idea how long the money they had saved would last. Two years? Three years? Bearing in mind his mother back in Amman and Salwa's family in Salt, and the financial aid they would all need, he was concerned that the money they had might not be enough to sustain them for too long.

Once again he put all his doubts to rest, and concentrated on the positive. A political new dawn was spreading beyond the Egyptian horizon. And for the moment that was enough for him to feel relatively restful.

"Flying to Kuwait two years ago," he confided to Salwa, "and thinking of all the civilizations that flourished on the land I was seeing from above, I found myself preoccupied with the ancient past. And now I'm obsessed with the present and the future."

"It's normal," Salwa said, leafing through a pictorial magazine.

"One minute I see miracles happening and turning our region into a new Garden of Eden. The next minute I'm full of doubts."

Without looking at him, Salwa said, "Again, normal."

"In my darkest moments I see us facing many threats, not just from our sworn enemy. I see us torn by jealousies and crumbling old systems, in addition to the certain meddling of foreign powers intent on colonizing us forever. I worry that the oil boom which should be a major source of income for our resistance, could dry up before we know it,"

Salwa put the magazine down and faced him. "We'll find other sources."

"Without substantial donations our transformation into a fighting force will be delayed. Perhaps indefinitely."

"Have faith. Our so-called transformation is inevitable. Isn't this what Amana is counting on?"

Substituting "revolution" for "transformation," Yousif appreciated her thinking. As the plane soared against the brilliant blue sky, he was convinced that the Return to Palestine itself would never be just a dream.

15

To Yousif in particular, Egypt was the Mecca of the arts, the center of Arab culture, and the land of political promise. Here the Nile had flowed, the pyramids had endured, and the Sphinx had beguiled for millennia. Here the singing of the incomparable Umm Kulthum, Abdel Wahhab, and Fareed El-Atrache intoxicated their listeners; here belly-dancers Tahiya Karioka and Samia Gamal shimmied and swayed their way to the hearts of cinema audiences; here the high priest of theatre, Yusuf Wehby, thundered from across the stage: "A girl's honor is like a matchstick—it lights up only once"; here the wide-mouthed and thick-lipped comedian Ismail Yaseen clowned and filled the cinema auditoriums with laughter. Here the wonderful and beautiful singer of Jewish faith, Laila Murad, was happily married to a matinee idol, Anwar Wagdi, of the Muslim faith. Egypt was the land of brilliant writers: the blind Taha Hussein, and the alleged misogynist Tawfiq al-Hakim. Their fiction and nonfiction appealed to highly sophisticated readers. Then there was the immensely popular Ihsan Abdel Quddous, whose romantic novels evoked engrossing portraits of life in modern Egypt. Not to be forgotten, of course, was the Emir of Poets, Ahmad Shawqi, whose verses soared like the great pre-Islamic odes. And here was the home of Al-Azhar, the renowned and perhaps the oldest university in the world, where the teachings of the holy Qur'an and Islamic theology were instilled in the hearts and minds of select students from all Islamic countries, and where the richness of the Arabic language was taught, perfected, and preserved.

In Yousif's imagination, no pilgrimage to any holy place or any world capital could begin to compare with his trip to Egypt. He was obsessed with Palestine but enthralled by Egypt. Salwa shared his feelings. From their childhoods, Egypt had been their window to the world. Much of their happiness had been derived from its children's books, comic books, novels, magazines, film journals, movies, and songs. Most of their textbooks were written and published in Egypt. Of the fifty or so dialects in the Arab world, that spoken in Egyptian films was the most familiar and admired. Yousif and his friends loved to pepper their conversations with its colorful words or expressions. Of particular interest to Yousif was the inimitable sense of humor. No one could phrase or deliver a joke better than an Egyptian. It seemed humor was in their genes. Oh, there was so much to love about Egypt. And because of the extreme popularity of the Egyptian cinema, its landscape was familiar from the beaches of Alexandria on the Mediterranean Sea to the magnificent Luxor columns in the south, an area which, to Yousif's bewilderment, was referred to as Upper Egypt.

And now in the land of Tutankhamen and Ramses II a new phenomenon had been born. He might not be one of the Pharaohs, but time would tell. For now they called him Nasser. To all generations of Arabs from Morocco on the Atlantic ocean and across North Africa all the way to Iraq, and from there down to Saudi Arabia and Yemen, and to Yousif and all those who worried about the future of their beleaguered nation, Egypt was now being singularly hailed as the birthplace of Gamal Abdel Nasser. *Yes Nasser*, the multitudes would shout. *Yes Nasser,* who voiced their innermost fears, addressed their clear frustrations, articulated their dreams and aspirations, loomed as the new Saladin, and who, like his legendary predecessor, would one day re-liberate Jerusalem.

CURIOUSLY, AFTER NEARLY FOUR years of marriage, and perhaps as a temporary escape from the horrific national trauma they were experiencing, Yousif and Salwa regarded their anticipated stay in Cairo as a period of relative bliss. Notwithstanding the roaring traffic below their windows, they considered their efficiency overlooking the fabulous metropolis as a lovers' nest. They rejoiced in knowing that for the next three or four years, there would be no more separations, no more searching for each other, and no more dingy dwellings crammed with relatives.

Then the issue of intimacy began to be a problem of a different sort. Salwa was amorous enough, but her appetite for romance was no match for Yousif's libido. Her preference was relatively average with bonuses reciprocated and granted on special occasions. Most nights she favored cuddling as an ideal expression of togetherness, while he desired more. For him, each morning had to start with passionate coupling to invigorate him to meet the challenges of the day, with another union to relax him before going to sleep. It was a hectic pace—especially on weekends.

"You're ruining my complexion," Salwa complained, standing naked in front of the mirror. "Look at the dark circles under my eyes."

"You've never looked lovelier," he answered, appraising her while still in bed.

"I stay sleepy," she said, opening drawers to fetch her underwear. "And they all think it's from studying late at night."

He picked up a rumpled pillow and placed it across his bare chest. "Why don't you tell them what a siren you really are."

"You're crazy," she laughed, snatching his pants off a chair and hurling them at him.

He jumped out of bed and went after her, but she beat him to the bathroom and shut the door behind her. Whether intentionally or not, she did not lock it. He stormed in and found her giggling and waiting for him. They embraced and kissed and she dropped the underwear she was holding. Then he led her to the shower where the warm water awakened their bodies, and where they lathered each other and again made love.

When it came to Nasser's speeches on the radio, there was never the slightest disagreement between them. That morning was no exception. They turned on Sout al-Arab as they sat down for breakfast. The announcer rebroadcast a segment of Nasser's latest speech. The two dropped their forks and knives and settled down to hear his folksy, warm voice: "Did you know that in this country the *gamoosa* is considered more valuable than a human being? A man earns fifteen piasters a day—and the *gamoosa* earns twice as much. The fellah is hired for less than his animal. *Da mish ma'ool. Da mish mazboot.* Allah frowns on such oddities. Such abominations, such gross injustices, have no place in our society. They must be stopped. They will be stopped."

A day later they heard their idol make another speech: "In Alexandria, before the end of the monarchy, Arabic was considered the language of the lower classes. The elite and the powerful spoke French and English. Even Greek and Italian. People like you and me, whose native tongue is Arabic, were people with whom the foreigners, and some of our own middle and upper classes, did not wish to associate. We were strangers in our country. Our own country was not ours. Allah . . . Allah . . . *da mai sahhish*. You must have heard the story about the foreign diplomat who arrived in Egypt and another foreign diplomat advised him to learn the native language as soon as possible. The new arrival complained that Arabic was a very difficult language and that it would be hard for him to master it in a short time. 'Arabic?' the older diplomat asked, rather shocked. 'Who's talking about Arabic? Learn French, mon cherie.' So on and so forth. That was Egypt under King Farouk . . . when we natives had to take insults from the foreigners and like it. No more. No more."

SPRAWLING CAIRO WAS CONGESTED almost to a standstill. But when the traffic moved it was ferocious. Drivers were like soccer players zipping across the field, from side to side, as if God had nothing else to do except look after them. Posters and more posters and posters galore were plastered almost on every wall high enough for a gigantic picture of charismatic Nasser. In Amman there had been two posters on public display: one of young King Hussein, the other of Nasser. In Egypt there was one and only one poster. Nasser was Egypt, and Egypt was Nasser. Nasser was the Arab world. Only the blind would fail to see it proclaimed on the sides of trucks and buses, even on store and car windows.

"How dangerous," Yousif said to Salwa as they strolled around Tahrir Square. "His pictures block the driver's view."

"Same as in Amman," she reminded him. "When we love, we really and truly love."

"This is hero worship."

At the university's coffee shop, Yousif and Salwa introduced themselves to a group of men and women from various regions of the Middle East and were invited to sit with them. All were students—some returning to complete their studies, and the rest freshmen like them. Both were delighted with the mix from so many Arab countries and looked forward to new friendships.

Above the hubbub, Yousif could hear Nasser's distinctive voice on the radio.

"... One people ... One policy ... One power ... One dream ..."

All activities around them stopped. Every conversation froze.

"It's time for us to rise and claim our place among the independent and free nations of the world. The Arab world is a rich world ... in history, in natural resources, in strategic location, in potential and, above all, in our people."

The airwaves crackled from the rousing applause of the crowds Nasser was addressing somewhere in Egypt.

"No more issti'maar. No more imperialism. No more colonialism. Al-issti'maar, in any shape or form, direct or indirect, will be rejected ... will be repulsed ... and will be defeated. Any future crusader, misguided or deliberate, no matter how disguised, will face in us a formidable foe. As united Arabs, we will no longer tolerate their chicanery, their mischief, their maneuvering, their manipulation, their deceptions."

The unseen crowd roared and those in the coffeehouse applauded.

"As a united people, we will stand up to aggression and free every inch of Palestine. We are ready and willing to engage in diplomacy and fair play. We demand mutual respect. We demand justice. We will trade only as equals and nothing else. If they treat us like new friends in a new world, and not like subjects in their old colonies, they will find in us willing partners. But if they revert to backstabbing, they will be the losers. They need to know that from here on we will deal in kind. Measure for measure. Measure for measure, indeed. God be my witness."

The on-air crowd thundered with the final exhortation of their own, "No more issti'maaar."

Caught in the euphoria of the moment, Yousif and those around him found themselves clapping and echoing, "No more issti'maar."

Salwa laughed and clutched Yousif's arm. "I just love the way he rolls the last 'r': *issti'maaarrrr*."

ONE OF THE FIRST Egyptian students Yousif met at Cairo University was Tahseen Salah. He was small with sparkling eyes and kinky hair and Yousif liked him the minute they introduced themselves.

They were walking out of a history class when Tahseen turned to him and said, "Have you heard about the man who was standing on a street corner when someone visibly upset ran up to him looking for his dog?"

"No," Yousif smiled encouragingly. "Tell me."

Tahseen plunged ahead: "'Have you seen my dog?' the upset man asked.

"'Is it a poodle—twice the size of my hand?'

"'Yes,' the dog owner replied, his face hopeful.

"'Is it white?'

"'Yes . . . yes . . .'

"'Does it have a brown leather collar?'

"'Yes . . . yes . . . yes . . .'

"'Does it have three tiny black spots on its nose and one large black spot on its tail?'

"'Yes . . . yes . . . yes . . . !'

"'I haven't seen it.'"

Yousif almost dropped the stack of books he was carrying. As soon as the laughter subsided, Tahseen said he had another one for him. But Yousif told him to save it till later, he needed to meet up with Salwa.

A FAR LESS RIBALD sense of humor awaited Yousif in his philosophy class. After enrolling in the course, Yousif had some second thoughts. In fact, his advisor had tried to steer him away from the night philosophy course, wanting him to concentrate on more basic subjects such as language or introduction to law. But Yousif had insisted, eager to plunge immediately into serious discussions. It took him only one period in Professor Ni'man's class to know that he had made the right choice. Ni'man was a short and lively man in his early sixties, afflicted with a spasm of sorts in his neck which made his head slightly gyrate right and left. More interesting was his unorthodox but refreshing approach to teaching.

Sitting behind his desk, arranging and rearranging his papers, the professor viewed the seventy or so students occupying a small auditorium.

"If I had my way," the professor began, "I'd be sitting on a hill somewhere in Italy or Greece—drinking wine and reading Ovid. But since I can't afford the luxury, I intend to spend the next few months trying to make you smart. And from the looks on your faces, I think I have my work cut out for me. If a first impression can be trusted, you look as motley a group as any I had the pleasure of confusing over the last thirty years."

The students giggled, and many seemed to anticipate, even welcome, such remarks, for they sat riveted in their seats waiting for the jovial sage to bestow upon them his golden nuggets. Yousif was perhaps the only one who had come unwarned and unprepared for such humor. Or, for the professor's visual eccentricity. He would pace the floor: his head shaking, his left hand stuck in the pocket of his baggy pants, his right hand grandly slicing the air, his half glasses perched on the middle of his nose, his gray hair tousled, and his eyes almost closed. He seemed to carry on a life-long, uninterrupted dialogue with Socrates, Marcus Aurelius, Ibn Rushd, Hobbs, Marx, and Russell as if they were his closest friends, and as if the students were merely eavesdropping on their conversation. He spoke nonstop for almost two hours without ever losing his thought or sense of humor or the attention of his grateful audience.

Over the next month, Yousif came to know more about his favorite professor's tastes and habits. His preferred meal: goat cheese, dark crusty bread, thin sliced apples, and white wine. His chosen pastime: washing dishes and thinking. Simultaneously, of course. His passion: browsing through libraries and old bookstores looking for rare books on philosophy. Yousif could understand most of those, but the dishwashing left him bewildered.

"Ah," the professor explained, sitting among a few of his students at a European delicatessen in a small dining area one night after class. "The more suds the better."

Yousif smiled. "Do you perhaps see life as full of suds—and bubbles?"

"Life often needs scrubbing," the professor answered, doing the impossible: nodding and shaking his head at the same time. "The only suds and bubbles in life are wine and poetry."

The affection between professor and student was mutual. Once Ni'man asked Yousif to accompany him to a bookstore on Tal'at Street, a few blocks from the National Egyptian Museum. The professor had an old Plymouth which sputtered and shook and threatened to disintegrate at any minute. But what was more remarkable about the drive to the congested heart of a city of over six million people was the fact the professor squinted his eyes while driving as much he did while lecturing. Because of the affliction in his neck the professor was unable to switch lanes safely without the help of the passenger beside him. How they managed to travel one block without an accident was a miracle in itself. Another miracle was that Yousif's heart did not stop.

"Do you ever drive alone?" Yousif asked, helping him navigate during a particularly busy noon hour.

"Alone, my boy?" the professor replied, nearly closing his eyes and hugging the steering wheel with both arms. "Never. Ovid is always with me."

Yousif grinned and turned in his seat to watch the traffic on both sides. "I have a feeling you like Ovid."

"Yes, yes, indeed. Marcus Aurelius is another constant companion. Have you read him?"

"Never heard of him until I came to your class."

"Pity, my boy. But we shall see to that immediately. I have fifteen rare copies of his *Meditations*—in six languages. I'm sorry I can't loan you any of them, but you're welcome to come home with me and see them. They are my most valuable possessions."

For several days, Yousif excitedly anticipated visiting this delightful professor. It would be interesting to see how scholars lived and how this eccentric one in particular managed to substitute for a hilltop in Italy or Greece. Even though Yousif's fellow students had known Ni'man much longer, none had been asked to visit his home. None had had that honor.

Surprisingly the house was extremely modest, on a nondescript street. The professor's wife—at least twenty years younger than her husband— reminded Yousif of the actress who played Ophelia in a film production of *Hamlet*. There were more bookshelves and bookcases and book stacks than furniture in the house: some open, some marked, and some piled up on chairs or on the floor. The couple was childless, and Yousif thought to himself that under the circumstances that was proper. Having married too late in life, the professor was too into books to care for little children. And the wife did not look well. Her pale skin, handwringing, and the readiness to withdraw, reminded him of Jihan Afifi.

What surprised Yousif most was the discovery that he was in a Jewish home. The menorah on the mantle and the portrait of a long-bearded rabbi on the wall brought memories of his frequent visits to Isaac's home back in Ardallah. His instant reaction was a mixture of pleasures: he was heartened by the professor's decency to avoid politics, by his inviting him to his home (no matter how casual the invitation might have been), by the Egyptians' differentiation between Jews and Zionists, and, above all, by the absence of rancor in his own heart.

Nothing that afternoon could equal the peace the visit had produced in him. Even Professor Ni'man's precious copies of Aurelius's *Meditations*—all yellowed and one dating back two centuries—failed to move him as much.

NEXT DAY YOUSIF AND Salwa had a concrete reason to appreciate Nasser's policies. They and a group of Palestinian students had been summoned to the Dean's office to be told that President Gamal Abdel Nasser had decreed that four-year scholarships would be granted to all Palestinian students now studying in Egypt and all those who would qualify in the future. Never dreaming of such a windfall, Yousif led vigorous applause. Standing behind the desk, the tall, stout, brown-skinned Dean relished the cheers as if they were meant for him personally.

In their mutual excitement, the students threw their arms around friends and strangers. Yousif was even kissed by an attractive girl standing next to him—a girl he had never met, but who was obviously so delighted that she could not help herself. Yousif was caught by surprise, but Salwa was totally understanding and offered her hand to the girl in friendship. Then someone suggested that Yousif should make a speech on behalf of the recipients. Yousif did not know why he was chosen for that honor, but then he thought, perhaps because he was the oldest of the group.

"Speech, Yousif," echoed a fellow student from history class.

Yousif did not need much urging. He thanked the Dean for being *rasool khair*, a messenger of good will. Yousif looked around. All eyes were focused on him and he did not disappoint as he made a brief, eloquent statement of gratitude on behalf of not only the students but also the Palestinian people.

WITHIN HOURS THE GENERAL public knew about Nasser's generous aid to the Palestinian students. Yousif saw a rush on newspaper kiosks to read the full announcement. In the cafeteria where Yousif and Salwa met for lunch, students were reading newspapers or gathering around them to discuss the incredible news. Yousif was again called on, this time to compose a telegram to thank President Nasser directly. Without waiting for his consent, Salwa took out a pen and a pad so he could dictate the message. After some revising, the telegram read:

> Your Excellency's memorable decision to grant aid to Palestinian students enthralled us beyond words. You have not only opened to us the doors of the great Egyptian universities—you have opened your arms and heart and the arms and hearts of our brethren, the Egyptian people. You have demonstrated solidarity with Palestinians' cause and struggle. In our tragic war for survival, you took up arms to defend us, and you were wounded to save our homeland. Now you shower more benevolence. As your beneficiaries, we salute your leadership and celebrate your wisdom.

Within twenty-four hours the telegram—and along with it the photograph of its author—was on the front pages of the daily newspapers.

Yousif was even interviewed on Sout al-Arab that was transmitted to the entire Arab world. His sudden thrust in the limelight was due to the telegram to President Nasser, but Yousif did not dismiss the possibility that Professor Galal Hilmy also had a hand in it. The forty-one-year-old Hilmy had a doctorate in political science from the University of Chicago. Yousif was impressed with him and his vast knowledge, and Hilmy had taken a liking to Yousif and encouraged his interest in politics.

In any case, Yousif was soon singled out as the unofficial spokesman for his Palestinian compatriots who were basking in Nasser's sun. Taking his public role seriously, Yousif tried to explain to readers and listeners the impact of the scholarship aid on the Palestinian society. Like an aspiring politician—which he was—he stressed that the Palestinians had lost their country not because they had less rights than their enemy, or that they had less courage on the battlefield. No, they lost because the enemy had been more educated and better prepared to argue their case in the halls of power and before the courts of public opinion. Again and again, he repeated that education was the key to the future; a nation that did not master the arts and sciences of the modern world was doomed to stagnate. More important, education was essential for national survival. Wise and visionary, President Nasser had set out to bridge the gap between the Arabs and the modern world. Nasser was the friend of the poor, the supporter of the fellah, the reformer of social injustice, the ally of the refugees, the defender of human rights. Look at him, Yousif said, aiding the just and honorable Algerian Revolution, and laying ground for the equally just and honorable Palestinian Revolution which was bound to follow. Education was the new battle cry—and Nasser was leading the holy march.

Little by little, Yousif was emerging as a thoughtful, well-informed young leader. Fellow students wrote to thank him for speaking on their behalf and for representing them so well. Congratulatory letters came from Cairo, from Alexandria, and from as far away as Tanta in northern Egypt. Telegrams from his mother and from Raja—and one from Amin in far away Kuwait—arrived one after the other. They had either seen his photograph in the newspapers or heard his interviews on radio and were proud of him. He felt like someone spearheading a movement that had been thrust upon him, but he was determined to live up to the principles of Amana Forever.

The crowning touch came in the form of a letter from President Gamal Abdel Nasser himself. It was nearly a full page in which Yousif's hero restated his commitment to help the education of Palestinian youth. They are the leaders of tomorrow, he said, and the redeemers of the enormous injustice that had befallen their parents' generation.

Yousif held Nasser's letter with pride and he and Salwa read it over and over. He made several copies and secured the original in a safe place. He showed it to his professors and to many of his close friends who did not hide their envy. What an honor, they all said, to have received such a letter from their idol himself.

That night he took Salwa to a fancy restaurant on the second floor of a luxury hotel, sat at a table near a window overlooking the glittering Nile under a full moon, touched glasses in Nasser's honor, and savored an exotic meal.

"You're a celebrity," Salwa whispered, dabbing her lips with her linen napkin. "Look how they're staring at you."

"No, *habibti*," he replied. "They're staring at you. You're dazzling."

She blew him a soft kiss. "Don't ever stop exaggerating."

He did not think he was exaggerating. He loved her white dress, her red silk scarf, her Nefertiti pendant, and her hair glamorously piled atop her head.

On their way out they walked past a few admirers, nodding at those looking at them, and feeling rather proud of each other. As they crossed under one of the enormous crystal chandeliers, Salwa smiled at him. "I hate to admit it," she confessed, "but I can easily get used to this kind of life."

"You deserve the best," he answered, squeezing her soft hand.

After a short pause and a deep sigh, she said, "Life is best in Palestine."

DAY AFTER DAY YOUSIF sat in classes and listened to fine lectures, his hunger for learning exceeding his expectation. He pushed himself vigorously and checked out many books from the library, wanting to be as informed as the men who taught him. He was usually the oldest student in his classes. His teachers welcomed his maturity, his firsthand knowledge of the Palestine tragedy, his familiarity with life in exile, and his travel in the Middle East. Many of the faculty became his friends (with the colorful professor Ni'man remaining his favorite), and he valued their strolls and talks and the occasional visits to their homes.

Whether with students or teachers, most conversations revolved around Nasser. One day he was a Bismarck who would unite the Arab world. Next day he was a Saladin who would re-liberate Jerusalem. They often strolled up and down the long and straight banks of the river Nile which were lined with palm trees on both sides. Occasionally Salwa would be with him, when they cruised up and down the river in a small felucca, and watched other gondolas silhouetted against the sunset, all the while talking about Nasser. Other times he and Salwa joined one of her professors and his wife at the fabulous Opera House or at an opening night at the theatre. On a couple of Fridays he went to pray with some of his Egyptian friends at Al-Azhar or Ibn Touloun mosques, always wishing for a glimpse of Nasser. There was no such luck. But if Yousif failed to see Nasser, Nasser's spirit was imbued in him.

In the middle of October, Nasser scored another triumph on the international scene. And as expected his popularity soared. While visiting in the office of history professor Galal Hilmy, Yousif and he got into a conversation about the Egyptian leader's successes.

"Nasser is incredible," said Hilmy.

"No wonder we all love him," Yousif said, sitting at the invitation of this friendly, articulate professor whose lean physique was fit for a soccer player.

"He accomplished two historic feats without a drop of blood," Hilmy said, his eyes blissful. "First, he ended the 150-year-old monarchy and let decadent Farouk leave Egypt with all his trunks of treasures and pornography—with zero violence. Two, look what happened this week! He forced Great Britain to evacuate from the Suez Canal after seventy-two years of de facto occupation—again without shedding one drop of blood. I've never seen anything like it."

For the next thirty minutes the professor gave Yousif a mini lecture on how the British descended on Egypt in 1882 under the pretext of "protecting" their shares in the Suez Canal. And from then until 1954, they acted as the real rulers of the country.

"In 1945," the professor continued, leaning back in his chair and lighting a cigarette, "there was a disagreement between the British in Egypt and King Farouk on who should be the next prime minister. Each side wanted a particular person, and neither would budge."

"And . . .?" Yousif probed, too polite to tell the professor that he was familiar with the story he was about to tell him

"When Farouk tried to defy them they surrounded Abdin Palace with tanks and their ambassador kicked the door of his private chamber and ordered him to come and look outside. 'Do as we tell you or else,' the ambassador warned."

Yousif pouted. "And they got their way."

"Of course they did."

"Well, those days are gone. Nasser is no Farouk."

The conversation turned to colonialism in general and Algeria in particular, perhaps because of the rumbling in the news about a nascent Algerian revolt.

"France colonized Algeria in 1830 and later on annexed it altogether," Dr. Hilmy said, tapping a pack of cigarettes on his desk. "They considered Algeria an integral part of France itself. In their opinion, the Mediterranean Sea was no more than a creek running between the main land and their territory in North Africa."

"The audacity!" Yousif said.

"Then they proceeded to wipe out Arab culture. First thing they did was stop teaching the Arabic language. Then they turned mosques into churches. At the beginning of World War II, they told the Algerians to fight with them against the Germans and after the war they'd get their independence. The Algerians lost over forty thousand casualties in that war, and then France reneged on her promise. Now the Algerians are waging a full scale revolution . . ."

"About time," Yousif said, thinking ahead. That was one revolution the Palestinians could participate in and learn from. "A number of Palestinians are already fighting with the Algerians right now."

"The more the better. You need training on the battlefield."

"Two of my best friends are doing just that. And I often wonder if I shouldn't be with them rather than in school."

"Each of us fights in his own way. Your time will come, I'm sure, and you'll do your share. Actually, the Algerian liberation movement started off and on since the 1920s. Let's see how long this latest attempt will last."

"And how successful it will be," Yousif added.

The fact that for over thirty years the Algerians had failed to launch a credible revolution was quite sobering. If Algeria was to become the paradigm for the Palestinians to emulate, the future of Amana Forever was bleaker than he thought. Obviously the Algerians had waited too long before rebelling. They should have been up in arms decades earlier. The Palestinians would never give the occupiers of their country such luxury. Soon enough they would be knocking at their own doors and entering their own homes, Yousif believed.

LEAVING DR. HILMY'S OFFICE, Yousif spotted Tahseen walking with a girl in front of the Students' Union. They waved at each other and met in front of the building. Yousif was ready for diversion from the stressful talk on the evils of colonialism. If anyone could provide that, Tahseen was the one. He could tell a joke like a hashish smoker.

"Have you heard . . . ?" Tahseen began.

Before answering, Yousif smiled and introduced himself to Lubna, the student with him. Her pretty face as well as cleavage dispelled innocence.

"No I haven't," Yousif finally said, smiling.

"Well," Tahseen began, "a few years back when Egypt and Sudan were feuding over unification, a demonstration broke out here in Cairo, urging the two sides to stop the nasty bickering and settle their differences. The young man who was leading the demonstration and chanting slogans louder and more enthusiastically than anyone else, soon found himself lifted on the shoulders of two strong men so he could be seen and heard better. And for about several city blocks he did not fail them. His chanting sounded more enthusiastic until his voice became hoarse. The crowd responded with equal fervor. He would chant: 'Long live Egypt. Long Live Sudan. Long live their union.' And the crowd would repeat the same, with equal enthusiasm. When he finally came down off the shoulders of those carrying him, he realized something was amiss. Instinctively he reached for his wallet in his back pocket. It was gone. Gone. He became furious and asked the two men who had carried him to lift him up again. This time around he began chanting different slogans: "Down with Egypt. Down with Sudan. And to hell with their union."

Yousif stared at Tahseen, not in the least amused.

"You don't like it?" Tahseen asked, bewildered.

Yousif shook his head. Turning to Lubna, he said, "The whole Arab world is euphoric with Nasser and his call for Arab unity. And here we're supposed to laugh at an idiot who runs against the grain. He shouts ruin on Egypt and Sudan just because he lost his wallet. What did you think of it?"

Lubna flashed her big black eyes. "It's just a joke."

"Not a bit funny," Yousif said. Then he put his arm around Tahseen's shoulder. "Your taste in girls is better than your political humor."

The ironic compliment escaped Lubna. "How sweet," she said, watching Yousif walk away.

STUDIES ASIDE, THERE WERE new political developments for Yousif to worry about. He and Salwa and some of their Palestinian friends anticipated it, and it surfaced to no one's surprise.

Predictably, the rise of Nasser's power was met with virulent threats from the northern aggressor. The idea that a hugely popular leader could promote a united Arab front against the occupier of Arab land was anathema to the prime minister of that government.

"If Nasser doesn't stop rallying the Arabs against Israel," its prime minister threatened, "we'll be in Cairo in ten hours."

More than anyone in the Arab world, Nasser knew the seriousness of that threat. After all, it was coming from a radical who headed the military outpost of Western colonial powers. They had supplied him with the latest weaponry and boosted his audacity to be more belligerent. Nevertheless, Nasser went on pleading with various nations to supply him with arms, not to attack Israel but to defend his country against an expansionist state led by that eastern European who dared to claim Palestine belonged to him and not to its rightful owners. The more Nasser argued for military assistance, the more incensed and blustering the prime minister became.

"Ten hours and we'll be in Cairo," he blustered over and over.

Yousif listened to the verbal exchanges and debated the war of words with friends. All his classes turned into political forums. The consensus was no doubt that the head of the enemy camp could deliver on his threat, but would he dare? Nasser, they were all convinced, would out-fox him. Nasser would turn that wild man's dream into a nightmare.

"There's a large map on the walls of the Knesset," Yousif told a group of friends sitting with him at the cafeteria. "And the only word written on it stretches from the Tigris and the Euphrates in Iraq all the way to the Nile. Do you know what it says? I—S—R—A—E—L."

All students expressed surprise—even shock. All except Lubna, who sat frowning and clutching the books against her chest. When the group got up to leave, Lubna seemed to tarry behind on purpose.

"Why do you say such rubbish?" Lubna asked Yousif, walking down the steps with him.

"What rubbish?" Yousif asked.

"About the map in the Knesset."

"Because it's true."

"How do you know? Have you seen it."

"No, but I have heard and read about it."

"But you have no proof?"

Yousif stopped and stared at her. Her oval face and large dark eyes were expressionless. What proof did she need?

"Have you seen Japan?" he quizzed her.

For a moment she appeared puzzled. "No, I haven't."

"Yet, I presume you believe there is such a country."

"It's not the same," she argued.

"Why not? There are million places in the world we haven't seen. Yet we don't doubt their existence. Besides, what a question is this? Even if there's no such a map on that wall, we all know that Eretz Israel is etched on the brain of every Zionist leader since Theodor Herzl. They will continue to expand until they reach their goal. You must be kidding. Their political writings are full of these intentions."

Lubna laughed and looked around. A few stragglers were hurrying to their classes.

"Oh, Yousif, don't be so naïve. There's no sense believing in such nonsense. Israel is a fact, and you need to learn to deal with it. The only way to stop the expansion you're talking about is to accept Israel now and avoid future wars."

Yousif could not believe his ears. An Arab girl telling him to accept Israel? What blasphemy! What sacrilege!

"If someone else told me this, I don't know what I would have done."

"Think about it."

"Think about what?" he said, holding back his temper.

"Israel is meant to be. You can't change God's will."

"Keep God out of it. It's Herzl, Balfour, Hitler, Truman, Ben Gurion. God isn't involved."

"They say God works in mysterious ways. He might have used these men to fulfill His will."

A cynical smile crossed Yousif's face. "Are you telling me that it's God's will for the refugees to starve and rot in their flimsy tents? And for the foreigners to occupy and enjoy their homes?"

"Oh, Yousif. I wish you'd listen to me. You're the brightest Palestinian I have ever met. You can help your people by showing them that there's no sense in fighting an inescapable fact. Israel is here to stay. Now, tomorrow . . . and forever."

Yousif looked at his wrist watch, beginning to feel that there was no sense in arguing with such an imbecile. He needed to return some books to the library and check out another one.

"Suddenly you're not one of us," he said, shaking his head.

As he began to ascend the steps of the library she stopped him. "I never was. And we want you to join us."

Her words jarred him. "Join you?! Who are you then?!"

"Have you heard of the Sons and Daughters of Zion?"

Yousif was stunned. "You're one of them?"

She nodded. "Full-fledged Zionist."

A chuckle forced itself on him. "And you're trying to recruit me. Is that it?"

"Only because we like you. If you give us a chance to explain things to you, you'll see that it's in your interest to cooperate."

He was not totally convinced that she was part of a network of spies but was willing to take her at her word. His impulse was to alert the authorities and have her arrested. He stared at her, measuring his next move. Thoughts impeded action.

"Don't do anything rash," she warned him. "You're being watched. Right now someone is taking our picture together. The same photographer who took your and Salwa's picture having a fancy dinner at the hotel by the Nile. The starving refugees back home would love it. Listen, Yousif. If you reveal my identity . . . or if any harm happens to me, they'll hold you responsible. You'll pay for it no matter where you go."

He leaned against the facade of the building, undecided whether to be angry or concerned. He felt drained, emptied. He watched her open a large coffee-table art book she was holding against her chest and pull out a large photograph. She handed it to him; again Yousif froze. It was an earlier photograph of himself at Casino de Liban being served a drink by a scantly-clad cocktail waitress.

"You'll never be alone working with us," she told him. "Our friends in Beirut took many pictures of you being wined and dined. Interesting pictures of the symbol of the refugees. You'd really like the one at the nude show. How would you like for Salwa to see it? Or the refugees for whom your heart is bleeding."

"The nude show," he said, realizing she was lying.

"Yes, the nude show."

Yousif remained silent. The victorious enemy was on the offensive, but this "agent" was an amateur. Still, he took his time to think how to respond.

"I will not be blackmailed."

Lubna pretended not to have heard him. "You lust for beautiful women," she said, her voice flirtatious. "And you're smart and fairly ambitious. Good things could come your way if you decide to become a friend. That's not asking you too much, is it? I might even come with the bargain. That wouldn't be too bad. I see how you admire my breasts. Be honest. You'd like to do more than just look."

He could tell that her bosom was twice as big as Salwa's. But she was not worthy to tie Salwa's shoelaces. He would not touch her if she were the Queen of Sheba and Cleopatra wrapped in one. The way she dressed was scandalous.

He fixed his stare on nothing but her eyes. The looks in them were icy.

BEFORE GOING HOME LATE that afternoon he debated within himself whether to tell Salwa, and he knew what course he should follow. He had never kept a secret from her and he was not about to start. Besides, it was safer that she was aware of Lubna's evil, should something happen to him. He even decided to show her the photograph of himself at the Casino de Liban and to explain to her the circumstances. They trusted each other implicitly and she would definitely understand. That Ali Bakri appeared in the background was also reassuring. It would prove to Salwa, if a proof became necessary, that they had been on a mission to check out some wealthy compatriots who were either hopelessly decadent or foolishly trying to recover their losses back home or to drown their misery at the gambling tables. But Lubna's blatant lie gave him some comfort. There was no picture of him at the nude revue. Because he had not attended such a show.

Salwa was undisturbed by what he told her, except for one fear. "I wonder how many she has tried to recruit," she said, studying on the sofa with her feet propped under her. "I doubt you're the only one."

"She mingles in a big circle. It's hard to tell who might have fallen in her trap."

"You mean her lap. Those fellows hunger for her charms. And she's not bashful about flaunting them."

They tried to think of the most likely targets, but no one in particular stood out as suspect. Perhaps the enemy was not really recruiting in their midst, but only stirring mental unrest or sowing mistrust among the Arabs.

"Come to think of it," Salwa said, pencil in hand. "I remember hearing her saying some outlandish things."

"Such as . . ." Yousif said, leafing through the *Al-Ahram* newspaper.

". . . that the Egyptians are not Arabs. Not really. When two other girls and I looked at her in shock and pressed her to explain, she didn't laugh it off or apologize. She was dead serious. She said they're descendants of the ancient pharaohs. And she didn't stop right there. She went on to say that the Lebanese also are not Arabs."

"What are they?" Yousif asked, bemused.

"Phoenicians. That's what she said. Phoenicians."

Yousif put the newspaper down and stared at his wife. "There's a pattern here. She was with Tahseen when he cracked that silly joke about Egypt and Sudan."

The more they talked about Lubna the more convinced they became that a subversive movement was afoot in their midst. Yousif called it a fifth column, which Salwa did not understand. He said it was a term used by the Allies in World War II to describe the native collaborators whose mission was not to shoot guns or drop bombs from the sky but to spread rumors, falsehoods, and misinformation within the enemy's territories to undermine their confidence in their own leaders and rattle their faith in themselves or their cause. "As I said, all of those troublemakers were natives who had been enlisted—bought, bribed, blackmailed—to aid the aggressor against their own people."

"You call them troublemakers and I call them traitors," Salwa said, closing the book and ready to talk.

"Well, of course. Lubna fits the type in many ways. She's Egyptian by birth—or at least I think so—Jewish by faith, and Zionist by indoctrination. She can move around unsuspected until she finds it necessary to take off the mask."

Next morning Lubna was waiting for him in front of his eight o'clock class. She handed him a large manila envelope without saying a word. He hesitated to take it, but his curiosity was too strong to refuse. She disappeared before he opened the envelope and slipped out what was in it. Someone had indeed photographed them together at the bottom of the cafeteria steps the previous day. It was black-and-white and sharply focused photograph—capturing the moment she was handing him the one from Casino de Liban. The camera angle intrigued him. It was taken from the roof of the science building or from the top floor.

He slipped the picture back in the envelope and tucked it in his history book and went inside. He took his usual seat in the third row, and listened to professor Hilmy's lecture on the evils of colonialism, without absorbing much of it. There was nothing incriminating in the pictures, so why worry? To prove to him that he was being followed? That she had others working with her? So what; he was not doing anything shameful or criminal. It struck him that Lubna and her cohorts were amateurs trying to practice playing the big game. Yet he could not dismiss them that easily. Perhaps he should alert the *mukhabarat* and take his chances.

After the three o'clock lecture, he rode the bus to the heart of Cairo and headed straight for the Egyptian Intelligence Headquarters. Without hesitation he told the officer in charge all he knew, letting him have the recent picture of himself and Lubna. Bushy-browed Captain Mustapha Azizi told Yousif that he recognized him from the newspapers. After two hours of intense questioning, he told him to return in a week. They needed time to check his file, Yousif surmised; in a sense that pleased him. It also disturbed him. Did he fall in a trap? What if there was indeed a network of collaborators in high places, and Captain Azizi himself was one of them?

Why had he not considered all the possibilities before revealing all he knew?

Coming out of the huge *mukhabarat* headquarters, Yousif wondered if someone was trailing or even photographing him? He looked about, but the absence of someone with a camera did not reassure him. The traffic policeman in the busy circle reminded him of another Tahseen joke. But he was in no mood to smile. It did occur to him that he should discreetly try to learn how much Tahseen knew about Lubna. Was he one of her targets? Had he compromised his loyalty to Egypt for the sake of her charms? He hoped that in time he would find out. For now, what was done was done and there was nothing he could do about it. In his judgment he had handled the situation as best as he could, and he would just have to bear the consequences.

He changed buses twice before he got back to the apartment. He found Salwa a little anxious, for she had no idea what delayed him. Without much ado, he sat down and told her where he had been. At first she was alarmed at Lubna's relentlessness, but then told him he had done the right thing. For the rest of the evening they were both tense. That night, and for the first time since their arrival in Cairo, they only held each other and went to sleep.

A week later he got his instructions from Captain Azizi. It was agreed that Yousif should play along with Lubna and try to infiltrate the ring—if such a ring did exist. He was no longer required to come down to Headquarters but to report directly to Lt. Khalil Bishara who was stationed at the Office of Admissions at the University.

"He's expecting to hear from you tomorrow morning at 10:15 at his office. He has your schedule and knows that you have a class till 10:00. Just go and introduce yourself, but make sure not to tell anyone about your appointment with him. It would be interesting to know if Lubna and her gang know who Bishara is. By the way, here's the photo you left with me. We made a few copies of it. We didn't think you'd mind."

Yousif shook his head and took it.

RUGGED-LOOKING BUT WITH SLIGHTLY sunken cheeks, Lt. Bishara was much older than Yousif. He wasted no time getting to the point. Yousif was to act as a double agent.

"See what's on her mind," he instructed Yousif. "Meet some of her friends. Take some of their money. See what kind of information they're seeking and how much they're willing to pay. In an emergency, call this number."

He handed him a piece of paper. "Memorize it right now and share it with no one except Salwa."

The scribbled number was 5151945.

Yousif tried to associate it with things and places but remembered it best by breaking it into 515-1945. Easy, he thought. 515 could stand for May 15, when Israel was proclaimed a state. 1945 was the end of World War II. Were these dates chosen at random? He did not care. He simply memorized the number, returned the piece of paper to the officer and watched him tear it up and throw the tiny pieces in the waste basket underneath his desk.

An hour later, ruby-lipped Lubna found him in a quiet corner in the library and seemed delighted that he was willing to cooperate. He smiled, and told her how well her yellow sweater contrasted with her burnt-almond skin. But he repressed his admiration for her cleavage.

"What brought about this change of heart?" she inquired, as she sat in the armchair next to his.

"Frankly, Salwa and I could use the money," he lied. "Also, I was intrigued by your suggestion that benefits could come to my people if we only stopped and listened. I'm eager to meet some of your friends and hear them out. In short, I am all ears."

"How interesting," she said, focusing on him.

"In brief, what do you expect from me?"

"Simple. Criticize Israel all you want," she said, crossing her shapely legs, "but tell us who is planning to do us harm. Who, what, where, when . . . that sort of thing."

He could not help but laugh. "You give me too much credit. Do you think I know all that?"

"No, not all of it. But some of it, yes. Tell us about Basim, for instance. What's he up to?"

Yousif's fingers froze on the page of the magazine he was holding. He shrugged his shoulder, pretending he had no clue.

"Don't act too innocent. We know you do. And we know about Abu Thabit, and the training camp."

He continued to feign ignorance, especially of Abu Thabit, and she reminded him of the only visit he had made to one of those training camps in Lebanon. He waited for her to say something about his friends Hikmat and Izzat joining the Algerian Revolution, but she didn't. And he wondered if she knew.

"So if you want to be helpful, stop dodging the issues," she told him. "In other words, come clean."

He put the magazine down, crossed his legs and looked her straight in the eye.

"First, come clean yourself. What exactly are some of the benefits we as a people expect to derive from our cooperation? And don't talk in generalities, please. Don't tell me there will be no wars and that peace will reign all over the region. Because it's not in your power, and you know it."

Lubna cast a wide look on the spacious library to see if someone were close enough to hear them. Then she re-crossed her legs. "I can see you're going to be tough to handle. For a start, tell us about Basim. What's on his mind?"

"How do I know. I haven't seen him in months."

"Weeks is more like it. Tell us, for instance, what's he up to."

"You honestly expect me to inform on my immediate family?"

"We'd like for you to help us change their minds."

"That's like asking you to turn into a man."

"That would be a pity, don't you think?" she said, winking.

Yousif did not answer. Questions tumbled in his head. The serious arrangement she wanted to make required time and space. Perhaps, he suggested, they could take a long walk away from people . . . say, in the open grounds around the Pyramids. Or have dinner at his apartment to let Salwa in on their discussion.

"She's the one who convinced me to cooperate," he said.

Lubna shook her head. "No dinners. No out-of-the-way places. All discussions right here on campus."

As much as he loathed her, he tried humor as a tactic. "You said you came with the bargain. How can that be if we don't meet somewhere else?"

She smiled and again re-crossed her legs, exposing much of her smooth inner flesh. "When the time comes, things can be arranged. A number of people you know can tell you I do keep my word."

Yousif gulped. Was she lying again? Were she and those behind her trying to sow animosity and suspicion among fellow students? He had seen her a couple of times with Tahseen. Was *he* one of her conquests? What could Tahseen offer her?

"Give us something substantial that we can verify," she said, and waited for him to gather his thoughts.

"You're asking me about people a thousand miles away. Can't you find someone closer?"

She stood up, ready to leave. "Yes, I can."

"Who?"

"The man you just left. Lt. Bishara. That was a mistake on your part. A baaaaaad mistake."

She looked down on him, not a hint of humor in her eyes. Before he could say a word—which he did not know what it would be, anyway—she left in a huff.

He looked around to see if anyone had noticed, but no one seemed to have paid them any attention. Two couples were flirting on sofas twenty or thirty feet from him. On the far end of the room was a lanky student busy copying pages from a large textbook, and an older female student was standing by the magazine rack, totally engrossed in whatever she was reading. Yousif knew that there was a phone in a small recess around the corner, near the main entrance to the library. But he decided against it. Often there was a queue waiting to use it; besides, it was too public.

He hurried up the spiral staircase next to the information desk, and within seconds he was on the second floor. He knew Laila, the girl behind the check-out counter, and he asked her to let him use the phone in the inner office. He must have sounded desperate for she let him in without asking any questions. The empty office was dark and he did not turn on the light switch. He quickly dialed Lt. Bishara's number to tell him that their identities were no longer a secret. The phone rang only once and then someone picked up the phone on the other end and said "hello." Before Yousif could identify himself, or even say "hello" in return, something hit him on the neck and on the side of his face. He fell to the floor, the black receiver dropping from his hand and dangling off the edge of the desk, and the urgent "Hello . . . Hello" getting fainter and fainter.

Two hours later he woke up at the infirmary with a concussion. Salwa was standing by the bed, holding his hand and her eyes moist. She smiled and bent down and kissed him. One week later, Lubna was still at large. Two weeks later, Yousif was in the news again. This time he was given credit for having tipped the authorities and helped them crack an espionage ring. Lubna was arrested at the airport with a fake passport . . . just before boarding. Her real name turned out to be Esther Mizrahi. She was a native Egyptian born in Alexandria, but with staunch allegiance to Israel. At no time had she been a registered student at the university.

"A snake does not go to school," Captain Mustapha Azizi was quoted as saying in *Al-Ahram*. "She was a second-tier recruiter. With bags full of bribe money, she had managed to corrupt a number of our students, both male and female. But thank God for Yousif."

Yousif stiffened when he read his name, and wished they had not revealed it. There was going to be trouble, he felt certain. Lubna's or Esther's friends probably were many more than the authorities had apprehended or identified and they would retaliate.

Upon release from the hospital a day later, he and Salwa were sequestered at a hotel, and the secret police guarded their apartment. When two local thugs burst in, they were arrested on the spot. Next day, these two confessed that they had been "recruited" by Lubna, and proceeded to squeal ten other names in the same ring.

"Egypt must be crawling with spies," Yousif told Salwa the first night they spent back at their apartment.

"She might've been truthful when she said many of your friends know that she kept her word."

"You mean sleeping with them as a reward? Oh, yes. Thank God Tahseen isn't one of them."

"Don't be too sure," Salwa said, slipping next to him in bed. "I'm beginning to suspect anyone who came in contact with Lubna."

"What I don't know is this: Lubna slept with the men as a reward. What about the girls she recruited? How did she reward them?"

Salwa was shocked. "I can't believe you said that. Go to sleep. . ."

". . . She told me it was part of the bargain . . ."

". . . Go to sleep," she repeated, turning off the lamp next to her bed, "and take your dirty mind with you."

She giggled and they tussled and both fell asleep, content in each other's arms.

RETURNING FROM SCHOOL NEXT day, Yousif could hear Salwa in the kitchen busy preparing dinner. When she heard him come in she came out wiping her hands with her apron. They met in the middle of the small all-purpose room and exchanged routine kisses. A stack of books, many loose sheets of paper, and two typewriters (one Arabic, the other English) sat at the far end of the dining table.

"I have two assignments due tomorrow. One biology and the other on bio-chemistry. Which one are you going to help me with?"

Yousif laughed. "It depends on what you have for dinner."

"Mujaddarah with labaneh, unless you prefer the finely chopped salad. . ."

". . . which I can make and season better than anyone else," he said, mimicking her anticipated flattery.

She giggled, nodded her head, wrapped her arms around his neck and planted a warm kiss on his receptive mouth.

When he untangled himself from her fervent embrace, he noticed an auspicious-looking letter by the radio. He picked it up and began to tear the large envelope open.

"Why haven't you opened it? It's addressed to both of us."

"It's from your mother. I thought you ought to read it first."

There were several papers inside the envelope: the three-page letter itself, and a clipping from *Amana Daily*, with a photograph of Jihan Afifi. The headline alone forced Yousif to drop in the nearest chair and stare at Salwa.

"What—?" she said before he handed her the newspaper clipping which announced Jihan's death. The headline said it all, THE SOIL OF PALESTINE: HER ETERNAL RESTING PLACE.

Their stares at each other were glazed. The oxygen in the room seemed to have evaporated.

The two read in silence, lumps in their throats. Even though Jihan's death had been imminent when they left Kuwait, it fell on them with a brutal force. Her obituary in the newspaper was longer than usual. It identified her name and place of birth, summarized the highlights of her background, then went on to admire her return from exile to fulfill her last wish: to be buried in Palestine. Her attachment to her roots and to her cherished memories of growing up in Palestine was hailed as it should have been.

His mother's long letter was newsy but very moving. She wrote that she had attended the funeral in East Jerusalem, together with Salwa's mother and some old friends from Ardallah (including Ustaz Sa'adeh and his wife). It was an emotionally gripping reunion on many levels. The sad occasion made it a lot worse. She described how heartbroken Dr. Afifi looked, and how much he sobbed when he saw his wife's coffin lowered into the grave. At the end of the ceremony all eyes were tearful. (I could only imagine what went through Salwa's mother's mind at that moment. I'm sorry, *habibti* Salwa, but my heart was torn to shreds.) Everyone was particularly touched by Jihan's attachment to Palestine. To be buried in East Jerusalem, the holiest city on earth, was a special honor.

Yousif wished his mother had not alluded to Salwa's father's death in the desert. He squeezed his wife's hand and pulled her down to sit next to him. He could see a pained look on her face, as she must have recalled leaving her father in the wilderness, unburied and prey to wild animals. When her chin began to tremble, he gave her a kiss on the cheek and patted her knee. They huddled closer as he read out loud the rest of the letter:

Jihan's death and return to Palestine for burial opened old wounds. Standing on that hilltop, many of us also cried as we looked at the Holy Places and named them one after the other as if they were literally our spiritual homes. As I was born and raised in Jerusalem, I could spot the direction of my home and the school I attended, and I couldn't help but wonder who is living in those buildings. How many homes can one lose in a lifetime, and how many of his roots must be cut off to make room for strangers? It is woefully unjust. Watching the part of Jerusalem that had been occupied by the enemy doubled our agony. Looking at the home of the British High Commissioner on the opposite hill from where I was standing filled me with anger. How dare they, I thought, give our country away as if we were not here!! A million times how dare they!!

Afterwards, Dr. Afifi took us, his immediate friends, to a mercy meal, and that is when he told us that he was establishing a long-range scholarship fund in Jihan's memory. What a generous gesture. But none of us was surprised. He is that kind of a man. And he asked Ustaz Sa'adeh to be in charge of it. His job is to select worthy recipients. The fund will subsidize their entire university education. Imagine that!

I can't tell you how proud I felt hearing him lavish praise on the two of you. He went on and on saying what a wonderful couple you are. And he was kind to say that Jihan had loved both of you dearly. Bless you, *habibeeni*.

Then came the biggest surprise: he turned to Ustaz Sa'adeh and specifically asked him to name the two of you as the first couple to receive such scholarships. May Jihan's memory be eternal, and may he, Dr. Afifi, find solace in honoring her name in such a lofty manner.

Salwa put the letter down and let her emotion erupt. Chewing on his lower lip and holding his tears back, Yousif put his arm around her shoulder and handed her his clean handkerchief with his left hand.

16

YEAR LATER the drums of war were beating for real. Egypt and the imperialist powers were at loggerheads. The issues of the Aswan Dam and the Suez Canal were looming as the core of the rising conflict. But Yousif and his professors saw these as pretexts for a Western desire to get rid of Nasser once and for all. His stature and prestige were so enormous, he could without even trying shut down activities throughout the whole Arab world on any night he was to deliver a major speech. Millions of people across North Africa and throughout the Middle East would sit glued to their radios ready to be mesmerized by his every word, eager for him to restore their hope and dignity. During the Cold War and the Red Scare, Nasser was making global alliances and adopting neutrality that did not please Egypt's former masters. To the West, he was the nemesis personified. To Israel he was enemy number one.

"War is imminent," said law Professor Hassan Omari, interrupting his lecture to answer the barrage of queries from his students about the troubling situation. "For years Nasser begged the West to sell him weapons to protect Egypt from the belligerent enemy on our northern border, but they all turned him down. His pleas with France, Britain and America fell on deaf ears. Then he dared to purchase weapons from the Soviet bloc. And that sealed his fate. Or so they thought. He became an irritant to the West. America slapped his hand and reneged on her promise to finance building the Aswan Dam, which was not only his pet project but a vital development for Egypt's economy. The Soviet Union was more than happy to step right in and provide all the financing he needed."

Despair descended on all the students as well as on the professor himself.

Coming out of class, Yousif ran into Dr. Ni'man in the crowded hallway.

"Ah, Yousif," his favorite professor said, several books under his arm. "I was looking for you. Do you have a few minutes to stop by my office?"

"I always have time for you," Yousif said, eager to shed his gloom.

Inside the L-shaped office, Yousif was surprised to see the professor drop his books on the desk and promptly extend his hand. Genuine concern covered his face.

"Look, Yousif," the disheveled professor said, his head gyrating, "I don't know what the outcome of this upcoming war is going to be. But no matter who wins or loses, I want us to be always friends."

"Of course," Yousif said, without a hint of animosity toward this gentle soul. Yet something in the back of his mind made him curious. He had never thought of the professor in terms of Arabs and Jews. Professor Ni'man was a man of all ages: Egyptian by birth, Jewish by faith and universal by attitude. Did he think that he, Yousif, would in any way associate him with Israel's belligerence?

Both remained standing in he middle of the cramped office. A moment of unadulterated rapport passed between them.

"As you know," the professor began, his head bobbing, "I am apolitical and basically agnostic. I know how you feel about the loss of your homeland to the Israelis. In all honesty, I empathize and sympathize with you and your people. How could my brethren do this to people who never did them any harm is unconscionable to say the least. But please don't let politics or religion stand in the way of true friendship. Politicians come and go. Causes change with the times. But human decency is to be cherished. I thought you ought to know how I felt before the horrors engulf us."

The endearing old man's sincerity touched Yousif. Outside that little enclave of learning, the echoes of war were resounding. Here, in the presence of the disciple of Ovid and Aurelius, the world stood still. All that moved were two hearts—and the professor's shaking head.

"If the world only had more like you," Yousif said, pressing the professor's hand and warmly patting it with his left hand.

Professor Ni'man leaned against an overstuffed bookshelf, biting his lower lip and looking forlorn. The sunlight, filtering through a dirty window-pane, wrapped around his head like a halo.

WITHIN WEEKS THE CRISIS broke out into war, pitching Britain, France and Israel against Egypt. The Arab masses seethed with anger, charging the three-pronged assault as an evil conspiracy. The hypocritical world waited to see if Nasser would be humbled, toppled or killed. Violent demonstrations broke out throughout the Middle East.

Yousif was incensed. Watching a demonstration pass before the statue of a former nationalist in front of the main entrance to the campus, he stood on the base of the statue and addressed a crowd of nearly fifty students.

"By now we should all be tired of all the well-meaning but useless demonstrations," he vehemently railed. "They have never won wars, not even small battles. Venting anger and boosting morale are never enough. The wolves are once again knocking on our door. The predators are out to prowl. Where is Arab solidarity?"

"*Wainkum ya Arab*?" a patriotic Syrian student hollered in agreement.

"Y-E-S. Where are you Arabs?"

"*Wainkum ya Arab*?" the crowd shouted back.

"Why aren't the Arab armies fighting with Egypt? Are they waiting for another catastrophe like the one in Palestine? Why aren't they here to stop the imperialists from returning to occupy our lands? Imagine the arrogance! They regard the whole Arab world as their own backyard. Their own banana republic. They can divide it, they can annex it, they can rule it as they wish, as if we weren't here. As if we didn't exist. The lesson we must teach them is this: Those days are gone. Gone. Gone."

The crowd in front of him began to thicken, numbering now close to a hundred.

"Gone . . . Gone . . . Gone..."

"Let us all do our duty," he said, shouting even louder and flailing his arm. "Let us volunteer. Let us all enlist. Let us sacrifice ourselves for the sake of Egypt. The Suez Canal is not the issue. Far from it. It's only a pretext for the aggressors' avarice . . . their greed. The real issue is Nasser himself. Nasser the liberator. Nasser the Reformer. They are out to topple him. Even kill him. Nothing, and I mean nothing, would satisfy them more than to see Nasser dead."

"No . . . No . . . No . . ." the crowd screamed . . . bellowed . . . roared.

"Let us capture their pilots when they parachute down. Let us challenge them face to face. Let us show them that Nasser is not alone. We are all Nassers."

"We're all Nassers. We're all Nassers. We're all Nassers."

A few days later Salwa and a group of classmates volunteered as nurse-aides and were sent immediately to Port Said. Yousif and his friends did not fare as well. They had blood drawn from their arms, but before they could be inducted into the Egyptian armed forces, the fighting had ended—thanks to Eisenhower and Khrushchev. Nasser not only survived—he triumphed. By having stood up to the three aggressors, and by demonstrating that he would fight to the last man to defend Egypt's sovereignty, he was a bigger hero.

"England's Prime Minister went down the drain, and Nasser is still in power," Yousif explained in the university quadrangle. "Eisenhower emerged as a true friend. And we should never forget his honorable stand. Maybe America is beginning to see the light. He told the three aggressors, including their darling, Israel, 'Retreat or else.' And what did the three do? They pulled back. Yes, indeed, they pulled back. That proves, if a proof is warranted, that America has the power and influence to restrain Israel whenever it wants to. Perhaps from here on they will stop giving her the green light every time the fingers of her leaders begin to itch."

The students listened and nodded. Some expressed their disgust over the invasion with gestures and words.

"Let's not forget Khrushchev," a student with a wide forehead reminded him. "He too sent the aggressors a stern warning."

"It's true," Yousif replied, "but the tight relationship between America and Israel is far more troubling. Eisenhower's quick and firm demand for a total pullback is also far more significant. Indeed, it's a glimmer of hope. That America, or rather Eisenhower, chose to go against Israel's wishes is unprecedented and most promising. Maybe Washington will start acknowledging our plight. No matter, the real credit for this victory belongs undeniably to President Nasser. Both Washington and Moscow realized two things: one, the aggressors needed to be stopped; two, that Nasser is no Farouk.

"Nasser is no Farouk... Nasser is no Farouk," the crowd began to chant.

Yousif let them vent for a few seconds and then motioned to them to let him finish. "Nasser is unbeatable," he said, "because he's the only one who can rally the whole Arab world behind him. Our supporters must've realized it's foolish—indeed dangerous—to alienate if not antagonize two hundred million of us. Not to mention a billion Muslims around the world."

A WEEK AFTER THE fighting stopped, a Palestinian delegation headed by Basim arrived to congratulate President Nasser on his triumph. Others were Abu Thabit, Hanna Azar, Raja Ballout, Ustaz Sa'adeh, Ali Bakri, Adel Farhat, and Hamdi Hamdan, a new member to the board. Meanwhile, Yousif was so exhilarated he couldn't contain himself: his wish had come true. He not only saw and heard Nasser—he even shook his hand in his own office. Nasser, with his imposing physical presence, infectious smile and Pharanoaic profile, was in a jovial mood. Why not, Yousif thought. He was the only leader who could send every Arab to sleep feeling safe and proud of being an Arab. Nasser laughed and joked as he moved from behind his enormous mahogany desk for souvenir group pictures with himself in his presidential office. Yousif was the youngest of those in the spacious office, and Nasser singled him out and bestowed upon him the honor of being photographed at his right side. As tall as Yousif was, he came to only a couple of inches above Nasser's shoulder.

But who, in Yousif's estimation, could measure up to Nasser? As the sacrilegious saying went, "Prophet Muhammad, *salla Allahu alaihi wa sallam*, might have erred once in his lifetime; Nasser never did."

"Take a picture of these two," President Nasser told the photographer, pointing to Yousif and Adel Farhat. "I did not see you two shake hands, and I'd like for your reconciliation to be documented in my office. I'll even stand between you as an eyewitness."

The former rivals were more than happy to oblige their idealized leader. They stepped forward and waited for President Nasser to stand between them. The photographer flashed and clicked his camera several times to capture the moment from different angles.

The entire delegation clapped at the end of the feud between these two. Nasser himself looked equally pleased.

Flashing his matinee-idol smile and tapping Adel and Yousif on their shoulders, President Nasser moved toward a sofa and invited everyone else to sit in the armchairs around him.

"The coming together of these two rivals should be a *rumz*—a symbol--for all of us," Nasser said, as if talking to friends visiting him at home. "May all our feuds be set aside for the sake of harmony. For the sake of our oneness of purpose. The Arab countries are one nation, regardless of some differences, and we should always remain one if we wish to withstand and frustrate the rivalries and ambitions of our old-age enemies. As we have seen recently, they are always looking for the slightest excuse, the slightest provocation—imaginary or otherwise—to come hurling at us their military might. But with the solidarity of our masses behind us, from the Atlantic ocean to the Arabian Sea, we have dealt them a defeat they deserve."

Yousif was intrigued on more than one level. First, how and why did this triumphant leader bother to know about him and Adel Farhat? Like his energetic *mukhabarat* he left nothing unchecked or un-utilized. More important, his praising the Arab masses without demonizing the Arab regimes that did not rush to stand with Egypt in her hour of need, was a nuanced diplomacy just as potent as pointing fingers or flexing muscles. Ignoring them was a deliberate warning they could not possibly miss.

"Pan-Arabism must not be a dream," Nasser elaborated. "It's a fact, a reality, if we are to overcome the dangers ahead. From the times of the Crusades till now the imperialists have harbored nothing but ill will toward us. They want to snuff our political awakening and keep us weak. No more, no more."

Yousif nodded with the others, and heard Ustaz Sa'adeh saying, "Amen."

"Only the deaf and dumb," Nasser continued, his tone full of pride, "are unaware of our contributions to world civilizations throughout the ages. And, indeed, we have abundant natural resources, huge markets, strategic locations, and yet all our enemies want is to belittle us. Subjugate us. Rule us, whether directly or indirectly. What nation would tolerate such bald-faced evil? And for how long? What nation would allow other nations to fragment it and occupy it as we have allowed the West to do to us? Would America, or Britain, or France allow us for a moment to meddle in their internal affairs?"

"Would Great Britain," Basim added, "allow us to advocate splitting it into three separate states: England, Scotland, and Wales? Not to mention northern Ireland."

"Absolutely not," President Nasser agreed. "Would America allow us to interfere in her racial problems? To play blacks and whites against each other? Yet, they feel they have the right and audacity to play us one against the other. And they feel free to draw Jews from around the four corners of the world and let the Palestinians—who were born and raised there for centuries and who are the rightful owners of the land—blow with the wind."

Those were Yousif's exact sentiments. And the camaraderie of the meeting emboldened him to speak up.

"Gather and scatter is their policy," he said, glancing toward his colleagues for consent.

"Precisely," President Nasser told him, nodding. "For centuries their policy toward us was based on the principle of Divide and Rule. In the case of Palestine, their new conquests are based on the principle which Yousif so aptly described: Gather and Scatter."

The phrase resonated with those present.

"Gather and Scatter," many repeated.

"And we're supposed to sit still and take it," Ali Bakri huffed.

Nasser resumed his tirade against the big powers. "Dare we tell France to end her 132-year colonization of Algeria! Dare we tell America to return

California to Mexico. Or Oklahoma to the Native Americans."

"Or any state for that matter," Basim sneered.

The unmasking of the big powers' hypocrisy and the trashing of their double standards were well received.

"We Arabs," President Nasser continued, "have been engaged in nearly thirty wars and revolutions in this century alone, trying to get rid of colonialism and post-colonialism. Their absolute avarice must cease. Look at all the waste in human life and treasure to say of nothing else. The solution to this problem is unity at all levels. Pan-Arabism is not a dream. It's our salvation."

"Liberation is Amana in our heart," Raja said.

"Your Amana is our Amana forever," President Nasser concurred. "It's every Arab's sacred trust. And Pan-Arabism is the right way to safeguard it. The only light to shine in this darkness."

After more handshakes, more slaps on the back, more promises of solidarity, more smiles, and more goodbyes, they left the presidential office of their colossal leader entirely buoyed. Nasser's visionary range hit Yousif like a thunderclap. He became a staunch believer that Pan-Arabism, articulated and championed by Nasser, would usher in a new dawn. A new era for peace, justice, independence and honor to be restored. It was a clarion call he must obey.

As they descended the wide spiral steps, Yousif spotted Salwa waiting for them in the rotunda of this magnificent Presidential Palace. As he nudged Basim and pointed her to him, he noticed that Adel Farhat was already aware of her presence.

Salwa rushed toward them, and hugged and kissed the ones she knew: Basim and Ustaz Sa'adeh. Noticing that Adel was standing nearby, she awkwardly shook his hand as well. One beat later, she kissed him graciously on both cheeks.

"Good to see you, Adel," she said, blushing.

"Likewise," Adel replied, putting his arm around Yousif's waist as a gesture of forgiveness.

Gleeful glances and smiles sealed a happy day for all concerned. Then

Ustaz and Adel politely pulled ahead as if to give the cousins a chance to be alone.

"I wish I could take you two out to lunch," Basim said, "but they're taking us to visit the Aswan Dam right now."

"I wish you could spend at least one night with us," Yousif said. "We have a lot to talk about."

"Yes, we do. How many more years do you need to finish?"

Yousif and Salwa looked at each other, grinning. It was hard to believe they were reaching their educational goals. One of them, at least.

"Soon I'll be an attorney," Yousif said. "A year later Salwa will become a doctor. And she has already been accepted to do her residency in pediatrics at the American University of Beirut."

Basim genuinely pleased. "Great news. What then?"

"Surprise!" Salwa said, grinning. "We intend to devote all our time and energy to Amana Forever . . ."

". . . and to Palestine," Yousif added, putting his arm around her waist.

"How strange!" Basim said, pretending shock. "I had no idea."

They laughed together, walked to the huge front door and saw the limousines lined up to carry the buoyant delegation to their destination.

After Basim had embraced and kissed his cousins goodbye, Yousif and Salwa watched him get in one of the limousines and be driven away.

Feeling utter satisfaction, Yousif nudged Salwa to look at the magnificent scene around. Cairo's sky was unblemished and as blue as the Nile. The palace garden was in full bloom. And the sun was extraordinarily bright.

THAT EVENING, YOUSIF SAT at their dinner table fiddling with his fork but hardly eating. He was in deep thought, and Salwa was more than happy to wait to hear what he had to say. Her own political impulse was also strengthened by her husband's meeting with Nasser in his presidential office and listening to him articulate his political vision. What a splendid honor, indeed.

"While Nasser is concerned with the big picture, we need to pay attention to the small picture," Yousif said.

"What do you mean?"

"While he is confronting diplomacy—and perhaps wars—on a regional and foreign scale, Amana Forever must make our story known to the world. We must convince our novelists, playwrights, filmmakers to document and reveal to our own people and to anyone willing to listen what catastrophe has befallen us."

"I see what you mean."

"Our enemies keep talking about their exodus from ancient Egypt. What about our exodus from modern Palestine? I don't know why the Pharaohs threw them out centuries ago, but I do know that we did nothing—absolutely nothing—to deserve this. They just came from all over the world and took our farms, orchards, shops, schools, and homes and left us penniless. For God's sake, why? Our writers and scholars and artists have to make it their duty to expose the injustice. Journalists and professors should visit the many camps and interview hundreds of refugees about their anguish, about their miserable existence."

Salwa nodded. "And a historian should write how well the Jews were treated in our midst. When they were expelled out of Spain after the Inquisition, where did they go? Not to England—"

"Shakespeare never saw a Jew in his life," Yousif interjected.

"—or France or Germany or Italy or any of the European countries. They went to Arab north Africa and ended up in the Middle East and lived among us as good neighbors. They ate the same food. Sang the same songs. And thrived in businesses we all supported. Someone should tell this story before the new arrivals start distorting the truth."

His appetite revived, Yousif scooped rice and green beans onto his plate and began to eat.

"Come to think of it," Salwa said, filling her own plate, "we never saw a photograph in any of the major American magazines showing the expulsion of our people. Hundreds of thousands of us trudged up and down our steep hills, fleeing the occupiers, and not a single photograph showed the world what we went through."

They ate in silence for a few minutes, then Yousif said, "I hear the young and brilliant film director now working here in Cairo is planning to make a film about an Algerian young heroine. He's a nationalist and a serious artist who just might want to tackle our tragedy."

"What will the film be called?"

"*Jamileh, the Algerian.*"

"How interesting."

"Maybe he could call the film about us: *Salwa, the Palestinian.*"

Salwa giggled. "What a beautiful title."

"It befits a beautiful heroine like you."

"Don't tease me. I'm no heroine."

"By the time he's ready to make the film you will be."

The young husband and wife looked each other in the eyes. They had experienced so much and seen so much, but at this tenderly domestic moment they saw only each other. Only each other, although it is true that their gazes also encompassed the past and future of their beloved Palestine. The past was memory, and the future was dream; both were real. Yes, Yousif and Salwa were ready to savor a respite from political drudgery, but it was neither tiredness nor despair that misted their eyes for a long heartbeat. They raised their glasses of water and touched them together, and their laughter lingered in the room and drifted through the open window out into the Arabian night.

~

ALSO BY **IBRAHIM FAWAL**

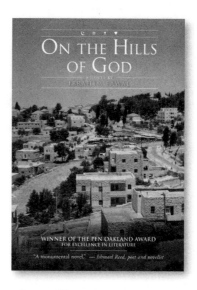

"A monumental novel." — ISHMAEL REED, poet and writer

June 1947 was the eve of the end of the world for eighteen-year-old Yousif Safi, for Yousif is a Palestinian. Author Ibrahim Fawal's debut novel *On the Hills of God* describes the year-long journey of a boy becoming a man, while all that he has known crumbles to ashes.

Yousif is filled with hopes for his education abroad and with day-dreams of his first love, Salwa, but he is frustrated by his fellow Arabs' inability to thwart the Zionist encroachment and by his own inability to prevent the impending marriage of Salwa to an older suitor chosen by her parents. As the Palestinians face the imminent establishment of Israel, Yousif resolves to face his own responsibilities of manhood. Despite the monumental odds against him, Yousif vows to win back both his loves—Salwa and Palestine—and create his world anew.

ISBN 978-1-58838-204-7
Available in hardcover and ebook
Visit www.newsouthbooks.com/onthehillsofgod